# O
# PONTIUS

## Lewis Ben Smith

eLectio Publishing

Little Elm, TX

www.eLectioPublishing.com

ISBN-13: 978-1-63213-140-9
Published by eLectio Publishing, LLC
Little Elm, Texas
http://www.eLectioPublishing.com

Printed in the United States of America

5  4  3  2  1    eLP    20  19  18  17  16  15

The eLectio Publishing editing team is comprised of: Christine LePorte, Lori Draft, Sheldon James, and Jim Eccles.

**Publisher's Note**
The publisher does not have any control over and does not assume any responsibility for author or third-party websites or their content.

# TABLE OF CONTENTS

*This novel is dedicated to
my longsuffering wife, Patty,
who only thought she was getting the computer back
when I finished my first book,
to my friend and muse Ellie,
who read it chapter by chapter
and supplied much constructive feedback,
and to the teachers and authors who inspired in me
a love for the Roman Republic and Empire,
that sophisticated yet barbaric culture
which fascinates me to this day.*

# PROLOGUE

"CRUCIFY HIM!" the crowd roared. The force of their rage was physical, gnawing and hungry, ferocious in its anger. It hovered over them like a sentient creature, sending black tendrils of hate into their midst, inflaming ordinary country folk and city dwellers into a blind, howling mob.

The Prefect of Judea was taken aback by their rage, and worn down by their persistence. It had started in the middle of the night, when his guards had roused him from a fitful slumber to inform him that his judgment was urgently required by the High Priest and his cronies. He had been surprised at first that Caiaphas had brought such an enormous mob with him, but its purpose soon became obvious. The old snake was not leaving Pilate any room to maneuver this time! It was very obvious that he wanted Jesus of Nazareth dead.

Of course Pilate knew who Jesus was—everyone in Judea and the Decapolis had heard of the wandering teacher and miracle worker who seemed to delight in turning the religious establishment of the Jews on its head. Pilate had ordered the itinerant teacher investigated by his agents, to see if he posed any threat to Rome, and had satisfied himself that the Galilean was nothing but a harmless religious mystic. Even when he had entered the city a few days earlier and a fawning crowd had offered to crown him as King of the Jews, Jesus had rejected their offer, leaving many of them shaking their heads in wonder and disappointment. Pilate had been relieved when he witnessed that moment; it confirmed his earlier judgment about the Galilean, and seemingly boded well for a quiet and uneventful Passover season—something anyone who had ever governed this difficult and rebellious province would recognize as a rarity.

But then the Supreme Council of the Jews had arrested Jesus on trumped up charges and grilled him for an entire evening. Pilate had heard of the arrest before he went to bed, and figured the Jews would try Jesus by their own law and order him beaten with rods and expelled from the city. Regrettable, perhaps, but the man had been provoking them for months, challenging their control of the Jewish religion that governed several million of the Empire's subjects and citizens.

Then they had shown up at the Praetorium, demanding that the Galilean be crucified—a death Rome reserved only for the worst offenders—rebellious slaves or non-citizens who had brought death and suffering to the people of Rome. This Galilean preacher had done nothing to merit such a fate, Pilate thought. He initially tried to dismiss the crowd out of sheer irritation, but it was obvious Caiaphas and his old father-in-law, Annas, who controlled the High Priesthood, were out for blood.

Pilate had interviewed Jesus privately, and emerged perplexed and distressed. This was no ordinary man or wandering fanatic! First of all, he required no interpreter, even though Pilate had secured one from among Jesus' disciples—the Galilean's Latin was as perfect and flawless as if he were born on Capitoline Hill! His calm, steady gaze and cryptic answers troubled the short-tempered governor, and the bullying tactics of his accusers angered Pilate. He had tried fobbing Jesus off to Herod's court, but the Tetrarch of Galilee had sent Jesus back to him in a couple of hours, roughed up a bit and wrapped in one of Herod's cast-off purple robes. As usual, Herod had refused to do anything useful, neither condemning nor protecting the Galilean.

Pilate had then ordered Jesus beaten by his soldiers, hoping to placate the mob's blood lust. The men had exceeded his orders, nearly flaying the Galilean with a cat o'nine tails, but even that had not satisfied the angry Jews congregated in the courtyard of the Praetorium. They saw the battered and bloody form, barely able to stand, and took up the hateful chant again. Pilate had pulled Jesus back into the building again and interrogated him a second time. Jesus proved reluctant to answer at first and Pilate burst forth in annoyance: "Do you not know that I have the power to crucify you, and the power to set you free?"

Jesus raised his battered head and looked straight at the governor. The bruises and swelling had not subtracted an iota from the power of his gaze as he said calmly: "You have no power over me, except that which is given to you from above. Therefore those who delivered me up to you have the greater guilt."

2

It was that statement, with its simple assessment, that haunted Pilate as he stood before the mob again. In one simple sentence, Jesus had placed *him* on trial, and pronounced him guilty—perhaps not as guilty as the religious leaders who still stood outside, urging the crowd to keep up that awful chant, but guilty still. Pilate sat down in the judgment seat overlooking the courtyard and held up his hands for silence. He could feel the rustling of a single sheet of papyrus that he had stuffed into the sinus of his toga, a note from his wife, Procula Porcia, begging him to have nothing to do with "the death of this righteous man."

Once more the governor pronounced Jesus innocent of any crime. The crowd's angry shouts immediately rejected his verdict. Suddenly from the back of the mob, the stern voice of Caiaphas the High Priest rang out.

"If you release this man, you are no friend of Caesar's!" he snapped. "For he called himself a king—and whoever makes himself a king is Caesar's enemy!"

Pilate turned to his servant, Democles, and whispered in his ear. The Greek slave nodded and disappeared into the Praetorium. Pilate slowly stood and walked to the edge of the raised platform where his judgment seat stood. The crowd slowly fell silent as they beheld the thunder on his brow. The Roman governor had been a terror to the local community for seven years, and had not hesitated to kill any Jews who defied him. At the same time, they knew that Emperor Tiberius had already reprimanded him more than once for his brutality and insensitivity to their customs. If they reported him to Rome again, they might secure his dismissal—although that would do them no good if they died here in the courtyard with a Roman gladius between their ribs! Half fearful, half angry, they stared at this man who was the embodiment of the mighty Roman Empire.

Democles appeared at Pilate's side with a basin of water in his hands and a white towel draped over his arm. Pilate nodded and dipped his hands in the water three times, then raised them to the crowd.

"Let all men see that I am innocent of this man's blood!" he cried aloud.

But then he looked in horror at his own hands. They were dripping with deep, crimson fluid! The drops pattered down on the white marble before him as the Jews recoiled in horror. Pilate cried in revulsion and looked in the bowl. It was an abattoir, filled with crimson. He struck it from Democles'

3

hands and it shattered on the marble platform, sprinkling his robes with crimson drops. He grabbed the towel and wiped his hands repeatedly, but the blood would not come off. However much he rubbed his hands, they were still soaked with the blood . . . the blood . . .

"THE BLOOD!!' he screamed, sitting up abruptly in his bed. His wife started next to him, then sadly shook her head and put her arms around him in sympathy. He accepted her embrace for a moment, but then shrugged free—no true Roman man fled to a woman's arms for comfort. He staggered to his desk and poured himself a cup of wine from a nearby flagon, relishing the sour taste for a moment. Forty days! Forty days since he crucified the Galilean—and the same dream had returned to him every night! Groaning, he put his face in his hands. How had he come to this?

# CHAPTER ONE

Lucius Pontius Pilate was born in the hills overlooking Capua in the fifteenth year of the Emperor Augustus, the firstborn son of an ancient and honorable plebeian family. His father was a career soldier and diplomat who had survived the civil wars between Pompey, Julius Caesar, Octavian, and Marc Antony by trimming his political sails and displaying an unerring instinct for picking the winning faction. He had been rewarded, after Octavian's victory, with a seat in the Roman Senate, and the governorship of a series of provinces. He also cultivated the friendship and trust of Augustus' right-hand man and son-in-law, Marcus Agrippa.

So it was that the eldest son of Decimus Pontius Pilate was destined to ascend the *cursus honorum*, the succession of offices young Roman men were expected to hold as they ascended the ladder of status and respectability. At age twelve, Pilate was sent to the Campus Martius, the nearest military camp to Rome itself, to train as a soldier. At sixteen he was assigned as a *conterburnalis*—a junior officer—in the Roman legions under Tiberius Caesar, the adopted son of the Emperor and Rome's leading general since the death of Agrippa twelve years earlier.

Pilate was not a natural soldier, but he was a hard-working and conscientious one. Wielding a blade didn't come naturally to him, so he spent long hours training and practicing until it looked natural. He didn't have that effortless ease with the enlisted men that had made Caesar and Pompey so beloved of their soldiers, so he tried to be stern and fair, and the soldiers respected him, even if they didn't like him very much.

Tiberius was much older than Pilate, and already an experienced soldier and a capable general. The sixteen-year-old Pilate looked up to him enormously at first, and the Emperor's heir apparent was impressed with the young officer's diligence. With Tiberius' support, Pilate had won his first elected office, being chosen as Tribune of the Soldiers for his legion. This made him the equivalent of a judge advocate, listening to the grievances from the rank and file, judging disciplinary hearings, and representing the legionaries in the officers' councils. It was a good start to a Roman political career, but what Pilate needed was a successful military campaign to burnish his record. Rome loved a war hero, and he aspired to become one.

The problem was that Tiberius was almost done campaigning. The Emperor's adopted son had spent several years pacifying Germany during the first part of Pilate's service with him, but he had appointed Pilate as his quartermaster in Rome—so Pilate's companions racked up honors and decorations while he stayed in the city, filling out requisitions and arguing with the censors. As the Emperor Augustus grew older and feebler, Tiberius returned to Rome, where he was being prepared for the succession. The political sinks of Rome were no place for a young officer on the rise to earn a military reputation, and after ten years as Tiberius' junior legate, Pilate was almost ready to request a transfer to leave the army permanently.

Then came the Varus disaster. Three legions, led by Publius Quinctilius Varus, had been ambushed and destroyed by an alliance of German tribes along the Elbe River in Germania. Most of the legionaries were slaughtered and captured, and all three of their golden eagle standards were taken by the enemy. Only a handful managed to escape, and the defeat was made all the worse by the fact that the enemy had been led by a German who was raised and educated in Rome. Arminius of the Cheruscii had posed as a loyal client prince, eager to please Rome at any cost, while secretly building an alliance of tribes to drive Rome out of Germania once and for all. Varus, a Roman of impeccable lineage with a reputation for cruelty, had fallen into Arminius' trap, and paid with his life and the lives of nearly 20,000 legionaries and auxiliaries. Augustus went half mad with grief when he heard the news, pounding his head against a wall and crying out: "Quinctilius Varus, give me back my legions!"

Now Tiberius was tasked with avenging Rome's defeat. For Pilate, the timing was less than perfect—he had just spent a small fortune to get himself elected as one of Rome's urban praetors, an important step on the *cursus honorum*. Now he would have to get permission from the Emperor himself to leave Rome during his tenure in office. But the chance for distinction on the battlefield was not something to be missed, so the twenty-six-year-old Roman was ushered into the presence of the man who was already a living legend—Gaius Julius Caesar Octavian Augustus, once simply known as Octavian. For over forty years this unflappable man had ruled the world's largest empire with dignity and simplicity, inspiring Rome's bards to proclaim him as the genius of the age.

Pilate's heart was in his throat as he approached the curule chair from which Caesar addressed the Senate. Augustus shunned the rich trappings of Oriental monarchs—he lived in a small, humble home on the Palatine Hill and dressed as any patrician senator might. But there was no mistaking the aura of power that radiated from him. This trim, white-haired man in the pure white toga with purple borders had single-handedly ended the Roman Republic and turned it into an Empire, becoming a monarch in all but name. Caesar was known for being a rational and humane ruler, but he could also be ruthless toward those who angered him.

Pilate stood before the Emperor and placed his fist over his heart in a soldier's salute. Augustus finished perusing the scroll in his lap and looked up. Pilate had seen him in public on many occasions, and had heard him address the Senate, but this was his first time to be close to the Emperor. His first impression was how tired the man looked. Caesar was past seventy years of age, and he was wearing those years heavily after the Varus disaster. The piercing blue eyes regarded Pilate with a look of mild amusement. The weight of the Empire seemed to ease for a moment, and Caesar gave him a warm smile.

"Pontius Pilate—so you are the young legate my son says he cannot do without!" he said. "I hope that you are as indispensable as he claims, since good urban praetors are very hard to come by."

Pilate allowed himself to relax just a bit. "I have served under your son's command for several years, sir, and we work well together. I have arranged for my fellow praetors to cover the duties of my district. The timing is somewhat regrettable, but an opportunity to campaign under a general like Tiberius is not to be missed!"

"And, of course, serving under a man who will one day be Emperor of Rome is not a bad path to advancement for an ambitious young pleb like yourself, is it?" asked Caesar, his gaze narrowing.

Pilate's nervousness instantly returned, but he knew better than to attempt a falsehood to this man who had survived Rome's treacherous political currents for over fifty years. "Of course, sir. The surest path for any Roman to advance himself is through service in a victorious army under a great general. I was born too late to serve under you or your father, the *Divus Julius*; but from what I have seen Tiberius inherited the family's military skills. My duties to him have kept me in Rome for several years now, but I would like to actually serve against the enemy at some point, and such a moment may not come again!"

Caesar Augustus nodded. "Spoken like a Roman!" he said. "I prefer a little honest ambition to false humility any day. I release you from your duties as urban praetor to serve as a legate under the command of my son, Tiberius. However, to compensate the city of Rome for the loss of your services, you will donate two hundred denarii to each of your fellow praetors, and donate an additional two hundred to the Temple of Mars for your safe return and good fortunes in battle. Thus your colleagues will be reimbursed for covering your responsibilities while you are with the army, and the god of war placated. Make sure that the amount is deposited before you cross the *pomerium* to join the army. That will be all."

Pilate swore to himself as he left the Forum. The Emperor was not letting him off cheap! There were twelve praetors in all, six of them assigned to Rome itself, and six scattered throughout the provinces. Twelve hundred denarii was not a fortune, but it was a considerable sum nevertheless, especially for a young officer who could not call upon his family's wealth. His father had been blessed with five children, two daughters who required a dowry to marry, and three sons to climb the *cursus honorum*. Simply put, the family did not have enough money to finance Pilate's German excursion, and he did not have the funds on hand himself after the expensive election he had just gone through.

But Rome's moneylenders were a thriving part of the economy, and Pilate knew that legates headed into the field of conflict were considered a good investment. He was senior enough in rank that the odds favored his safe return, and foreign campaigns invariably meant foreign plunder—treasures from enemy temples, proceeds from the sale of captives brought back as slaves, and money earned by selling the military equipment of fallen enemy soldiers. Soldiering was a profitable business for Rome's officers, and the moneylenders knew it.

Before nightfall Pilate had sufficient funds borrowed, and the next morning he called on his fellow praetors and handed them the letters of credit from his bank—wealthy Romans had long since ceased carrying coin of any significant amount in the city itself. However, he did withdraw two hundred newly minted silver coins after that to take to the Temple of Mars. Offering a letter of credit to a god was considered very poor taste! As he entered the temple, he saw that the fires of the altar were lit once more, signifying that Rome was at war. It was a point of great pride to Augustus that he had extinguished those fires more often, and for longer, than any ruler in Rome's history. It was the Emperor's preference for diplomacy over war that made opportunities for advancement, like Pilate was about to enjoy, so rare. As the young officer donned his scarlet legate's cape and mounted his horse, he thanked Fortuna, the goddess of luck, that he had made such a good impression on Tiberius. With any luck, this German campaign would mark the beginning of his rise to power. Who knew where that path would take him, or how far? These thoughts made good companions as he steered his course northward.

Pilate joined the army at Tolosa, where Tiberius was mustering his forces. They would have to cross four separate provinces to get to the German frontier. The barbarian tribes of the deep forests had launched a series of raids on Roman colonies after the defeat of Varus, leaving burnt-out farmsteads and charred corpses in their wake. Tiberius was advancing with four full legions under his command, three veteran and one newly recruited—all told, over twenty-four thousand infantry, cavalry, and auxiliaries. It was a force small enough to move with great speed if need be, but formidable enough to deal with a very large enemy host. The two great military men of the previous generation, Gaius Marius and Julius Caesar, had taught Rome that her legions need not be huge to be victorious. A well-commanded, mobile, smaller force was more than capable of fending off vastly superior numbers. What really counted was not so much the quality of the army as the quality of the commander, as Varus had demonstrated. Fortunately for them all, Tiberius was no Varus!

Pilate was appointed second-in-command of the newly recruited Sixteenth Legion, under the leadership of Flavius Sixtus, a hoary old veteran who had marched with Tiberius and Agrippa in their famous campaign to Armenia thirty years before, when Tiberius had been younger than Pilate was now. The veteran soldier regarded the young Pilate with a keenly appraising eye. "Tiberius has taken a liking to you, young legate," he said, "and he and I go way back. If he says you're able to do the job, then I'm inclined to respect his judgment."

"Thank you, sir!" said Pilate. "I hope that I will not disappoint either of you."

The march through the three Gallic provinces proved uneventful. It was fall, the crops were being harvested, and the harvest had been good enough that the army did not lack for food. By the time they reached the land of the Belgae, though, they were entering the zone where the raiders from Germania had done the worst damage, and food became scarcer. The veterans tightened their belts and scrimped on their rations, and the new recruits did their best to emulate them, albeit with more grumbling.

"*Legatus!*" called one of the legionaries as Pilate rode by. "When are we going to see some of those blond German Amazons the old-timers keep telling us about? Not to mention the famous German bread and mead?"

"Idiot!" snapped his centurion. "You won't see a German lass until you feel her dagger slip between your ribs!"

Pilate nodded his approval at the centurion's riposte, but then addressed the soldier anyway. "This province cannot feed us as well as the Gauls to the south, because the accursed Germans stole all their food, their livestock, and their women! So if you want bread, and mead, and meat, and women, you are going to have to beat the Germans to get them, son!"

"Bring them on, then!" shouted the soldiers. "We're getting hungry!" Laughter ran through the ranks, and Pilate allowed himself a tight-lipped smile before he rode on. They were good boys, he thought, and had the potential to become good soldiers. He wished he had the effortless ability to inspire love in his troops, as the great soldiers of previous wars had. A simple jest with the ranks taxed his social skills to their limit, but he knew from experience that such exchanges were worth the effort. Soldiers would die to please a general who treated them with respect and affection.

Flavius Sixtus was such a general, and Pilate knew it. He studied the old veteran carefully as the army proceeded northward, determined to learn all he could from this man who had served Rome for over forty years. He noticed that Sixtus rarely rode for long when the army was on the march. He would ride to the rear of the legion and dismount, sending his horse back up to the vanguard with a servant, and then proceed to march alongside the soldiers, working his way up the legion, taking a moment or two to visit with every century, and calling every centurion by name. It might take him half the day, but when he was done, every member of the legion would be able to say that their general had marched alongside them and bantered with them. So, after a day or two, Pilate dismounted and made the walk with him, carefully learning the names of the legion's fifty centurions in the process.

The real wonder of the Roman army, reflected Pilate, was its ability to turn a rural meadow into a fully fortified camp in a matter of a couple of hours. Supply wagons hauled the portable timbers and joists, and when Tiberius spotted the site he wanted them to camp for the night, the legionaries went to work with a vengeance. Palisades were erected, trenches were dug, and tents pitched in perfect order. Guard towers were assembled, and watches posted for the night. In the morning, the same process was followed in reverse—the tents were packed away, the guard towers disassembled and their parts neatly stacked on wagons, along with the palisade walls, and in a matter of an hour and a half, 24,000 men were ready to resume the march.

If the generals intended to occupy the same location for more than a night or two, the portable fortifications would be reinforced with timber felled locally, and the walls doubled in height. The site would be chosen based on the availability of water—usually the camp would straddle a spring or stream—and in a matter of a week, the army's camp would be transformed into a miniature city, with streets and gates and tents that came to resemble small houses more and more as the soldiers added wood floors and walls. Of course, such long-term camps usually meant the army was going into winter quarters, and would be in the area for an extended stay. No chance of that until they had come to grips with the enemy, Pilate thought.

But the enemy was seemingly reluctant to put in an appearance that winter. Once the army arrived along the border with Germania, a strange quiet descended over the region. Less than six months had passed since the Germans had destroyed Varus' legions and captured their standards, but now that Tiberius and his legions were on their doorstep, they withdrew into the dark forests of Germania and bided their time. The four legions marched up and down the border for over a month, and then went into winter camp along the east bank of the Rhine in December.

Not long after that, Flavius Sixtus died in his sleep one night, and Pilate found himself in sole command of the legion. Tiberius, grown increasingly dour and glum in the bitter cold, nonetheless spoke encouragingly to the assembled legions at Sixtus' funeral pyre.

"Flavius Sixtus was a Roman of the Romans, a man of courage and skill, whose love for his legionaries was matched only by his skill in commanding them," Tiberius said. "He died as he lived—in a military encampment, defending the honor of Rome against her enemies. Do you think such a noble soul would depart for Elysium without leaving his beloved boys in the most capable of hands? Sixtus would not have felt content to abandon this world unless he was certain that Lucius Pontius Pilate would lead his legion with the same skill and care that he always displayed. So even as we mourn the passing of our beloved general and friend, let us take courage in the skill and leadership of the successor he leaves to take his place!" The men cheered, and even though Pilate knew that they were cheering the memory of the beloved general, he felt his chest swell with pride all the same.

Six weeks later, the Cheruscii—the same tribe that had destroyed Varus' army the previous year—came screaming down from the forests and launched themselves at the Roman defenses. Sixty thousand Germans—tall, their blond hair stiffened into fantastic spikes, and wielding iron-tipped spears—stormed the palisades as the Roman legionaries used all their ingenuity to keep the camp from falling. Scorpions and ballistae were fired into the howling masses as fast as they could be reloaded, and the fighting on the wall grew furious.

Tiberius was in the thick of it from the start, grimly stalking the walls and barking orders to his centurions. As the fighting grew more intense, each of the senior legates took one side of the encampment, staying on the wall constantly. Pilate discovered that he enjoyed battle very much—the fear of death was like a drug that kept his nerves on a razor edge, intensifying every sensation. Near the climax of the fighting, a particularly persistent band of Germans got over the wall Pilate was guarding, and into the Roman camp. Sextus Dividicus, Pilate's *primus pilus* centurion, was borne to the ground by the crush and disarmed. A huge German warrior stood over him, about to skewer the hapless officer with a spear, when Pilate launched himself at the barbarian and drove his gladius deep into the man's belly. The German gave a howl of pain, and Pilate yanked the sword free and stabbed him again through the throat, ending the howls abruptly. Three more Germans hurled themselves at him, and Pilate slashed and parried like a madman. In a matter of moments, all three of them lay dead, and Sextus was back on his feet and fighting by his side. The demoralized troops rallied around their general, driving the Germans back across the palisade. Pilate ordered the scorpions brought up and began pelting the German ranks with stinging stone missiles.

The huge barbarians roared in fury and massed for another charge. Pilate looked at his thin ranks and knew that this moment could turn the tide of the battle one way or the other.

"Archers!" he shouted. A hundred crossbowmen leaped to the walls as the Germans began rushing the fortifications again. "On my command— FIRE!" roared Pilate, and a hundred bowstrings twanged at once. Nearly every bolt seemed to find its mark, and a good portion of the enemy's front rank crumbled to the ground.

"Flamepots!" he shouted next. A row of catapults hurled a dozen pots of boiling oil at the enemy, and a company of Gallic bowmen followed with fire arrows which ignited the fluid that soaked the advancing barbarians. Screams of anguish went up and down the ranks as the flames scorched flesh and clothing.

"Now! Scorpions! Let them have it!" Pilate ordered, and a shower of lead and stone pellets, each the size of a duck egg, was launched at high speed, denting helmets and shields and breaking bones where they struck. Howls of pain and frustration welled up from the enemy, and then, as suddenly as the attack had come, it ended. Within a few minutes, the last of the Germans fled the field. An eerie quiet descended over the Roman camp, broken only by the groans of the wounded.

"By the gods, sir—that was as neat a bit of fighting as I have ever seen!" said Sextus as he cleaned his blade on the cape of a fallen Cherusci. "I must confess, I thought of you as a bit of a dandy when we first met, but Julius Caesar himself could not have turned back that assault any better."

Pilate allowed himself a grin. "Thank you, centurion!" he said. "Things did get rather intense there, didn't they?"

The veteran soldier looked at Pilate respectfully. "That they did, sir, and you saved my life—and you held your ground and killed several of the enemy with your own hands. Didn't he, boys?" Sextus asked the men around them.

They cheered in the affirmative, and then grew suddenly quiet as a familiar figure in a red cape approached. Tiberius Caesar looked at the sprawled bodies of the enemy and the battered survivors with satisfaction. "Well, Pontius Pilate, you have repaid my confidence in full!" he said. "The enemy threw his toughest men at your wall, and I had no reinforcements to send you at that moment. But it looks as if you did not need them!"

Pilate gave a respectful bow, and suddenly Sextus spoke up. "Sir, I would like to recommend the legate receive the Civic Crown! He saved my life and held his ground throughout the battle, and personally killed at least five of those big fellows lying there."

Pilate was stunned. The *corona civitas*! There was only one higher honor that Rome could give! The Civic Crown carried with it a full membership in the Senate and an exemption from all taxes, and its holders were always honored at public events when every Senator present rose when they entered. Tiberius looked at Pilate and nodded.

"It sounds as if you have earned the honor, Legate!" he said. "Now have a drink and wash your face. I want to see all the officers in my tent in half an hour. Now, men, throw the enemy bodies back over the wall, post sentries, and have some dinner!" The men cheered as the general departed, and the centurions surrounded Pilate and congratulated him on his honor.

Half an hour later he and the other legates and lieutenants stood in Tiberius' tent and faced the general, whose usual grim demeanor had returned. At his side was his second-in-command, Julius Caesar Germanicus. Germanicus was Tiberius' natural nephew and adoptive son and heir, but there was little love between them. He was, however, Rome's best young general, and one of its most beloved public figures. He would make his mark in the years to come, but for now, he was a loyal subordinate to a prickly and difficult general.

14

"An excellent effort today, gentlemen," said Tiberius. "The enemy threw about sixty thousand of his warriors at us, and as near as I can tell, left about half of them lying on the ground outside our camp. We lost about a thousand killed and perhaps as many wounded, but considering the odds and the suddenness of the attack, those losses are actually minimal. The enemy only breached our walls at one point, and thanks to young Pilate here, they were thrown back quickly and forcefully!" He nodded at Pilate, who flushed and bowed. The other legates grinned and thumped him on the back.

"But I didn't come to Germany to fend off attacks; I came here to avenge our fallen comrades and *destroy* those responsible for their deaths!" Tiberius' face darkened, and he pounded his fist on the table for emphasis. "Now we have a dilemma on our hands. My scouts followed the retreating Germans, and I am waiting for them to return and tell us where their camp is. I want to set out in pursuit and catch them at dawn and destroy their army, as they destroyed Varus and his legions! But at the same time, we are the only army Rome has north of the Alps right now, except for two understrength legions in western Gaul. If we should perish, there is nothing to keep the Germans from harrowing all our provinces from here to Italy!"

The men nodded. The loss of Varus' legions, and the cost of the dreadful campaign into the Balkans three years before, had left Rome's armies stretched thin. Another victory by the Germans might throw all the northern provinces into rebellion, and destroy the *Pax Romana* that Augustus had worked so hard to achieve.

"So we must temper our desire for vengeance with caution," said Tiberius. "I want to take ten thousand men out of our camp about six hours from now, as soon as I hear back from our scouts. Germanicus, you will command the remainder until I return. If I do not return, fortify this camp even more strongly and send to Rome for reinforcements. Then, next spring, you can retrieve my skull from whatever tree the Germans have it nailed to—unless one of their kings uses it for a drinking cup!" He laughed, but it was a humorless laugh. The awful fate of Quinctilius Varus had been told from one end of Rome to another. Tiberius continued: "Of course, I have every intention of returning, and if Fortuna smiles on us, I will come back bearing all three of Varus' standards! Pilate, Verbinius, and Cassius—pick

15

the strongest, least exhausted men from your legions and tell them to get some sleep while they can. We march before dawn!"

Pilate wound up taking about half of his legion—he had several hundred dead and wounded, but considering the ferocity of the fighting, they had gotten off pretty lightly. The Gallic scouts came filtering back into camp at midnight. These men were walking forest spirits, Pilate thought as he beheld them, wrapped in black fabric with twigs and leaves protruding from them at every angle. You could walk right by them in broad daylight and not realize they were there!

They reported that the Germans were encamped some twenty miles distant, exhausted and demoralized. Their camp was guarded, but not heavily so, because they were counting on the Romans being too battered and worn out to pursue them. Pilate sent the centurions to wake his men, and an hour after midnight, the expedition set forth. Two stripped down legions, double timing through the forest, ready to wreak havoc on a foe they despised—Pilate would not have wanted to be in the German camp when they arrived!

As the sun cleared the horizon they could see the smoke of the campfires rising before them. Tiberius gave the order, and Pilate sent two dozen of his best Numidian archers forward. In a matter of moments, the German sentries were dropped where they stood, and not a single one lived to give an alarm. The legionaries formed up, the archers rejoined their ranks, and then Tiberius raised his sword and lowered it dramatically.

With a roar of pure fury, the Roman legionaries charged into the German camp, unleashing their *pilae* at short range, then wading in with gladius in one hand and shield in the other. The rain of spears had skewered dozens of Germans, and the sight of the Roman army descending on their camp dismayed many of them. Some of the forest warriors had already begun to break and run before the legionaries came to grips with the host.

But most of them stood their ground and tried to defend their camp. They knew the reputation of the Romans, and were determined to die on their feet rather than live on their knees. For the second time in twenty-four hours, Pontius Pilate felt the joy of battle as he threw himself into the enemy's ranks, slashing and stabbing at the huge warriors. The clash of arms sounded like a hundred blacksmiths hammering their forges at once— except that molten metal did not scream when the hammer struck it!

The battle lasted less than an hour. Another ten thousand Germans lay dead when it was done, and at least five thousand warriors, plus a host of women and children, were taken prisoner. The victory was not without cost, though. Another thousand Romans lay dead or wounded, and Varus' eagle standards were nowhere to be found. However, in the general's tent, three large chests full of gold coin and jewels were recovered, as well as the mistress and young son of Arminius, the German mastermind.

The march back to the Roman encampment was much slower and more exhausting than the trip in had been. The adrenaline had subsided, and the men were feeling the full effects of fighting two pitched battles within twenty-four hours. The mournful wailing of the captives only added to the gloomy atmosphere—the German women knew what fate awaited them when they were turned over to the legionaries, and pleaded with their menfolk to save them. The vanquished warriors ignored their pleas, marching forward grimly with their heads down and their fists clenched. Before sunset, the legions were within sight of the camp. They turned their captives over to Germanicus' soldiers and tumbled to their tents, exhausted but victorious.

Two days later, Tiberius assembled the entire army to hand out the decorations and awards that the men had won. In accordance with tradition, Tiberius' own decorations were displayed for the men to see, drawing whistles of amazement from those who had not seen them before. The only honor the Emperor's adopted son had not won was the *corona granica*, the Grass Crown, which was only given to those who single-handedly saved a legion from destruction, and then helped it defeat the enemy. Only a handful of soldiers in Rome's storied past had won this coveted honor—a simple crown woven of the grass from the field where the deed was done.

But many other decorations were handed out that day—two Civic Crowns; one for Pilate and one for Germanicus, and many gold, silver, and bronze *phalerae*, as well as several golden *torcs* and *armillae*. These were medallions, necklaces, and armbands that all signified specific acts of valor on the battlefield. Pilate received one golden armband and one gold and three silver medallions, in addition to his Civic Crown. He was now a legitimate war hero, honored by law and custom as a true son of Rome. Many other soldiers were decorated that day, and Tiberius was hailed as

17

*imperator*, or conqueror, by his men for the fourth time in his career, guaranteeing him a triumphal march when he returned to Rome.

That was the end of the fighting for the season. The Germans withdrew into their forest and contented themselves with small raids and acts of arson, and the Romans withdrew their line of settlement back west of the Danube and fortified their strongholds all up and down the frontier.

It was a couple of nights after the battle that Pilate made an uncomfortable discovery about himself, triggered by a common accident. His Greek servant Sosthenes was an inoffensive, mild-mannered slave given to occasional clumsiness. Pilate had just finished an oil bath and had changed into a comfortable tunic to spend the evening writing letters to his family when Sosthenes stumbled and spilled a cup of wine all over the fine linen garment.

"You dolt!" snapped Pilate. "This tunic is ruined!"

"I'm terribly sorry, master!" stammered the Greek, but his apology did no good. Pilate balled up his fists and struck him hard in the face. The slave wailed and tried to cover himself—no Roman slave would dare lift a hand to his master, for fear of crucifixion—but Pilate waded into him, punching and kicking with a fury he did not know he had. Half an hour later, he threw himself on his bed exhausted, and the weeping slave crawled from the tent, leaving several teeth on the floor.

The next day, Pilate did not know what to think. His educated, urbane half was horrified at the savagery of his own temper, and by the damage he just had inflicted on a loyal and well-mannered servant. But another part of his mind—a baser part, a slavering beast coiled around his psyche like a serpent—relished the memory of each blow landed, and each drop of blood shed. To his horror, Pilate had discovered that since his initiation in battle, he *liked* being cruel—and that discovery shook him to his core.

There in the bitter cold German winter, the two halves of Pontius Pilate emerged together for the first time—the brave, competent, and intelligent soldier who had learned to inspire loyalty and respect from his men; and the angry, vengeful, and petty martinet who delighted in harming those powerless to defend themselves. As Pilate pondered the events of the evening, he wondered which side of his character would be the one he was remembered for. Only time would tell, he supposed.

# CHAPTER TWO

The next year in Germania was uneventful. Tiberius pulled back all the remaining Roman colonies and farms to the east side of the Danube, consolidating Rome's position within a more defensible border. Germanicus did more and more of the actual soldiering, leading his men on punitive raids against the Cheruscii and seeking clues as to the location of Varus' lost eagles. As for Pilate, after winning honors on the battlefield, he now found his legion mainly involved in helping Roman colonists relocate, and finally building a permanent fort on the banks of the Danube where they would be able to protect several large communities that were less than an hour's ride away. Garrison life was boring, for the most part, he found. But he kept the men whipped into shape with stern discipline, for one never knew when the Cheruscii or their allies might come calling.

Pilate was listening to the report from a patrol across the river when Tiberius came riding into his camp late that fall, with a dozen lictors preceding him and two squads of soldiers riding behind. The rail-thin, dour general dismounted and entered the tent, brusquely returning Pilate's salute.

"By all means, Legate, finish your business!" he said, so Pilate nodded to the centurion to continue.

"Well, sir, things seemed pretty quiet for most of our patrol, but we found evidence of a pretty large camp about three miles east. Too big for one of the small raiding parties we've been getting through lately—more like a full cavalry reconnaissance. They appeared to be headed southward as far as we could trace their trail," the patrol leader finished.

Pilate nodded. "Thank you, centurion," he said. "You and your men have earned some rest. Report back for duty tomorrow morning. Dismissed!"

The soldiers saluted and left the room, and Pilate turned toward Tiberius. "To what do I owe the honor, sir?" he asked.

Tiberius did not answer. He was looking around Pilate's tent, studying the map of the frontier that was spread out on the table, and Pilate's Spartan sleeping chamber. Finally he turned and spoke. "So, how do you like garrison duty, Legate Pilate?" he asked.

"Not as much fun as actually fighting the enemy, but it is a necessity," said Pilate. "So I try to keep the men sharp and keep my eyes open for mischief from the other side of the river."

The general nodded. "You have done all I could ask of any legion commander since the unfortunate loss of Flavius Sixtus," he said. "You have earned the respect of your men, and been a true lion in combat. But this post is enough to rot any man's brain! I have been asked to return to Rome—my father is feeling his years and wants his successor close by. Germanicus will take over the war on this front, and I have no doubt he will make the Cheruscii rue the day they betrayed Varus!"

Pilate kept his thoughts to himself. Germanicus was indeed a fierce and brave soldier, but he was also very close in blood to the Emperor—in fact, rumors said that Augustus had actually preferred him for the succession, but the old Empress Livia had persuaded him to name Tiberius instead. No wonder Tiberius was willing to leave him in this gods-forsaken frontier on the back side of nowhere!

"I am going to need some reliable men at my back when I return to Rome," said Tiberius. "Men who know how to command, and who also know something of Roman politics. Your election to *Praetor Urbanus* was a neat bit of work, from what I have heard. Your Civic Crown guarantees your life membership to the Senate, but do you aspire to higher office?"

Pilate swallowed hard. Tiberius could be a ruthless enemy, but he would also make a splendid ally. In all likelihood, he would be Emperor within a year or two. The highest offices of the Republic—tribune, consul, and censor—did not wield the power they had before Rome's civil wars had brought the old government crashing down and given birth to the office of Emperor. Still, those offices carried a great deal of honor and *arctoritas*, that indefinable Roman term for a man's sum total of influence and social status. Tiberius could indeed lift him high up on the *cursus honorum*—but he could also cast him down just as fast if he did not perform well. Finally he spoke.

"I would like to be consul someday," he said. "There has not been a consul from the *Pilatti* in three generations, and my father has always hoped that I would bring that honor back to the family."

Tiberius nodded. "It is a worthy ambition and an important office as well. You might well do it honor! But for now, I have another post in mind for you—one that will serve your ambitions and my purposes equally well. I would like you to run for Tribune of the Plebs."

Pilate gasped. Tribune of the Plebs! That was the one office from the era of the Republic that still retained some of its political clout. The Tribunes represented the People of Rome, and they had the power to veto any action by the consuls or the Senate. Theoretically, they could veto the Emperor as well, but as the Emperor kept at least three Tribunes as his personal clients, that option had never been put into effect—since the ten Tribunes could also veto each other. So Tiberius was getting a jump on his responsibilities as Emperor by making sure that he had a loyal Tribune in his pocket! Very clever, thought Pilate. Augustus had trained his heir apparent very well.

"I think that is a job that I would enjoy, and perform quite well," he said. "But the Tribune's elections are enormously expensive!" Indeed they were. The People of Rome did vote for the ten Tribunes every year, but their votes could always be bought. It was a rare Tribune who won his election on popularity alone.

Tiberius laughed—a rather short sharp barking sound. "Fear not, Lucius Pontius!" he said. "If you are going to be my man, of course I will help you secure your election. Probably for more than one year, in fact. I do not know yet exactly what I will need from you, but all I ask is that, when the time comes, you propose the legislation I request, or impose your veto when I need it."

Pilate squared his shoulders and faced the heir to the Imperial throne. "But what if your request violates my conscience, and my principles as a Roman?" he asked.

"Then you will have to act as your conscience dictates," said Tiberius. "However, if you cease to be useful to me, then I will cease to support your advancement."

Pilate nodded. "I would expect nothing less," he said.

"Good!" said Tiberius. "And I do not expect that you will have anything to worry about. I am no Lucius Cornelius Sulla! I anticipate no purges and proscriptions, only sound legislation and a few needed reforms. My honored father has taken the creaky old machinery of the Republic and made it fly again. My job will be to make sure that what he has done is not undone after he departs from us. With your help, I plan to achieve that. I leave for Rome in three days. Decimus Tullius will succeed you in command of the legion; please introduce him to the men and show him the ropes over the next couple of days, and be at my camp at dawn three days hence!"

With a swirl of his crimson cape, the general swept from the room, leaving Pilate to mull over his fate. Tribune of the Plebs! This was an unexpected kiss from Fortuna indeed! Pilate straightened his breastplate and strode from his tent to meet the Legate Tullius. It would not do to keep his successor waiting!

* * *

The trip back to Rome was a nightmare. The fall rains had come early, swelling streams and soaking the ground. The dirt tracks in Nearer Germania had not yet been replaced with good Roman roads, and the horses slipped and tripped for the first hundred miles or so, throwing all the riders into a foul temper. Tiberius was a glum and quiet man at the best of times, and he simply withdrew into himself under these deplorable conditions.

Pilate hated mud, and he hated being cold and wet with no hope of shelter before nightfall. His mood grew fouler and fouler as they rode on through the interminable rain. He had done his best to control the raging impulse that had led him to beat poor old Sosthenes half senseless—in fact, he had freed the slave not long after the episode, so great was his guilt over what he had done—but the misery of his current condition made him long to punch, beat, kick, and gouge at someone. He found himself wishing that one of the legionaries would commit some horrible breach of discipline so he could at least watch a good flogging! But the soldiers feared the wrath of Tiberius as much as a Vestal Virgin feared being alone with a man, so no opportunity presented itself.

They arrived at a miserable hamlet called Barasinium, in the south of Gaul, and spent an uncomfortable night in its sole inn—the beds were so crawling with vermin that the officers threw all the bedding into the fireplace and slept on the bare floor, wrapped in their capes. The next day was cold and cloudy, with a promise of rain in the air, and all of them were stiff and sore as they mounted up and set out southward. At least the Alps were in sight now, and soon they would be through the high pass and down into the warm and fertile country near Tolosa, from which they had departed two years before.

So intent were they on the last leg of this journey through Gaul that the bandits' attack caught them nearly by surprise. The arrows came whistling from the woods on their right, dropping several of Tiberius' lictors and military escorts as they marched. Then with a howl, some twenty bandits came leaping from the trees, swords at the ready. Pilate's gladius fairly leaped into his hand as he spurred his mount toward the scruffy-looking horde.

The battle was short and sharp. The bandits had apparently mistaken the general's convoy for some sort of valuable shipment—Tiberius' personal goods only took up two wagons, downright Spartan for a general, and there was one more wagon carrying their food and supplies—and so had not realized they were attacking hardened Roman combat veterans. Pilate split two skulls with his blade before an arrow struck his horse in the flank and he was thrown. Fortunately, he landed well, not breaking anything, and was on his feet in a trice. A huge bandit wielding a Gallic spear was charging straight at him, and he ducked the thrust and drove his blade clean through the man's throat. However, he had a devil of a time yanking it back out, and another bandit was on him before he could free the blade. The man had a large dagger raised overhead, and Pilate caught his arm as he tried to bring it down. He used the man's own momentum to overextend the arm, and then delivered a smashing blow to the elbow while holding the man's wrist tightly, completely dislocating his arm. The dagger flew out of the screaming bandit's hands, and Pilate threw himself on his opponent, pinned him, and then quickly surveyed the scene. The legionaries and lictors were fully engaged with the bandits, and making short work of them. He was in no immediate danger, nor was there any threat close by that needed deterring. He had a moment to enjoy himself, so he did. Using his fists, he pummeled the bandit's face, relishing each blow as he felt the nose breaking under his fists. When the man was unconscious, Pilate finished him off with his own dagger, then stood up and dusted himself off. He found Tiberius Caesar eyeing him coolly.

"Impressive fisticuffs, Legate!" he commented.

Pilate walked over and planted a foot on the shoulder of his fallen foe, yanking his sword free of the man's throat at last. "When blades are not handy, bare hands have to do!" he replied.

Tiberius nodded, but there was an odd twinkle in his eye, a look of— understanding, perhaps? There were dark rumors about Tiberius to be sure, whispered about the camp: that he had a murderous temper when crossed, and that he was known to watch floggings with just a little bit too much enjoyment. The same kind of rumors, had Pilate but known it, that were whispered about him!

By now all the bandits were dead or captured, with no further loss to Tiberius' party than the five men who fell in the initial assault. Tiberius gestured Pilate to follow him as he surveyed the four captives. One of them had a legion tattoo on his forearm—none other than the fabled Thirteenth, one of Julius Caesar's old legions! Tiberius glared at him fiercely.

"I sincerely hope, thief, that you had that tattoo done in an attempt to masquerade as a legionary, for I would hate to think that any soldier of Rome would be so foolish as to attack a general's escort, no matter how long ago his service was!" snapped the general.

The man's eyes bugged out as he recognized his interrogator. "Legate Tiberius!" he said. "I was with you and Agrippa in Armenia! By Jupiter, sir, I had no idea this was a general's escort! My mates and I were hoping for a pay wagon—times has been hard since I was drummed out of the legion!"

The heir to the Empire narrowed his eyes. "They are about to get a lot harder, fool!" he said softly. "Legionaries! Cut me some beams, and quickly! I want all four of these men crucified within the hour!"

The captives howled in protest—three of them did, anyway; the fourth one had taken a hard blow to the skull and was knocked senseless, although Pilate imagined he would wake soon enough when the nails drove through his wrists. The lictors kept them bound and guarded while the soldiers procured the necessary wood to do the grim deed. As for Pilate and Tiberius, they paused there by the road and ordered their cook to prepare lunch for the entire party. They were just tucking into the hastily prepared meal as the

24

soldiers began nailing up the offending bandits. Pilate found their screams made his meal that much more enjoyable, and when he looked over at Tiberius, seated across from him on the back of the supply wagon, he saw that the dour old general was actually smiling. Not only that, the clouds were parting, and the sun was starting to shine again. Things were definitely looking up!

That was their only real adventure on the road homeward. The journey across the Alps took three days, and the weather held nicely, although the high passes were bitter cold. But the mild winter south of the mountains gave way to a glorious spring as they neared the city of Romulus, and the local inns got more and more comfortable and luxurious as they got nearer to home.

Tiberius owned a pleasant, if small, villa just north of the city; the party stopped there for the night just before their arrival. They sent the lictors ahead to inform the Senate of their arrival, and Pilate had the chance for a long and luxurious soak, followed by a massage and scraping of his tired skin. Clad in a crisp white toga, with a goblet of excellent Samnian wine at his elbow, he felt like a true Roman gentleman again. Tiberius joined him a short while later, likewise cleaned off, freshly shaven, and clad in a fine toga. Pilate rose to greet him, and then they reclined on the couch together as a servant brought in a tray of sweet fruits and fresh baked bread.

"Tomorrow you will enter Rome and discuss the date of my triumph with the Senate," Tiberius said. "I also want you to take a letter to the Emperor for me, and receive any messages he may wish to send. Once you have reported back to me, you may tend to your own affairs for a few days. But do not leave the city—I want you to march with me in my triumphal parade!"

Pilate nodded. By longstanding tradition, Tiberius could not cross the *pomerium*, the city's sacred boundary, until after he celebrated his many victories in Germania. Crossing that line beforehand would require him to lay down his *imperium*, the authority by which he governed his legions, and disqualify him from having a triumph. So, like many a victorious Roman before him, he would wait outside the city walls for the day the Senate had appointed, receiving visits from his clients and taking care of his affairs through proxies.

Pilate wondered if Tiberius' wife, Julia, would attend the parade. Probably not, he thought. Her dislike of her husband and his distaste for her was well known to all. At one point her infidelities had become so flagrant that Tiberius had fled to Greece in embarrassment and loathing, and had to be coaxed back to Rome by the Emperor himself. So Pilate did not even bother asking if there was any message for her. He and his patron dined together in comfort and elegance, and after some light conversation they retired for the evening.

The next morning Pilate dressed himself in his full Legate's uniform, but left off his military decorations—he would wear them publicly for the first time in Tiberius' triumphal parade. He took the letters from Tiberius to the Senate and to the Emperor and headed toward Rome. The white walls and teaming markets rose up before him like a mystical kingdom in a story of old, and he had to pause and drink in the view. What better lot was there in the world than to be a Roman in this age? The civil wars of the past were done, and the peace Augustus had so carefully forged through a combination of war and diplomacy had created a time of unprecedented prosperity.

Soon he found himself riding toward the Forum, with the dome of the Senate building coming into sight. A few in the crowd recognized him, and as he mounted the steps toward the Curia Julia where the Senate met, a familiar face came down to greet him.

"Proculus!" he exclaimed. "How good to see you!"

"And you likewise, Lucius Pontius!" said the older man. He and Pilate's father had been longtime friends, and he had helped Pilate conduct his campaign for praetor before Pilate left for Germania.

"How is my family?" Pilate said. "I have not had a letter in several months."

"Your father is not well," said his old comrade. "He has lost weight, and his color is off. I suspect that he may have the Crab's Disease, to tell you the truth. It will do him good to see you again. Your brother Cornelius is in Sicily and your two younger brothers are serving with the army in Africa. Your sister Pontia has married a wealthy Senator twice her age, and is expecting her first child."

Pilate nodded. "And Cornelia?" he asked.

26

The old man looked at him sadly. "She was married to my son last year," he said. "Such a delightful girl! But she died last month after delivering a son. My household, and your father's, are still in mourning for her."

Pilate hung his head for a moment. Little Cornelia, gone so soon! She had been only seventeen when he left two years before, still ecstatic over her betrothal to Marcus Proculus. She had been the prettiest of Pilate's siblings, and his favorite. He swallowed hard, and looked up again. The old man was regarding him sadly.

"That is a difficult blow," Pilate said. "But I must mourn her later. My business right now is with the Senate, and then with the Emperor."

"A word to the wise, young Lucius," said Proculus. "I would reverse the order of those visits if I were you. Augustus is not the man he once was. At one time, your seeing the Senators first would have been considered perfectly proper and in accordance with the *mos maorum*. But age has not been kind to Augustus, and he is greedy for news of his kin. But after you have discharged your official business, perhaps you could dine with me and my family?"

"It will have to be tomorrow," Pilate said. "Tiberius wants me to return with news before the day is done."

Proculus nodded. "I assumed as much. I shall look for you tomorrow evening. But do try to see your father soon! He has been most concerned about you."

Pilate nodded and turned his steps from the Forum toward the Palatine, where Augustus' simple home was located. He remembered his last visit to the man, two years before, and found that he was not nearly as nervous. Two years had passed, by the calendar, but he felt at least a decade older than he had that day. No wonder, he thought. He had been an ambitious and rather callow youth of twenty-six when he had galloped away to join Tiberius at Tolosa. Now he was a legion commander and a decorated hero of Rome, with one major battle and numerous skirmishes under his belt. He did not forget the awesome power of Augustus, but he felt that he could at least hold his head up in the man's presence now.

There was a long line of clients waiting, but Pilate's uniform and the source of his message ushered him to the head of the line immediately. A servant showed him into Augustus' small receiving chamber, and he was shocked at his first sight of the Emperor of Rome. The man had physically shrunk since Pilate last saw him. Caesar had never been a big man, but he had always been well-proportioned and broad-shouldered, and carried himself so rigidly upright that he appeared to be larger than he actually was.

But that was no longer true. Augustus' hair was now snow-white and visibly thinning, the lines on his face deeper, and his eyes a bit more unfocused than they had been. The razor-sharp mind that had forged a failing Republic into a functional Empire seemed to be slowing down visibly, like an exhausted horse near the end of its race. He sat on his curule chair, his hands in his lap, staring downward, appearing to be almost asleep.

But then the old man looked up and saw Pilate, and the vision of decrepitude vanished like a dream. The shoulders squared, the eyes focused, the head snapped upright, and the old Caesar was back, with all of his majesty and humility. "Lucius Pontius Pilate!" he exclaimed. "Back from the wars, I see, and looking a good bit more seasoned than when I saw you last. My son says you acquitted yourself very well against the Cheruscii and their allies, but I have not had a letter from him in many weeks. Do you bring me news?"

Pilate saluted and stepped forward. "Yes, Caesar," he said. "Tiberius has returned to Rome, and waits outside the *pomerium* until after his triumph. He asked me to bring this missive to you." He handed the letter to the Emperor.

Caesar broke the seal and unrolled it, reading through its contents quickly and nodding here and there. When he finished, he gave a snort. "Just like the boy!" he said. "Two terse pages of official business, and not a word to me or his mother about how he is actually doing! I assume you rode with him on the homeward journey, Legate. Tell me, how fares my son?"

Pilate thought for a moment. "Tiberius is a hard man to read, Caesar. He is a rather morose person, at least in my experience of him. Brave, yes, and thoroughly competent at all he undertakes to do. But he does not allow any of us junior officers to be—well, to be his friends. All things considered, though, he seems to be feeling well enough."

Caesar nodded. "A man in power must choose his friends very carefully, young Pilate," he said. "I taught Tiberius that when he was very young, and he learned the lesson well. Too well, in fact. I have been careful in my friends, but I have still had them—a few, at least. None as close as my dear Marcus Agrippa, now gone from us for far too long! But a man must have a few choice individuals with whom he can occasionally set aside ceremony and simply enjoy life with. That is a lesson I fear that my Tiberius has not yet learned. Well, I suppose you must go and deliver his letters to the Senate now, eh?"

"Yes, sir, I must. May I bear any reply to Tiberius from you?" he asked.

"No," said the Emperor. "But you may bear me to him, when your business with the Senate is done. It has been too long since I sat on a horse and got outside these infernal walls! Come back for me in three hours. Perhaps I shall be done with all these pestilential hangers-on by then." Pilate bowed and turned to go, when the Emperor spoke again. "By the way, young man, you know that protocol really should have taken you to the Senate first, before you came to see me."

Pilate paused. Old and frail or not, the man did not miss a trick!

"I suppose that is true, my Emperor," he said. "But Tiberius is their political superior. He is your son."

The old man laughed, and the weight of the years seemed to fall from his shoulders. "By Jove, I like you, young fellow! Come back soon, and escort me to my son!" he said.

Pilate delivered Tiberius' message to the Senate and spoke with a number of the men there, discussing the details of the triumphal march and taking several letters from various senators to deliver. Then he was asked to give a personal account of the events in Germania over the last two years, and answered some pointed questions from a couple of curious politicians. After two hours, he extricated himself from the crowd and returned to the Palatine Hill. The line of clients outside the door was gone, and two saddled horses waited out front. Something struck him as odd about one of them, but it took him a minute to realize what it was. The horse had three toes on each foot instead of a normal hoof!

"Do you like Toes?" a familiar voice said.

Pilate turned and saluted the Emperor as Augustus came down the steps, wearing a crimson and purple mantle over a gorgeously trimmed bronze breastplate.

"I had heard that the Divus Julius rode a three-toed horse into battle, but I did not know there were any of them left in Rome!" Pilate replied.

"Caesar's Toes was this horse's grandsire," said Augustus. "It is a difficult trait to breed—perhaps one out of every five colts from a three-toed horse will inherit it. But they are the most sure-footed and courageous mounts in the world. I don't know where old Sulla found the first one, but he gave it as a gift to my divine father when he set out for his first provincial governor's seat, in Spain. This old fellow is probably going to be the last of the bloodline—he has sired dozens of colts, but none of the ones with toes instead of hooves lived to adulthood."

The two men mounted and rode down the streets toward the north gate of the city, flanked by six guards from the Emperor's own household. Pilate was astonished to see how quickly the bustling street cleared as they advanced. They reached the gate in a matter of ten minutes, when the same ride would have taken Pilate nearly an hour had he been alone.

The Emperor was in a loquacious mood, and the afternoon's conversation was one Pilate would never forget. Every temple, every hill or clump of woods, seemed to hold some significance for the old Emperor, and he told Pilate stories of his adoptive father, Gaius Julius Caesar, and his archrival for the succession, Marcus Antonius. He explained how it was his firm belief that Cleopatra, last of the Ptolemy Queens of Egypt, was in fact a dark sorceress who cast a spell on Rome's greatest soldier. "He was a man's man, was Antony, and a Roman of the highest ancestry!" said the Emperor. "And yet she unmanned him and turned him into a simpering Eastern potentate! He wore eye make-up and worshipped snakes and baboons, and according to the palace servants, she made him crawl on all fours like a beast while she rode on his back drinking wine from a golden goblet!"

"Remarkable!" said Pilate.

"I was never so glad to see anything as I was to see her lying there with two fang marks on her breast," Caesar continued. "What my father saw in her I will never know, but I saw a great threat to Rome, and to me. I lived in fear of her dark witchcraft the whole time I was in Egypt!"

30

"Whatever happened to the son she had by Caesar?" asked Pilate, and then snapped his mouth shut in horror. Whatever had possessed him to ask such a tasteless question?

But Augustus did not seem offended. "Many people have wanted to know the answer to that question, lad, but you are one of the very few who has had the audacity to actually ask me!" he said with a chuckle. "The truth is, I do not know. I don't even know for sure that he was Caesar's child, although his Greek tutors assured me that he was, and that he looked so much like Caesar as to be his twin! He slipped out of Alexandria in the confusion of the war, and was never seen again. I like to think that perhaps he made off to the desert and is living somewhere in peace, perhaps as a shepherd—or maybe as the prince of a nomadic tribe. Certainly, wherever he is, I wish him well. If Caesar was indeed his father, that would make us brothers, and I could never harm a brother." His voice trailed off, and Pilate had the distinct feeling he had just been lied to.

Moments later they arrived at Tiberius' villa, and he walked beside the Emperor up the stairs. Tiberius was dictating a letter to a scribe, but rose in surprise when he saw them enter.

"Father!" he said. "You should not have come out here!'

"Well, my boy, is not an old man allowed to come and see his son and heir after an absence of two years?" the Emperor asked.

"Of course," said Tiberius somewhat stiffly. "I was merely concerned for your health—"

"Nonsense!" snorted Augustus. "I know I am seventy-three years old, but I am not going to break in half just because I get on a horse. Everyone around me has turned into a gaggle of clucking old hens here lately!"

Tiberius actually smiled. "That is one thing I have never been accused of before!" he said. "So how are you, my father?"

Augustus said, "I am tired, my son. I have carried the weight of this Empire on my back for nearly forty-five years now, and I am ready to pass it on soon, I think. Your man Pilate was kind enough to escort me here when I asked him. He seems a decent fellow, if you ask me."

"Lucius Pontius has been quite useful to me," said Tiberius. "And I have kept him from his family far too long. Pilate, why don't you leave me with my father so you can go visit yours? I will summon you when I need you."

Pilate bowed. "Thank you, General," he said. With that he left the two most powerful men in the world to their own devices, and spurred his horse toward Rome and his family.

# CHAPTER THREE

The next few weeks passed quickly for Pilate, as he reconnected with his family and coordinated the preparations for Tiberius' triumphal parade. Only two of the legions that had fought under Tiberius in Germania were in Italy—the rest remained on the frontier under Germanicus. But they would march in the parade, following behind the ancient triumphator's chariot and their mounted officers. Pilate would ride in the first rank of those officers, directly behind Tiberius himself. Behind the legionaries would come the captives—not just the five thousand that had been captured in the battle Pilate took part in, but another ten thousand from Tiberius' first few years in Germania, including two kings and four tribal chieftains. The more valuable captives would be held in Rome as hostages; the ringleaders would be strangled in the Temple of Mars following the parade, and the common soldiers and civilians sold as slaves. Behind the unhappy captives would come wagon after wagon of captured treasure, idols, and weapons of war. Triumphs were the highlight of the season for the masses of everyday Roman citizens; men who had never been near a battlefield could feel, for a moment, that they had taken part in Rome's victories.

Pilate was enjoying the time in Rome, seeing his family again. His father was clearly not long for this world, but was determined to see his son riding in Tiberius' parade, so Pilate rented a box window in a friend's house overlooking the parade route, where the sick man could sit in comfort. Pilate also was enjoying spending time with the family of Gaius Proculus Porcius—most especially with his eighteen-year-old daughter, Procula Porcia. She was a classic Roman beauty with hair as dark as night and lips as red as strawberries in the high summer, but she was also highly intelligent and politically astute. She had several suitors at the moment, but was committed to no one, and Pilate was planning to ask for her hand once the triumph was over and done.

Tiberius was growing increasingly glum as the day approached. Pilate did not pry into his general's personal business, but he could see that relations among the Imperial family were strained. Augustus seemed genuinely fond of Tiberius, but at the same time frustrated by him. The Empress Livia doted on her son, who alternately seemed to adore her or despise her, according to his mood. As for Tiberius' wife, Julia, she remained away from Rome, disgraced after her father's sentence of banishment for her serial infidelity to her husband.

Pilate's star still seemed to be rising, however. Tiberius called him to the villa almost daily to plan the triumph, and also to discuss the future of Rome.

"It is no easy thing, being the heir of Augustus," he commented one afternoon, a week before the parade. "My father has cultivated an atmosphere of worship around himself which has drawn an enormous number of sycophants and fools to his side. During his prime, he could easily sort the fools from the useful clients, but age has clouded his judgment, and all too often he heeds the voice of flattery these days. I want to clear Rome of the useless sycophants and replace them with competent administrators!"

"What about those who are shameless sycophants and competent administrators?" asked Pilate.

Tiberius let out his barking laugh. "You mean those like you?" he asked. "You have a long way to go before you sink to the level of those I am speaking of! You have yet to write a single poem comparing me to Jove, Adonis, Mars, or any other god I can think of, and you are not trying to talk me into marrying any of your kin!"

Pilate nodded. "So I am either a very incompetent sycophant, or else I am a man who knows the limits of his usefulness," he said.

Tiberius shook his head. "I have a feeling, Lucius Pontius, that you have not begun to reach the limits of your usefulness to me! But more importantly, I think that you shall prove to be of great use to Rome. In the end, that is the standard by which I will judge you, and all my other clients. My father is handing down to me the greatest Empire the world has ever known. I intend to preserve it, to improve it, and to hand it down better than I found it! If you can help me do that, then you will rise high indeed!"

Those words were still ringing in Pilate's ears when he donned his uniform and decorations the morning of the Triumph. It was the first time he had actually worn the Civic Crown since he won it in Germania. With

34

the golden torc on his arm and his medals riding over his gleaming breastplate, he donned his crimson cape and mounted his horse feeling like Julius Caesar himself.

Tiberius waited in the ancient chariot that had carried every triumphator for the last four centuries, and the legions formed up neatly behind their centurions as all prepared to enter Rome through the ancient triumphal arch. The general's face was painted a deep red, and a golden crown of leaves was held over his head by a slave. For this day, the triumphator became the living incarnation of Mars, the Roman god of war, and all Rome congregated in the streets to pay homage to him.

Tiberius looked at Pilate and the other legates and spoke softly, moving his lips as little as possible to avoid causing the thick make-up to crack and flake off. "Enjoy this, my friends, because this is the one event that many Romans of great rank and prestige never get to take part in!" he said. "This chariot carried Scipio Africanus, Gaius Marius, and Julius Caesar. Today it is my turn to ride in it, but someday it may be yours. For now, enjoy the day!"

He turned and took his position, standing straight upright in the chariot, one hand on the rail, the other raised to salute the crowd. The slave held the crown of golden leaves above his head, and then leaned forward to whisper the ancient warning in his ear: *"Recordare, tu quoque sunt mortalia!"* Remember, you, too, are mortal!

The procession wound through the ancient streets of the city one district at a time before ending at the Forum. In the Suburba, thousands of people from every corner of the Empire stood in the streets, cheering themselves hoarse as the parade wound by. The legionaries smiled, waved, and winked at the pretty girls, while the officers rode straight and proud, glancing left and right, but making no gestures of greeting, as befitted their rank. The crowds were not so restrained—they howled, whistled, cheered, and gestured at the soldiers. The captive kings and princes were jeered and hissed at, but their escort of seasoned troops protected them from any violence. The rank-and-file captives had it worse—they were pelted with fruit and mud, and occasionally jostled or shoved. But that was all; everyone knew that these unfortunates would be showing up in the slave markets soon, and deliberately damaging them would be harming another person's property.

It took the better part of the morning for the procession to arrive at the great Roman Forum, and once there, Tiberius stepped up onto the platform to receive the adulation of the Senate. Then he sat in the high triumphator's chair, and his legates took their positions on either side of him. One by one, the captive kings and officers came and made their obeisance, then were hustled off to the Temple of Mars. After that, the legions marched by, saluting their general as they passed, and then breaking into the usual ribald and vulgar marching songs. For once they refrained from lyrics that would have slandered Tiberius himself—whether out of respect or fear of him, or simply from the fact that Tiberius had no known vices which made for funny rhymes, only the troopers knew.

Once the sacrifices to Mars were complete, the crowds surged toward the great open market, where tables groaning with food had been set out for them. At last the officers were freed from their stations, and Tiberius retired to his home on the Palatine to wash the red from his face. Pilate stepped toward the Senate's banquet hall, realizing that he was suddenly famished.

"A most satisfactory triumph for the Emperor's heir, don't you think?" came a voice at his elbow.

"Ave, Proculus!" said Pilate. "Indeed it was. This was the first triumph I have witnessed since I was fifteen, and it was most satisfying to be marching in it instead of standing in the crowd!"

The older man nodded. "I watched it from the window with your father," he said. "He was very gratified to see you so close to the triumphator's chariot!"

Pilate smiled. "I am glad he was well enough to see it," he said. "I fear he does not have long left with us."

Proculus nodded. "I will be surprised if he lives past midsummer," he said. "There is one more thing he told me he would like to see before he crosses the Styx."

"His eldest son's marriage?" asked Pilate.

"Exactly!" said Proculus.

"I have been meaning to speak to you about this," Pilate said. "With your permission, I should like to propose to your daughter, Procula Porcia."

The older man beamed. "Her mother and I have been hoping you would ask," he said. "She has been fond of you for many years, long before you went to Germania."

"That is gratifying to know," said Pilate. "I did not notice her much then, except to see that she was growing into a beautiful young lady. I will speak to her tomorrow morning. For now, how about if I join the feast with my future father-in-law?"

The two Romans linked arms and walked toward the couches that had been set up inside the Forum for the members of the Senate and senior army officers. As they stepped into the chamber, the members of the Senate rose as one and applauded the newest winner of the Civic Crown. Pilate returned their salutes with a generous bow, and then reclined at the table. Being shown such respect by men who were far his senior in years and rank filled him with a deep joy. His rise in the world was truly well begun!

The next morning Pilate went calling at the home of Gaius Proculus Porcius, dressed in his finest toga and bearing a fine, jeweled necklace as a gift for his lady. He was shown to the atrium, where Procula Porcia waited for him. Her carriage and posture were flawless, as befit a Roman lady, but her eyes were demurely cast downward, as befit a maiden unbetrothed.

"Good morning, Procula Porcia," said Pilate. "I trust you are well?"

"I am quite well, Pontius Pilate," she said. "It has been a joy to see you back in Rome, and I was very proud to see you honored before the city yesterday."

"I have spoken to your father, Porcia, to ask for your hand in marriage," said Pilate. "That is, if such a union is suitable to you."

She looked him in the eyes and smiled. "Nothing would suit me more!" she said. "Oh, Pilate, I was so hoping you would ask, and so afraid that you would not! Of course, I would marry whoever my father asked me to, but I was so afraid he would choose some fat old Senator thirty years older than me!"

"A Senator would be a fine match for your family," said Pilate. "And he could probably keep you in better style than I will be able to. Should I withdraw my request?"

"Silly man!" she said with a giggle. "You are a Senator, only younger and better looking than the majority of them. And the only way I want to be kept is by you!"

"Then kiss me, sweet girl, and we will call it a betrothal!" said Pilate. She did kiss him then, and it was a most satisfying kiss—enthusiastic but not overly erotic, as befit the virgin daughter of a respectable Roman family. "Now let me see how this looks on you!" he said, and placed his gift around her neck. The rubies and emeralds in the necklace shone against her lovely pale skin, and she embraced him again in gratitude for such a lavish gift. He held her close for a moment, then offered her his arm and went to the peristyle garden, where Proculus and his wife Marcia were waiting.

"Your daughter has accepted my proposal," said Pilate.

"Excellent!" said Proculus, clapping him heartily on the back. Marcia hugged their daughter and gave Pilate a guarded smile. "Have you given any thought to where you will live?" asked the father of the bride.

"I will be taking my captives to the slave market tomorrow," said Pilate. "I got first pick of the lot, and they should fetch top price. I also should be receiving my share of the plunder we took from the Germans soon. That will provide me more than enough wealth to purchase a nice house. I am thinking I should like to live outside the city walls, but close enough to easily ride into town."

"There is a nice house for sale in the Aventine District," said Marcia.

"I was not aware there were any nice houses in the Aventine!" said Pilate—the district was mainly known for its large markets, stores, taverns, and brothels.

"That's not entirely true," said Proculus. "The heart of the district has gone to seed, but along the east side there are some very nice homes. Understand, we are not making any sort of conditions—but we would appreciate your taking a look, at least. It's the most suitable residence we have found yet."

"Exactly how long have you been looking?" asked Pilate.

"Roughly speaking, since you returned to Rome and had dinner with us," replied his future father-in-law.

So it was that, a week before midsummer, Lucius Pontius Pilate and Procula Porcia were married in the garden of her parents' home. Tiberius himself presided over the ceremony in his office as Pontifex Maximus, and the Emperor sent a beautiful pair of silver drinking goblets as a wedding gift to the happy couple. Pilate then took his bride to his new home in the Aventine, which, as his in-laws had promised, was comfortable, well-appointed, and in a respectable neighborhood. Procula was a delightful spouse—attentive and always proper in public, affectionate and even sensual when they were alone. Pilate would always remember those first few weeks in their new home as some of the happiest days of his life.

Two weeks after the wedding, Pilate's father collapsed at home, and died the next day. He had been growing steadily weaker all along, and was unable to stand during most of the wedding ceremony, which he insisted on attending even though it tired him. Pilate's oldest brother, Cornelius Septimus, had made it back to Rome in time for the wedding and was still there when the elder Pilate passed away. The two brothers took care of the funeral arrangements and staged gladiatorial games in their father's honor, as befitted a Senator and former praetor. After the games were concluded, they discussed the disposal of the family home. As eldest son, Pilate had been given the choice in his father's will to either take the home for himself, give it to one of his younger brothers, or sell it, as long as he provided a place for his mother to live for the remainder of her days. He would never have considered turning her out of the home she loved, but since he had just purchased such a suitable residence for himself, he agreed to sign ownership of the family home over to Cornelius.

That fall Pilate stood for election as Tribune of the Plebs, with discreet financial backing from Tiberius. He finished second in the polls, which meant that he would be second in seniority out of the ten tribunes elected. It was a very respectable finish for a relative political neophyte, but Romans were always fond of young war heroes. Pilate found that he enjoyed the job immensely; crafting legislation and debating public policy were satisfying activities. He found that Tiberius was not a demanding patron at all; only once did Pilate have to employ his tribunician veto at his request. He did, however, employ his veto purely on his own authority once, to block legislation that would have raised taxes on the sale of captive slaves from Rome's wars. The sale of captives was a critical source of wealth for officers returning from the conflict, who often ran up considerable debts during their long absences from Rome. Charging extra taxes on their greatest source of income, Pilate argued, was like penalizing victory. The crowds cheered his spirited oration, and none of the other tribunes overrode his veto.

About a year after Tiberius returned from Germania, the Emperor of Rome died in his seventy-fourth year. The entire world was stunned by the news—Augustus had ruled over the Empire for forty-five years, and had been co-ruler for five years before that! Men had been born, married, and had children and grandchildren without ever seeing any other figure at the head of the Empire. Many old-timers, however, regarded the passing of the Emperor with trepidation, remembering the civil wars and struggles for succession that had followed the death of Julius Caesar nearly sixty years before.

After he heard the news, Pilate made his way to the home of Tiberius to offer his condolences, and to see if he could be of any service. He found his patron looking unusually shaken, and Tiberius quickly dismissed his other attendants and poured a glass of wine for each of them. He gestured for Pilate to join him on the couches in the dining chamber, and for a while the two associates sipped their drinks in silence. Finally it was Tiberius who spoke first.

"I never really expected the old man to die," he said. "Logically, of course, I knew that he was mortal, and that his body was failing. But emotionally, all I could see was that Rome had always had Augustus, and I thought it always would."

"You are far from the only one who feels that way, your Highness," said Pilate.

"By the gods, please do not call me that!" snapped Tiberius. "I hate flattery! I hate how it takes otherwise honorable Romans and unmans them, reducing them to shameless sycophants and toadies. If I am truly your Emperor, Lucius Pontius Pilate, then I command you—always speak your mind in my presence!"

"Very well, sir," said Pilate. "Then let me say this: you are the Emperor now. The moment Augustus joined the ranks of the gods, you became the most powerful man on earth. Men are going to flatter you. They are going to do everything in their power to buy, seduce, or compel your affections. Nothing you can do or say will change that, and complaining about it helps nothing. You need to make up your mind what kind of Emperor you are going to be. Your father's reputation is already secure and established; it is time for you to begin creating your own."

Tiberius nodded. "That is excellent advice, Lucius Pontius," he said. "You are a good counselor, and I will have need of such in the days to come. It is odd, you know—I never really loved Augustus as a son should love his father. He was a very closed man in many ways. You know, of course, that I was adopted when I was only a child. My natural father, Tiberius Claudius Nero, hated Octavian so much! He had always sided against the Caesars, first with the assassins of Julius Caesar, then with Marc Antony—anyone but Caesar's heir. He spoon-fed me with hatred for the Julii when I was too small to understand any of it. Then when my mother had the temerity to fall in love with Octavian, and both of them already married! I do believe he would have beaten her had she not been pregnant with my brother. To this day I do not know what stratagem Octavian used to force Nero to divorce my mother, but it worked. I remained at my father's house until he died a few years later, along with my baby brother. You cannot imagine the hateful rants he spewed forth when he was in his cups!"

Pilate listened, enthralled. The personal lives of Augustus and Livia had been a subject of gossip to generations of Romans, but they were both intensely private people who furnished little grist for the gossip mill. To actually be hearing the story of that complex marriage from one who knew it better than almost anyone was something many in Rome would die for! A shame, he thought, that he would never be able to share what he was hearing.

"So when my father died, I was about nine and my brother only four. Suddenly we were taken to live in the house of this monster who had stolen our mother. I don't really remember what I was expecting, only that I knew it would be horrible," Tiberius continued, taking another drink of wine. His glass emptied, he called for more. After the goblet was filled, he went on. "But it wasn't horrible—not at all. I think that Octavian felt bad that my brother and I had been forced to grow up with no contact whatsoever with our mother, because he treated each of us with exquisite kindness. It was bewildering to me, to see that everything my natural father had told me about this man was not only false, but the direct opposite of the truth. In time, I came to be grateful—very grateful—that Octavian had taken us in and adopted us as his sons. But I never loved him. In fact, truth be told,

Lucius Pontius—" Tiberius drained the goblet again and held it up for more. His butler poured the cup full, and Pilate realized that the Emperor of Rome was getting drunk before his eyes. He took a very small sip of his own cup, determined to keep a firm grip on his own wits this evening.

Tiberius went on, oblivious to Pilate's train of thought. "I am not sure that I can love," he said. "There are people I am fond of, don't mistake me. But I have never known a single person that I would lay down my life for, except for Vipsania. Ah, Pilate, I would have opened a vein for that woman in a heartbeat. Isn't that the definition of love? Someone you care about more than you care about yourself? I could feel that for Vipsania, but I couldn't even feel that for my father—neither my natural father, nor for the man who adopted me and treated me like a son! No matter how kind he was to me, I always held back my heart from him. Then he forced me to divorce the only woman I ever cared about and marry his vile daughter instead. I was so angry, and he tried so hard to make it up to me. Now the old bastard is dead, and I never even once thanked him for all he did for me! Is there something wrong with me? Am I somehow broken inside, that I cannot feel love anymore?"

"We all have our regrets, Caesar," said Pilate as neutrally as he could.

"Listen to this!" said Tiberius. He crossed the room, staggering a bit, and returned with a beautifully written scroll. "This is his will," said the new Emperor. "He gives the usual blather about Rome, and his wife, and leaves me all his offices and honors—but then there is this, that he wrote just for me: 'To Tiberius Caesar—I have left you the greatest inheritance ever bequeathed. Guard it jealously, yet handle it with care. It can make you into a god, but it can also destroy you, my son. Govern with justice, but with caution, and when the need for ruthlessness should arrive, do not hesitate to be as ruthless as the occasion demands. May the gods give you wisdom!' You know the saddest part of it all, Lucius Pontius? He never asked me if I wanted any of this! Emperor of Rome! Ruler of the world! I have no desire to govern the world—it is all I can do to govern myself!"

He tossed his goblet aside and grabbed the flagon from his butler, drinking directly from it. Then he struck the slave across the cheek. "What are you looking at?" he roared. "Get out of here!" The servant scuttled out of the chamber quickly.

Pilate spent three hours there, watching as Tiberius got steadily drunker and drunker, roaring in anger at times, and weeping at others. Reflecting on how glum and morose the man normally was, Pilate figured that he was seeing the accumulated stress and misery of many years being released in one mighty bender, triggered by the stress of the Emperor's death. Finally, around midnight, Tiberius began to wind down. Pilate helped him to his bedchamber and out of his toga, and then pulled a light blanket over his exhausted form.

"Thanks you sho much!" Tiberius drawled. "You a good man, Looshus Ponchus Whatsis. Are you my friend?"

"I suppose I am, Caesar," said Pilate, tiptoeing to the door.

"That's just funny," Tiberius whispered. "I've never really had a friend before."

Neither of them ever referred to that night again, but Pilate never forgot it, either.

Over the next few weeks, all of the city of Rome and the citizens of the broader Empire mourned the death of the Emperor. Augustus was proclaimed to be a god, just as his own adoptive father Julius Caesar had been. He was cremated in an impressive public ceremony, with Tiberius reading off a beautiful oration that left many Romans weeping for the loss of their beloved leader. The funeral games and feasting that followed were the most impressive seen since the death of Julius Caesar himself.

When the month of mourning was over, the Senate convened and ratified the will of Augustus, bestowing on Tiberius all the titles and honors that the former Emperor had held, and naming him Princeps, the First Citizen of Rome—the same title it had created for Augustus after his defeat of Marc Antony had left him as the sole ruler of Rome. Rome's leaders never wore a crown, yet they were considered superior to any king or potentate. For good or ill, Rome ruled the known world, and those kingdoms it had not yet conquered paid enormous tributes to avoid that fate. From the chilly northern shores of Gaul to the burning sands of Egypt, Rome ruled supreme. So it was that Tiberius Julius Caesar Augustus became the second Emperor of Rome, and the entire world waited to see what manner of ruler he would be.

# CHAPTER FOUR

The next few years were busy ones for Lucius Pontius Pilate. He served three terms as Tribune of the Plebs, each lasting a year, and not consecutive with each other. At one time it had been positively forbidden for a tribune to seek re-election, and more than one would-be demagogue had been torn apart by angry mobs for trying to do so. The rules were less strict now, but it was still considered unlucky and a bit improper for a tribune to succeed himself in office. Pilate also finally got to serve a full term as Urban Praetor, and sat with every session of the Roman Senate. He became a respected member of the legislature, with a reputation for efficiency and intelligence.

His marriage to Procula Porcia was everything a Roman aristocrat's family life was supposed to be: affectionate, respectful, and happy. Unlike most Roman husbands, Pilate rarely sought the affections of other women. While adultery by men was not forbidden, or even particularly frowned upon, by Roman law or religion, he was not a slave to his sex drive, and his wife was a satisfactory partner to him. Only during the latter stages of her pregnancies did he occasionally stray, and he never formed lasting relationships with his paramours. Porcia's pregnancies proved the only regret he had about his marriage to her—she seemed incapable of bringing a son to term. They had one healthy daughter, and another who died as an infant. After that, Porcia became pregnant twice more, but miscarried both times. They both agreed that if she did not bear a son by the time she was thirty, they would adopt a child from another family. Adoptions were very common in Rome, and completely binding in every way. Many an impoverished family of ancient blood and impeccable lineage could not afford to raise more than one son, so they adopted their younger boys out to those who were wealthier and less fertile.

The other relationship that continued to be successful in Pilate's life was his ongoing political relationship with the Emperor. It became obvious early on that Tiberius was never going to enjoy the love of the Roman people as Augustus and Julius Caesar had. His glum and morose nature forbade familiarity, and his disdain for flattery stymied those who sought his favor.

His relationship with the Senate was awkward, to say the least—rather than regard them as a tame body of legislative consultants, as Augustus had, he seemed to want them to actually govern, at least at first. But their confusion about his wishes and uncertainty as to their political independence rendered them ineffectual, so Tiberius gradually took up the reins of power his adopted father had wielded, but he never held them as easily or as competently as Augustus had. As time went by, it was more and more evident that the new Emperor of Rome simply did not like Romans very much at all—or the city itself, for that matter. Tiberius had moved into the house of Augustus at first, but the presence of his mother, Livia, drove him to distraction, so he retired to his villa outside the city. When she continued to visit him there once every week or so, he took to going on long rides around the countryside, staying in the homes of various senators and notables. Eventually he discovered the Villa Jovis, a magnificent summer palace that Augustus had built on the Isle of Capri, and took to spending several months of the year there. Pilate came to see him occasionally there on business, and he noted that Tiberius never seemed happier than when he was on the lightly populated island, enjoying the company of a few select servants and close associates.

"Look at this place!" he said one evening as he guided Pilate through a lovely atrium, open to the Mediterranean breeze on the north end. Tiberius was leaning against a column, surveying the sea. The moon was setting, turning the water into quicksilver flames. "This is the only place I find peace anymore, Lucius Pontius. I dread every time I have to leave here and return to Rome, and yet my duties keep me going back to that horrible city. There are times I wish I could stock up a boat full of food, water, and a few musicians and servants, and sail west until I could find the place that the sun goes when it leaves our skies in the evening."

Pilate stood beside him, thoughtfully. "I suppose, Sire, that you would eventually find another land somewhere out there beyond Spain. Of course, it would be filled with people, and noise, and politics, and all the other things you left here to escape."

Tiberius glared at him. "That is a terrible way to speak of another man's dream!" he said in mock anger.

"Well, sir, you did always ask me to give a candid opinion," said Pilate. "And right now, my candid opinion is that the Senate is getting restive at your absence. Some are even whispering that Germanicus might have been a better successor to your father after all!"

"They are, are they?" asked the Emperor, suddenly dead serious. "The issue of Germanicus is quite troubling to me, Pilate. He is a brilliant general and a beloved figure by the people, but he is also my adopted son and a loyal family member. He inherited the natural charisma that is the Julian trait—one I did not inherit and have never been able to cultivate. I give the Empire peace, and prosperity, and sound legislation, and they call me a sour old man. He slays enemies on the battlefield, and he is the darling of Rome! If I were a more vindictive man, young Germanicus might not live to become old Germanicus!" he snapped.

He walked across the polished marble floor to the far wall. A huge staircase swept upward to the next floor of the villa, but a small door opened in the wall under it. From the outside it looked like a storage closet, but inside was a lacquered teakwood desk with an inkwell and papyrus, and a small curule chair for the Emperor to sit on. Pilate leaned on the doorjamb, looking in as the Emperor seated himself—the room had no other seat, and was so small as to be somewhat cramped with two men inside it at once.

"Give me a few moments to write," said Tiberius, "and I will have two letters for you to take back to Rome. One is for the *Princeps Senatus*, to let him know I will be returning to the city soon. The other will be some new orders for Germanicus—which may or may not be to his liking."

"This is a tiny chamber," said Pilate. "Why not use your library upstairs?"

"I like this little room," said Tiberius. "When I sit down here, I know I am the only one present. It is small, and plain, and lets me focus on what I am doing. Now begone! I will send Mencius for you when I am done. He will serve you some food while you wait."

As Pilate ate the excellent fish and warm bread the steward brought him, he reflected upon his rise in the world. With any luck, he would soon be ready to run for Consul of Rome, the office he had long dreamed of holding. His friendship with the prickly old Tiberius had indeed been a political asset! The Emperor rarely asked Pilate for any political favor, only to be kept informed of the mood of the Senate, and any developments that might merit Tiberius' concern. He often wished the Emperor were a happier man, but he also knew that men could not change their personality, even when they wanted to.

His own secret life was ample proof of that. Upon his return to Rome five years before, he had buried the savage love of cruelty he had discovered in himself during his stint in Germania. But it could not be forever repressed; he found himself growing angrier and more sullen the longer he went without hurting someone. Yet he did not want to hurt those he cared about, nor those who could possibly do him some favor or benefit later on. So he took to disappearing into the sinks of the Suburba, Rome's poorest and most densely populated district, every few months. He would wear the clothes of a commoner, slip a sturdy dagger into his belt, and find some seedy tavern where fights broke out with regularity. After a night or two, he would pick a fight with someone and usually beat them senseless. He was in splendid physical condition, and his combat experience made him a deadly opponent. On the rare occasion that he misjudged his foe, he could always resort to the dagger. However, there was a risk in that. While bar fights were a common occurrence, killing someone outright was a sure way to draw the attention of local magistrates. It simply would not do for a close associate of the Emperor to be arrested for killing someone in a drunken brawl. So Pilate contented himself with pummeling whatever unfortunate he chose for his latest venting session, and usually tossed a gold coin or two at the tavern's owner to pay for any damage. His wife might occasionally cluck over his bruised face and cut up knuckles, but she was too discreet to question him when it was obvious he did not want to talk about it. There were times when he wondered what created this dark and violent streak in him, but over time he came to regard it as a sort of wild beast one might keep as a pet—safe enough if fed, but dangerous if allowed to grow too hungry.

After he finished the meal Mencius had brought him, he walked through the Emperor's library. There were hundreds of scrolls there, but one shelf was full of codices—an innovation in recent writing, where the pages were cut short and bound together with cords at the back, so that they could be readily perused without taking up the space that a scroll did when unrolled.

Pilate despised the things—an innovation of the lazy that should never catch on!

On the opposite wall was a weapon rack, holding several swords and spears. The blade at the top caught his attention at once. The richly styled Corinthian leather scabbard had a small silver plate woven into it with a clear inscription in Latin: *"Ad Romae mundissimo filius, gerunt cum honore – Aurelia Cotta Caesar."* "To Rome's Finest Son, wield it with honor – Aurelia Cotta Caesar."

"I see you found the gladius of Divus Julius," said a familiar voice behind him.

"I did not know it was still in existence!" said Pilate, turning to face the Emperor.

"Caesar was unarmed the day he was murdered," said Tiberius. "His armor and blade were with his other gear at his home above the Vestal Virgin's quarters. My father told me there was a tremendous row when Caesar's will was read—Marc Antony was so sure that he would be Caesar's heir that he was already trying on the cuirass that Caesar had worn during his campaigns in Gaul. Father was only about eighteen then, and slight of build. He came into the home of Gaius Julius Caesar and found Antony trying to buckle on the cuirass over that massive torso of his, and ordered him out of the house on the spot! Octavian, as he was simply known then, was a small slip of a lad, and Antony was a huge burly brute who did not like him one bit. But my father drew this sword from its scabbard and chased Antony out of the house with it. He told me that he was terrified that Antony would simply wrestle it away from him, but all he did was curse my father before running away into the night! From that day forward, my father never let Caesar's armor and sword out of his sight. He wore them on every campaign until he gave them to me twenty years ago. For all our differences, I believe that when I am no more, I shall pass them on to Germanicus. He has the military abilities of a Caesar, and I imagine that he will be my heir one day, since my natural son Drusus shows little talent for governing or leading men in battle."

"Germanicus is a talented general, and beloved of the people," said Pilate. "I think that, in the long term, it is best for Rome that you and he remain cordial in your official relations, despite any private difficulties."

"In other words, as long as the Senate believes that I am going to leave my titles and honors to Germanicus anyway, they will be less likely to try and raise him up against me?" asked Tiberius.

"Quite so," said Pilate. "That being said, I do not think that Germanicus would ever come out against you publicly. He may privately disagree with you on some accounts, but he is a loyal Roman and a loyal son."

"I believe you are right," said Tiberius. "This letter will recall him to Rome to stand for election as Consul next year. Perhaps if I allow some of the powers of that office to be restored, Germanicus can shoulder some of my duties and allow me more time away from the infernal city!"

But that was not to be. When Pilate returned to Rome, he found the city reeling in shock from the news that Germanicus had died in Antioch, while in the midst of a furious dispute with the Governor of Asia, Gnaeus Calpurnius Piso. From his deathbed, Germanicus had accused Piso of poisoning him. The entire city of Rome was grieving the loss of the beloved young general whom many called "The Roman Alexander." Pilate roamed the streets and the Forum for a day, listening to the voices of all he encountered, from the eldest members of the Senate to the shopkeepers in the Suburba. That evening, he drafted a letter to the Emperor and sent it to Capri by the fastest couriers he could hire. Its contents were short and simple:

*To the Emperor of Rome, Tiberius Julius Caesar Augustus:*

*Sire, you must return to the city immediately. Germanicus is dead, as I am sure you have already heard. From his deathbed, he accused the Governor of Syria, Calpurnius Piso, of poisoning him. The people of Rome are saying that Piso would not have dared to do such a thing except on direct orders from you. There are such rumblings as I have not heard in the city in my lifetime! It is imperative that you arrive here quickly, and in full mourning attire. Only the most extravagant show of grief will convince the people that you were not a party to this dreadful act. Piso should be arrested and tried immediately in order to completely clear your name, and make it clear who, if anyone, was the responsible party. Forgive the impertinence of this letter, but the circumstances do not allow for ceremony. If you do not return to Rome within the week, the grieving mob will become an angry mob, and things could get very ugly very fast.*

*Your faithful client,*

*Lucius Pontius Pilate*

Tiberius was already halfway to Rome when the letter found him, having received word from Antioch of Germanicus' fate, and arrived in the city two days later. He was clad in a black toga, and his attitude was one of profound sorrow and regret—an expression that came naturally to his gloomy countenance. Piso, who had been ordered out of his province by Germanicus the previous year, had compounded his already compromised position by moving back to Antioch with his legions as soon as he got word that Germanicus was dead. Tiberius ordered the arrest of the governor and his wife, and their immediate transport to Rome for trial on charges of murder.

"This is a bad business," he said a few nights later as he and Pilate shared a cup of wine at his villa just outside the city. "I cannot believe that Piso would have been so stupid, and yet at the same time, his every act screams of guilt! The people are angry—there is graffiti all over the city showing me standing over Germanicus' body with a cup of poison in my hand! No matter what I do, I am sure to be blamed for this by the people. They have never loved me, and now many of them hate me. How I long to be away from this dreadful city forever!"

"It does no good to long for what we cannot have," said Pilate. "We must figure out how to put the mobs to rest before their grief gives way to rage."

"Any suggestions?" said Tiberius.

"The more you show your respect for Germanicus and grieve before the people, the more likely they are to believe you," said Pilate. "I think some kind gesture to the family of Germanicus would be well received."

"That will not be difficult," said Tiberius. "I have always been fond of his wife Agrippina, and their son Gaius is but a tot. I believe Agrippina is expecting another child at the moment. I feel for the baby, coming into the world without a father. Children are the only things that seem to bring me pleasure anymore, Pilate. Their laughter is the only music that I love. Sometimes on Capri I hire the local boys and girls to come out to the Villa

Jovis and dance and sing for me." His voice grew wistful and sad, and Pilate felt guilty for steering the conversation back to its course.

"I think that appearing publicly and mourning with them would help improve your image with the people immediately," he said. "Are any of Germanicus' family in Rome right now?"

"Well, there is Claudius, the fool," said Tiberius.

Pilate knew Germanicus' reclusive brother by sight only, but had heard whispers that he was either simple, or somehow afflicted. "Is he truly a simpleton?" he asked the Emperor.

"No," said Tiberius. "He actually has a first-rate mind, if you can understand him. But he has a serious speech impediment that makes every conversation with him an ordeal. Most of the family tries to avoid him, and leave him to his scrolls and inkwells. He fancies himself a historian of some sort. Last I heard, he was writing a chronicle of the Etruscans."

"I shall go and fetch him," said Pilate, "and tomorrow the two of you will ride into the city together and offer sacrifices to the memory of Germanicus."

Tiberius scowled. "Why do I work so hard to win the affections of a people I despise?" he asked no one in particular.

"Because you are their Emperor," said Pilate, "and if they do not love you, you cannot rule them!"

Tiberius drained his wine glass and called for another. "I dislike you sometimes, Lucius Pontius," he said. "You have a most annoying habit of being right all too often!"

Pilate rode rapidly into the city and made his way to the Palatine Hill, where Claudius lived in a small house next to that of Livia, the widow of Augustus. He had to bang on the door for some time before a scruffy-looking Greek steward answered.

"What do you want?" he asked Pilate insolently. "The household is trying to sleep!"

"At the moment, I want to cut that sniveling tongue from your mouth and feed it to the dogs!" Pilate snapped. "But my wishes are irrelevant—as long as you obey me, and quickly. Now fetch your master!"

The servant paled and scurried back into the apartments. Moments later, a rather plump young man appeared. His eyes were red and his face puffy, and it was obvious he had been weeping a great deal.

"Claudius Caesar?" said Pilate.

"Y-yes s-sir," the young man said. "You are P-p-pilate, correct?"

"I am," said Pilate. "The Emperor has need of you. Do you have a horse you can follow me on?"

The dumpy young fellow straightened his tunic and squared his shoulders. "Yes, I shall have Demetrius saddle him up. M-may I offer you some w-wine?"

"Water it, please," said Pilate. "I have no wish to get drunk this evening."

A shy maidservant appeared out of the corner bearing a goblet, and Pilate took a sip.

"What d-does my uncle r-require of me?" said Claudius.

"He wants to offer his comfort and support in your time of grief," said Pilate.

Claudius choked back a small sob, and then his expression soured. "And allay the s-s-suspicions that he is a m-murderer of his kin, no doubt!" he snarled.

Pilate raised an eyebrow. Stammerer he might be, but this young man was no fool. He wondered if Claudius, too, suspected the Emperor. "Surely you do not believe the idle gossip of the marketplace, do you?" he asked.

Claudius looked at him sharply. "Do I b-believe my beloved uncle is c-capable of m-murder?" he asked. "Of c-course I do. B-but do I believe he killed my b-brother?" A spasm of anguish crossed his face as he said those words. "That would be foolish and impolitic, and my dear Uncle T-Tiberius is no fool!"

Pilate smiled. "I have served your uncle for several years," he said. "And he is indeed no fool. Indeed, I think he loved Germanicus after his own way. But if the people do not see a very convincing show of grief, things could become very difficult for him—and for all of Rome. So you and I are going to help the Emperor convince the people of Rome that he is devastated by this tragic and untimely loss. And, when peace and order are restored, the

Emperor will remember which family members stood by him in his time of need."

Claudius nodded and began pulling on his toga. The classical Roman garment hung slackly off his rotund figure, and he looked more like a piglet wrapped in a bedsheet than a Roman aristocrat. But his reply was classically Roman: "I suppose it would not do to d-disappoint a family member then, would it?" he asked.

The next morning Claudius and the Emperor rode through the city gates and publicly sacrificed an ox to the beloved memory of Germanicus, and Tiberius gave an oration that was flawless in its eloquence, reminding some of the oldest members of the audience of the great orator Marcus Tullius Cicero. Even hardened veterans of Forum assemblies wept as he recounted the many victories and sterling character of Rome's favorite son, and reminded them that Germanicus was his own beloved son by adoption.

What happened next astonished the Emperor and Pilate both. When Tiberius was done speaking, Claudius stepped forward and gave a speech of his own. He held forth for over a half an hour on his love for his brother, and his appreciation of the outpouring of grief that the people of Rome had honored him with. Remarkably, he did not stutter a single time throughout! Tiberius remarked on it as the three of them rode back to his villa by chariot.

"By the gods, Claudius, I did not know you were capable of such eloquence!" he said.

"I c-can speak without stuttering when I h-have a ch-chance to memorize what I am going to say in a-advance, and practice it," said the young Caesar. "That's what I was d-doing when your man P-Pilate came to get me."

Tiberius smiled for the first time in several days. "There is more to you than meets the eye, Claudius Caesar Germanicus," he said. "You may have a political future before you, despite what my mother says!"

The portly youth paled. "Gods!!" he said. "I hope not!"

Pilate looked at the Emperor with an amused eye. "He is definitely related to you, Sire!" he said.

Tiberius actually laughed out loud this time.

# CHAPTER FIVE

The day after their funeral offering, Tiberius sent for Pilate urgently. His message read: "Come to my villa at once! See to it no one observes your arrival!"

It was very early in the day, so Pilate saddled up his horse and rode out of Rome by a different gate than usual, traveling eastward away from the Emperor's estate, making sure that his route passed several carts and drovers on their way into Rome with livestock and wares to sell. Then, where the road passed through a dense copse of trees, he steered his mount off the road and took off cross-country, traveling quietly through fields and farms until he approached Caesar's villa from the east, a half mile from the road. He tethered his horse among the trees and then discreetly approached the villa through its vineyards, slipping in through the back door without even a servant noticing him.

He heard some commotion in a storeroom and found the chief butler there, attempting—with some apparent success—to seduce one of the kitchen maids. The man immediately abandoned his quest and bowed to Pilate as the girl scurried out, straightening her clothes.

"Praetor Pilate! Whatever may I do for you?" he said.

"Conduct me quickly to your master, and let no one know you saw me here!" snapped Pilate.

"Of course, sir," said the butler. The Emperor's servants lived in terror of his irascible temper, and were known for their discretion. The slave conducted Pilate down a corridor and through a curtain to a small room where Tiberius reclined on a couch, devouring a breakfast of sweet rolls and fruit. With him was a man Pilate recognized immediately.

"Prefect Sejanus," Pilate stated coolly. "An unexpected pleasure." He then turned to the reclining figure and bowed. "*Imperator* Tiberius, it is good to see you again so soon."

"Were you seen?" asked the Emperor, his drawn features weary and sorrowful, but with a note of anger in his voice.

55

"Not by anyone outside your household," said Pilate. "Among your servants, only by the butler and a kitchen maid."

The Emperor turned to Sejanus, the Prefect of his Praetorian Guards. "I told you he was dependable," he said, to which the obsequious sycophant nodded.

Pilate, like many Romans, did not like or trust Lucius Aelius Sejanus. The man had attached himself like a leech to Tiberius even before Augustus' death, and had risen alongside Tiberius. He was as ruthless as Julius Caesar and as evil as Cornelius Sulla, but had somehow managed to worm his way into Tiberius' affections years ago. Tiberius claimed to hate greedy hangers-on, but as the years went on he became increasingly blind to Sejanus' faults. This was a man, thought Pilate, who could cause great grief to Rome someday. But he was also on the Emperor's rather short list of close personal assistants, so Pilate went out of his way to treat him with respect, if not with trust.

"We have a situation," said Tiberius. "I have figured out who is responsible for Germanicus' death."

"Then they must be publicly tried immediately!" said Pilate.

"That will not be possible," Sejanus said laconically.

"What do you mean?" asked Pilate.

"The man responsible is me," said Tiberius wearily.

Pilate was stunned, but looking at Tiberius' face, he saw the truth graven in the deep worry lines around the Emperor's nose and mouth.

"How?" he asked, not sure he wanted to hear the answer.

"It was not intentional," said the Emperor. "I doubt that anyone in Rome will believe that, but I never intended Germanicus any harm. You know, Pilate, that from time to time I indulge my fondness for wine a bit too deeply."

"I have observed that on rare occasion, Sire," said Pilate cautiously. The fact was that, since becoming Emperor, Tiberius had on a number of occasions gotten royally drunk. It seemed to Pilate that this morose and intensely private man could only unbend when he had drunk too much, but he kept that observation to himself.

"About a month ago I was at Capri, dealing with a series of impossible demands from the Senate and trying to mediate in the ongoing squabble between Germanicus and Piso," said the Emperor. "I was tired and impatient, and after writing several letters that I knew would do no good, I began to drink. My only company that evening, besides my slaves and a few children brought in to dance for me, was Sejanus here. Apparently, during the course of the evening, I said something to the effect of—what was it again, Sejanus?"

"You said: 'Will no one rid me of this impudent whelp!'" Sejanus said. "As always, I took your wishes as an order."

Tiberius glowered at the lanky prefect. "WHICH YOU SHOULD NEVER HAVE DONE!!" he roared. "I was drunk and babbling, and not to be taken seriously!" He cuffed Sejanus across the top of the head, and the Commander of the Praetorian Guard meekly submitted to the blow.

Tiberius turned to Pilate. "So this moron wrote a letter to Calpurnius Piso, urging him to 'do something about Germanicus' immediately. Believing the order came straight from me, Piso gave Germanicus a dish of poisoned figs, knowing my son loved the fruit dearly. Germanicus ate a dozen of them, and then felt the pangs of the poison almost right away and knew what had happened. So he accused Piso, who is on his way to Rome to stand trial. If he stands trial, I have no doubt he will name Sejanus, and everyone knows that to name Sejanus is to implicate me."

Pilate nodded slowly. "Then he must never be allowed to stand trial," he said.

Tiberius nodded grimly. "He is currently in custody on his way back to Rome. Someone needs to . . . persuade him . . . to fall on his sword before he gets here."

"I could be that someone," Pilate said. "Where is he?"

"Still in Antioch, awaiting favorable winds to sail for Rome," said Tiberius. "The further from Italy he dies, the better."

"And if he should leave a letter confessing his crime and begging Caesar's forgiveness for the death of a beloved son?" Pilate asked.

"So much the better," said Caesar.

"What about his wife?" asked Pilate.

"My august mother assures me that she can arrange for Munatia Plancina's silence," said the Emperor. "But could I trouble you to pay a discreet visit upon the honorable Proconsul Piso?"

Pilate bowed to the Emperor. "I shall be as fleet as the winds and as subtle as a fox!" he said.

As he left the Emperor's chamber, Sejanus followed him. "Lucius Pontius," he said.

Pilate turned. "Yes, Prefect?"

"In taking care of this small matter, rest assured that you shall have my own gratitude as well as that of the Emperor," he said.

Pilate nodded. "Like you," he said, "I am the Emperor's man. What I do, I do for him. But in the process, if it pleases you as well, I am glad to make your life easier."

Sejanus nodded. "And so you shall. I was . . . shall we say, a bit overzealous this time in interpreting the Emperor's wishes. He is most unhappy with me. Erasing the consequences of this error in judgment will hopefully restore me to his favor."

Pilate slipped out the back door and through the vineyards to his horse. He spurred his mount south and east until he joined one of the roads entering Rome from the east side and rode home. When he got to the house, he went to the study to find Porcia reading a scroll of the Greek poetry she loved.

"Good morning, dear," she said. "You were out early. Is anything amiss?"

"I am afraid so," said Pilate. "I am quite ill. In fact, I shall be ill for the next week or so—too ill to receive guests, and too irritable to tolerate the sight of our servants. You shall bring me my meals in our bedchamber, and forbid all visitors. After a week, you shall convey me by covered litter to your family's estate in Samnia. Do you understand?"

She looked at Pilate standing before her, the picture of health, and slowly nodded. "You have to be somewhere else, but give the impression you are still here," she said. "It may be difficult to sustain that illusion for too long, you know. Would it not be better to simply say that you have gone on a short trip—to somewhere other than the place you are actually going?"

Pilate thought a moment. "The fact of my absence would in itself be noted. I think an illness is more likely—something contagious, which will keep well-intentioned visitors away."

She nodded. "Do you ride into danger?" she asked.

Pilate shook his head. "Unlikely," he replied. "It is just a matter that cries out for . . . discretion."

"More of the Emperor's business, I suppose," she said sadly. "He has been generous in his favors, but I worry that one of these missions for him is going to go awry someday."

"That may come to pass," said Pilate. "I just hope this is not the occasion! I shall return as speedily as I may, but it could be a while."

With that he went to his quarters and donned a hooded mantle and his riding gear. Then he went to his bank and withdrew a substantial sum to book passage on the fastest conveyance he could find. Antioch was far off, and he did not know how far toward Rome his quarry had come. By noon he had left the city gates and was galloping eastward toward the busy port of Asculum.

He chartered a fast bireme to take him eastward as quickly as sail and oar could make the journey. Fortunately, for Pilate's sake, the same strong northwest wind that kept Piso from sailing toward Italy pushed the bireme eastward quickly. Pilate had ordered his captain to put in at every major port along the way, to make sure he and Piso did not pass each other in opposite directions. To avoid drawing attention to himself, Pilate let the Captain, Sullemius, make inquiries for him, and at Rhodes they finally had a bit of luck.

"I just found an Egyptian vessel that put in yesterday," he said to Pilate after returning to the ship. "Had a rough voyage, against the wind all the way, and had to put in at Paphos to make repairs to the mast and sails. One of the passengers was a courier come from there with an express message to the Emperor from Calpurnius Piso, who is holed up in Paphos waiting for the winds to change!"

"Excellent!" said Pilate. "I don't suppose there is any chance we could get a look at the message, is there?"

The scar-faced captain grinned. "Just so happened the courier boasted that the message was so important he kept it on his person at all times, so prying eyes could not get a peek at it! Well, after a few drinks, he set out to return to his ship, and the poor fellow was set upon by cut-purses. I was too late to save him, but I did manage to retrieve this from his pouch."

He handed Pilate a sealed papyrus scroll, with a bit of crimson stain on one corner. Pilate took it from him with a wry look. "Cut-purses indeed!" he snorted. "You are a talented man, Quintus Sullemius. You waste your abilities as captain of a small ship like this."

"Perhaps you could find other employment for me in the future?" the captain asked with a grin.

"I can probably find a use for a sharp blade and a quick mind," said Pilate. "Provided they are not accompanied by a wagging tongue!"

The seagoing scoundrel looked at Pilate askance. "By the gods, sir, you wound my feelings!" he said. "I am merely a humble sea captain, transporting a roving scholar to Cyprus to consult the histories of the House of Ptolemy that are stored there."

Pilate tossed him a small purse of gold coins. "Then come to me in Rome, and I will find work for you that you will enjoy—and profit from. Now, begone with you, rascal, and get this ship underway for Paphos immediately!"

As soon as he had the tiny cabin to himself, Pilate opened the scroll and quickly perused its contents. Piso was in trouble and he knew it, apparently. He wrote:

> To His Excellency Tiberius Caesar,
>
> I am mortified to find that I have offended in my actions. By all the gods, I thought that an order from Sejanus was as good as an order from you! The poison should have acted much more swiftly—I had no idea that the arrogant whelp Germanicus would live long enough to name me a suspect in his demise! But does his death still not serve your purpose? Your rival and would-be successor is gone, and you may now rule Rome uncontested for years to come! I recognize that the Senate and People are unhappy and may require that someone pay the price for this crime, but I warn you—if I stand trial before the Senate, I WILL let them know who gave me the order

*to dispatch Germanicus. If you do not want the odious task of explaining to the Conscript Fathers how your offhand remark somehow got translated into a death warrant for a member of the Imperial family, you had best find a way for me to avoid public trial. I am a talented and wealthy man. I do not mind in the least disappearing into the east, or the south—wherever Caesar tells me to go. I am still loyal to you, Emperor Tiberius—but not so loyal as to die a traitor's death to atone for your actions and words!*

*Rome's humble servant,*

*Gnaeus Calpurnius Piso*

Pilate shook his head. He knew Piso only by reputation, but that reputation was confirmed by the contents of the letter. Related by blood to the last wife of the Divus Julius, the Calpurni all had a reputation as rather stupid, venal social climbers determined to cash in on their family connection to the Julio-Claudians. But the breathtaking arrogance of Piso's letter was truly shocking. Did he really think that the Emperor of Rome would let himself be blackmailed by a jumped-up mushroom from a minor noble family? As the ship's crew made preparation to set sail for Paphos, Pilate decided that performing this particular task for the Emperor might be somewhat enjoyable.

The northwest wind continued to push the ship swiftly through the waters of the Mediterranean, and they covered the 300 miles from Rhodes to Paphos in just over two days. Pilate sent Sullemius to find out where Piso was staying. The Governor, it turned out, had hired out a small vacant villa just outside of town while he waited for the winds to change—and, probably, to hear a reply from his frantic missive to Rome. Fortunately for Pilate, Piso had only his wife and one loyal slave with him, so confronting him would be relatively easy. There were also four Roman legionaries outside the estate, making sure that Piso did not make a run for it, but Pilate knew the habits of legionaries well enough to avoid them. After all, they were there to keep someone from getting out, not from getting in.

After dark, Pilate pulled on his hooded mantle, strapped on his gladius and a dagger, and hired a mount from a local stable. He rode quickly to the remote villa and tied his horse up at an inn a mile down the road, booking a room for the night. He had to spend an extra denarius to get the chamber to himself, but it had a window that faced away from the road, so it was money well spent. He ate a quick bite and pretended to go to bed, then slipped out the window just before midnight. The four legionaries were living in a large tent pitched in front of the villa. Two of them were sleeping, while the other two slowly patrolled the grounds. Pilate waited for them to both pass out of his field of vision, and stealthily ran toward the building, ducking behind a column just as one of the sentries rounded the corner coming toward him. Swathed in his dark mantle, he carefully spied out the rooms of the villa. Fortuna was smiling on him—Piso's wife, Munatia Plancina, was gone from the villa for the evening. The servant, an elderly butler, was snoring in a deep sleep in the servants' quarters, with a jug of wine at his elbow. Pilate smiled. It was time for some fun!

He slid into Calpurnius Piso's bedroom, silent as a shadow, and drew the dagger from his belt. Then, in one smooth motion, he clapped his hand across the portly governor's mouth and put the blade against his throat. The eyes started awake and stared about the room in terror. Piso tried to scream, but Pilate's hand reduced his cries to a muffled squeal.

"SILENCE, fool!" he hissed in Piso's ear. "Listen to me very closely. You are a dead man. The only thing remaining to be seen is whether you die like a Roman, quickly and cleanly, or squealing like a wench being raped by a legionary! Do you understand me?"

Slowly, Piso nodded his head, and Pilate released him.

"I am the governor of Syria, little man!" snapped Piso. "How dare you lay a hand on me!"

Pilate laughed softly. "Really?" he said. "It is a bit late in the game for false bravado. I come to you directly from Tiberius. You have made things very uncomfortable in Rome for our Emperor. The people blame him for the death of their beloved Germanicus."

"As they should!" snapped Piso. "Sejanus wrote me that Tiberius wanted his adoptive son gone, and I made it happen!"

"In a way that was so obvious a child could see who was responsible!" snapped Pilate. "Not to mention the fact that Sejanus foolishly interpreted a drunken rant for a direct order. Be that as it may, there is only one way for the Emperor to salvage his reputation now. You must die, cleanly and by your own hand, leaving behind a letter acknowledging your guilt and exonerating Tiberius completely. You killed Germanicus in anger because of your dispute with him, not because you thought the Emperor would reward you!"

Piso's eyes shifted rapidly. "If I give the alarm, the sentries will come running!" he said.

"And find you a gutted corpse!" said Pilate. "Not to mention that I would then have to kill all four of them and set fire to the villa. Trust me, in this matter, you need to remember your honor as a Roman and act for the good of Rome. An uprising against Tiberius would be brutally crushed, and hundreds if not thousands killed. Your wife and children would be stripped of their citizenship and crucified, or sold into slavery to the Parthians. Do you relish the thought of your son being turned into a toy for some perverse Parthian nobleman?"

Piso gritted his teeth. "Who are you to speak to me so?" he snapped.

"I am the Emperor's man," said Pilate. "That is all you need to know. Now, I believe you have a letter to write."

The Governor of Syria gave a sigh of resignation. "May the guilt of your deeds hang over your head like a cloud of doom all your days, stranger!" he snapped. Then he withdrew a piece of papyrus from his wardrobe and dipped a pen into the inkwell and began writing. When he was done, he handed the finished note to Pilate.

"Excellent!" said Pilate. "Now lie down on your bed while I read it!"

He placed the point of his dagger against the man's throat and held it there while he quickly read the suicide note. It was short and quite effectively phrased.

> To His Excellency Tiberius Caesar,
>
> I regret deeply that I have wounded you and your family by ending the life of Gaius Caesar Germanicus. His acts against me as governor of Syria wounded my pride and inflamed my temper, and in a fit of anger I had him poisoned without thinking of the cost to Rome. I am deeply grieved that any would dare to think I did such a thing under your orders. Murdering your son was a selfish act, and I apologize for the grief I have inflicted on you, and on the

*children of Germanicus. May the ending of my life be a satisfactory atonement for my misdeeds.*

*Gnaeus Calpurnius Piso*

Pilate removed his dagger from the man's throat. "Now all that is left is to do the deed," he told Piso.

The governor gave him a look of pure hatred, and drew his gladius from its scabbard. "I should charge you here and now!" he snapped. "I'll wager I could hold you off until the guards came!"

Pilate laughed, a long, low, mocking laugh. "Look at yourself!" he hissed. "Life in the debaucheries of Syria has made you soft and fat! I won the Civic Crown for killing five Germans in as many minutes, every one of them ten times the man you are. Do you think I cannot cut you down in a matter of seconds, no matter how loud you yell? Then your wife goes to the cross and your children to the slave markets. Is that what you want?"

The resistance in Piso's eyes slowly drained away. "In the name of all the gods, I curse you—Pontius Pilate! When you mentioned the Civic Crown I knew immediately who you were. Tiberius' bloody-handed message boy! See how long you last once you have fallen from the tyrant's favor!"

Pilate yawned. "Oh, do get on with it!" he snapped, showing more sangfroid than he felt—the curse of a dying man was not something to be taken lightly. But he refused to give the man the satisfaction of knowing that his words had carried any weight whatsoever.

Piso went to his knees, placed the point of the gladius against his chest, and fell forward. The razor-sharp blade slipped between his ribs and drove clean through his chest. His eyes widened and his body spasmed. He opened his mouth to cry out, but Pilate's hand was there again, blocking the sound. The anguished eyes writhed in Piso's face as he twisted in Pilate's grasp.

"Missed the heart, apparently," said Pilate. "Fear not. You have skewered your lung, and you will expire in a matter of moments. They will find your letter; your wife will be treated as the tragic widow of a man whose ambitions got the better of him. Your children will grow to adulthood with a chance to redeem your family name, all because you did the honorable thing."

Piso nodded weakly, and his eyes ceased rolling so wildly. As Pilate watched, he saw consciousness begin to fade. Unable to resist the temptation, he whispered in the dying man's ear: "That is, unless I choose to slaughter them myself!"

Piso's eyes widened in alarm, and he twisted in Pilate's grasp one more time. Then, with a final gasp of bloody froth from his lips, he died.

Pilate stood and surveyed the chamber. The spreading pool of blood covered the marks his feet had made near Piso's body, and the suicide note was neatly placed on the small writing desk. There was nothing there to indicate that the Governor of Syria had not written the note of his own free will, and then fallen on his sword in fine Roman fashion. He yawned and stretched, then silently slipped from the room. He hid behind a colonnade until the sentry passed by, and darted into the woods. Just over an hour after he had left it, he returned to his chambers in the tiny inn through the window he had left by, and slept soundly all night long.

The next day the winds changed abruptly, blowing stout and strong from the southeast. The small bireme got underway, its scholarly passenger having copied the passages he needed from the chronicles of House Ptolemy. They enjoyed a swift and uneventful voyage back to Rome, and a month after he had been summoned by the Emperor, Pilate rode to his father-in-law's country villa in Samnia. Proculus Porcius was gone way on business, but his daughter was there, sitting down to breakfast as Pilate arrived.

She greeted him with an affectionate but proper Roman kiss. "Greetings, husband," she said. "It pleases me to see you well again."

"I am feeling much better," Pilate said. He returned her kiss with enthusiasm and walked her outside, away from the ears of her father's servants. "Does anyone suspect that I have been away?"

Porcia smiled. "No!" she said. "I had your young slave Democles take your place, and brought him soup twice a day. His groans from the sickroom were very convincing! I told everyone you had the spotted pox."

Pilate beamed at her. "Very clever," he said. "That would definitely keep visitors away! But how shall we explain the absence of sores?"

She looked at him shrewdly. "Sometimes the malady only afflicts certain parts of the body," she said. "I told them that you were mainly broken out on your lower torso, with just a few small spots on your face. We may have to—well, do something to create those spots, though."

Pilate winced. "I suppose you are right. Two or three pokes with a burning taper should generate pretty convincing blisters on my face, and perhaps one or two on my shoulder, where my toga leaves it bare. I shall ask double reward of Tiberius for this!"

She kissed him again. "Fear not, my dear," she said. "I will not mar your manly beauty!" With that, they retired to their bedchamber, and did not emerge until the next day.

# CHAPTER SIX

"By the gods, man, what happened to your face?" Tiberius asked in horror.

Pilate smiled instinctively, and then winced. His face was marked with a half dozen or so angry red blisters, with several more on his shoulder, where his toga left it bare. "We needed a convenient reason why I have not been seen in public for the last month," he said. "A case of the spotted pox seemed as likely an excuse as any."

The Emperor looked at him and shuddered. "How on earth did you . . ." he began.

"A lit taper, and the steady hand of my wife," said Pilate. "She assures me they will heal with minimal scarring."

The Emperor looked at Pilate again, and slowly broke into a rare smile. "I shudder to think what my accursed wife would do if I let her get a lit taper anywhere near my face! Now, tell me—what of your errand?"

"Piso is dead," Pilate said. "By his own hand, leaving a note full of remorse for the death of Germanicus and the grief he caused the Imperial family."

"Well done, sir!" Tiberius said. "I shall see you elected Consul for this!"

Pilate bowed. "It is my pleasure to serve Rome," he said.

The Emperor nodded. "And serve you have," he said. "Tomorrow I shall greet Germanicus' wife and children and conduct them to the funeral games that are being held in his honor. I should ask you and your wife to be part of the official entourage for the day. I shall remain in the city for at least another month or so, until I am sure that the public unrest is quieted. Then I shall return to Capri. The consular elections are a ways off, but I shall have Sejanus begin quietly lobbying my clients in your favor—the fool needs to be put to work, to atone for his dreadful error in judgment!"

Pilate's mind was racing. Consul of Rome! In the days of the Republic, the consuls had been chief executives, leading the Senate, conducting foreign policy, and commanding the armies in time of war. Since Augustus had ended the Republic, all the old offices were still in place, but much reduced in power and authority. But still, being consul ennobled his family for life, and guaranteed him the governance of a nice, profitable province when his yearlong tenure was up. His years of diligent service to Tiberius had finally paid off—Pilate would no longer be a minor noble from an honorable but obscure plebeian family. Instead, he would be a respected statesman and leader of the greatest nation on earth. Piso's blood was well spilled, he thought. He would have willingly bathed in the blood of a dozen such idiots in order to climb this high!

Even as he thought that, Pilate paused a moment, listening to this violent inner voice. Where had it come from? He was a cultured Roman, a sophisticated man who read Greek philosophers and spoke three languages. Like all Romans, he understood and appreciated the need for violence and armed might to sustain the power and authority of the Empire. But where had his own savage love of cruelty come from? He recalled the vile words he had whispered in the ear of the dying governor, and was repulsed—not only by the sheer vindictiveness of what he had said, but by the savage glee that had filled his heart as he said them. Yet now that part of him slept, satisfied and content. He could not find the least desire within himself to do violence to anyone at the moment—but he also knew that, at some point, that hungry beast within him would awaken again, and when it did, another person would pay with blood and ruin for this part of his nature he did not understand.

"Praetor Pilate!" The Emperor's voice snapped him back to the present. "My word, man, did you doze off with your eyes wide open? I was speaking to you!"

Pilate bowed once more. "I beg your pardon, Sire, but my face was throbbing and my mind wandered for a moment. May I trouble you to repeat yourself?"

The Emperor looked at him, gruff but sympathetic. "You have paid a high price for obeying my orders," he said. "Sejanus will want to speak with you for a moment, and then by all means go home and rest. Put ointment on your burns—I mean, on your blisters. Make your wife tend you well! And then join us tomorrow in the Amphitheater of Taurus."

The Prefect of the Praetorian Guard looked at Pilate's ravaged face and nodded thoughtfully. "Nice bit of work, that!" he said. "I keep my ears to the ground throughout the city, and there has not been so much as a hint that you were anywhere other than at home, in your villa, deathly ill. With Piso gone and the Emperor cleared of suspicion, the crowd will weep for Germanicus and move on. You have helped Tiberius, Lucius Pontius, but you have also helped me. I must learn to be more cautious and thoughtful in carrying out our master's wishes from now on, and I might not have gotten the opportunity for this lesson had you not taken care of the situation so well. I know what the Emperor has promised you, but I want you to accept this gift from me alone." He handed Pilate a very heavy purse, and when he arrived home, Pilate discovered therein a talent of gold, a beautiful and ornately inscribed man's sapphire ring, and a lovely ruby and emerald necklace for Procula Porcia.

The next morning Pilate, the burns on his face already less painful, donned his formal toga and traveled with Porcia to the Amphitheater where the funeral games would be held. It was a longstanding Roman tradition to commemorate the fallen of the upper classes with funeral games sponsored by the family, for the amusement of the masses, after the funeral ceremony had been held. Pilate had returned to Rome a day too late for the actual funeral, but would make his first public appearance since his "illness" at the Games of Germanicus.

In earlier days, before the Republic had fallen, gladiatorial matches were contests of skill and showmanship featuring dazzling swordsmanship and weapons handling, but were rarely fatal to the gladiators themselves. If someone had to die, condemned prisoners would be herded into the arenas and armed, providing the crowd with the blood they howled for while rarely damaging the skilled and valuable gladiators themselves, who were highly prized by their masters.

In recent years, however, the gladiators were often expected to go after each other in death matches. The owners might protest the loss of such valuable property, but there was never a shortage of slaves with military experience, and the crowds loved seeing two skilled and deadly warriors face each other upon the sands.

Tiberius was already there, waiting to escort his guests into the luxurious platform from which the imperial family would watch the games. Pilate and Porcia carefully mounted the steps, and Pilate took his wife's hand and walked very slowly, remembering that he was supposed to be recovering from a serious illness. Sejanus stood behind the Emperor, formally decked out in his black and gold finery as the Prefect of the Praetorians. He greeted Pilate with a cool nod and a quick wink, and Pilate returned the gesture with gravity and civility.

Moments later Agrippina, the wife of Germanicus, arrived with her children in tow. There were six of them, three boys and three girls, ranging in age from ten years old to a babe in arms. The older children were solemn and still obviously grieving the loss of their father, while the younger ones were enjoying the occasion, oblivious to its meaning.

Tiberius introduced Pilate to Agrippina, and he nodded his head in polite acknowledgment of this legendary Roman matron. Still quite lovely at thirty, she was taller than average, with raven-black hair, a high bustline, and a proud Roman nose. But her eyes were a bright and sparkling blue, betraying her close blood ties to the Emperor Augustus. She obviously did not care much for Tiberius, but was taking great pains to be civil.

"Lucius Pontius Pilate," she said. "I do not believe we have met before."

"No, madam," he said, "but I had the privilege to serve with your husband briefly in Germania. He was a good man and a fine soldier, and Rome is all the poorer for losing him."

"No doubt you say true, Pontius Pilate," she said, "but Rome's loss pales beside my own. Germanicus was the owner of my heart, and now my spirit is dust and ashes without him. Only my love of the children he gave me keeps me in this world." Her face paled slightly, and Pilate saw that here was a Roman matron who had truly loved her husband. Such matches were uncommon, since most marriages among the upper class were arranged affairs, done for purposes of establishing political alliances and bringing rival families together.

She regarded Pilate's face with some interest. "They tell me you are recovering from the spotted pox," she said.

He nodded. "Yes," he replied, "It kept me bedridden for nearly a full month! I have never been so miserable."

"Strange," she said. "My children have all had the malady, but their sores did not resemble the ones I see on you."

Pilate felt the Emperor's eyes flick toward him and his heart sank. He kept his expression carefully neutral. "My physician says that the disease frequently takes very different form with adults than with the young," he said. "Many times it is actually far worse, and slower to heal. He told me I was fortunate that my case was a relatively mild one. I replied that if my case was mild, I prayed the gods might never send me a severe dose!"

She nodded. "Well, once you have had it, they say it can never recur, so I imagine the gods will grant your wish. Thank you for coming to honor the memory of my husband, Pontius Pilate," she said, and moved on. Once she was out of range, he let out a faint sigh of relief.

"I think your face looks rather funny!" said a small voice. Pilate looked down at the smallest centurion he had ever seen. About six years old, blond-haired, and with the striking blue eyes of the Julio-Claudians, he was obviously the son of Germanicus. He was dressed in a complete replica of a military uniform, right down to the finely tooled leather boots, the smallest ones Pilate had ever seen.

He knelt down so that he was eye to eye with the youngster. "And who might you be, young sir?" he asked.

"I," said the boy, his voice swelling with pride, "am Gaius Julius Caesar Germanicus! But my father's soldiers call me Little Boots."

"Caligula!" said Pilate. "Well, Centurion Caligula, may I congratulate you on your uniform. It is most impeccable, as a true soldier should always keep it on formal occasions."

"Gaius!" said Agrippina. "Come now, the games are about to begin."

Tiberius led the necessary prayers to Mars and Bellona, and then sat down, with Agrippina and her children at his right hand, and his own son, Drusus, returned to Rome from his province of Illyricum on business, on his left—an honor sure to impress the crowd, since Drusus was now heir to the Imperial purple as the only son of Tiberius. Pilate sat in the row behind the Emperor, watching the interactions of the Imperial family with far more interest than he gave to the games.

Not that the games were unimpressive, however. Tiberius had hired some of the best gladiators from the legendary training facilities at Capua. Almost a hundred years before, Capua's gladiators, led by the legendary Spartacus, had revolted and led thousands of slaves to slaughter their masters and challenge the armies of Rome. Nothing so terrified a slaveholding society as the prospect of a widespread slave revolt, so Rome had dispatched four legions under the command of the wealthy Senator, Marcus Linnaeus Crassus, to defeat the *Spartacanii*. He had done so in impressive fashion, leaving thirty thousand of them dead on the battlefield and crucifying the twenty thousand survivors. All of Rome's slaves—over a hundred thousand of them—had been forced to walk down the Via Appia past the screaming, moaning rebels to see the price of raising a hand against one's master. Since then, Rome had never seen another slave revolt.

Over the next hundred years, Capua had rebuilt its training facilities and its reputation as a home of the best gladiators in all of Italy—although the owner of Rome's *Ludus Magnus* might argue that distinction. This day the group from Capua lived up to that reputation, wielding weapons with the utmost skill and with such raw courage that, even when one of them finally lost his match, the crowd howled for his life to be spared. The next losing contestant was not so lucky, however. He suffered a nasty gash to the ribs early in the contest that weakened his right arm, and was unable to wield his trident effectively. His opponent, from a rival *ludus*, slowly backed him across the arena, dodging the jabs of the trident and inflicting more minor cuts on him. The unfortunate *retarius*, steadily weakening, resorted to wild jabs with the trident in a vain effort to catch the sword of the *secutor* and tear it from his grasp. The wily blademaster refused to be drawn into a foolish thrust, however, and let his opponent slowly wear himself out. Finally the *retarius* lunged too far and stumbled, and the swordsman spun past him and cut his hamstring with one quick slash. The anguished opponent grasped the back of his leg with one hand, trying to hold his weapon steady with the other. It was the moment the *secutor* had been waiting for. He thrust his blade forward and jerked it upwards, catching the trident and tearing it out of his opponent's hands. He tossed it away and grabbed the man by the hair, raising his blade to the Imperial box and waiting to see what the Emperor's command was.

Little Caligula had been watching the match with great excitement, shouting encouragement throughout. Tiberius watched him with an approving eye, enjoying the child's excitement and enthusiasm. As the crowd grew silent, waiting for the Emperor's decision, Tiberius looked down at his adoptive grandson.

"What do you think, young Gaius?" he asked.

"That *retarius* did not fight well at all, did he?" the young Caesar asked.

"Not particularly," said the Emperor. "His wound prevented him from using his weapon very effectively."

"Then he should not have let himself be wounded so early in the match," said Caligula gravely. "Perhaps he might serve as a lesson to others."

The Emperor nodded sagely and then looked at the victorious *secutor*. He gave the man a curt nod, and the blade descended in a blinding arc, shearing through the throat of the defeated *retarius* and spilling his lifeblood onto the sand. The winner of the match bowed deeply at the Imperial box, then shook his blade at the roaring crowd. Slaves came out and removed the body, then raked the sand clean for the next match. Caligula drank in every detail with a look in his eyes that Pilate knew all too well. Here was a lad, he thought, whose instinct for cruelty might someday surpass his own. He wondered how well Caligula would control that fierce appetite.

By the end of the day, dozens more gladiators had faced one another on the sands, although only three more lost their lives. The matches were played out with such skill and cunning that the crowd, for the most part, cheered winner and loser alike. But the true star of the show was young Gaius. He yelled himself hoarse, prancing around the Imperial box and waving at the crowd until he finally tired out around midafternoon and crawled into his mother's lap. When the games officially ended at sunset, the Emperor's party left the box and its members were borne home by their respective litters. Pilate was tired but strangely energized, his face throbbing slightly, but the events of the day still shining in his mind. The Senate and People of Rome had seen the Imperial family standing together, and their Emperor paying proper honors to the memory of his slain adoptive son. Pilate wondered if it would be enough to allay their suspicions about Germanicus' death.

For the moment, it was. Whatever doubts Agrippina might have still harbored about the Emperor's role in her husband's death, she kept them to herself for the time being. Tiberius remained in Rome for another month, busying himself with affairs of state, and then returned once more to Capri, where he was spending more and more time of late. He left his loyal Prefect, Sejanus, in Rome to keep his finger on the pulse of the city, to monitor the

Emperor's enemies, and to reward his friends. Sejanus excelled at both tasks, as Pilate found out that fall when he put his name before the Senate as a candidate for the office of Consul. While the elections were pretty well rigged and decided in advance by the Emperor and his allies in the Senate, they still were an exciting time for the Tribes and Assemblies of the People, who cast their votes eagerly. Pilate returned second in the polling, with the Emperor's son Drusus as his consular colleague. Drusus, however, was still the Proconsular Governor of Illyricum, and once the elections were done, he returned to his province, leaving Pilate alone to hold the highest office in the Roman *cursus honorum.* It was a proud moment, he thought, restoring honor to his ancient family and holding an office no Pilatti had held for over a century. The powers of the office had declined, to be sure, since the days of Gaius Marius and Lucius Cornelius Sulla, but the title was the same, and the *arctoritas* it carried still impressive.

Pilate's term as consul was uneventful, and when it was concluded, he was assigned by the Emperor as the Governor of Further Spain, a fairly quiescent province. Pilate was allowed to take his wife and daughter with him on this assignment, since Spain was not a war front. He was pleased with this prospect, since Porcia Minor was already nearly six, and he did not know how long his proconsulship would last. Pilate left Rome at the head of his legion, with his slaves instructed to bring the family by ship to Gades, where the governor's residence was built, at the earliest fair season.

Governorships were generally reserved for consulars—Senators who had held the office of consul at least once. They were granted *Proconsular imperium* the minute they crossed the *pomerium,* the sacred boundary of Rome, and held it until their authority was revoked by the Senate or until their successor took office and they returned to Rome. Governors had ample opportunities to do quite well for themselves—they controlled tax policy, issued all permits for merchants, miners, slave traders, and bankers within their province. Those permits cost money, and by longstanding tradition, governors were allowed to set their own prices—although a governor who charged too much and generated complaints to the Senate might well find himself hauled before the extortion courts upon his return. Governors who tried to squeeze the people of the province too hard could spark revolts, which never boded well for their future employment. All that being said, however, a clever governor could still accumulate a tidy fortune without ever generating a complaint. Rome wanted efficiency and order above all, and governors who maintained those things tended to do well for themselves while doing good for the Senate and People of Rome.

Pilate's tenure as governor of Spain ran for three years, and he enjoyed his time there. While the province was mostly pacified, he did have to lead his legions out twice—once to clean out a nest of pirates who had established themselves near Iria Flavia, and a second time to repel an invasion of Celtic warriors from the distant, legend-shrouded island of Britannia. Other than that, Pilate issued decrees, heard local cases, and generally made sure that the province stayed on an even keel. He received regular letters from his clients in Rome, and particularly from his favorite scoundrel, Quintus Sullemia, who had, upon his suggestion (and on Pilate's payroll), taken up residence in the Suburba and was now a regular Forum frequenter, following political events quite closely.

In the spring of Pilate's second year as governor, he received this missive from Sullemia:

*To His Excellency Proconsul Pontius Pilate of Spain,*

*Well, things have been lively here in the city of Romulus of late. Your master, our beloved Emperor, becomes increasingly short-tempered and irascible, and those closest to him pay the price. It's mostly Agrippina's fault, of course—she has never forgiven Tiberius for the death of her husband, and still thinks he had a hand in it (you and I know, of course, how ridiculous such an accusation must be!). Matters between them are steadily eroding, and I look for a proper dust-up in the near future. Foolish woman! How can any female defy the will of an Emperor of Rome? I hear that she is longing to re-marry, but I doubt Tiberius will allow it.*

*But the juiciest gossip of the moment is not about her at all. Rather, it concerns our beloved Emperor's natural son, the esteemed proconsul and sot Drusus Caesar. You know, I trust, what a drunken brute Drusus is, and how little love is lost between him and his spouse Livilla, even if she did bear him twins a few years back. Of course Tiberius adores his son, the only issue of his much-loved first wife Vipsania, whom he still moons over even though their divorce is twenty years in the past. Now that Germanicus is gone, all Rome knows that Drusus will one day ascend to the purple—if he lives that long!*

*Now why would I say such a thing, you may wonder? After all, Drusus is a relatively young man, in good health despite his choleric temperament and penchant for too much wine. The answer is simple—Drusus has made himself a very deadly enemy. I refer to none other than your friend and mine, the erstwhile commander of the Praetorians, Lucius Sejanus. He and Livilla have been carrying on a torrid affair for several years now, and Drusus knows it. Last month he openly mocked Sejanus in the Forum, and actually punched him in the face in the presence of half the Senate! Sejanus may smile and scrape and bow before his imperial master, but when Tiberius is out of the room he is as vicious as a hyena. I personally think that Drusus signed his death warrant that day—although I could be wrong. And if he is man enough to survive the wrath of Sejanus, maybe he will be a better emperor than any of us suspect.*

*Your family is well—although Cornelius is up to his eyeballs in debt at the moment, trying to run for Urban Praetor in a crowded field. Do not be surprised if you get a letter requesting financial assistance in the very near future! Your sister Pontia seems to be making a career of fertility, bearing her husband yet another son two months ago. That is a total of six children for her, and four of them surviving the early years—something not many Roman matrons can boast.*

*I hope this finds you and yours safe and well. Please find me some interesting work in the future—I miss the sea and the feel of a pitching deck beneath my feet! But I remain your loyal client until we meet again.*

*Kill some pirates for me! Quintus Sullemius*

Pilate read the letter with interest. It sounded as if Drusus was indeed living on borrowed time—Sejanus was not a man to cross! He wondered how Tiberius was faring. He had come to have, if not affection, a certain respect for the gloomy, aging Emperor. Tiberius cared not a fig for the affections of the mob, but he did seemingly care a great deal that the machinery of the Roman state should continue to run smoothly and efficiently under his watch. His cultivation of men like Sejanus and Pilate was all for one common purpose—to eliminate potential sources of strife and dissent. Yet, for all his detached nature, Tiberius seemed unable to see that his own son might be the source of all those things. Drusus was ill-tempered, often drunk, and notoriously short-sighted. He had inherited most of his father's vices, but none of his redeeming virtues.

Sure enough, not long after that, Pilate received word from official channels that the Emperor's only son Drusus had died, apparently of natural causes, after a heavy bout of drinking. Tiberius, it was said, was heartbroken at the loss of his beloved son, and was so overcome with grief he could not officiate at the funeral games. Apparently, if Drusus had been murdered, it was done with such skill and finesse that not even the suspicious old Emperor imagined that his son's death was not an accident. Sullemius himself could not find direct proof of poisoning, although he was convinced that Livilla was responsible.

Pilate found himself wondering who on earth would succeed Tiberius now. Germanicus had three sons, but his widow had become such a thorn in the Emperor's side that Pilate could not imagine him choosing one of them to be his successor. Still, Tiberius was awfully fond of young Gaius Little Boots. He remembered the boy's disturbing enthusiasm for the bloody games, unusual even for a Roman, and wondered what kind of Emperor he might make.

The next message he received from the Senate informed him that his term as Governor would not be prorogued a third time, and that he would be free to return to Rome and take up his seat in the Senate again as soon as his successor, Lintus Antoninus, arrived in Gades. It was with some regret that he informed his family about the upcoming move; Spain had been good to him, as his bulging bank accounts could attest. But still, he thought, Rome was where the action was. If he was going to continue to be the Emperor's man, and rise even higher in Tiberius' service, then that was where he needed to be. He also found himself interested in seeing his family again— he missed his brother Cornelius and his sister Pontia. His two younger brothers, Gaius and Marcus, had been away from Rome so long on military and political assignments that he rarely thought of them anymore, although the occasional letter from Cornelius informed him of where they were and what they were doing.

He decided to return by ship with his family, if the season permitted—there was about a month's worth of favorable weather left when he received notice from the Senate, so the travel arrangements would depend on how quickly Lintus Antoninus arrived in Gades. Pilate knew Antoninus on a social basis; the man was a brusque, humorless Roman functionary who was adequate at many things and exemplary at none; dividing his time between the Senate and the army in a slow and unimaginative hike up the *cursus honorum.* But he was punctual; Pilate had to give him that. He showed up exactly two weeks after the letter from the Senate informed Pilate of his impending arrival.

Pilate took the time to show him around and introduce him to the local civic and tribal leaders. "The pirates and the Celts are pretty well subdued for the moment," he said as they reviewed the local legion together. "We killed several hundred of them and burned their ships last year, and the Britons in particular had to limp their way back up the coast and find a way back to their infernal island. But they are a persistent bunch, and there is much gold still being mined in the northern parts of the province. That will always draw them like moths. My lads here are good soldiers, most with several years to go yet on their enlistments. They are always ready for a good scrap, and their centurions are seasoned veterans."

Antoninus slowly nodded; efficient he might be, but conversation was not his long suit. "It seems to me, Lucius Pontius," he said, "that you have left this province thriving and in good order. I shall try not to do anything to upset the situation, and I thank you for your services, as I am sure that the Senate will likewise do."

Pilate nodded. He was nearing forty and had already completed a career that many a Roman would envy. He found himself wondering if he had not peaked already; if he would become one of the Senate's elder statesmen, always deferred to in debate but overlooked when real opportunities sprang up. He hoped that was not the case—he enjoyed action, and command, and executive power, and wanted to taste more of them in his future. Perhaps a good old-fashioned Roman war of conquest? Unlikely, he thought, as long as the miserly Tiberius was running the Empire. But Tiberius was well past sixty now, and the gloomy old cuss could not live forever. Perhaps the *Pax Romana* would not outlast him for long.

78

There was one other thing he wondered, as he and his family boarded the ship for Ostia. How would he feed the ravening beast that lurked within him once he returned to the respectability of life in Rome? It had not been that hard in Spain—battling the Celts and crucifying captured pirates had given him ample opportunity to sate the monster that lurked in his bosom. It had been one thing for a junior praetor to go incognito into the fleshpots of the Suburba and pummel strangers into unconsciousness, he thought. But how could a respected consular and former governor get away with such un-Senatorial behavior? The thought vexed him as the ship weighed anchor and got underway. But then his daughter, Porcia Minor, came running up, nearly ten years of age now and bubbling over with questions. As he took her by the hand and showed her how the mast and sails were connected by intricate rigging, and how the rudder steered the ship, he almost forgot about his strange taste for human suffering and pain. Almost.

# CHAPTER SEVEN

Rome might be the Eternal City, thought Pilate as he looked at the sprawling metropolis that covered seven hills, but it could just as easily be named the Noisy City—or the Noisome City, he thought with a small smile at his pun. A mile away from the gates, the sounds of the people of Rome about their daily business carried clearly to him—as did the smell of the huge city: a combined odor of dung and urine, sweat and cooking food, the smell of cloth and oxen and fish and fountains and sheep and a million other things. To Pilate, it was the smell of home.

He looked back at the litter and wagons carrying his family and his household goods. They were bound for the family home on the Aventine, but he must go to the Senate and hand in the official report on his province before he, too, could return home. He reined his horse in and brought it up beside the litter chair where his wife and daughter rode. Porcias Major and Minor drew back the curtains and looked at him together; their faces were so similar he smiled involuntarily.

"I must go and take care of business before I join you at our home," he said. "The house has been opened and aired, and there are slaves waiting to move our property back into place. I shall join you as soon as I may."

His wife smiled back at him. "It is good to be home," she said, "but it will be better to have you at home again! Tarry not too long, husband, and I shall make your homecoming a memorable one!"

Their daughter rolled her eyes. "You two are insufferable," she said. "*Tata*, I wish you would take me to the Forum with you!"

Pilate looked at her face—already assuming the shape and lines of womanhood—and smiled. "You know it is not proper for grown women to frequent the Forum, much less children!" he said. "Now be a good girl and perhaps mother and I will let you go to the market when I get home. You need some new dresses, as quickly as you are outgrowing your clothes these days."

She gave him a pouty look. "You just want me out of the house!" she said. "Know that it will cost you!"

He laughed and spurred his horse toward the city gate. His daughter was a precocious thing, already on the brink of her teen years. He supposed that he should begin casting about to find her a husband; Roman girls did not generally marry until they were seventeen or eighteen, but the matches were usually arranged well in advance of that. Traditionally, it was purely the decision of the father, as *paterfamilias,* to choose who the groom would be, but most Roman fathers generally made that decision after at least consulting the daughter's wishes. While the father could make his daughter marry anyone of any age, it made for a better marriage and a more trouble-free life at home to make sure that the girl at least did not despise her chosen groom.

The thoughts of his daughter grown and married, as well as the soreness of the long ride, made Pilate feel his years more than usual. Roman men typically lived into their sixties, provided they dodged the many maladies of childhood and the rigors of military service. Practically speaking, Pilate knew his life was two-thirds done—yet he did not feel like an old man most of the time. He wondered what the next few years would hold for him, and if he would rise any further in the Emperor's service than he already had. Consul was as high a rank as many noble and wealthy Romans ever reached, but there was something in him that hungered for more—to make sure that, like the former lions of Rome, his name would be forever remembered for posterity. But what could he do that he had not already done? About the only option left was to lead an entire army against an enemy of Rome and its people, but Tiberius' foreign policy had just about put an end to the wars that had raged along Rome's frontiers for centuries. The Parthian Empire was at peace with Rome, and had been for a generation. The Gauls were long since conquered, as were the Celtiberians of Spain. No one cared about the damp and foggy island of Britannia, although the Divus Julius had landed and briefly established a Roman presence there eighty years ago. The border with Germania, now marked at the Rhine River, was relatively peaceful, with Rome showing no desire to expand further north, and the tribes of Germania not raiding to the south as they once did. Pilate, it seemed, had no handholds above him that would allow him to climb further. It was a depressing thought.

He sent his horse to the public stables and walked across the Forum to the Curia Julia, where the Senate met. Gaius Pollio, that year's senior consul, was addressing the Conscript Fathers of the Senate as he entered.

"While peace and prosperity have indeed been good for Rome's public treasury and for the People themselves," he said, "they present those of Rome's governing classes, patrician and pleb alike, with a unique set of problems. Fewer military commands against enemy forces, less plunder from wars of conquest, and fewer able-bodied slaves on the market. It makes it more difficult for us to distinguish ourselves and rise among our peers, and therefore it increases the temptation to engage in corruption and graft in order to raise the money necessary for the annual elections," he continued—mirroring some of the things Pilate had been thinking earlier.

"We must not give in to these temptations!" he said. "Corruption poisons politics, and the Conscript Fathers of Rome must be above such common vices!"

Pilate took his seat next to his father-in-law, Gaius Porcius, who smiled in pleasure and greeted him in a whisper. The old man was more wrinkled, and his hair whiter and thinner, but there was still a crackle in his voice as he greeted his daughter's husband. "Good to see you back, lad!" he said. "I trust the journey was not too troublesome."

"Sailing conditions were excellent, and the family enjoyed the voyage immensely," said Pilate.

"Good!" said Gaius Proculus. "Sorry you had to get back in time for one of Pollio's tiresome sermons. He might as well preach the virtues of chastity in a brothel!"

"Surely my honored father-in-law is not suggesting the Conscript Fathers of Rome would engage in illegal profiteering!" said Pilate in mock dismay.

"No more than the Emperor would drink too much, or engage in wanton acts of cruelty!" whispered Gaius.

Pollio droned on for another half hour. Half the Senate was either reading scrolls, snoring, or talking among themselves. Pilate recognized that the current Consul was a boring pedant, but still, he found himself reflecting on the old tales, from the days when the Senate actually meant something. He doubted any of the Senators snored when Gaius Marius or Marcus

83

Cicero were consuls! At the end of his harangue, the Senior Consul finally recognized Pilate.

"It is with joy I see that our esteemed proconsul, recently Governor of Further Spain, has returned from his province. Lucius Pontius Pilate, would you care to enlighten us about the state of affairs in Iberia?" he asked.

"The province is peaceful and prosperous; the pirate threat is subdued for the moment, and the Celts received a proper lesson on why NOT to invade Roman provinces. I have the official report on budgetary matters to be handed over to the censors, as well as my expense accounts as governor," he said.

"Excellent!" said Pollio. "If there is no further business, then, I believe I shall call on the *Princeps Senatus* to dismiss us."

The elderly Senator who held the title stood and gave a short invocation to Jupiter Optimus Maximus, the chief god and protector of Rome, and then dismissed the assembly.     Several Senators, either clients or friends of Pilate, stopped by to welcome him on his return to Rome. When he had spoken to them all, he turned and found his father-in-law still waiting.

"Would you care to join me for a quick bite?" he asked.

"I am famished from my journey, but I do not need to fill up," said Pilate. "Porcia is planning a celebratory dinner, I believe. Still, a bit of bread and a cup of wine would be most pleasant."

They walked toward a small shop not far from the Forum and Proculus purchased each of them a hot fresh loaf and a cup of wine. Pilate filled his father-in-law in on the details of the family's time in Spain, and the doings of his wife and daughter, for several minutes. When the old man's curiosity seemed sated, Pilate turned the conversation toward events in Rome.

"So how is Tiberius faring these days?" he asked.

Proculus scowled. "Angrier and gloomier all the time," he said. "I understand the gods give each of us a unique disposition and personality, and that our life experiences shape our person. But I cannot help but think that a man who rules the entire world could find something to take joy in occasionally! Right now he is still grieving the death of Drusus, but even more so, he has had it up to his *podex* with Agrippina! She has never forgiven him for the death of Germanicus, and is now saying that Drusus' death was actually the gods' way of settling the score for her! Her friends urge her to silence, but she never quiets down for long. She has never taken another husband, or another lover, and lives vicariously through her children. I do not know how much longer Tiberius will take it."

Pilate nodded. "What of Sejanus?" he asked.

Proculus raised an eyebrow. "He has become very powerful, since our Emperor spends less and less time in Rome of late," he said. "But that being said, he is riding for a fall. He is carrying on with Drusus' widow, Livilla, even more openly now that her husband is dead. Rumor has it he plans to ask the Emperor for permission to marry her! That would make him the stepfather of Drusus' children, who may well be in line for the Imperial purple someday—if in fact they are Drusus' children, which many doubt."

"It sounds as if Tiberius has reason for his gloomy character," said Pilate. "What a tangled mess his family is!"

Proculus lowered his voice. "I will tell you the truth, son-in-law," he said. "We were very fortunate to have Augustus as Emperor for so long. He may have done a foul deed or two early on, in order to secure himself in power, but for most all of his life he was a clement and honest ruler and Rome thrived under him. Rome has prospered under Tiberius, but he is becoming increasingly vindictive as he ages. One of the younger Senators made a rather impertinent speech last year, ridiculing Tiberius and Drusus, right after Drusus died. Not too long thereafter, as he was leaving the Forum, he was set upon by bandits—at least, they said it was bandits—and murdered in an alley not a half a *stadia* from here. Not only did they cut his throat, they stripped him naked and cut his tongue out!"

Pilate thought for a moment. Could the Tiberius that he knew so well, and had fought under in Germania, have committed such a deed? Then he recalled how he and Tiberius had eaten lunch together as the bandits were crucified only a few feet away, and the gusto with which the normally abstemious Caesar had tucked into his meal. It took one to know one, he supposed. Tiberius was quite capable of ordering the tongue of someone who displeased him cut out, he thought, just as Pilate was perfectly capable of obeying such an order. He gave a mental shrug. It was a cruel world, and it took cruel men to rule it.

He and Proculus chatted awhile longer about Senators they both knew, and affairs in Rome's provinces, and after an hour's conversation, Pilate excused himself. The sun was tipping past midafternoon, and he was eager to be home. It took about a half hour or more to walk to his home in the Aventine on a typical day; the streets of Rome were bustling with people of all descriptions and races, all come to the capital of the world to ply their trades and seek their fortunes. Between the Forum and his home he rubbed elbows with Syrians, Scythians, Greeks, Gauls, Jews, Ethiopians, and Arabs as well as countless ordinary citizens of Rome. Occasionally a litter chair was carried past him by slaves, curtains usually drawn, the occasional giggle or whisper betraying the presence of some wealthy Roman matron or maiden.

He stepped through the gate of his home and a servant immediately relieved him of his toga, slipping a comfortable house robe over his tunic. It was spring, but the air still had a slight chill as the sun crept westward. Procula greeted him with a smile. "Home before sunset!" she said. "You must have conducted your business quickly."

"Not so quickly that your father didn't bend my ear for an hour with the latest gossip," Pilate said, pulling his wife close for a quick kiss.

"The servants have an early supper prepared," she said. "I thought that Porcia might enjoy a trip to the market before the merchants close up shop, and perhaps you and I could take a nap after a stressful day."

Pilate smiled at the prospect. "That sounds quite pleasant," he said. "Now where is our daughter?"

"Right here, *tata*!" she said. "Now, how long do you want to be rid of me? I figure one new gown per hour is an acceptable rate, don't you?"

"I pity whoever you wind up married to, you little mercenary!" he said with a mock scowl. "You will drive the poor man to debtor's prison!"

"Only if he wants me out of the house so he can 'take a nap' with someone else," she said impudently.

Pilate tried very hard to look stern, but found himself chuckling at her matter-of-fact tone. He reached into his purse and drew out several denarii. "This should purchase two gowns, if you spend it wisely," he said. "I will expect Democles and Stephenia to go with you and watch you most closely! But first, let us recline at the table together."

The meal was simple but tasteful and not filling; Roman fare tended to be heavier on fish and poultry, but lighter on beef and pork, than the Spanish dishes the family had grown accustomed to. A hot loaf of fresh-baked bread finished off the meal, with olive oil and garlic for dipping. When they were done, Pilate sent the two slaves off with his young daughter and instructions to give himself and Procula an hour or two to themselves. Once they were gone, his wife slid into his arms and looked up at him. "Why is it so hard for us to find time to be a couple?" she said.

"I believe the correct answer to that is: We have a daughter!" he answered, and bent to find her lips.

"I'm terribly sorry, Master," came the voice of his steward, Aristion, from the door, "but you have a guest who requests audience."

"Tell him to come back tomorrow!" snapped Pilate in irritation.

"He comes with a message from the Emperor," said the steward.

Pilate groaned and looked at his wife. "I am sorry, my dear," he said.

She gave him a brief pouting look, then a quick hug. "Go, then, deal with your precious business," she said. "I know that the Emperor cannot be refused!" She muttered something under her breath as she whisked off to their bedchamber. Pilate thought it sounded like "Tiberius *interruptus*!" He chuckled as he stepped into his study.

A stern man a bit older than Pilate in a Praetorian's uniform was waiting for him, and saluted him as he entered. "Greetings, Proconsul!" he said. "I bear express greetings from Emperor Tiberius Caesar, who requests that you join him for supper at his home on the Palatine."

"Tiberius is in Rome?" Pilate said. "I had not heard. Of course I am at his disposal for the evening. Tell him I shall be on my way momentarily."

"I brought a spare horse," said the soldier. "I am instructed to wait for you and escort you to his presence."

Pilate nodded. "I see," he said. "And who might you be?"

The Praetorian bowed. "I am Quintus Sutorius Macro, Tribune of the Praetorian Guard, second in command to Legate Lucius Sejanus," he said with a clear sense of his own importance.

"Very well, Macro, have a cup of wine while I get dressed," he said. "We shall ride for the Palatine momentarily."

"I thank you, sir, and I apologize for the intrusion," Macro replied.

Pilate donned his formal dinner toga and a mantle to keep it clean as they rode through the streets of Rome. By now the crowd was clearing, and they went clopping on toward the Palatine at a good clip.

"So can you tell me what the Emperor wants with me on my first night back in Rome?" he asked Macro.

The tribune looked at him and replied, "He did not say specifically, but between you and me, it probably involves a rather sensitive errand. I have often heard him lament your absence over the last three years. He seems to think you quite dependable."

Pilate nodded. "I thought Sejanus more dependable for the Emperor's purposes than I would be," he said.

"He usually is," said Macro. "But—well, I should say no more. Sejanus is my superior officer and my friend. I will say this much—the Emperor needs all the dependable clients he can get! Rome is not only a sewer; it is a dangerous sewer these days."

Pilate mulled that over as they dismounted outside the Emperor's rarely used house in Rome. He wondered if Tiberius' mother, the aging but redoubtable Livia Drusilla, would be present. She was ancient by Roman reckoning, eighty-two years of age, and still full of spite and mischief. Tiberius had never gotten along with her, and she was one of the main reasons that he avoided Rome for months at a time. Pilate had seen her on occasion and had one brief conversation with her in his whole life; frankly, he understood Tiberius' ambivalence about her. In a world ruled by men, she was a truly formidable woman.

The Emperor's household steward escorted him to the dining room, where Tiberius stood talking to Sejanus. Pilate had a moment to study the ruler of the world before he was noticed, and took full advantage of it. He was shocked and somewhat saddened by what he saw. Tiberius had aged, and not well. He had always been rail-thin and sour of expression, but his close-cropped hair had now whitened and thinned. His once sharply erect posture was stooped slightly, and his hands were beginning to show the telltale signs of arthritis. Pilate remembered the brave, experienced general he had served under twenty years before, and felt suddenly, unhappily old. But then, he wondered, how must Tiberius feel?

As if hearing his thoughts, the Emperor turned and faced him. "Lucius Pontius Pilate!" he said. "It is good to see you again!" He smiled, and for a moment Pilate caught a glimpse of the man he might have been, had not the weight of family and Empire crushed his spirit.

He bowed deeply. "Caesar," he said. "It is good to see you too, sir."

Tiberius scowled. "Pilate, we have known each other far too long to stand on formalities! You may always simply call me Tiberius when we are alone. So how was your time in Spain?"

Pilate began to explain his duties as governor and the state of the province, but the old Emperor scoffed aloud. "I can read official reports any time I like!" he snapped. "Tell me about your campaign against the pirates! How many of them were there? Did they put up much resistance?"

Pilate smiled. "There were about six hundred of them, plus four hundred of their women and children," he said. "They had found a sheltered cove with a steep canyon, far from any town, and made it their headquarters. One of my patrols happened to see their ship emerging from the mouth of the harbor, or we might never have found them—the place was very hard to spot from sea or land, unless you were looking for it. The legionary in charge of the patrol rode straight for Gades and reported to me what they had seen, and I assembled a single legion and made a beeline for the site. I ordered two triremes to follow us up the coast, and they blocked the exit of the cove even as we descended upon the pirate village. When they realized there was no escape, they put up a terrific resistance! They knew the fate that awaited them, and were determined to go down fighting. My boys were starving for a good scrap, and made short work of them. I fought and disarmed the pirate king myself, and then we nailed him and all the surviving men up right there on the beach, and burned their ships. The women and children went to the slave markets, and all the loot that could be identified was returned to its proper owners, while the rest was kept on deposit to be returned to the Treasury here in Rome."

"Splendid!" said Tiberius, rubbing his gnarled hands together. "So what sort of fellow was the pirate king?"

"A big man," said Pilate, remembering the deadliest opponent he had ever crossed swords with. "He was armed with a Syrian-style scimitar and a dagger, and wielded them both at once. He called himself Brandir, I think.

Something like that, a barbarian name if you ever heard one. He already had killed two of my legionaries when I singled him out, and I told the boys he was mine. I almost regretted that decision—he was half a head taller than me and very strong!"

"You could have gotten yourself killed," said Tiberius. "That was a foolish risk."

Pilate shrugged. "My blood was up, and I wanted to take him down myself," he said. "I'll admit, it took every bit of skill and training I had, but fortunately I had been practicing with the men for a year, waiting for the day we would find the pirates' stronghold!"

"How did you prevail?" said Tiberius.

"I pretended I was wearing out," said Pilate. "I began to swing with half strength, and panting heavily, and letting myself look a little bit afraid. He got overconfident and extended himself too far, and I got inside his swing and hamstrung him. He dropped his dagger to grab at his calf, and I brought my blade down on his wrist, hard—nearly severed his hand, but he dropped his blade and the men jumped him. You should have heard him cursing me as they nailed him up!"

Tiberius cackled. "I always said you had more guts than anyone I ever soldiered with," he said. "Those kinds of battles are easy, Pilate—you know who your enemy is, and you know he wants to destroy you! All you have to do is kill him first. The battles I am fighting now—pah!" He spat upon the marble floor. "They surround me day and night, some of them leeches and some of them serpents. I don't know who wants to poison me and who wants to simply drain off little bits of me until there is nothing left. And my family is the worst of the bunch!"

"Families are a blessing and a curse, Tiberius," he said.

"Mine has been a curse throughout," said the Emperor. "My mother wants to rule Rome, my daughters-in-law want their children to rule Rome, and Sejanus wants to rule me! It is enough to drive a man to distraction—or, in my case, to drink. I don't even distract easily anymore!"

Tiberius walked over to the couch and reclined in front of the table. He held out his hand, and a slave quickly poured him some wine. "Leave the flagon on the table," said the Emperor, "and dismiss yourself—and the others—for the evening. I would have a private time with my old friend

Pilate." He gestured, and Pilate joined him on the couch, pouring himself a cup of wine and then watering it. He had no desire to get drunk this evening.

"How can I ease your burdens, old friend?" Pilate asked.

Tiberius let out a long sigh. "Would that one of my sons had lived longer than me!" he said. "Germanicus and I quarreled, but he had the makings of a true Emperor. Drusus—well, I was not blind to his faults, but he was not a bad person. He was my heir by birthright, and with Germanicus gone, it eased my heart to think my own natural son, born of the only woman I ever loved, might succeed me as Emperor. But now he is gone too. His widow is sleeping with Sejanus—they think I do not know, but I do! They want to set up Drusus' boys as my heirs, and control the Empire through them. I do not even think they are Drusus' children, if you want to know the truth! I will see myself neck deep in Tartarus before I let either of them wear the purple when I am gone!" He emptied his wine cup, and Pilate refilled it for him. "That brings me to Agrippina," said Tiberius. "She hates me, and is raising her boys to hate me as well—all except little Gaius, who adores me. He is a piece of work, that child. Mean as a snake at times, but as charming as a courtier at others. He has the makings of a true Caesar!"

Pilate remembered the pint-sized centurion striding up and down the Imperial box, shouting encouragement to the gladiators, and his enthusiasm for seeing the losing contestant put to death. "Do you really think so?" he asked Tiberius.

The old man cackled again. "You don't miss a trick, do you?" he said. "The boy has a mean streak, no doubt. But you have to be a monster to run this monstrosity called Rome! He will be the leader the people deserve someday, I think."

"Does anyone know that he is your choice?" said Pilate.

"Not yet," said the Emperor. "That is where you come in."

Now for it, thought Pilate. "What would you have me do?" he asked.

"Agrippina will not speak with me anymore," said Tiberius. "She thinks I want to have her killed."

"Do you?" asked Pilate.

"You'd do it for me if I asked, wouldn't you?" said the Emperor. "But no, I have no desire to be rid of her—not yet. However, I do want to adopt young Gaius. Since she refuses invitation to my home these days, I am going to ask you, as my personal representative—and someone whose loyalty I completely trust—to broach the subject with her and get her reaction. You will report back to me every word, every expression, and her posture—anything that will reveal how she feels about such a move."

Pilate grimaced. "Are you sure I am the right man for this job?" he asked.

Tiberius looked at him, not unkindly. "You are the man I trust to do it," he said. "I do not envy you, however. Agrippina is a difficult woman! But not every assignment can be as enjoyable as dueling a pirate king, or forcing a provincial governor to fall on his sword!"

Pilate nodded. "I think I would rather deal with a dozen of Calpurnius Piso than one irate Agrippina!" he said.

"You are a wise man," said Tiberius. "Now, tell me of your encounter with the Celts!"

Pilate launched into a quick account of the attack on the north Spanish coast, and Tiberius demanded more details. All told, it was two hours later before Pilate finally left, his borrowed horse trotting him down the Palatine Hill toward his home in the Aventine. Procula Porcia had already gone to bed and was sound asleep when he slid between the sheets beside her. Pilate sighed, kissed her neck, and went to sleep. This evening had definitely turned out nothing like he envisioned it!

# CHAPTER EIGHT

The next day he sent one of his servants with a message to Agrippina, requesting permission to call upon her at her earliest convenience. She sent a reply back by her servant, telling him that she was at his disposal during the evening meal. Pilate explained briefly to his wife why he would be absent, and spent the day attending to his many clients, all of whom wanted something—a favor, a bit of legislation, another month to pay rent, sponsorship for their son who was taking the first steps on the *cursus honorum*. It was the price of *arctoritas*, Pilate knew—having a wide circle of influence, in Rome, meant that you would never lack for people who wanted something from you. But every favor granted was a favor owed; by being gracious and accommodating to those who were beneath him, Pilate ensured that they would be useful to him in the future.

After his clients finished, Pilate had a bite of bread and olive oil with a piece of grilled fish for his luncheon, and then walked up the hill to the Forum. The Senate was not in session today, but the popular assemblies had met and were listening to the senior Tribune of the Plebs hold forth on a proposed agrarian law. Tribunes of the Plebs had been promulgating agrarian laws since Tiberius Gracchus over a hundred years before; all of them promised Rome's poor and downtrodden a chance to own land of their own, somewhere outside the city—and most of them never delivered. Yet the people still cheered, and tribunes still got elected, by promising land to the landless. Pilate wondered if that would ever change.

He returned home late that afternoon and enjoyed a cup of watered wine with his wife. Porcia Minor was off at her tutor's home, learning to read Greek poetry, and Procula enjoyed the chance to simply visit with her husband for a while, discussing all the latest gossip of Rome and what had happened in the neighborhood during their long absence. About an hour before Pilate had to leave on his errand, his daughter came bursting in, full of life and energy.

"Hello, *tata*!" she exclaimed. "See, you and mama got to spend an afternoon together, and you didn't even have to send me away to the market!"

He smiled. "We were having a very pleasant conversation until a small cyclone tore into our living quarters!"

She batted her tiny eyelashes at him. "I am sure I have no idea who you are referring to," she said.

"So how were today's lessons?" he asked.

"Boring!" she exclaimed. "I think that Odysseus was not particularly bright, personally."

"Do you now?" Pilate said, her thought processes always interesting to him. "How so?"

"Why would he insist on hearing the song of the sirens if he did not intend to go to them?" she asked. "Wouldn't it fill all the remainder of his days with a longing for something he could never have?"

Pilate raised an eyebrow. So mature, yet so naïve at the same time! "Well, my dear," he said, "it is wanting that which we cannot have that drives us to excel! If we did not seek to rise above ourselves and become something more, then no man would ever excel at anything. It is the longing for that we can never possess that makes us become more than we thought we could!"

"Unless it is longing for a siren," she said. "Then it just makes you drown."

Pilate was still chuckling over that one an hour later when he pulled on his toga and headed out to see Agrippina. Her home on the Palatine was not far from Tiberius' dwelling, and he was met at the door by a huge, muscular slave who conducted him to the dining room without a word. Agrippina entered the room from the interior passageway opposite just as Pilate came in from the entry corridor. She was still a handsome woman, although the strain and grief of the last five years had added deep lines to her face.

Pilate gave a polite bow. "Lady Agrippina," he said. "It is kind of you to see me on such short notice."

94

"I fear I do not have much of a social life at the present," she said. "It is good to have company—my children are dear to me, but they are a handful and I long for adult conversation sometimes. Will you join me at the table?"

They reclined at the table together, and Pilate looked around. "Where are your children this evening?" he asked.

"They are with their grandmother, Antonia Minor," she said. "She enjoys seeing them, and I enjoy an occasional relief from their . . . exuberance. So tell me, what brings the former Consul to my door this evening?"

Pilate took a small sip of wine and began. "As you may know, I do enjoy the confidence of the Emperor," he began.

"I know you are one of his lackeys," she replied.

Pilate blinked at her abruptness. There was no hostility in the tone, just a dry assertion of fact. "I assure you, madam, I am no lackey," he said.

"Lackey, client, errand boy, call it what you will," she said. "You are the one who silenced Calpurnius Piso, are you not?"

Pilate's eyes widened for a moment. This woman was indeed formidable! "My dear lady," he said, affecting nonchalance, "whatever gave you such a bizarre idea?"

She laughed grimly. "The Emperor is not the only one who has spies," she said. "I know that Calpurnius Piso poisoned my husband. I also know that he was on his way back to Rome with every intention of defending himself vigorously at trial. He sent a letter to the Emperor by special courier—but that courier was found dead in an alley at Rhodes, with all his personal effects stolen. Not long after, Piso falls on his sword at Ephesus, leaving a suicide note confessing to the murder of Germanicus, but specifying that the Emperor was not to blame in any way for it. Now, out of all Tiberius' closest servants, you and you alone were completely out of sight during that entire time—suffering from the spotted pox, according to your family. But those sores on your face at my husband's funeral games were not like any pox I have ever seen! Hence, I believe you had a hand in making sure Piso would never stand trial!"

Pilate decided to fight bluntness with bluntness. "Without confessing to the truth of any of your allegations, Lady Agrippina, let me assure you of

95

one thing," he said. "I do know Tiberius well. I have served under him for many years, and I have had occasion to perform some errands for him—some much less pleasant than this enjoyable dinner meeting! I can say this as truth before all the gods of Rome: Tiberius Caesar neither desired nor ordered the death of Germanicus. May the Furies take me if I am lying!"

She looked deep in his eyes and nodded. "I believe you are telling the truth," she said. "Or, at the very least, what you believe to be the truth. So tell me then—why do you come to my dinner table this evening?"

Pilate took a bite of fish from his plate, ate a bit of bread to go with it, then sipped his wine and spoke. "Since the death of Drusus, the succession of the next Emperor has become a matter of some concern," he said.

She arched an eyebrow. "I figured that Sejanus and Livilla Julia had that all wrapped up," she replied.

"The Emperor has no desire to see either of the twins inherit his power," said Pilate. "Frankly, he does not even believe them to be Drusus' children!"

"He is not as blind as I thought, then," said Agrippina. "So who does the Emperor propose to elevate when he is no more?"

"That is why I am here," said Pilate. "The Emperor is very fond of your young son Gaius, and proposes to legally adopt him and begin grooming him for the succession."

"Gaius!" she said. "*Ecastor!* He must hate Rome more than I thought!"

"That is an odd thing to say about your own son," Pilate remarked.

"My son is an odd creature," she replied. "Not without virtue, but with a great many vices. It may be that he can overcome his flaws, with careful training. He can be very charming and gracious when he puts his mind to it. But there is—I do not know what to call it. There is darkness in him, Lucius Pontius, which, if allowed to take control, could turn him into a monster. Either of my other sons might be better qualified to be Caesar someday."

"Tiberius does not choose them," said Pilate. "He thinks they hate him. He is fond of little Gaius, and Gaius Little Boots seems to return his affection. It may simply be that Gaius is the youngest. The Emperor is fond of children, you know."

She nodded thoughtfully. "He is indeed," she said. "That may be his only redeeming virtue."

Pilate frowned. "You are too hard on the man, Agrippina!" he said. "He is a sad old soul, it is true, but he is not a monster. There is courage and honor in him as well as anger and bitterness."

She sighed deeply. "I think, Pontius Pilate, that I know things about him that you do not—and you may well know other things about him that I do not. Be that as it may, this is not an easy decision. I assume that the Emperor will be waiting to hear my answer from your lips?"

Pilate nodded. "He is most anxious about the matter, to tell the truth," he said.

"Then tell him this," she said, looking him in the eye. "I do not give my permission for him to adopt my son—nor do I withhold it. I would speak with him in person about it before I make a final decision. And, since my son is now nearly eleven years old, I also feel as if I should discuss the matter with him as well."

"I imagine that your answer will not displease him," Pilate said. "He is tired, Agrippina—tired of bitterness and suspicion and disappointment. I truly believe that he wants to do right by you and your children."

She gave her low and bitter laugh again. "Doing right, as you put it, has not been a Julio-Claudian tradition of late," she said. "Perhaps that may change. Come, let us finish our dinner." She looked at the burly slave who had escorted Pilate to her dinner table. "Theseus!" she snapped. "Bring us some music!"

The huge Greek bowed and left the chamber. "Do you always discuss things so freely in front of your slaves?" asked Pilate. "Slaves' gossip is the source of much mischief in Rome."

"That is not a problem with him," said Agrippina. "He was my husband's loyal servant, and the Germans captured him during the last campaign my dear Germanicus waged against them. They tortured him for two days, trying to get him to disclose the location of the Roman camp, and he would not talk—so they cut his tongue out! My husband rescued him when he attacked the German camp a few days later. He freed Theseus for his loyalty and sacrifice, but Theseus chose to remain with us of his own free will. He manages the household slaves quite well, and is married to my chief maid, Dorothea."

Pilate digested this bit of information and mentally filed it away while enjoying the remainder of the dinner—an excellent serving of Tiber River bass, eels, and snails served with copious amounts of garlic and butter, and small loaves of delectable bread, with plates full of fresh grapes and cheeses alongside. He chatted with Agrippina about her children and their personalities the whole time. Nero, the eldest son, was eighteen and currently serving under Pilate's successor in Further Spain as a *contraburnalis,* or junior lieutenant. Drusus, who was a year younger than Nero, was about to don his toga and legally become a man. He, too, was planning on serving as a junior officer under the new governor of Syria. The three girls, Agrippina Minor, Julia Drusilla, and Julia Livia, were all in their early teens and living at home. Caligula, about to turn twelve, was the liveliest and most mischievous of the lot, according to his mother. She told Pilate several stories about the young Gaius that made him sound both endearing and a little bit fearsome.

Finally, when the last morsel was consumed and their wine glasses emptied, Pilate returned home and thought long and hard about all that he had heard and seen from the wife of Germanicus. It took him several hours to wind down enough to go to sleep, and when he finally dozed off after midnight, he dreamed of seeing the twelve-year-old Caligula on the Imperial throne, laughing as he stared at the body of a withered and frail Tiberius. It was not a comforting dream.

The next morning he made his way to the Emperor's home and found Tiberius waiting for him. Sejanus was nowhere to be seen.

"I sent him on an errand to Capri," said Tiberius. "Now, come, let us go riding together. I have not been on horseback in a month or more, and some country air will do me good!"

Pilate was a bit surprised—Tiberius was normally not one who enjoyed exercise for its own sake—but he said nothing until they were beyond the city walls and trotting across open farmland. Once they were cantering across a fertile hay meadow, he turned to the Emperor with a quizzical look. Tiberius made a wry face and spoke.

"I no longer trust my servants—at least, not the ones here in Rome. Sejanus knows far more of my business than I am comfortable with. On Capri, I do not worry as much—Mencius runs a tight ship and those slaves have been with me for many years. Here in Rome, I do not even know everyone that scurries around my villa. Now, tell me, what was your impression of Agrippina?"

Pilate gave a wry grin. "If she had been born a man she might have made a most impressive emperor!" he answered.

Tiberius laughed. "You may be quite right there. If she were a man, I doubt my head would still be attached to my neck! But she is not a man—so I do not fear her becoming Emperor anytime soon. Seriously, how did she respond?"

"She is a remarkably perceptive woman, Caesar. Despite all our precautions, she has deduced that I am the one who silenced Piso," said Pilate.

"*Edepol!*" swore Tiberius. "How did she—hell, never mind. So she is convinced I had Germanicus killed?"

"Not really," said Pilate. "For one thing, without admitting that she was correct, I swore to her before the gods that you neither desired nor ordered the death of Germanicus."

"That is true," said Tiberius, "and well said on your part. But did she believe you?"

"I think she did," replied Pilate. "Or at least, as she put it, she believes that I believe it to be true."

"So will she allow me to adopt young Gaius as my heir?" asked the Emperor.

"She did not grant her permission, nor did she refuse it," Pilate answered. "She wishes to discuss the matter in person."

Tiberius nodded sagely. "You have done your work well, old friend. She has refused all invitations to see me for nearly a year now. If she is now willing to talk, I believe progress can be made. For your services, and your loyalty, I thank you."

Pilate nodded. "She did express some reservations about your choice of young Gaius from among her children, however," he said.

"Really?" said the Emperor. "No doubt she would prefer I choose Nero or Drusus instead, since they are both well-nigh men already, with their own tastes and desires fully formed. And of course those tastes include a distinct distaste for me, the old tyrant who may have murdered their father! I have seen the way they look at me when I have appeared in public with them—a mingling of fear and loathing that neither of them can hide. Do you think I would be safe for a moment if I named either of them my heir?"

"I seriously doubt either of them would dare to—" Pilate began.

"Oh, I don't doubt it for a minute!" said Tiberius bitterly. "And even if they dared not try to take my life, do you think for a minute that I could shape either one of them into the Emperor that I want them to be? Gaius is young and still teachable. If I take him in now, I can mold him and shape him—teach him the principles of governing an Empire, so that it does not all fall apart as soon as I am gone!"

"I think," said Pilate, "that the Empire you and your father created has grown and stabilized to the point that it is greater than any one man. Of course it is better when the Emperor's office is held by someone who has been trained and groomed for it—but unless I miss my mark, I believe that Rome will endure far beyond the time of your successor—or his successor."

Tiberius nodded. "You may be right, old friend, but I want Rome to do more than endure. I want Rome to thrive, even if I do not care much for her people. I cannot stand Romans, truth be told, but I do love the idea of Rome! The thought that our single city grew into a Republic and went on from there to rule the world is unique in history. I want Rome to be a light for generations to come, an eternal city that will set the standards of civilization and decency in a world of squalor! My father spent a good part of his life training and shaping me for the duty of governing this mighty engine that he created. I have tried to train and groom two different successors now, and both of them are dead! Gaius is my last chance to leave Rome in capable and well-prepared hands—I am running out of time, Lucius! I am sixty-six years old. Most of the companions of my youth are long dead."

"Your mother still lives, Caesar," said Pilate.

"That old witch will never die!" snapped Tiberius. "Her continued existence is no comfort to me. She cannot govern the Empire—even if she once thought to do so. I need an heir, and Gaius Caligula is my choice. I need to make Agrippina see that, and I thank you for giving me that chance. Now, I have a small gift that I wish to give you—a reward for your continued faithful service. I own a small villa near Ariminum—a gift from some noxious seeker of favors. I give it to you to do with as you like. Let it be your retreat from Rome, or rent it out—sell it, for that matter, if you ever need the coin. Your services to me have been invaluable over the years."

Pilate bowed as best he could from horseback. "You are too generous, Caesar!" he said. "I serve you because in serving you I serve Rome, whom I, too, love—although I am fonder of the Romans themselves than you are, I think!"

Tiberius gave his grim laugh. "It would not take much fondness for that mob to surpass mine!" he said. "Now let us turn back toward the city—my servants will be wondering at my absence."

They turned back toward the massive gates of Rome, and before they cantered onto the roadway, Tiberius turned and faced Pilate again. "How old is your daughter now, Lucius Pontius?" he asked.

"She is ten, Caesar," he answered.

"Is she spoken for yet?" asked the Emperor.

"No," said Pilate. "Porcia and I are just beginning to discuss arranging a marriage for her, but our long absence from Rome has not given us much opportunity to seek an appropriate match."

"What kind of girl is she?" asked Tiberius. "And more importantly, what kind of woman do you think she will become?"

Pilate reined his horse to a stop and looked at his master closely. Tiberius was focused intently on him, and he understood that this was no idle inquiry. Choosing his words carefully, he said: "She is highly intelligent, mischievous, and quite precocious for her age. She will never be a dowdy Roman matron, but I do think that she could be a clever and cunning political ally for the right husband."

Tiberius nodded. "Is she kind?" he asked.

An odd question, thought Pilate. "Yes, sir," he finally said. "She can be mischievous, as I said, but her mischief is directed more at making people laugh at the absurdity of a situation than it is at making them laugh over someone else's pain or humiliation. She loves her pets, and is always kind to the servants."

Tiberius nodded thoughtfully. "Gaius shares one attribute with us both," he finally said. "He can be quite cruel on occasion. That is not necessarily a bad trait for one who must govern a hard and cruel world, but left untempered, it could turn him into a tyrant. I think a kind and clever bride might do much to mitigate his less savory tendencies, don't you?"

Pilate swallowed hard. His Porcia, wife of the next Caesar? It was an honor he had never dared dream of! But could she be happy with someone like young Gaius? And should that even be a consideration? It was something to be thought over very carefully. Finally he spoke.

"You do me too much honor, Tiberius," he said, meaning every word. "I am not sure how to respond. Both of them are still children, and it might be good to observe them together and see how compatible they are—you and I both know that a good marriage can be a wonderful and stabilizing factor in a man's life, but a bad one can be a horrible curse and a burden!"

Tiberius looked very solemn. "I am sure I have no idea what you are talking about, Pontius Pilate," he said, keeping a straight face for a moment, and then breaking out into his barking laugh again. "I need to spend more time with you; I can see that—I have not laughed this much in a fortnight! Now let us each return home, and think on the future of our families!"

They trotted together back to the gates of Rome, and Pilate took his leave of the Emperor at the gate of Tiberius' home, and then turned his horse toward the stables at the Aventine. His mind was racing. Father-in-law of Rome's future Emperor? He wondered what his own father would have thought of that! More importantly, he thought as he turned his mount over to the grooms, what would his wife think?

The next year or so was a busy time for Pilate, and generated much gossip in the Roman Forum. First there was the public reconciliation of Tiberius and Agrippina—it did not last long, but for a few months, she once more attended imperial banquets, and her children were welcomed at court once more. Then Pilate stood as consul for a second time, losing narrowly to a pair of rich patricians who were able to out-bribe the Tribal assemblies. The provinces were growing increasingly restive, and Pilate knew that before long he would be sent off to govern once more. He was hoping to be appointed governor of Egypt—still Rome's richest province, and one of the most prestigious Proconsular appointments.

The adoption of Gaius Caligula was not formally announced yet, but he did spend more and more time with his adoptive grandfather Tiberius, even after relations between Tiberius and Agrippina began to sour again. The betrothal between Porcia Minor and Caligula was not yet announced, either, but the two children were allowed to spend some time together and seemed to get on well enough. Caligula was growing into a gangly youth, all knees, elbows, and pimples, but with a mop of curly light brown hair and piercing blue eyes that promised a rather handsome man in the making. He was awkward socially as well—one moment laughing and fawning on his elders, the next moment screaming in a furious temper tantrum over some slight, then laughing as if none of it had ever happened.

Pilate and his wife were somewhat divided about the betrothal of their only surviving child to the Emperor's adoptive heir—Pilate, as he got to know the boy better and see the two of them together, was more prepared to see the match go through. Procula Porcia Major, however, never trusted Gaius.

"There is something bent in that lad, Lucius!" she exclaimed on more than one occasion.

"You are just being overly protective of your child, my dear," Pilate would reply soothingly. "Young Gaius has had a difficult life, caught between a formidable mother and a doting grandfather who happens to be the Emperor of Rome. He has some rough edges, but I do think that he will make a decent young man in the end—with our daughter's help."

She sighed deeply. "I hope you are right, husband!" she finally said.

He wasn't.

# CHAPTER NINE

By the spring of the twelfth year of Tiberius' rule over Rome, Pontius Pilate felt secure in his ascension to the peak of Roman society. He was a distinguished consular of the Senate of Rome, a confidant of the reclusive and somber Emperor who had very few friends, and the prospective father-in-law of the next Emperor. He and his wife were happily married, and their twelve-year-old daughter was becoming a beautiful young woman. However, all of that was to change in the course of a single day.

Tiberius was spending the spring on Capri, enjoying the Mediterranean sun's warmth after a particularly bitter winter. Young Caligula was with the Emperor, while his mother and siblings remained in Rome. Agrippina was out of the Emperor's good graces once more, mainly because of her desire to marry again, which Tiberius found unacceptable. Her adult sons were both ascending the *cursus honorum* into the ranks of Roman nobility, as befit those of Imperial lineage, but both of them were foolishly vocal in their criticisms of Tiberius. Pilate had taken a moment to speak to each of them in private, but their scorn for him and the Emperor was such that he simply walked away. If they were determined to blight their futures by defying the ruler of the civilized world, then let them do so, he thought.

One afternoon he was returning from a session of the Senate in the Forum when he was intercepted by a courier—a uniformed member of the Praetorian Guard, no less! The letter the man bore was from Tiberius himself. Pilate took it to the atrium of his home and sat down at a bench by the fountain to read it.

> *Julius Tiberius Caesar Augustus, Princeps et Imperator Romagna,*
> *to Lucius Pontius Pilate, Former Consul and Tribune, Greetings!*
>
> *I hope that the spring finds you and your bride doing well together. I welcome the return of the sun's warmth—these arthritic old joints feel the bite of winter a bit more every year. I wonder sometimes how many more winters I will live to face, but my strength still holds up well for a man approaching seventy, so I fear I shall not be released from my earthly responsibilities anytime soon. I enjoy my*

*time here on Capri more and more each year, and dread my return to Rome so much that I am giving serious consideration to not coming back to the city at all this year—and maybe never again!*

*I am going to ask you and Sejanus to be my eyes and ears in Rome for the coming season, and to help me to govern the Empire in absentia. There is much about this arrangement that will bear discussion in person—my little writing nook is designed to be uncomfortable, so as to keep my correspondence brief, and there are many details to be worked out between us that I do not want to commit to papyrus.*

What that means, thought Pilate, is that he wants to tell me things that Sejanus cannot overhear. Tiberius had told him a year before that he suspected the chief Praetorian of reading all his outgoing letters. Sejanus was riding for a fall, thought Pilate. He continued reading.

*Young Gaius is here with me, and he is longing to see your Porcia again. I believe that we have made a good match there! I would like for you and your family to come and visit me on Capri at your earliest convenience. It is a pleasant time of year to travel, and the island is beautiful. Come join us and stay awhile, and perhaps you can, once more, be of some service to your Emperor—and therefore to Rome. I anxiously await your arrival. May Fortuna smile upon you, old friend!*

Pilate put the letter down with a smile. Helping the Emperor to govern the Empire! That was yet another step up the ladder of respectability for the son of a minor diplomat and soldier who had never even served as Tribune of the Plebs! He began mentally calculating the cost and time of the journey, and then called for his wife.

Porcia was not as thrilled about the journey as he was, but she was not as displeased as she pretended to be, either. Although she still did not like young Gaius, he had been enough of a gentleman around their daughter that she had come to accept the future union with a sense of hopeful resignation. The phrase *que sera, sera* would not be coined for another fifteen hundred years, but it summed up her feelings aptly nonetheless. She ordered the servants to begin packing up the family's effects for a summer on Capri.

106

As for Porcia Minor, she was thrilled to be making a journey, and even more excited about seeing Gaius again. Over the last year she had begun to mature physically, and knew that her womanhood was nearly upon her. She had fallen in love with Gaius at first sight—he was so tall, and his eyes were so blue! She knew that his pimply countenance and awkward posture made other girls turn their noses up at him, but she could see past those temporary flaws to the man he would become someday, and knew that those selfsame girls would be swooning with jealousy when he was the handsome young Emperor and she his bride and consort.

She also knew that their unofficial engagement had made her father a very important man in Rome, and she took pride in her father's *arctoritas*, knowing that its aura illuminated the whole family with a *dignitas* that many Romans never achieved. Pilate was a doting father whom she greatly adored, and the idea that her love for Gaius would elevate him to a status he might never have otherwise reached filled her with pride. She was sure that this trip to visit the Emperor and his adopted son at Capri would be the finest moment of her life!

Pilate sent a letter ahead so that the Emperor would know when they were coming, and two days after meeting the courier, he and his family, along with three trusted servants, began the journey to Capri. Spring was running rampant in the countryside, and Porcia Minor frequently left the litter she and her mother were riding in to chase butterflies and baby rabbits. They were in no particular hurry—Capri was only two days' hard ride from Rome, and Pilate had told Tiberius they would be there in a week or so. He and Porcia spent the first night of their journey at the country estate of Marcus Fabricius, of one of Pilate's clients, who was currently back in Rome. Their daughter had worn herself out on the road that day and was falling asleep at the dinner table; Pilate carried her to bed and kissed her forehead, then joined his wife in the master bedchamber.

After making love, he held Porcia and they talked far into the night about everything and nothing—bits of Forum gossip, memories of a marriage that was nearing fifteen years' duration, silly moments from their childhood—the kind of talk that only two people who truly enjoy life together can share. It was long past midnight when they fell asleep.

The next day started off lovely, but clouds came rolling in from the Mediterranean around noon, and by the second hour past it was pouring buckets and the wind was blowing the rain horizontally. Pilate pulled his old campaigning *sagum* from his bags and placed it over his clothes, but even the oiled leather could not keep the water from pouring in at his neck and soaking his tunic. Porcias Major and Minor were even less able to keep the floods at bay, and both were soaked to the skin inside their litter within the hour. By that time the cobblestones were so slick with mud and water that the bearers were having a hard time keeping the litter on the level, so both ladies mounted up in most un-Roman fashion on the extra horses and rode alongside Pilate. Finally they came to an inn about three hours before dark, and Pilate rented two rooms for the family and servants. He paid an extra denarius to get a hot tub of water brought up so that they could shake off the chill of the journey, and that night he, his wife, and his daughter all shared one bed for the sake of warmth as a cool north wind reminded them all that winter's hold had not been completely relinquished.

The next day, though, the clouds had rolled away, and the morning sun dawned doubly bright—determined, it seemed, to apologize for its absence the previous afternoon. Dressed in clean, dry clothes, Pilate's entourage set out once more for Neapolis. They made excellent time, and by the end of that third day were only twenty miles from the seaport from where they would set out to reach Capri. Pilate was very anxious now to get to their destination, and decided about midday to ride on ahead and secure lodgings for the night on the outskirts of the city. He made the journey in a little over an hour once he was free of the litter bearers' pace, and found a large and comfortable villa for rent just outside the city. The owner was puzzled that Pilate only wanted it for one night, until he explained that he was on his way to Capri to see the Emperor.

"Of course," said the merchant, Fabius Caprilius. "Any guest of the Emperor is welcome to use my weekend home! We are all quite fond of Tiberius around here!"

Pilate was puzzled. Most of the people of Rome were at best indifferent and at worst downright hostile to the gloomy old Caesar, but this man's affection was obviously genuine. The man must have seen Pilate's expression, for he burst out laughing.

"Probably don't hear that sentiment up in the Forum very often, do you, sir?" he asked.

Pilate nodded with a slight smile but did not speak.

"Those Senators have never seen the Emperor around children," the merchant explained. "He has all the local boys and girls out to the island on a pretty regular basis—lets them have the run of the palace, watches them dance and play, and sends them home with a bellyful of candy and sweets and a gold sestercius each! If he were a Greek, I would wonder about it all, but my boy has been out there a half dozen times and swears up and down the old coot—er, begging your pardon, the noble Emperor, I mean—never does anything unseemly with any of them. He just loves to watch them being happy!"

Pilate smiled. "The Emperor has often told me how much he loves children," he said. "He claims it's a shame they must grow up to be people!"

"That sounds about like him," said Fabius. "Enjoy your stay for the night—I will have my servants prepare supper for your household, so that you have no worries for the evening except rest after a long day's journey."

Pilate paid the man and rode back down the road, finding his family only about ten miles from town. The litter bearers were looking quite exhausted, and he told them about the evening's accommodations, and then invited his wife and daughter to give the tired slaves a rest and ride with him for the last stretch. He told his steward, Democles, to bring the entourage along at a relaxed pace. He took a fresh horse and set Porcia Minor in front of him, while his wife rode alongside—riding sidesaddle, like a proper Roman matron, this time.

They arrived at the villa a little over an hour later, and found that the servants had bath water heating and supper laid on the table. Pilate made sure provisions had also been made for his own household slaves, and then he and his family cleaned off the dust of the road and enjoyed a pleasant meal. After supper they lit a charcoal brazier in the villa's receiving room and curled up on a stone bench covered with pillows and blankets. Pilate read several selections from Homer's *Odyssey*, and when Porcia Minor grew sleepy, he carried her to bed and then retired with his wife. All of them slept soundly, and did not stir until long after the sun was over the horizon.

It was a beautiful morning, and the harbor at Neapolis was teaming with ships of every size and description. Pilate chartered a small vessel to carry his family and three domestics across—he paid off the litter bearers, who had only been hired for the journey—and the party were all aboard before noon. With a light north breeze blowing and the rowers keeping good time, they took about four hours to get out to the island's harbor. Pilate sent a runner to inform the Emperor of their arrival, and then he rented a litter for his ladies and a horse for himself. The road up to the huge Villa Jovis, where Tiberius spent his summers, was fairly steep but well maintained, and both the horse and the bearers seemed used to the journey. By the time the sun had begun to lower in the sky, they had arrived at the Emperor's residence.

"Villa" was quite an understatement, thought Pilate as he stared at the huge structure. It had been built by Augustus early during his reign as an escape from the noise and distraction of Rome. Built on top of a mountain, the Emperor's summer home was in fact a huge and luxurious palace, four stories tall in places, with magnificent colonnades overlooking the island on one side and the Mediterranean on the other. It was easy to see why Augustus and Tiberius both loved the place so much—it was designed to be both beautiful and comfortable.

The Emperor met them at the top of the majestic staircase, leaning on a cane and looking weather-beaten and careworn but still healthy for a man of his years. Young Gaius stood by his side, taller by two inches than the last time Pilate had seen him. If he kept growing at this rate, thought Pilate, he would near six feet before he was done—quite tall for a Roman, but not unusual for the Julian line.

"Welcome, Pontius Pilate!" called the Emperor. "And welcome to your lovely family! It is good to have guests here on the island. Gaius, show the family to the guest quarters. Supper shall be served in an hour; come and meet me in the main banquet room. There will be music and dancing, and I have told my chef to make the meal memorable!"

"Caesar is most kind," said Pilate. "We are delighted to come and visit you at any time, but most especially at your beautiful island home."

Porcias Major and Minor bowed graciously, and young Caligula stepped forward and gave the younger of the two a wide smile. "Hello, Porcia, it is good to see you again!" he said. "You are almost as lovely as your mother now!"

Pilate's wife gave him a stern glance. "Your future bride should always rank above her mother in your eyes, young Gaius!" she said with mock severity.

Caligula gave an impish grin. "Well, I am sure she will surpass you soon enough," he said. "But you are looking most lovely today, Procula Porcia! I think the sea agrees with you!"

She rolled her eyes at his shameless flattery, and Caligula showed them to the guest chambers—which were almost as large as their entire house back in Rome. They washed their hands and faces and donned clean clothes for dinner; then the servants came to conduct them to the main dining hall.

The table was at least fifty feet long, and laden with all sorts of dishes and delicacies. Sejanus, Macro, and a few other people Pilate did not recognize joined them near the center of the table. It obviously was made for many more guests, but from what Pilate had seen, for Tiberius eight guests were a large number indeed. Gaius sat next to his adoptive father and waited on the Emperor attentively, handing him choice morsels and whispering the occasional comment or private joke to him. Tiberius nodded and occasionally let out a low chuckle.

They ate until they could eat no more, and then the Emperor clapped his hands and ten small children came scampering out from a nearby doorway. Dressed in white tunics, they danced to the music of a lute, played by a lovely Greek maidservant, for about a half an hour. They were not particularly talented and frequently burst into giggles when they missed a step or got off beat. At one point, two of them collided with each other and collapsed in a tangle of arms, legs, and laughter. The Emperor laughed in amusement, and when they began to tire, he clapped his hands once more and the music stopped. The boys and girls lined up to face him, and Tiberius rose stiffly from the couch where he reclined and spoke.

"I thank you for entertaining my guests, and you may now go to your rooms. Selena has some sweets and fresh squeezed grape juice for you. Tomorrow the ship will take you back to your parents. Thanks for gladdening an old man's heart once more!" he said. They bowed, and one small girl came up and gave him a shy hug. The Greek girl who had been playing the lute had ducked back into the kitchen, and came back out with a large dish of sweetcakes and a flagon full of juice. With excited voices, the children followed her out of the room, and Tiberius watched them go with a fond look.

"If only all citizens were so easy to satisfy, and so eager to please!" he said. "But life is what we are stuck with, not what we wish for. Sejanus,

111

Pilate, if you would be so kind as to join me in my study? The rest of you enjoy whatever delicacies you have not filled up on, and when you are ready to retire, my servants will show you to your chambers."

"Can I come too?" asked Gaius.

Tiberius shook his head. "No, dear grandson, you will have to have enough boring and tedious conversations about politics when you are older. Trust me, it is not something you want to rush!" he said.

Caligula stuck out his lower lip in a pout, and then returned to the table. He was thirteen now and looked more like fifteen. His eyes were a very intense blue, thought Pilate, with an icy coldness at the heart of them that his smile never seemed to touch. He wondered if his daughter would melt that iciness away someday.

Moments later, they arrived in Tiberius' study, and he gestured for them to be seated. He leaned upon his desk and looked at them both very carefully. Finally he spoke.

"I am the Emperor of Rome," he said. "The problem is that I despise Rome. Not the Empire, not the system of government, and not necessarily the people—although I would be lying if I said I was fond of them. It is the city of Rome I despise. Every time I set foot in it I feel the life force sapped from me, and the longer I stay there the more miserable I become."

He began pacing about the room, running his fingers across the scabbard of Julius Caesar's gladius where it hung on the wall. "It has occurred to me that, since I am the Emperor, perhaps it is time I simply exercise Imperial prerogative and choose to stay away from the city altogether. I will be happier and the citizens of Rome will be indifferent. However, in order to do this, I will need loyal clients—not that nest of vipers in the Senate—to be my administrators, my instruments, and my eyes and ears. Sejanus, you have the loyalty of the Praetorian Guard and are keenly attuned to the thinking of the legions and the Equestrian Order. Pilate, you are a respected Consular and a senior member of the Senate. Between the two of you, I will want to be aware of every political current that wafts through the city. I want each of you to develop an extensive network of confidential informants who will keep you apprised of all developments that might impede or imperil the ongoing smooth governance of Rome. I will need regular reports on all matters that might be of concern. When it is necessary, you may have to act in my name quickly—and, if need be, ruthlessly. I am not abdicating my control over the Empire—only my presence in the city of Rome. Should anyone have reason to question my control, it is up to the two of you to give them a reminder of its thoroughness."

Sejanus bowed deeply. "Rest assured, Caesar, Rome will still tremble when the name of Tiberius is spoken!" he said.

Pilate also bowed, albeit less obsequiously. "I shall keep a close eye in all the affairs of the Senate, sir," he said, "and I shall keep you informed of all matters as events may warrant. You know that I have had some success in the past in making your burdens a bit lighter. It shall be my privilege to do so again, if it is necessary."

Tiberius nodded, then stretched and yawned. "Sejanus, I need to confer with Pilate about some family matters," he said. "Would you please excuse us?"

The Prefect of the Praetorian Guard rose and bowed. Tiberius turned and looked at Pilate. "Walk with me to my balcony," he said. "The moon is rising over Our Sea." Together they walked out of the study and onto the massive stone balcony that looked westward, across the quicksilver waters of the Mediterranean. Tiberius leaned out over the rails for a moment, then quickly turned and surveyed the balcony all down its length, and looked at the windows around it. Finally he peeked through the curtains back into his study. Then he approached Pilate and leaned close. When he spoke, his voice was a soft but urgent whisper.

"All that I just said is true," he told Pilate. "But I will add one other charge to your list of responsibilities. Watch Sejanus! He is thinking to elevate himself by marrying Livilla Julia and setting up her brats as my heirs. I am biding my time and waiting to compass his downfall, but any information that you can gather that will give me just cause for his removal will be most welcome. Macro is a much more decent and loyal soldier; I will be elevating him to take Sejanus' place one of these days."

Pilate nodded. He had never liked Sejanus, but he still chose his words carefully. "All you command I will do, Caesar," he said. "But if I may add a small word of advice—be cautious! Sejanus is clever and ruthless. If he believes you intend to remove him, I would not put it past him to try and strike first."

"Don't think I haven't considered that," said Tiberius. "I live on my guard every day. But here on Capri, I am safer than I am in Rome. My servants here are chosen most carefully, and are loyal to me, not him. I think. I suppose I cannot be too sure of anyone, though, can I?"

Pilate gave him a long, careful glance. "You know that you may always count on my loyalty, Tiberius Caesar," he said.

"You know, Lucius Pontius, I actually believe you!" said Tiberius, and clapped him on the shoulder. "Now go and get a good night's rest!"

The next morning Pilate and his family woke not long after sunrise. The sky was clear of clouds and a light south wind promised a warm and lovely day. A servant brought them hot bread and cold juice for breakfast, and a note from the Emperor stating that he was going to be occupied all morning, and inviting them to enjoy the island's beauty until the evening meal. Pilate pulled on a sturdy pair of sandals and invited his wife and daughter to walk down to the harbor with him. They set out with no particular goal, simply enjoying the sunshine and each other's company. As they passed through the atrium, young Caligula spotted them.

"Good morning!" he said. "I think Caesar is sleeping in today; he has one of his headaches. What are you doing for the morning?"

"We are going for a walk," said Pilate.

The young Caesar nodded. He was leaning on a display case where a large group of flint knives, anywhere from four to eight inches long, were resting. Porcia Minor noticed them and stepped forward for a closer look.

"What on earth are those?" she said.

"They were found fifty years ago, when the foundations for this villa were being dug," said Gaius. "There were some enormous bones with them, but those have almost all crumbled away. The locals say that they were crafted by a race of giants who lived here thousands of years ago."

She stared at the sharp blades with interest. "I have heard tales of giants, but I always thought they were mythical," she said.

"They may well be," said Caligula. "That is just a tale the locals tell." He looked at Porcia and smiled. "I am going fishing with some of the village children before they catch the boat for home. Would you like to join me—if it's all right with your *paterfamilias*?" he asked with a sidelong glance at Pilate.

114

Pilate looked at his wife, who gave him a slight frown. "Will there be adults with you?" he asked.

"Oh, yes, grandfather does not allow us to go near the cliffs without slaves to help us bring the fish in and Praetorians to keep an eye on things," said Caligula with seeming sincerity. About that time several of the older boys and girls from the night before came down the steps, with fishing lines and hooks. Two servants brought up the rear.

Pilate smiled. "Be careful, Porcia, and bring me a big fish!" he said.

The flock of children, with the tall young Gaius in the lead, headed down the steps, with the servants bringing up the rear. Porcia leaned her head upon Pilate's shoulder.

"Well, it appears we have the morning to ourselves," she said. "What would you like to do?"

"There is a small village at the base of the mountain," said Pilate. "Why don't we walk down there and see if there is anything in the shops that you might like?"

"That sounds delightful," she said.

So the two of them walked down the narrow road together to the small village by the harbor. Many of the people who lived there were employed in one capacity or another by the Villa Jovis—some were paid servants, accountants, or groundskeepers, while others raised crops or herds or caught fish to supply the Emperor's needs. There were only two or three shops worth visiting, and one small inn that sold roasted fish. Pilate and his wife ate a light noontide meal, and he purchased two matching necklaces, both made up of pearls and seashells, for his wife and daughter. Not long after noon the two of them began the walk back up the mountain road to the Emperor's home. It was at that moment that Pilate's life and future were forever changed.

There was a rustling in the bushes beside the road, and then a bloody and battered figure emerged. It was Porcia Minor, but she was barely recognizable. Her lovely tunic was gone, and her shift was torn down the front so that she had to hold it together with one hand. The other arm was bent in half midway down the forearm, as if someone had tried to give her a second elbow. Her nose was bloodied and one eye was already swelling, and blood ran down her thighs. She walked in a painful, slow hobble, legs slightly apart—as if every single step was agony. Pilate knew that walk, having seen it in enemy villages when the soldiers were turned loose on the local womenfolk. Porcia was whimpering in pain, and when she looked up and saw him she cried in anguish: "*Tata!!*"

He was at her side in a moment, scooping her up in her arms. Her mother was also there instantly, stroking her forehead and making soothing noises.

"What happened, child?" she asked.

"Gaius!" she said through her tears. The story came tumbling out of her, interrupted by sobs and whimpers of pain. "We went fishing with the other children, like he said we would. But after a little while he said he was bored and asked if I would walk him back to the villa. But then we wound up on another trail and came out in a small clearing I did not recognize. He turned and asked me if I would give him a kiss. I said he could have one . . . that was all!" She started sobbing again, so heavily that she could not speak. Pilate felt his heart turn to lead in his breast. "But then he started kissing me again and again, and I tried to push him away. He grabbed my arm and threw me to the ground so hard I felt my bones snap! Then he was on top of me, tearing at my clothes and punching me in the face. I tried to stop him, but he HURT me! Oh, *tata*, it hurt SO BAD!" Pilate hugged her close and looked at his wife, seeing the anger behind her tears.

His daughter tried to continue. "He laughed, *tata*! The more I cried, the more he laughed! Then he . . . he raped me! It hurt so much. I thought I was being split in two! I thought he loved me, *tata*. I . . . oh, mama, I know it is wrong, but if that was what he wanted, I might have let him do it if he had only been NICE! I thought he was nice! *I thought he loved me!*" she wailed, and then her tears overwhelmed her, and she could not speak anymore.

For the rest of his life, Pilate could not recall exactly what happened next. One moment he was holding his daughter in his arms, the next he was in the Villa Jovis, running from room to room. He grabbed a terrified servant and demanded to know where Gaius Caligula's rooms were. The servant pointed toward a chamber opening into the hallway near the Emperor's chambers, and Pilate burst through the door. There stood Gaius Caligula, wearing a fresh white tunic. The one that was crumpled on the floor beside his bed was grass-stained and had specks of blood upon it—his daughter's blood, Pilate realized.

*"Mentula!!!"* he screamed in rage. "You ravaged my daughter!"

The gangly youth looked at him coolly. "Oh, please!" he said. "Don't be ridiculous. The little slut threw herself at me!"

At that moment the beast that Pilate had kept penned up inside himself since his return from Spain burst from its bonds and seized control of him. He was not aware of crossing the room, only of his hands seizing the boy by both wrists. Caligula squawked in rage and fear as Pilate bent him backward until he fell onto his bed.

"Unhand me, you common brute! Don't you know I will be your Emperor soon?" he blustered.

Pilate spoke through gritted teeth. "Tell me, Gaius Caligula, when you broke her arm, did it sound like this?" He wrenched the youth's arm to full extension and then struck it with his palm as hard as he could. The bone snapped like a dry twig. "Or was it more like THIS?" He repeated the process on the other arm as Caligula shrieked in pain, then he threw the writhing teen to the marble floor and fell upon him.

"Did she squeal like you are squealing now when you struck her in the face?" he said, demolishing the boy's nose with punch after punch. He relished each blow. "You nasty little whelp, I will see to it that you never ravage another man's daughter as long as you live!" he snarled, grabbing a dagger he had seen by the bedside table. He tore the boy's tunic away and exposed his body, but before he could use the blade on the screaming teenager's member, he caught a movement out of the corner of his eye. He turned just in time to see Sejanus swinging the butt of a gladius toward his head, and then he knew no more.

# CHAPTER TEN

Pilate woke to the rays of the late afternoon sun slanting in through an unfamiliar window. The back of his head was throbbing, and he could feel his pulse pounding in his eyeballs. He tried to remember where he was, and how he had gotten there. Then the memory of his daughter's anguished cries came flooding back, and he sat up abruptly. The sudden movement worsened his pain, but then when the room swam into focus he saw Tiberius seated next to his bed, looking straight at him with eyes full of anger and pain. Sejanus stood behind him, one hand on the hilt of his sword.

"My daughter?" was his first question.

"She is being tended by my personal physician," said the Emperor, "as is my grandson and heir. What in the name of Hades were you thinking, Pilate? You assaulted a member of the Imperial family! If you were any other man, I would have already had you thrown from the cliffs!"

"He . . . raped . . . my . . . daughter!" said Pilate slowly and clearly, fury filling his heart again. The beast within him slavered and gnawed at the bonds that held it in check.

"He claimed his conjugal privileges a little early!" said the Emperor. "Most of the men in Rome do the same!"

"When their betrothed bride is twelve years old?" asked Pilate viciously. "Tell me, Caesar—when you were claiming your conjugal privileges, did you ever snap your bride's arm? Or beat her face so severely her own mother could barely recognize her, and then set her to wander in the woods, ravaged and stripped? I only regret your man here found me before I could make a eunuch of the little monster!"

Tiberius bowed his head and put his face in his hands for a moment. When he looked up, there were tears in his eyes. "It wasn't supposed to be like this!" he said plaintively. "I knew the boy had a wild streak, but I thought she would help him tame it, not become a victim of it! Oh, Pilate, my old friend, you should have come to me with this! I could have punished him appropriately, and tried to recompense your family for the injury done

119

your daughter. But by taking things into your own hands, you have imperiled your entire family!"

Pilate frowned. "What do you mean, Tiberius?" he finally asked in what was an almost normal tone of voice.

"That boy whose arms you broke; whose face you did your best to ruin—he will be Emperor of Rome someday! And not in the far distant future either! I am nearly seventy and will not live forever. Do you think he will not try to find you when he comes into the purple?" Tiberius asked earnestly.

Pilate's jaw dropped in disbelief. "You would still make him your heir? A man who would rape a twelve-year-old?"

Tiberius groaned. "I have no choice now!" he snapped. "I am too far committed. If I back out now, I will be a laughingstock. Tiberius, the Emperor who could not give away his Empire! It has to be Caligula. Drusus' two sons are worst fit to rule than he, and Gaius' brothers hate me with a passion. Caligula is my last chance to groom an heir fit for the seat of Augustus. But you have broken him, Pilate—physically, and possibly mentally as well. I do not know yet what manner of man he will be when he recovers from his injuries. You may have created a monster!"

"The monster was already there, Caesar!" snapped Pilate. "You know that as well as I do!"

Tiberius nodded. "That may be so, but this monster is going to be thirsting for your blood as soon as he comes to. I cannot undo what has been done, but I can remove you two from each other's proximity, and that is what I must do. You and your family will leave at first light."

"Leave for where?" Pilate asked.

"Judea. I am appointing you as governor there," said the Emperor.

"Judea!?" Pilate asked in horror. It was the armpit of the Empire, the worst posting any proconsul could receive.

"Judea is ideal as a place of exile. It is the one place which will put you out of Caligula's immediate reach, while the appointment will also show all of Rome that I am displeased with you," explained Tiberius. "As Caligula heals, I will try to mitigate his desire for vengeance. In the process, I may have to pretend that I am just as angry with you as he is. But my goal is to eventually enable you to return to Rome without fearing for your life. You have been a loyal friend and client, Lucius Pontius Pilate. You doubtless deserve better than this. But it is the best I can do for now."

"Doesn't Judea already have a governor?" Pilate asked. "What about Valerius Gratus?"

"Gratus has been begging me to return him to Rome for a year," said Tiberius. "He has interfered in the local government so many times that all the factions hate him, and the Zealots—you'll need to watch out for those nasty buggers while you're there, by the way—have tried to kill him twice. You will have a chance to make a new start for yourself, and clean up one of the worst provinces in the Empire."

Pilate groaned. His daughter was ravaged, her innocence stolen by a monster. He had done what any *paterfamilias* in Rome would have done, and now he was being punished. All of his dreams for himself and his family were shattered beyond repair. It was too much!

"Sejanus has chartered a ship for you and your family already. Your personal goods will be delivered from Rome; in the meantime, I have here enough coin to see you set up properly in the governor's home. I need you to be an exemplary governor, Pilate. If you can demonstrate your usefulness, perhaps I will be able to convince Caligula that you are indispensable. But above all, I need you to be gone from here as soon as possible. It grieves an old man to do this, but it must be done. For your sake, for your family's sake, and for the sake of the Empire," the Emperor concluded.

Pilate sat up and rubbed the knot on the back of his head. "I suppose I have no choice," he said bitterly. "Let me go to my family. And let me speak plainly—I am barely in control of myself. You had better make sure that little monster is well guarded, because if the sight of my daughter makes me lose control, I may very well kill him!"

Tiberius' face darkened with anger. "If you would see your wife and daughter hurled from the cliffs, touch Caligula again! I have dealt with you as kindly as I could. Do not presume too much on our friendship!"

Pilate wearily got up. "Forgive me, Caesar," he said. "My heart is broken and my spirit still enraged. I do not understand why you feel that this horrible young man is your only viable choice to be the next Emperor. Rome will bleed because of your decision, mark my words. But you have been kind to me since I was a teenaged *conterburnalis*, and your kindness continues through this horrible situation. For that, I thank you. Now let me go to my family."

He rose and bowed to the Emperor, then left the room. Sejanus followed behind him, and when they were out of earshot, he grabbed Pilate by the shoulder and turned him around. There was a wolfish grin on the Praetorian commander's face.

"So the mighty Lucius Pontius Pilate has fallen at last!" he sneered. "You do not know how much I have longed for this day. Don't think I did not know that the Emperor wanted to set you up against me! Now I will control him and his heir, and one day my children will rule the Empire!"

Pilate looked at him wearily. "I am sure you think that, Lucius Aelius," he said. "But do you think Tiberius so foolish? I go to exile, sure enough, but you will go to your grave a traitor before I return to Rome. Now get out of my way. I promised the Emperor not to harm Caligula any further. I made no such promise about you, and frankly, I am longing to kill someone right now!" The beast had returned, staring out through Pilate's eyes, longing to destroy the Praetorian commander.

Sejanus paled and stepped away, and Pilate continued down the corridor to the guest chambers where his family waited. His daughter lay in the bed, eyes closed and covers pulled up to her chin. One eye was blackened and swelled nearly shut, and her bloodied lips were scabbing over. Procula Porcia was seated next to her, gently stroking her brow. An elderly Greek physician stood nearby, and Pilate gestured for him to follow and took him into the hallway.

"How is she?" he said.

"Her nose is broken," said the physician, "and I have set and splinted her arm. It is a fairly simple fracture that should heal cleanly in a few weeks. There will be a good deal of pain, and I have recommended milk of poppy mixed with mulled wine to help keep it under control. As for her . . . womanhood—well, there was a good deal of tearing and bleeding, but I cannot say if there was permanent damage or not. I have seen young girls who have been assaulted in such a manner that recover fully and go on to marry and have children, and others who never fully recover physically or

122

emotionally. She seems like a strong young lady, and I am sure she will be well cared for, so I would give a hopeful prognosis."

Pilate nodded. "Can she travel?" he asked.

The physician nodded. "It will be a bit painful, but if you handle her carefully, she should be able to make a journey. She will gain back a bit of strength every day."

Pilate thanked the man and re-entered the room. His wife stood and came toward him. He tried to embrace her, but she pulled away, glaring at him.

"You knew I never trusted that little monster!" she snapped. "Now look at what your ambitions have done to our daughter!"

Pilate nodded. He could not deny the truth behind her allegations. "I never dreamed it would end so badly," he said. "For what it is worth, I am sorry. Sorrier than I have ever been for anything in my life."

"Did you kill him?" she asked. "No one will tell me anything!"

"I was . . . interrupted by a rather sharp blow to the head," said Pilate. "But he has two broken arms, and no girl will call him handsome for some time. I intended to make a eunuch out of him, but I was stopped short of that goal."

Porcia finally stepped to his side and touched the knot on the back of his head. He winced.

"It does not look too bad," she said. "I have seen you come home from the Suburba with worse."

Pilate smiled ruefully. "Back in my younger, wilder days, eh? All that is behind us now. We must leave this place at first light, so let us pack up quickly. Send for Democles and the other servants to remove all our effects to the ship."

She nodded. "Porcia will heal more quickly at home, away from the horrible memories of this place," she said.

"That might be true," Pilate replied, "but we are not going home."

She looked at him incredulously. "What do you mean?" she said. "Our daughter is too grievously injured to travel anywhere else!"

"That no longer matters," he said. "The Emperor has decided, for our safety, that I must be sent far, far away, and that you must come with me."

"For our safety?" she said. "Safety from what?"

"From who, you mean!" said Pilate. "The heir to the Imperial throne lies in a bedroom nearby with two broken arms and a smashed face that I gave him. I doubt little Gaius is going to tearfully realize the error of his ways and cry pardon! So Tiberius sends us far, far away to Judea, and hopefully young Gaius, by the time he is Emperor Gaius Caligula, will have forgotten this episode."

Procula Porcia's face slowly crumbled into tears. "So no matter how barbarically he acted, it is we who must be punished for his crimes!" she exclaimed. "Why on earth does Tiberius insist that such a worm must be his heir?"

"That I do not know," said Pilate. "I begged him to change his mind and name someone else, but he feels trapped into following through with his current course of action. I have a feeling that young Caligula is going to be an absolute disaster, but Tiberius no longer listens to me. So our only choice is to take our daughter and go to Judea. I have been appointed governor there, so at least it is not a punitive exile."

"Judea!" she said. "We both know that vile little province is a dumping ground for Senators too incompetent to be trusted with the governorship of somewhere important!"

"That is why I am being sent there," said Pilate. "It is my punishment, my place of atonement. Tiberius thinks if he makes a show of being angry with me, it will be easier later on to make Caligula forget my offense."

She snarled. "I wish you had killed the little *culus*!!" she snapped.

"Such language, dear!" Pilate said. "Where did you learn such a horrible word?"

She gave a tiny smile, her first since their daughter's attack. "You don't live in the Aventine for so many years and not pick up a little of the local lingo," she said.

"*Tata*?" came a tiny voice. Pilate looked at the bed and saw that Porcia Minor was awake, looking at him with her one good eye. The other was barely visible beneath the purplish swelling. Pilate rushed to her bedside.

"I am here, my little sparrow," he said, kissing the top of her head.

"I hurt," she said. "Everything hurts, especially . . . down there." She gestured at her hips.

His fury boiled up white-hot within him, but he suppressed it. "I am so sorry for what he did to you," he said. "He will not be hurting anyone else for a good long while, if that is any comfort."

"Did you kill him?" she asked. "I shouldn't say so, but I hope that you did!"

Pilate sighed. "No," he said, "they interrupted me before I could finish. But your broken arm and smashed face are repaid double! Now, let me give you something to take the pain away." A flagon of sweet wine had been set near enough to the charcoal brazier to be nicely warmed, and he poured her a cup and added a few drops of the milk of poppy to it. He held it up to her bruised, cracked lips and she took a few sips.

"Tastes funny," she said.

"It will help you sleep, and numb the pain," said Porcia Major. "And tomorrow *tata* is taking us far, far away, where you will never have to look on the face of Gaius Caligula again."

"That will be nice," said Porcia in a very soft voice. Moments later her eyes closed, and her breathing became deep and regular.

Meanwhile, Democles had arrived and was hovering at the door. Pilate gave instructions for all their personal goods to be packed away and loaded onto the ship the Emperor had chartered for them, and for the family to be woken an hour before dawn. Then he and his wife lay down on either side of their bruised and broken daughter and tried to sleep, but their thoughts and memories ran through their minds for hours to follow, and sleep eluded them both.

It was still quite dark when Democles woke them—or at least, got them out of bed. A litter had been prepared for Porcia Minor. The drug she had taken made her so groggy she barely whimpered as he lifted her from the bed and placed her in the litter and covered her with blankets. He and Porcia donned clean robes and their sandals, and Pilate ordered that his sword and dagger be brought to him and strapped them on. He would not go unarmed in the future, he decided. The walk down the mountain trail was very quiet, as Pilate and his wife were locked in their own thoughts.

The ship Tiberius had chartered for them was fairly large and comfortable. The captain showed them to a cabin which was, if not spacious, at least less cramped than most shipboard accommodations Pilate had used over the years. There was one large bunk bed that two people could fit in if they were fond of each other, and a smaller one off to the side. Pilate carried his daughter to the smaller bunk and laid her there, then paid the litter bearers off and went topside to talk to the captain while Porcia unpacked their personal items.

The captain was a huge Persian named Diomyrus, with arms like oak trees and skin like copper. He bowed when Pilate came topside.

"Journey to Judea this time of year takes two months or so," he said. "We will take on cargo at Rhegium, and then land at Crete, then straight shot eastward to Joppa. From there, short ride up the coast on horseback to Caesarea. You are to be new governor of Judea, yes?"

Pilate nodded. The captain scowled.

"Bad people, the Jews," he said. "Invisible gods and their followers cannot be trusted. Our gods—they are made of marble and gold and wood. You can see them, leave offerings at their feet. Our gods laugh and cry and fornicate with mortal women. Our gods are like us! Their god big, invisible. Float in the clouds, demands burnt offerings, does not make love to their women. Who wants a god that does not love fun?"

Pilate filed that away for future reference. He had very little experience with Jews, but knew that their province was home to fewer than half of them. The Greeks had liked them, apparently—there were millions of them living throughout the old Greek dominions, especially in the territory of the Ptolemies. Alexandria, it was said, was home to more Jews than Judea! But the province of Judea was a poor, blighted region whose inhabitants hated Rome with a passion. No governor had yet been able to make the place peaceful and obedient. Pilate decided that he would do his best to make Judea a model province, and so redeem his reputation. It was the best he could make of a bad situation.

When he went below, Porcia Minor was awake and holding her mother's hand. He smiled at her and sat at the foot of her narrow bunk.

"Where are we going, *tata*?" she asked.

"I have been made governor of Judea," he said. "You and your mother will accompany me to the province."

"Judea—isn't that a bad place?" she asked.

"It's a difficult province to govern," said Pilate. "That is why the Emperor is sending me there. I am to get things into shape."

"Is it my fault?" she asked.

"What do you mean?" said Pilate.

"Are you being sent away because of me?" she said.

"No, precious!" he said. "What happened to you was no one's fault except for Gaius Caligula, and what has happened to me is completely unrelated. The Emperor needed a good governor for a bad province, to make it run better. That is all."

She looked at him, her bruised and swollen face still full of pain. "I think he is sending you away because you hurt Gaius, and you hurt Gaius because he hurt me. So it is my fault!" She turned her face to the wall and began crying. Pilate bowed his head in grief for a moment. Procula Porcia took his hand and squeezed it, and gave him a look that was full of regret—but also of compassion. Despite their current predicament, Pilate thanked the gods that he had married so well. But the atmosphere in the room was oppressive, so he turned and went back up topside to watch the ship get underway.

The first week of the journey was uneventful. The winds were light and southwesterly, and the ship was headed almost due south, so most of the sails were furled and the crew rowed the ship steadily southward, using the aft sail for steerage. It took them four days to reach Rhegium, an important seaport near the toe of the Italian boot. There they took on two hundred amphorae of wine and many bolts of fine Italian linens, which they would sail to Crete with.

The ship had a crew of fifty or so, of whom about twenty-four would man the oars at a time, working in eight-hour shifts. The first mate was a wiry little Greek named Demosthenes, and the crew was a polyglot assemblage of mongrels from all over the Empire. After making a few inquiries, Pilate found that two of them were from Judea. He questioned each of them separately, trying to get a better feel for these people he was going to govern for the next few years.

"We are the Chosen People," said Simeon, a forty-year-old Jew with the massive shoulders of someone who had manned the oars for many years. "That is the blessing and curse of the Jews. Our Scriptures teach us that God called our ancestor Abraham to the lands around Jordan two thousand years ago, and promised to give those lands to him and his descendants forever and ever. Abraham's son and grandson lived there all their lives, until Jacob, whom we name Israel, went as an old man to live in Egypt with his son Joseph."

"Wait a moment," said Pilate. "Is not Israel the name you give your entire nation?"

"Exactly," said the man. "Jacob had twelve sons, whose descendants became twelve tribes, and so the sons of Israel are numbered as twelve tribes to this very day. I am of the tribe of Asher myself."

"So why did Jacob go to Egypt?" asked Pilate.

"His younger son Joseph was hated by his brothers, because his dreams foretold he would rule over all of them," explained Simeon. "So they sold him into slavery, and he wound up becoming the Grand Vizier of Egypt, the Pharaoh's most trusted servant. When a great famine struck all the lands, Joseph was forewarned by God and made sure the lands of Egypt would have food in abundance by saving up in advance. When the lands of Israel began to starve, he revealed himself to his brothers and father as their long-lost sibling, and invited them to come and stay in Egypt as honored guests of the Pharaoh."

"But weren't the Jews slaves in Egypt?" asked Pilate, recalling a story he had read long ago.

"They were," said Simeon, "but not right away. A new Pharaoh, from a new dynasty, saw how numerous the descendants of Jacob had become, and feared their might, so he enslaved them all long after Joseph's time. They were treated most cruelly, and cried to God for a deliverer. So he sent them Moses, who called down mighty plagues on Egypt until Pharaoh agreed to let them go back to the land promised to Abraham. Moses also was given a code of laws by God on Mount Sinai, and wrote for us the Torah, which became the heart of our Scriptures."

Pilate nodded, and dismissed the man back to work. What an odd mythology the Jews had! He wondered if the story of Romulus and Remus would sound equally strange to someone who had never heard it.

He talked to Simeon several times, as well as to Zakariyah, the other Jewish crewman. Zakariyah was more cynical and less religious than his companion, but in essence his description of Jewish culture and history was very close to what Pilate had already heard. At the very least, Pilate thought, he would not arrive in Caesarea completely ignorant of the strange nation he was to govern.

He spent so much time trying to learn about the Jews, at least in part, to take his mind off his worries about his daughter. Porcia Minor was recovering physically, but her spirit seemed broken. Pilate and Procula Porcia took turns trying to reassure her and make her feel loved, but she was convinced that the entire family was being punished because she had somehow failed as Gaius' betrothed spouse. Pilate could not convince her that the assault was not something she had brought on herself. In some childish way, she still refused to believe Gaius could have done something so awful without being provoked by her in some way.

Dealing with her depression left Pilate feeling angry and frustrated. The job of the *paterfamilias* was to make things right, and he could not seem to do that for his daughter. The hungry beast within him that thrived on bloodshed and pain threatened to rise to the fore each time he saw his little girl crying again, and it was harder and harder for him to keep control.

It was in this frame of mind one night that he returned to his family's cabin. Procula Porcia was going to give Porcia Minor a bath, and Pilate had absented himself from the chamber to give them privacy. Romans were not prudish about nudity, but since his daughter's ordeal she had been obsessively modest, and Pilate wanted to give her space. But later that night, when he swung down the hatch and entered the short passage that led to their quarters, he saw the hunched figure of a man at the door, trying to peek in through a crack between the boards. The beast in Pilate's breast burst its cage immediately, and he was on the man, his hand over the bearded mouth and his blade at the throat, in a heartbeat.

Mindful of noise, he dragged the crewman topside. "Not a word!" he hissed, and spun the man about. He recognized him as one of the rowers, an Italian nicknamed Strabo for his crossed eyes.

"What were you doing?" he demanded.

"Begging your pardon, sir, but it's been two weeks at sea with no womenfolk to look at!" said Strabo. "I meant no harm—I just wanted a peek at the girl!"

"That girl has been through enough misery without a common toad like you leering at her while her mother gives her a bath!" snapped Pilate.

"I meant no harm, Excellency, and she would never have known—" the crewman tried to protest, but his comments were cut short as Pilate's blade severed his windpipe. A sharp kick to the chest sent the gurgling corpse overboard, and Pilate made his way to the captain's quarters.

"Here," he said, throwing a few silver denarii down on the captain's small desk. "For the loss of your crewman. And tell the others to keep their prying eyes away from my family's cabin!"

Diomyrus pocketed the coins and nodded. "Peeping at keyholes, eh?" he said. "Sailors will be sailors, I suppose, but they should not intrude on their betters! Which man was it?"

"The Italian Strabo," said Pilate.

The captain shrugged. "He was a shirker and a weakling," he said. "I can hire a better and stronger rower when I get to Joppa, and his absence will be little noted before then. My apologies for your inconvenience."

Another week saw them arrive at Malta and offload their cargo. Pilate took his daughter topside and tried to interest her in the operations of the ship, but she showed no curiosity about anything. He thought of the lively ten-year-old who had explored every part of their vessel on the return voyage from Spain, and wept for the child that Caligula had murdered with his vile deed, leaving only this blighted and frail wraith in her place.

Three days later, even that pale shade of his daughter was taken from him forever. One night, as Pilate and his wife slept, Porcia Minor slipped out of her bunk and stole topside, where she threw herself into the sea. She left a short note behind, tucked under her pillow.

*Tata and mama*, it read.

*Forgive me for what I am about to do. I cannot sleep, I cannot heal myself inside, and I know that the two of you are being punished because of me. My life has no joy and no hope; every time I close my eyes I hear his mocking laugh and see his evil smile as he thrusts himself into me again and again. I go to the one place where I hope he can never follow. Leaving the two of you behind is my only regret. Do not blame yourselves; I do this of my own free will. No girl ever had more loving parents. I shall wait for you in the land of the shades.*

*Your loving daughter,*

*Procula Porcia Minor*

Pilate ordered the ship turned around, and they meandered about the sea for three days, but her body was never sighted. The Mediterranean had swallowed his only child without a trace. Diomyrus commented that one of the ballast weights was missing from the hold, and theorized that the girl may have tied it around her waist before throwing herself into the deep. Procula Porcia wept for days, clinging to her husband for comfort. Pilate was devastated beyond words, but like a true Roman man, he showed his grief to no one except his wife. By the time the ship anchored in the magnificent artificial harbor at Caesarea, his tears had all been shed. It was time to make the most of his exile, and get on with his life. His daughter's smile and voice he kept in a locked chamber of his heart, where he could visit them in his dreams for the rest of his life.

# CHAPTER ELEVEN

Prefect Valerius Gratus was overjoyed at his unexpected relief from duty as Governor when Pilate landed in Caesarea. Gratus was a chubby, middle-aged Roman of mediocre talent and limited intelligence, whose rise to proconsul had been largely achieved through family connections. He had repeatedly pestered Tiberius and the Senate for an appointment as a provincial governor, hoping to restore the family fortune he had squandered on expensive artworks and prostitutes. Tiberius had appointed him as Prefect over Judea as a grim joke—it was a poor province, having been squeezed of its gold by a succession of corrupt client kings, priests, and conquering empires for almost a thousand years. Valerius had still tried to line his pockets through aggressive tax farming and an excessive entanglement in local religious politics, but had only succeeded in making himself despised among the Jews.

"They are an impossible people, Pontius Pilate!" he said after welcoming Pilate to the governor's palace. "Illogical, irrational, and altogether too devoted to their religion! Won't work on Saturday, won't go near certain animals, and they seem to take off work for religious festivals on a near-constant basis!"

"We do have religious festivals in Rome, too," said Pilate, sipping a glass of wine to wash the dust of the town's busy streets from his throat.

"But our festivals are joyous!" said Valerius. "A time to drink and sing and fornicate to our heart's content, all to the honor of our gods! They come together and mourn and wail for the forgiveness of their sins, and pray for their god to send the Messiah to restore their fortunes!"

"What on earth is a Messiah?" asked Pilate.

"A huge part of their religious mythology," said Valerius. "Supposedly he will be a human descendant of their great warrior-king David, but also will be an incarnation of their invisible God—who, incidentally, does not have a proper name. At least, not one that they are allowed to say. They use substitute names like 'Elohim' or 'Adonai' instead. At any rate, this Messiah-King is supposed to be from David's line and will drive away the evil Gentiles—that's their term for us, and for all foreigners—and then restore the kingdom to its former glory, and bring about the rule of their God on earth."

Pilate nodded. "What kind of shape is your legion in?" he said.

"Bored, lazy, and corrupt," said Valerius. "I parcel them out into the countryside, a few dozen to a hundred in all the major villages and towns, and keep a cohort or two here in Caesarea in case of trouble. Half of them are criminals from the worst stews of Rome who live to make trouble with the locals; the other half are decent soldiers. Some of them have gone native and married Jewish girls; a few even worship Adonai or whatever his name is."

"Why do you tolerate laziness and corruption among your soldiers?" Pilate asked rather sharply.

"I am not much of a military man, I'm afraid," said Valerius. "I can see the problems, but I have no idea how to fix them. I hope you will have better fortune than I have had!"

"It seems to me, Gratus, that the majority of your problems are self-inflicted!" said Pilate. "Tell me, who is your senior Legate?"

"Don't have one at the moment. Titus Vorenus was the last one I had, and he got his throat cut by a Zealot over a year ago. Rome has not seen fit to send a replacement," said Valerius.

Pilate snorted. He wondered if Valerius Gratus had even bothered to ask. "So is your *primus pilus* centurion worth his salt?" he asked.

"Cassius Longinus?" he said. "A decent fellow, but he is one of those who have gone native since he has been here. He lives in a village called Capernaum with a Jewish wife, and even owns a copy of their Scriptures and reads them to his children from time to time. But he is a first-rate soldier, and seems to understand the local culture as well as anyone."

This means, thought Pilate, that he would probably be a better governor than you! But he held his silence.

"Do you suppose that I could use the ship that brought you here to return to Rome?" asked Gratus.

"Of course," said Pilate. "But the captain wants to put out to sea within the week. Will you have your effects gathered and your report to the Senate ready by then?"

"I can and I will," said Gratus. "I am more ready to be out of this place than you can possibly imagine! Let's see, what else do I need to tell you—oh, yes! Festivals! Jewish religion demands that all the faithful who can must gather in Jerusalem at their great temple to celebrate their high holy days. It is always good to have a strong presence in the city at that time—it seems to be the moment that trouble is most likely to flare up. Now, they do not like having Gentiles in their holy city during festivals, so I usually keep most of my troops inside the Fortress of Antonia except for the necessary patrols. That way, if trouble breaks out, I can respond quickly and forcefully."

Pilate nodded. That was the first piece of useful advice the toad had given him. After a few more minutes of discussion, he asked to be shown the governor's personal quarters. The chambers were luxurious enough, but Valerius Gratus seemed to have the personal hygiene of a pig, and not a very neat one at that. The bedclothes were stained and stale-smelling, there were scrolls and official reports scattered haphazardly about the room, along with the governor's personal reading material—which, from the quick glimpse that Pilate got before Valerius rolled the scrolls up and stuffed them into his trunk, seemed to be primarily erotic poetry and stories.

To give the man his due, however, he did vacate the chamber quickly. Two trunks held all his personal effects, and a large, locked strongbox in the corner contained his valuables. Within a half hour, Valerius told Pilate he was done.

"What about the furniture and bedding?" Pilate asked.

"Do what you will with it," said Gratus. "I have far nicer furnishings at my villa in Rome."

Pilate looked around the room in disgust. The furniture was old and battered, and he would never ask his wife to sleep in that bed. Perhaps some shopping would be good for her, he thought. He told Democles to bring her from the ship and have their effects delivered. While his servant was gone, he called in a couple of legionaries from the governor's personal detail.

They were unshaven and hung over, their uniforms wrinkled and stained. Time to start work, thought Pilate as he looked at his men.

"Are you two what passes for soldiers around here?" he snapped angrily.

"Who wants to know?" grumbled the older one. Pilate slapped him, snapping his head halfway round.

"Your new prefect, that's who!" he snapped. "You call yourselves Romans? Look at you! Slovenly, lazy, unshaven, uniforms a disgrace! Your governor was a pig, so you thought you could get away with being pigs too, is that it? Well, things are changing, starting NOW!"

"Yes, sir!" said the two legionaries. He had their full attention now.

"First of all, I want you to haul all this furniture and the curtains and bedding out of here and burn them. Then I want both of you to go down to the barracks and shave, then bathe, and wash your uniforms. Tell all the legionaries that I will be inspecting the ranks tomorrow, and I had better find them well turned out, or there will be hell to pay! Make sure they know that there is a new prefect in town!" he said. They got to work very quickly as he sat in the windowsill and watched. At least, he mused, he had not lost his talent for commanding troops. It was something he had worked hard to develop, and he hoped it would help turn the province around.

The soldiers were just hauling out the last of the previous occupant's soiled personal effects when Procula Porcia came in with her maid, Stephenia, and Democles in tow, carrying one of the trunks. She cast a wary eye around the chamber.

"I see our predecessor favored a rather Spartan lifestyle," she finally said.

"More a bacchanalian one," he replied. "I had his furniture burned—it looked as if you might get the pox just touching it! There are some large markets between here and the harbor, though. Could I prevail upon you to purchase us some furnishings and bedding, my dear?"

Porcia looked at him. Her grief for their daughter was enormous and still overwhelming at times, but their loss had driven them closer together rather than further apart, and Pilate was very grateful for that. Life could be short and hard in the Roman Empire, but the loss of a child who had survived all the dangers of infancy was still heartbreaking. Many marriages would not have survived such a loss. Porcia finally nodded.

"I suppose it would do me some good to be busy," she said finally.

He tossed her a purse full of sesterces. "Be frugal, my dear," he said. "This is not Spain. We shall make no fortune here, I fear."

"Have I ever wasted your money?" she asked, and left the room before he could answer.

After she left, Pilate walked down the corridor and outside. He spotted a couple of servants and ordered them to wash and scrub out the governor's chambers, then strode over toward the barracks. The two soldiers were still burning Valerius' old furniture, and several of their comrades were watching, laughing and poking fun at them as they worked. Pilate decided to see what they found so funny.

"Legionaries!" he said. The two men who were burning the furniture and bedding snapped to attention. The others slouched to a semi-erect posture. He looked at the men he had disciplined earlier, and nodded. These men were soldiers at heart, he thought. They had just been stuck with a governor who had allowed them to forget their training. He walked up to the biggest of the five who had been spectators and looked him up and down. The man was a head taller than Pilate, and muscular enough, but there was a sheath of fat over his belly and an air of indolence which told Pilate he had traded on his size alone for too long. But the others were watching him with an air of respect and awe, so it was clear that he was the top dog in the barracks. Good, Pilate thought. Breaking him would bring the others into line quickly enough.

"So, are you a soldier of Rome, big man, or are you just a circus freak who stole a legionary's uniform?" he asked with a sneer.

The burly soldier glared at him and spat on the ground. "I am three times more a soldier than any rump-kissing Roman Senator!" he said with a laugh.

"If I were a rump-kisser, as you so eloquently put it, I would not have been sent to this particular posting, now would I?" Pilate asked in a deceptively soft voice.

The big man looked at him contemptuously. "Maybe you just weren't doing it right," he said, and then after a long pause, added: "Sir!"

"Very amusing," said Pilate, turning his back on the man. Then he drove his elbow backward and up as hard and fast as he could, catching the unsuspecting behemoth square under the chin and snapping his head back hard. His arms flailed out to grab Pilate, who had already spun out of his reach.

*"Mentula!!"* snapped the legionary. "I'll send you back to Rome in pieces!" With that he lunged forward, and Pilate snapped his foot up in a straight-toed kick to the man's solar plexus, knocking his wind out. As he doubled over, Pilate grabbed his greasy locks of hair and yanked the man's head forward and down, where it collided with Pilate's knee, which he was bringing up as hard and fast as he could. The soldier's nose crunched audibly, and blood gushed from his face as he crumpled to the ground, holding onto his middle and groaning. The other four soldiers looked at Pilate with shock and fear—this was not the outcome they had expected. Pilate gave them a wolfish grin.

"Anyone else want to try their luck?" he said.

"Not on your life!" said one of them. "If you can take down Brutus Appius that quickly, I doubt any of us would stand much chance."

"Brutus Appius, eh?" Pilate asked, nudging the doubled up giant at his feet. The big man gave a groan and nodded.

"Well, my name is Lucius Pontius Pilate, and I am the new prefect of Judea," he said. "I have commanded legions against Germans, Celts, and pirates in my time, and I've probably seen more combat than any of you. You men have been allowed to forget that you are legionaries in the service of the Roman Empire. Trust me, you will not be allowed to forget it again! Tomorrow morning there will be an inspection of all the troops here in Caesarea. Your faces will be shaven, your uniforms will be clean, and you will carry yourselves like soldiers! Is that clear?"

"Yes sir!" said five terrified voices at once. Pilate smiled inwardly. Legionaries were much like children, he thought. They will push their boundaries as far as they are allowed to, but once they are reined in, they become as docile as sheep.

"Dismissed!" he shouted, and they scurried into the barracks.

Brutus Appius slowly climbed to his feet and surveyed his new commander. "I suppose you will want to have me flogged?" he said in a rather tired voice.

Pilate looked the big man in the eye and saw resignation there. "No," he said. "You were acting as your previous commander allowed you to act, and in a manner I am sure you have gotten away with for some time. Are you going to be insolent and disrespectful to me in the future?"

"No, sir!" said Appius.

"Then I see no need for further punishment," said Pilate. "Do you know why I singled you out?" he asked.

"Because I am biggest and strongest," replied the legionary without hesitation. "If you can take me down, the others will fear you and obey you."

Pilate nodded in appreciation. "So there is a brain inside that large and thick *calvarium* of yours!" he said. "Excellent. Tell me, Brutus Appius, how is this army supplied with centurions?"

"Poorly, sir," said the big man. "Our *primus pilus*, Longinus, is a good man and a good soldier, but he could not stand Prefect Gratus, and so was given permission to live in a village not far from here, on the north shore of Lake Tiberius. Other than him, we have about twenty other centurions, some of middling quality, many poor, and two who are decent besides Longinus—Titus Ambrosius here in Caesarea, and Marcus Quirinius in Jerusalem."

"How strong is the legion then?" he said. "That is not nearly enough centurions for six thousand men!"

"We are severely understrength, sir," said Appius. "Last full count was taken two years ago, and at that time we were three centuries over four thousand. We've lost dozens of men since then. I'd be surprised if we even number four thousand now."

Pilate was appalled. Four thousand men to control one of Rome's most rebellious provinces! This place needed some serious shaking up, he decided. Best to get the men into shape first, though, and then see how many reinforcements were needed. He looked at Brutus Appius again. The big man was watching him with curiosity, but without hostility—a sign of intelligence, Pilate decided.

"Brutus Appius, I am going to need good soldiers who are looked up to by their fellow legionaries if I am going to whip this army and this province into shape," he said. "And I am going to need some centurions who are known and feared by the rank and file. As of now, I am appointing you to centurion's rank on a provisional basis. Your first job is to make sure that the men are ready for inspection tomorrow morning. And one more thing — send a fast rider and fetch me this Cassius Longinus. I need to take his measure quickly."

The tall legionary looked at Pilate in wonder. "Yes, SIR!" he said, saluting neatly. "I'll get right on it!" He turned on his heel to go, and then looked back at Pilate. "You know, Prefect, that I probably could have taken you in a fair fight!" he said.

Pilate laughed. "That is exactly why I did not fight fair!" he replied.

The Roman army's newest centurion grinned at him. "You're all right, sir!" he said. "For a politician!"

"You're not bad yourself, Brutus Appius — for an inbred idiot!" The big man guffawed at that and sauntered off toward the barracks. Pilate nodded to himself as he returned to the governor's quarters. Not a bad start, he thought.

He found some unused parchment in the quartermaster's office and sat down in the windowsill of his quarters and began drafting a letter to Quintus Sullemia. He was about halfway done when two wagons pulled up in the courtyard below, both filled with furniture, fabrics, and bedding. His wife hopped out of one and began ordering the slaves to carry the goods up to their chambers — grabbing a heavy basket herself to lead by example. The sight made Pilate smile.

Before night had fallen, the chambers were set up with a new bed and crisp clean linens, a large writing desk with numerous drawers and cubbies to hold Pilate's correspondence, and a conference table with detailed maps of the province and its major cities. There was also a low table and couch for private dinners, several lovely rugs from Persia, and a complete set of goblets and flagons, as well as a few unopened amphorae of the better local wines.

Pilate sat at the new desk and finished his letter to Sullemia, then wrote a short and very businesslike letter to the Emperor, informing him that the new governor of Judea was now in place, and that his utterly incompetent predecessor was heading home to justify his mismanagement to the Senate. Finally, he added a brief postscript about his daughter's death. Knowing how fond the Emperor was of children, Pilate hoped that maybe a stab of guilt would strike Tiberius in his cold old heart. In his mind, he imagined seeing Caligula's neck bared to his sword for a moment, and smiled at the thought. It would never happen, but a man must have his fantasies, he decided.

Finally, after a late supper of warm bread, salted fish, and some delicious figs and grapes from the local market, Pilate and Porcia climbed into their new bed and lay side by side. They did not talk much these days—their grief at their daughter's death was still too fresh. But he hugged her tight and she rested her head on his shoulder as the warm breeze blew in their window from the beach a half mile away. Both of them were nearly asleep when the chamber door was pushed open, and an overwhelming odor of cheap perfume filled the room.

"I'm here, my lovely Prefect!" came a slurred feminine voice, and a stout figure approached their bed. Pilate scrambled to light the lamp, and when it flared up, he saw a fat woman wearing too much eye makeup—and not much else—blinking in the light and looking at him with an air of drunken curiosity.

"Where is the governor?" she said plaintively.

"I am the governor!" snapped Pilate.

"You're not my voluptuous Valerius!" she shouted.

"Your Valerius is no longer governor!" shouted Pilate. "He is staying at the inn by the docks, waiting to take ship for Rome tomorrow!"

The drunken prostitute tried to take it all in, but it was too much for her limited intellect to grasp all at once. "Well then," she finally said, "I don't suppose you and the missus would want any company, would you? For a denarius I will—"

"GET OUT!" roared Pilate, leaping out of bed, spinning her around, and kicking her in her ample *podex*. She staggered out the door, wailing in dismay, and he slammed it shut behind her.

Procula Porcia looked at him somberly. "Lucius Pontius!" she exclaimed. "I was curious to know what it was she would do for a denarius!" He looked at her, and then, for the first time since their daughter's death, both of them burst out in hysterical laughter. They held each other and giggled for an hour or more before finally falling asleep.

The next day Pilate inspected the double cohort that was stationed at Caesarea. Ideally, it should have numbered eight hundred legionaries and two hundred auxiliaries, but the neglected army of Judea was indeed understrength—barely six hundred men and fewer than fifty auxiliaries awaited his inspection. He was pleased to see that most of them had made at least some effort to make themselves presentable, although many of their uniforms were threadbare and stained, and several of them were missing vital components, such as helmets, *pilum*, or bucklers. Most of the men snapped to attention, and he was pleased to see that Brutus Appius was handsomely turned out in an impeccable uniform, with his centurion's horsetail carefully knotted to his helmet. A few of the men still slouched or stared at him defiantly, but a brisk slap across the face or kick in the shins got them to stand tall and straight—all except one drunken lout, who roared in outrage and charged at Pilate, who neatly sidestepped and gave his attacker a slight push; the man's forward momentum sent him sprawling in the dust. Pilate kicked him hard in the temple with his iron-toed boot as the ruffian tried to get up, and the man slumped to the ground, limp as a rag. Pilate looked at the two legionaries who had stood on either side of the man, and they stared back at him, wide-eyed.

"Drag him back into the barracks, and when he regains consciousness, see to it that he receives fifty lashes!" he snapped.

The two broke ranks to lift the man from the ground, but he did not move or make a sound when they grabbed his arms. One of the legionaries looked at the side of his head and felt for a pulse, then turned back to Pilate. "Sir, do you still want us to flog him if he is dead?" he asked in a trembling voice.

"Not necessary," said Pilate. He could feel the eyes of every single soldier upon him, and could feel the fear and awe in their gaze. "Well, legionaries, I don't know if any of you egged that man on or not—if you did, you bear the burden of his blood on your hands! Let him be an example. You will find I am not an ungenerous commander, as long as I am scrupulously obeyed. But if you disobey me, there will be a price to pay! And if you dare think to assault me—" He gestured at the limp figure on the ground. He ran his gaze up and down their ranks.

"Many of you do not have complete uniforms. I don't care if you lost them gambling or gave them to some tavern wench, by this time next week I will see every one of you properly attired, is that clear?" No one stirred. They were learning, he thought. "This province has been allowed to go to seed, and I intend to fix that. But before I can repair a neglected province, I will repair this neglected army. You are understrength, poorly disciplined, and without enough centurions. What that means for some of you is an opportunity for advancement. For most of you, it has meant an opportunity to drink and carouse and shirk your duty. That time is now over. But let me make this clear to all of you: while I demand your obedience, I will also reward it! Now, how many of you have not received proper pay in the last few months?"

About half the hands present went up. Pilate nodded. "I will not see my men uncompensated for their service," he said. "But do not let me catch you in a lie, either! Starting this afternoon, we will begin full military training. I will not command men who are not prepared to do battle at any time. If any of you know men in the other cohorts and centuries who are not stationed here in Caesarea, be sure to make them aware that they have a new commander, and the old ways will no longer be tolerated. That will be all. Centurions, I want to see you after the men are dispersed. Dismissed!"

The men rendered a straight arm salute, and he returned it crisply, and then watched as they filed back into the barracks. Five centurions, plus Brutus Appius, stood before him. Pilate took their measure carefully. One of them was a grizzled old veteran of perhaps forty; his uniform was worn but clean and neatly turned out, and he bore himself like a soldier. Pilate looked at him closely—he seemed somewhat familiar.

"Have we met before, Centurion?" he asked.

"Not formally, no, sir. My name is Titus Ambrosius. I was with you in Germania—fighting on the wall of our encampment not far from you, the day you won your Civic Crown," the man said. "And if I may say so, it is a pleasure to be commanded by a real soldier again!"

Pilate nodded his thanks and looked at the next officer. He was young for a centurion—not more than twenty-five by the look of him—and seemed intimidated. "How long since you earned your tassel, Centurion?" he asked.

"Less than a year, sir!" he exclaimed nervously.

"Who promoted you?" Pilate inquired.

"Prefect Valerius Gratus, sir!" came the reply. Pilate arched an eyebrow.

"Really? And what service merited promotion to centurion in one so young?" he asked.

The young officer actually blushed at this, and Pilate glanced sidelong at the other officers and saw that they were choking back laughter. "Oh, out with it, man!" he said. "Don't be so embarrassed!"

The other centurions could no longer hold their mirth, and laughed out loud. The miserable young officer glared at them and snapped: "Oh, do shut up! I never asked for it!" Then with resignation he turned to Pilate and said: "I am the one that fixed him up with his favorite doxie, Fat Fatimah!"

Pilate stared at him. "Fat Fatimah—is that the whale that tried to barge into my bedchamber last night and woke my wife?" he finally asked.

The wretch nodded. "Yes, sir! Sorry, sir! She was passed out drunk most of the day and did not know—"

Pilate threw back his head and laughed hard and long. "Well, Centurion—what is your name, by the way?" he said when he could finally speak.

"Antonius Hadrian, sir!" said the young man, actually smiling now.

"For now you will remain a centurion; however, I expect you to do a centurion's work—which incidentally, will not include whaling expeditions for your new prefect! As for the rest of you, I will expect you to teach this young officer his responsibilities, and also to treat him as a colleague and fellow officer, not as a butt for your jokes. At least," he said, "not in front of the men. Although, to tell the truth, young Antonius, you will need to be a very brave warrior in order to live down the means by which you gained promotion!"

He looked at the other three. All three met him with a firm gaze and a fairly straight bearing. "Are you men prepared to help me turn this legion around?" he finally asked.

"Yes, sir!" they all replied in unison.

"Give me your names, then!" he said. They were Lucius Andronicus, Marcus Pullo, and Metellius Macro. They all looked to be about thirty, and seemed to know their duties—although there was something about Pullo that Pilate instinctively disliked. He brushed that aside for the moment and gave them their directions.

"At the third hour past noon I want all legionaries not on watch to assemble here in the courtyard for two hours' worth of practice with gladius and buckler!" he said. "They will be decked out in full combat gear, and I want you to push them hard!"

Ambrosius spoke up. "Begging yer pardon, sir, but do you know how hot it gets here at midday? They'll be dropping like flies!"

"Battles are not always fought in the morning cool, or in the last hours of evening," Pilate said. "I will make sure that plenty of water is available, but these men have been allowed to get fat and lazy! It is time to change all that. And I will be training alongside you, every day, swinging my blade and bashing with my shield. I will, in fact, probably spar with every centurion before the week is out. I want to know personally what kind of fighters my officers are. Now, that will be all. Enjoy the noon meal, and make sure the men have proper gear. Dismissed!"

That afternoon Pilate's Caesarean cohort drilled hard for two hours. Several men fell out from heat exhaustion, and were dragged into the shade and dowsed with water. Everyone sweated profusely, and many of the younger soldiers got bashed on the head with the flat of a blade for not remembering basic combat steps and postures. Pilate made a point of crossing swords with every single centurion, and was not displeased with what he saw. Young Hadrian was terrified at first, but he was quick and nimble, and a natural with the blade. Brutus Appius was a beast, charging in and bellowing like a bull, but he had no subtlety about him. Pilate disarmed him twice, and the big man was clearly growing frustrated.

"Calm yourself, centurion!" Pilate said. "The problem, as I see it, is that you have relied on strength and size for too long, and forgotten the use of cunning. Don't signal your every lunge with a bellow, and don't be afraid to lunge one way and strike another. Now, pick up your blade and come at me again."

And so it went. By the end of the session, Pilate was the commander of the Judean legion not just in name but in fact. There were still the scattered cohorts of his army to be pulled together and brought to heel, but the men of the first two cohorts were now his to the death. As he bathed away the sweat and dust of the day that evening before supper, he thought that he had done a good day's work.

# CHAPTER TWELVE

On his second day in Caesarea, Pilate made two important discoveries that would have long-term consequences on his tenure as governor. The first was that his *primus pilus* centurion, Cassius Longinus, was as solid and obedient a soldier as he could have hoped for. The other discovery was that Pilate absolutely despised the Jews he had been sent to govern—or at least, their leaders.

Pilate had woken early, his joints stiff and aching from his swordplay the day before. It had been a while, he thought, since he pushed himself that hard. He stretched his weary frame and rinsed his mouth out with clean water, then used a small, bronze-handled brush to clean his teeth. Moments later, his steward Democles brought him a freshly baked bread roll and two pieces of dried, salted fish.

"Off to teach soldiers their craft again?" asked Porcia, sitting up in bed. The morning sun slanting in the window illuminated her face clearly, and Pilate saw the beginning of gray tinting the hair at her temples, and the lines of care and sorrow the loss of her daughter had graven in her face. She was not yet an old woman—far from it! But in that moment, he saw the old woman she would one day become, and was moved with a deep sense of love and compassion for her sorrow. He crossed the room to kiss her forehead.

"Only if I have to," he said. "Yesterday was hard on this old frame of mine. But they are not bad soldiers, really—just neglected ones. I think they began to remember their trade yesterday."

"And you only had to kill one of them to jog their memories!" she said.

Pilate raised an eyebrow. He had never concealed the brutal nature of the soldier's trade from her—it was not the Roman way—but she had never commented on it before either.

"Were you watching from the window yesterday?" he asked.

"No," she said. "But word travels fast in this small town. Some of the locals seem glad that you are whipping these men into shape. Others are laying odds on how long before one of the soldiers slips a dagger between your ribs."

"And what say you, my wife?" he asked, kissing her again.

"You need no advice from me on how to command soldiers," she said. "You learned that craft well, long before we were wed. But do be careful! I have no desire to lose husband as well as daughter."

Pilate nodded. "I have yet to see a man here who could best me," he said. "But in another week none of them will wish to. Soldiers are like children, my dear. They may grumble about their parents' strictness, but all they really want is structure and discipline. Break them to your will, call them every name in the book, then pat them on the back and hand out a few awards after a battle—and they will be ready to lay down their lives for you in a moment!"

She gave him a sad smile. "I wish that I had something to keep me as busy and motivated as you seem to be!" she said.

Pilate gave her a long look. He knew that the Roman world was unfairly stacked in favor of men, but had never really thought about it much before. After all, that was the way things had always been. Men ruled the world, while women kept house, raised children, and pleased their husbands. But for the first time in his life, he tried to put himself in his wife's place. She had no children to tend to, and her husband's hours would be long. Servants would take care of the physical labor of the governor's home, for the most part, so what would she have to do? He racked his brain and could think of nothing—unless? He voiced his thoughts to his wife.

"I think we should try to have another child," he said. "That is, if you want to."

"I do not carry children well, my love," she said. "Four pregnancies and only one girl who survived infancy. I would love to embrace another baby, but I fear it is not my fate to be a mother."

"In the past," he said, "we have simply let nature take its course and abided by the result. Perhaps it is time to help nature a bit. In every culture there are wise women who know the ways of childbirth and assist mothers who have difficulty conceiving. In Rome we never consulted with such— but perhaps it is time we did."

"Would you give me another child for Caligula to destroy?" she asked, her expression bleak.

"Never!" he said. "But I would give us a child who can one day avenge the death of his sister. Or at least, a son or daughter who can flee with us into exile and grow into adulthood far out of Gaius Caligula's reach."

She looked at him with a very small smile. "If that is your wish, I cannot object to it," she said. "You are the *paterfamilias*, after all."

"But is it the choice you desire?" he asked.

She nodded. "I cannot stand the hole in my heart that was torn open by Porcia Minor's departure!" she replied. "That wound can never heal completely, but having a baby to hold in my arms and nurse at my breast would at least keep it from blighting my life completely. I shall give you another child, my husband, if the gods are kind."

"The gods owe us a little kindness!" said Pilate. "This evening we shall go to bed early." He kissed her firmly—a kiss with much love and a bit of desire behind it, then fastened on his cape and left their chambers.

The men were done eating breakfast in the barracks, and the guards had just changed shifts. As Pilate looked around the governor's residence, he saw that uniforms were clean and the men were moving with a spring in their step and a sense of purpose. Titus Ambrosius saw him entering the courtyard and came over to report, rendering a sharp salute.

"Good morning, Prefect!" he said. "Men are up and about their duties, and they seem to be in good shape overall."

"Excellent!" said Pilate. "Tell me, Centurion, what is the security like in the countryside here? Are there bandits or revolutionaries about?"

"Banditry is a constant problem on the desert roads," said Ambrosius. "Merchants have to travel with a considerable escort if they wish to arrive at their destination with their throats and purses intact. But the biggest problem is the Zealots. They single out Roman soldiers and citizens, and wait for an opportune moment to cut them down. That is why Romans do not travel unprotected in this country."

"Do they have a commander?" asked Pilate. "Or a known headquarters?"

149

"Not that we have been able to discover," said the centurion, "although Longinus would know more than I do. From what I have seen, they are not a well-organized force. More a clustering of fanatics than a private army in the making."

Pilate nodded. "I want the men patrolling all the roads in the province," he said. "Spread the orders to each detachment in every small town and city. There should be a patrol on every road at least once a day. If you know that merchants, or Roman citizens, or any other prospective target for these bandits and Zealots should be traveling the roads, then make sure a patrol shadows them, out of sight. I don't want these brigands inconvenienced — I want them dead! Or captured alive, so that I can crucify them as a warning to others. Banditry and marauding will not be tolerated while I am here!"

Titus Ambrosius grinned. "That's more like it, sir!" he said. "When your illustrious predecessor heard of bandit and Zealot attacks, his response was to pull our patrols in and warn Roman citizens not to travel alone. Makes you wonder, doesn't it, what he thought soldiers were here for?"

Pilate nodded. "Apparently, he favored sending them on whaling expeditions to the local brothels," he said. "Now, send those patrols out. And send word to every cohort and century that is not stationed here in Caesarea that I will be touring the province soon, and expect to find good order and discipline in every unit I inspect! And they can be assured — if good order and discipline are not in evidence when I arrive, they will be when I leave!" Ambrosius saluted and laughed as he walked back toward the barracks.

Pilate began walking around the perimeters of the governor's palace, taking the time to talk briefly with the legionaries stationed at the various watch points, and then left the facility and walked through the town. Caesarea, named after Caesar Augustus by his client king Herod the Great fifty years before, was a bustling seaport and trade center. Camels laden with merchandise entered the three gates at all hours of day and night, some bound for the large marketplace, but most for the docks where ships anchored daily to load up on the wines, spices, and perfumes produced locally, as well as fresh produce and meat for the crews. Like most seaports, it was a noisy, smelly, busy place. Sailors who had been recently paid staggered down the streets, looking for cheap wine and women, while those still seeking to earn their wages carried heavy crates and sacks from vendors to ships and vice versa. Caesarea was a tiny microcosm of the trade network that was the source of Rome's vast wealth.

At all three gates, patrolling among the docks, and standing guard at the marketplace were Pilate's soldiers. They regarded him with interest, snapping to attention as he approached and watching his back as he departed. He made a point to compliment them on their uniforms and their sharp appearance, and told them he looked forward to training with them again soon. Their attitude seemed to be a healthy dose of fear, respect, and perhaps just the beginnings of some real affection. He wished that there was an enemy he could lead these men against! One solid campaign against a foreign foe would make them his forever. But Judea, though grumbling and rebellious, was largely a province at peace—or at least, a province without organized hostility.

But there was hostility there all the same. And as Pilate toured the city, it was obvious to see whence it came: the Jewish citizens of the region. They glared at him when he passed, and again and again he caught the same word—*goyim*—whispered among them. Although every one of them that he spoke to addressed him with the appropriate respect and courtesy, it was obvious that he—or, truth be told, Rome itself—was an unwelcome guest in the land of the Chosen People. That hostility was utterly irrelevant, as far as Pilate was concerned. The Jews had proven to be stubborn and inflexible subjects for every people who had ever conquered them. Let them hate Rome, he thought, as long as they feared her in even greater measure.

As he passed by the docks, he saw his predecessor preparing to board ship for Rome. Valerius Gratus was trying to climb onto the gangplank, sweating in the morning heat, as his slaves carried his luggage aboard. But his progress was impeded by the rotund prostitute Fatimah, who clung to his arm and begged him to take her to Rome. The former governor shook his head repeatedly, which set her off wailing all the more loudly.

"It just isn't done!" snapped the angry Gratus.

"Oh please, my precious Prefect!" she begged. "No one else here will treat me as well as you do, and I promise to be so very discreet! Don't leave me in this awful place!"

151

"You did fine for yourself before I arrived, and I am sure you shall continue to prosper after I am gone," Gratus said, and managed to twist his arm out of her grasp. "I have a wife and a Senate seat back in Rome, and you shall never see me here again. For your time and your . . . efforts, I thank you. But they are no longer necessary. Now take this and go!"

He tossed a small bag of coins her way and nearly ran up the gangplank to escape her. Her wails turned to curses and imprecations, but neither was heartfelt enough to keep her from grabbing the coin purse and stuffing it into her ample bosom. Then, mustering something approaching dignity, she made her way past the snickering sailors and tradesmen and headed toward the nearest tavern.

Despicable, Pilate thought. No wonder these people hate Rome, if the likes of Valerius Gratus have been sent here as her official face!

When he arrived back at the governor's residence, he was greeted by his newest centurion. Brutus Appius still bore a huge bruise on his chin from the impact of Pilate's elbow, but he strode up and saluted the Prefect with all the enthusiasm of a first-year *conterburnalis*.

"Good morning, sir!" he said after Pilate returned the salute. "Cassius Longinus has arrived from Capernaum and is waiting to see you."

"Excellent!" said Pilate. "I have been looking forward to meeting him."

He mounted the steps to the office which adjoined his private chambers. There he found a clean-cut, neatly dressed Roman officer in his mid-thirties who snapped to attention and saluted with admirable respect.

"*Primus Pilus* Centurion Gaius Cassius Longinus, reporting for duty, sir!" he said.

Pilate surveyed him for several seconds before speaking, taking the measure of the man, as he was sure that Longinus was taking his. After he had thoroughly inspected the centurion, he spoke.

"So tell me, Gaius Cassius, how is it that the *Primus Pilus* centurion of the Judean Legion absents himself from his post in Caesarea to take up residence in some tiny, pathetic village nearly fifty miles away?" he asked sharply.

The centurion returned his gaze with complete frankness, and then spoke. "The men tell me that you are a real soldier, Prefect, and that you also seem to be a man of honor, so I will extend you the courtesy of presuming they speak the truth. I stayed here as long as I could stand it. The grasping, incompetent nature of your predecessor was matched only by his corrosive effect on proper discipline. He tolerated an inappropriate degree of contempt and familiarity from the men, and made an open display of his slovenly and disgusting predilections. I tried to keep order and discipline for the first year, and he threatened to break me in rank if I persisted—said that I was 'making him look bad' in front of the men. I told him that it would be impossible for me to make him look any worse in their eyes than he himself did—but I also agreed to leave the fortress. I have tried to keep the men posted in the villages from being infected by the corruption that he unleashed among the legion, but I am only one man. If it is your intent to remind these men that they are soldiers of Rome, and force them to act like it, then I am your man to the death!"

Pilate nodded slowly. "It seems to me, then, that you have acted with as much honor and discipline as any man could, serving under Valerius Gratus. But what is this I hear about your going native? Do you really ascribe to the Jews' religion? Do you have a Jewish family?"

Longinus looked testy. "I am a Roman of the Romans, sir!" he said. "It is true that I am a man of the Third Class, but my folks have served in the military since the Punic Wars! My great-granddad won the Civic Crown under Gaius Marius himself. I have marched under the standard for nearly twenty years and never disobeyed an order. But as far as my religion goes, yes sir! I do accept that the God of the Jews makes more sense than any of our bewildering array of Roman deities. I have not gone the full limit of conversion—I can't quite work up the nerve to be circumcised—but I am what the Jews call a 'God-fearer,' and proud of it! I also am married to a local girl, Abigail by name. She is raising my two sons, Cassius David and Gaius Moses."

"So where do your loyalties lie?" asked Pilate. "With Rome, or with Adonai, or whatever it is he is called?"

Longinus looked at him for a moment before speaking. "My first duty will always be to Rome, sir. And if there ever comes a time when my duties to my God and my country conflict so badly I cannot reconcile them, I shall lay my gladius at your feet and resign my office."

Pilate nodded and extended his hand. "Spoken like a man of honor!" he said. "I shall need you, Longinus, if I am to successfully govern these people I know so little of. Still, I should like to have you nearer at hand than Capernaum. Can you relocate your family?"

"I have built them a comfortable home near that of my wife's mother. If you can allow me leave to see them periodically, I see no need to trouble them with a move at this time," said Longinus.

"As you wish," said Pilate. "But I may keep you too busy to see them for months at a time!"

"Were my wife Roman, she would be accustomed to my absences being measured in years, not months," said Longinus. "My Abigail is a good girl, and will do fine while I am gone. Now, sir, what do you require of me first?"

"I intend to inspect every cohort and century that is posted in every village in the province over the next month or so," said Pilate. "I want to see their condition for myself, and I want them to see what kind of commander I intend to be. I will also use this inspection tour to introduce myself to the local political and religious leadership. They need to see what a true Roman looks like! You can accompany me on this tour and be my liaison to the local Jewish communities."

Longinus nodded. "That sounds like an excellent plan. You will need to make sure that you travel with an escort, however. The Zealots have made this province a dangerous place for unguarded Roman citizens."

"Tell me more about these Zealots," said Pilate. "Even the Emperor warned me about them, but I know very little about who they are."

For the next two hours, Pilate listened in fascination as Longinus explained the complicated and tortuous religious and political web that was the Judean province. He had heard some of the ancient history of the Jews on his way to the province from the two Jews onboard Captain Diomyrus' ship—he knew of Moses and Abraham, David and Solomon, and the various kings and prophets that the Jews reverenced. But now for the first time he got a detailed account of the current events in Judea—of the house of Herod the Great, the cruel and paranoid monster that had ingratiated himself to both Mark Antony and Augustus, and been granted the title "King of the Jews" for his troubles. He also got a rundown on the complicated politics that surrounded the Jewish High Priesthood, and the

House of Zadok that controlled that office. By the end of the interview, his head was spinning with the names of Maccabees and Hasmoneans, of Pharisees, Sadducees, Essenes, Zealots, and Samaritans, and of the complex network of religion and intermarriage that bound them all together.

By the time Pilate called it quits, the hour for the noon meal had long passed. The governor and the centurion walked down to the marketplace together, purchasing some bread and cured meat, as well as a bowl of figs and grapes. Rather than recline at the table in Pilate's quarters, they ate with the soldiers in the barracks. The sight of the senior centurion, whom they all knew and respected, having lunch with the Prefect on such good terms, set the men's minds at ease and erased many of the lingering doubts they had about the new man in charge. After the meal, Pilate marched them out into the courtyard and set all those not going on watch to drilling with sword and shield again. Their movements were crisper, sharper, and more professional than the day before. Longinus was obviously pleased at the change; several times he looked over at Pilate and nodded as the men demonstrated their skills.

After practicing with the men for an hour, Pilate left Longinus and Ambrosius in charge of finishing up the drills, and returned to his office to write a letter to Quintus Sullemia. However, he had barely begun when Brutus Appius, who was commanding the watch for the hour, reported that he had visitors from Jerusalem—priests, by their dress. He told Appius to have Longinus report to his chambers immediately, and then see the visitors up. If he was going to deal with the local leaders this soon, he wanted to have someone who understood them handy.

Longinus joined him momentarily, but before they had time to confer, three bearded men in black robes entered his chambers. The tallest of them approached Pilate's work desk and gave a polite bow.

"I am Joseph Caiaphas, son of Matthias, High Priest of the Temple, son-in-law of Annas the former High Priest," he said. "I bring our express greetings and best wishes to the new Prefect and Governor of Judea."

Pilate returned his bow. "It is good to meet you, and I hope you will convey my greetings back to the former High Priest Annas and let him know that I look forward to meeting him soon, in Jerusalem," he said.

The second priest stepped forward and deposited a heavy bag on Pilate's desk. "On behalf of the Levites and priestly classes of Jerusalem, we present this offering and hope that the relations between the governor and the Temple can continue to be as mutually amicable and profitable as under your predecessor," he said.

"What is this?" asked Pilate, looking in the bag and finding it to be full of gold coins.

"Your stipend, of course," said Caiaphas. "As your predecessor pointed out to us on more than one occasion, the Empire does not pay its governors a sufficient salary to defray their expenses. So we supplement the governor's income in exchange for certain . . . considerations."

"And what would those considerations be?" asked Pilate, his tone icy.

"Valerius Gratus always allowed our Supreme Council, the Sanhedrin, a wide degree of latitude in local governance," explained Caiaphas. "In turn, we would keep him apprised of what situations required Roman intervention, and which ones we felt were best handled by our own ways and means."

Pilate walked to the front of his desk, grabbed the heavy bag, and dropped it back into Caiaphas' hands. He was furious, not so much at the Jews as at Gratus, who had seemingly done nothing right while he was Prefect. No wonder the province was rebellious and ungovernable! He approached Caiaphas until his face was only a few inches away from that of the priest, who paled and stepped back until Pilate managed to corner him against the wall of his office.

"Let me make one thing perfectly clear, Caiaphas son of Matthias," he said. "I work for the Senate and People of Rome, and for our Emperor, Tiberius Caesar. I do not work for you. I do not work for your father-in-law Annas. I do not work for your Sanhedrin, nor do I work for your Temple. I am here to see this province properly governed and pacified. My predecessor was a corrupt and incompetent fool. He took your gold and was happy to look the other way when you violated Roman law and policy. I am not him. While I have absolutely no problem using the governor's office to enrich myself, I will do so by the time-honored means of destroying and pillaging the enemies of Rome, and selling their wives and children into slavery. I am not for sale! But if I do want your gold, at any time . . . I will find a reason to take it!"

Caiaphas was opening and shutting his mouth in amazement, like a fish out of water—if fish had beards, Pilate thought as he finished his statement, keeping his voice icy calm the entire time, and then backing away. The astonishment on the Jewish priest's face gave way to a harder, angrier expression.

"My apologies, Pontius Pilate, if our well-intentioned offering gave offense," he said. "It was not our intent to question your honesty, or to seem as if we wanted to give you orders. We merely desire an amicable relationship between Rome and Jerusalem. Peace is mutually profitable, while war and rebellion are sordid and unpleasant. If you are here to keep the peace, we will be your willing partners, with or without financial inducement."

"I am here to uphold Rome's laws and traditions, and her governance of this province," said Pilate. "Of course I intend to do so by peaceful means—unless I am given reason to invoke my Proconsular *imperium*. But let your people know that attacks on Roman citizens and property will NOT be tolerated any further! Those who carry them out will only bring suffering on the people of Judea that they claim to be fighting for!"

"I cannot be held answerable for the deeds of brigands and outlaws!" snapped Caiaphas, his mask of affability completely gone now.

"You personally?" said Pilate. "No, I will not demand an account from you. But those who shelter and protect these villains—they will feel the heel of Rome's boot on their neck, until they give up those who are preying upon Rome's people!"

The three priests sidled toward the door. Caiaphas spoke one more time.

"I would beg you to reconsider your proposed policy, Prefect!" he said. "If you enact reprisals upon the poor people of Judea for the actions of a heinous few, you will only add to the ranks of the rebels and Zealots who currently trouble Rome!"

Pilate favored him with a wolfish grin. "If I have to, I will make a desert and call it peace!" he snapped. "But I imagine very few examples will be necessary. One or two small villages destroyed, and the locals will be falling all over themselves to give us the Zealots' heads!"

The three Jews scurried out, and Pilate returned to his desk and took a sip of wine. He then looked at Longinus, who was staring at him with a slight grin.

"Well, Prefect," he drawled, "you spent a good part of this morning painting a very pretty picture of how you intend to run this province—and in the process, you managed to paint yourself as a Roman of high principles and honorable intent. I must admit, I found myself wondering if all of it was nothing but a lot of pretty words. But after that little exchange, I see that you are pretty much who you make yourself out to be. I think I will enjoy working with you!"

Pilate scowled. "Was Gratus really so big a fool as to take bribes in front of his subordinates?" he asked.

Longinus made a scoffing sound. "Sometimes he did," he replied. "Other times the honorable Valerius Gratus sent his subordinates to collect his stipend—and encouraged them to charge the High Priest for their service as couriers!"

Pilate shook his head in wonder. "How can the Rome that bred men like Augustus also breed such worms as Valerius Gratus?" he asked.

"With great regularity, I would say," commented Longinus. "You don't really intend to go burning any villages down, do you? Please don't judge all the Jews by the actions of their priests and these fanatical Zealots! Most of the people here are simple and surprisingly virtuous. They deserve better than that."

Pilate nodded. "I was mainly trying to show them that I am deadly serious about crushing the Zealots," he said. "But if I catch a village giving them aid and comfort, I will raze it to the ground. I doubt I will have to do it more than once."

"Agreed!" said Longinus. "Truth be told, most of the common folk of Judea hate the Zealots for making their lives so difficult. It is all well and good to dream of seeing David's kingdom reestablished, but in practice all these fanatics do is harm the people they are trying to help. There is one thing you should know, however," he added.

"What would that be?" asked Pilate.

"Most of the Zealots congregate north of us, in Galilee. If you really want to go after them, that is where you will need to focus your efforts," explained the centurion.

"Isn't Herod Antipas the tetrarch there?" Pilate growled.

"Yes, but he is worthless militarily," said Longinus. "Jews won't enlist in his ranks, for the most part, so his soldiers are a mix of Syrians and Samaritans. The local Jews hate them as much as they hate Herod, so he keeps his troops concentrated around his various palaces and uses them as bodyguards. He is politically shrewd, and well-connected back in Rome—but he is no general."

"I intend to end this Zealot movement, so we will see if we can root them all out, or at least chase them back into the remote areas," Pilate said. "I want our roads to be safe for travelers, be they Roman, Greek, or Jew! I thank you for your time. I need to write some letters now, but why don't you go ahead and pick a reliable squad of men to accompany us. I want to start my inspection tour tomorrow."

"Very well, sir!" said Longinus. "I look forward to accompanying you."

That night Pilate told Procula Porcia of his absence over the next month, and she nodded with the resignation of a soldier's wife. "It will be difficult for me to conceive another child if you are going to be gone from my bed for months at a time!" she said.

Pilate nodded. "Perhaps we can get started on that before I leave," he replied. And so they did.

# CHAPTER THIRTEEN

Over the next few weeks, Pilate was on the road a great deal. With thirty legionaries in tow, commanded by the redoubtable Cassius Longinus, he rode from one end of Judea (admittedly a rather small province) to the other. He found that the further the soldiers were from Caesarea, the more professional and less lazy they seemed to be. Part of the reason for that state of affairs was that they had been more removed from the corruption tolerated and encouraged by Valerius Gratus, but a good part of it also seemed to be that they were living in much more dangerous conditions and they knew it. Everywhere Pilate went, the Roman citizens and merchants he talked to were living in fear of the roving bands of Zealots who targeted anyone and everyone associated with Rome.

The Jews distinguished between the two groups of Zealots: those they termed Zealots directed their violence against Romans only, while the *sicarii* also attacked Jews whom they regarded as insufficiently sympathetic to their cause, or suspected of collaborating with the Romans.

"Nothing but ruffians is all they are!" said Eleazar ben Shimon, an innkeeper in one of the small towns where Pilate stayed. "They could care less who rules Judea—all they want to do is kill and rob anyone who has more than they do! Them other Zealots—now, I might disagree with their methods, you understand—but at least their motives are honest. The *sicarii*—as far as I am concerned, you should gut the lot of them!"

Pilate listened with interest and sympathy. He had discovered that, as long as he kept his mouth shut, bought wine for the locals, and affected an attitude of commiseration, the Jews were a very vocal people. He absorbed all he heard, nodded occasionally, and acted when he felt he needed to. All the while he was debating within his own mind about the best possible way to strike a blow against the Zealots and send a message to the entire province that Rome was no longer asleep at the helm.

It was while they were approaching the sleepy little town of Nazareth that an idea occurred to him. Galilee seemed to be a hotbed of Zealot activity—no doubt due to Herod's refusal to go after them—and thus an excellent place to teach a lesson to these violent revolutionaries. All Pilate needed was to draw them out. He halted the detail for lunch and pulled Longinus to one side to explain the idea to him.

"What I want to do is send two men dressed as merchants ahead of us down the road. Let them be leading a couple of mules, heavy laden with bags of goods, and throw some gold around at the local tavern," he explained. "The rest of us will camp outside the town—preferably in a barn or cave where we can be undetected. When the merchants leave town the next morning, we will shadow them along the road some distance back—hopefully far enough to avoid detection. If the Zealots attack, we shall swoop in and bag the lot of them!"

Longinus nodded. "There have been several attacks along the road between here and Mount Carmel," he said. "But if we send these men out completely unguarded, it will draw suspicion. Everyone knows these parts are dangerous for Roman citizens. I would say give them a small escort—big enough to show that they are aware of the danger, small enough to still be a tempting target. I bet I could talk a half dozen of the lads into posing as mercenaries. The men all hate the Zealots with a passion!"

Pilate thought a moment. "Very well," he said. "That sounds like an excellent idea. Pick men who are willing to bear the danger, and can do a passable imitation of rich merchants. We will remain in the hills south of Nazareth, and send them on into town to establish their cover story there. When they set out the next morning, I want to follow them at a distance of a mile and a half or so. We must be far back enough to avoid easy detection, but close enough to intervene when they are attacked. I don't want to lose the whole group!"

Longinus thought a moment. "We may need to acquire some clothing somewhere," he said. "I don't know if we have enough local garb among the men to pass eight people off as civilians. We can't go into Nazareth; it will tip the locals off as to what we are planning. It's not too far back to the village of Nain where we spent last night; let me dress up as a local and hotfoot it back there. I know a tailor who lives there; I can purchase six or seven garments from him and be back in a few hours."

Pilate frowned. "What if there are Zealot scouts trailing us?" he asked.

Longinus shrugged. "I've had flankers going before and behind to watch for any curious eyes on our march and we haven't seen any in several days. The Zealots know this is too big a patrol to ambush, so they have melted into the countryside. But I imagine they will know when two men come into Nazareth with heavily laden mules and spending large amounts of coin!"

Longinus shed his centurion's armor, helmet, and plume and pulled a homespun robe and mantle from his saddlebags. He also produced an odd necklace with a small wooden box on it and tied it around his neck. It looked somewhat like the *bulla* amulet young Romans wore around their necks before they reached the age of manhood, but it was different in shape and more solid than the leather or fine linen favored by the Romans.

"Whatever is that thing?" Pilate asked.

"It is my copy of the *shema*," said Longinus. "Something Jews and God-fearers wear to remind them of their faith."

"What is in it?" said Pilate.

"A small piece of papyrus with a sacred verse from the Book of Moses written upon it," said Longinus. *"Shema Y'srael! Adonai elohainu Adonai echod!"*

"What does that mean in our language?" asked Pilate.

"Hear, O Israel! The Lord Our God, the Lord is One!" said Longinus.

"I suppose he is," said Pilate. "Be careful, and return quickly!"

Longinus rode off like the wind, looking for all the world like one of the natives of this strange and arid land. Pilate ordered the men to pitch tents next to a small spring one of them had found and make ready to camp for the night. He then pulled the men around him in a tight circle and explained why they were halting for the night and what he planned to do.

"After Longinus and his escort head into Nazareth, it will be VERY important for no one to know that the rest of us are near," he said. "So we will camp away from the road, and there will be no fires tonight. If any locals stumble upon us, we will detain them until Longinus and his crew leave town tomorrow morning. We are throwing them out there as a big, juicy bit of bait—but it is important that we be in position to spring the trap when the moment comes."

"No worries, Governor," said one of the legionaries. "There is not a one of us that hasn't lost a friend to those damned Zealots. It will be nice to deal out a little payback to them!"

"Aye," said another. "And we have no wish to see Centurion Longinus come to harm. He's a bit funny with the Jewish religion stuff, but he is as fine an officer as I have ever served under. I'd hate to see someone else replace him!"

Pilate looked at the men with some affection. Longinus had chosen well—these fellows were all veterans, and eager to get at their enemy. He had them set up tents and shelters on the slope of the hill above the spring— there was no need to build a more formidable camp if they were trying to be undetected. One of the men found a small cave on the far slope of the hill; it would be a sheltered spot where about a dozen or more could sleep at a time. The rations were on the dreary side—salt fish and dried figs—but the countryside around the little spring was quite lovely, so Pilate posted guards and then found a rock to sit upon. He unrolled a blank piece of papyrus and began thinking about what he would write to Sullemia this week. He was anxious to know how things were going in Rome, and for any news he could get about Gaius Caligula. Would it be too much to hope for the little maggot to die of his injuries?

A few hours later, just after sunset, Longinus came riding back into camp. His disguise had worked, apparently, or else no Zealots had been patrolling the road. He brought along several sets of clothes, including tunics and mantles for his "mercenary" escort. He chose several men to play the role, and instructed each of them to put on the loose-fitting garments over their breastplates.

"Zealots frequently take out armed guards with arrows before attacking a caravan," he said. "Barring a lucky hit to the head, these should protect your vitals. Just fall down if you feel an arrow hit your torso, and be ready to spring up and surprise them when they charge at us!"

"What about you, Centurion?" asked the youngest legionary, Marcus Quirinius.

"They won't waste an arrow on an old merchant who is unarmed," said Longinus. "And by the time they close on us, I will no longer be unarmed!"

"This is going to be dangerous work, men," said Pilate. "Play your roles well! Don't walk or act like soldiers. Be unprofessional and slipshod. Let the enemy think they have nothing to fear from you until it is too late—then send them to Hades! Now off to Nazareth with you!"

He watched as the "merchant caravan" left their hidden camp by the spring and headed down the road. Light in the sky was failing, and it would be just a few hours before midnight when they checked in to Nazareth's lone tavern. He ordered the men to turn in early, except for the night watches, and left instructions to be woken two hours before dawn. The ground was hard and the night cool, but the exertion of the day had tired him out, and his eyes closed almost right away.

He knew it was early when he was woken up—far earlier than the time he had asked. The moon had only advanced a few degrees in the sky—it was maybe an hour since he had fallen asleep.

"What is it?" he asked the sentry who had called him out of his slumber.

"A young Jew has wandered into our camp," he said. "We took him into custody, but did not harm him."

Pilate rubbed his eyes and gave a sigh of exasperation. "Very well," he said. "Let me see what he has to say for himself."

The moon's light was more than bright enough for him to make out the boy's features. He was barely old enough to sport a rather scraggy beard— no more than twenty, thought Pilate. He was trying to look indignant, but the fear in his eyes belied the defiance he was trying to project. He spoke as soon as Pilate drew near.

"What is the meaning of this?" he demanded, speaking passable Greek. "Why have I been arrested? I am no criminal!"

Pilate arched an eyebrow. "You are not under arrest," he answered in the same language. *Koine* Greek was the universal trade language of the Mediterranean—not as lovely and poetic as the Attican Greek of Homer, but a simple language, easy to learn and understand. "But you will be if you lie to me. Who are you, and what are you doing out this late in such a remote area?"

"I am James, the son of Joseph," he said. "I live in Nazareth, where I run a carpentry shop with my brothers. I am looking for my older brother. He wanders off periodically, claiming he needs time to pray. Hmmph!" he snorted. He did not seem to care much for his brother, thought Pilate. "He is usually back earlier than this, and my mother is worried sick about him, so she sent me out to search. He likes to frequent this spring, so it was the first place I checked. Instead of Yeshua, I found your soldiers. What brings a band of Romans this far from Caesarea?"

"Keeping the peace," said Pilate. "A mission which your presence here makes more difficult. I cannot let you tell anyone where we are until we leave in the morning."

"Prefect, just let me kill him," said one of the men. "You can't trust any of these Jews!"

Pilate shook his head. "No," he said. "We are here to protect these people, legionary, and show them that Rome's governance is for their good. If I thought he was one of our Zealot friends, we would not be wasting time bandying words with him. We shall detain him overnight here in our camp, and in the morning, we will take him with us until we are in sight of our merchant friends. Then we shall send him straight back to Nazareth—and if he tries to warn anyone, then he will join his Zealot companions on the cross!"

The young Jew shuddered at the mention of the cross. Pilate recalled Longinus telling him that crucifixion was particularly loathsome to the Jews, who believed being hung on a tree was to be cursed. But James squared his shoulders and addressed Pilate directly.

"If you are laying a trap for the Zealots, sir, then I will not breathe a word to anyone. Those cursed vagabonds have brought a thousand woes upon the poor people of our land!" he said.

"So your loyalties lie with Rome?" asked Pilate.

"My loyalties are to my God and to my family," said James. "But I am intelligent enough to know that it will take an act of God, not a mob of thieves, to remove Rome from these parts! The Zealots say they want to restore the throne of David—pah!" He spat on the ground in contempt. "They don't even know who the heirs of David are! There has not been a king of David's line in this land for six hundred years, but if the Kingdom were to be restored, my brothers and I would be the strongest claimants to the throne! My father, who has now gone to the grave, was a direct descendant of the royal line, father to son, all the way back to King Jeconiah! And my mother, Mary—why she also traces her lineage all the way back to King David himself! And you know what all that royal blood has got us?" He seemed even angrier than he had been when Pilate first confronted him. "A house where five brothers sleep in one bed and my mother and sisters in the other! A carpenter shop that barely earns enough to feed us and keep a roof over our heads! That's what being the heirs of the true king of the Jews has done for my family. Romans, Ptolemies, Herods—I do not care who rules Judea between now and the time Messiah comes. All I want is to go back to my bed and my shop and my trade, and hope that one day I earn enough money to build a house of my own and marry my sweetheart."

Pilate listened in some amusement. This young Jew certainly seemed to have a grievance with the world, he thought.

"Well, James son of Joseph," he said, "until your God decides to throw us back into Our Sea, this province belongs to Rome. And as your new governor, it is my job to keep the peace and put down rebellion. You seem harmless enough, but I will hold you till tomorrow. My men and I will be riding out before dawn to hopefully catch some Zealots in the act of attempted murder and brigandry. Who knows? If I take a few of them alive, I might even have to do a little business with you. Good wood is scarce in this country, and I may well need to make a few crosses."

The young Jew paled. "Please, sir," he said. "I have no sympathy for the Zealots, but they are sons of Abraham still. Do not hang them from a tree! Cut their heads off or burn them alive if you have to—but hanging them on a cross will curse their souls forever!"

Pilate allowed the beast that lived inside him to show its fangs for a moment. "They should have thought of that before they began murdering Romans!" he snapped. "Now good night, James son of Joseph!" He stalked back to his tent and went to sleep almost instantly, wrapped in his cloak and using his bedroll for a pillow.

It seemed like only an hour, but the moon was low in the sky when the sentry shook him again. All over the darkened camp, soldiers were rolling up their bedrolls, donning their cloaks, and checking their gear. The young Jew, his hands tied before him, stood and stretched next to the sentry who had guarded him all night. Pilate got an idea.

"You probably know the country around here better than any Roman," he said. "I need to be watching the road that runs westward from Nazareth toward Mount Carmel by sunrise, and I need to watch it undetected. Is there a suitable location?"

James looked troubled. He obviously had no love for the Zealots or the Romans, but the talk of crucifixion still seemed to bother him. However, he had seen enough of Pilate the night before to know that the governor was no man to be trifled with. Finally he spoke up. "There is a ridge just outside of town," he said. "There are some sheepfolds and shepherd's huts on top of it, but the shepherds have all moved westward for the summer, grazing their flocks on the slopes of the mountain. From those huts you can see the road trailing off westward for at least five miles or so. The ridge runs parallel to the road for twice that distance at least, so you can shadow your caravan for a long ways toward Mt. Carmel."

"I wonder if the Zealots use those shepherd's huts to monitor the road?" Pilate wondered out loud.

"I doubt it," said James. "The huts are too close to town, and young folks like to sneak up there sometimes."

"Are you sure the 'young folks' you mention aren't spying for the Zealots themselves?" asked Pilate.

The young Jew blushed furiously. "I am pretty sure they are not the least bit concerned with what happens on the road while they are there," he finally stammered. Pilate threw back his head and laughed.

"Well, James son of Joseph," he finally said, "you are the first one of your people that I can honestly say I have liked! Conduct us to these huts quickly and quietly, and once our caravan passes, I will allow you to return to Nazareth unharmed. I will wager your brother has already beaten you home!"

James' eyes narrowed. "He probably has," he grumbled. "And Mother will be so glad to see him back safe she won't even notice I've been gone all night!"

The squad of soldiers followed the young Jew and the Prefect cross country, staying in the wooded creek bottom for a couple of miles. Soon they could see a small cluster of stone houses and shops on the right, and a long grassy ridge on the left. There was a large sheepfold, nearly a hundred feet in diameter, surrounded by a low stone wall, and several ancient stone huts next to it. Pilate and his men jogged up the ridge as the light began to grow on the horizon, and before the sun's first rays split the sky, they were hidden from view. As James had promised, the huts afforded a splendid view of the road stretching off toward the west. The rising sun's rays illuminated the slopes of Mount Carmel, some twenty miles distant. The road from Nazareth ran almost straight toward the mountain, and then jogged north toward the bustling seaport of Ptolemais as it reached the foothills of Mount Carmel.

Most of the soldiers clustered inside the sheepfold, where the summer grasses had mostly covered the layers of dung and hay at the bottom of it. Several of the more experienced men joined Pilate and James in the largest hut, whose window openings faced out toward the road. He spoke to the men as they filed into the sheepfold.

"Sit quiet, eat some breakfast, and if you are tired, close your eyes," he said. "But keep your gear on and your weapons at the ready. When we move out, we may have to move very quickly!"

"No worries, sir!" said one of the old-timers. "Give us a shot at the Zealots and we'll run like we were wearing Mercury's boots!"

Pilate favored the man with a grin and returned to the hut. James was staring wistfully out the window toward his home village. Pilate felt somewhat sorry for the poor country boy who had not asked for any of this trouble, but comforted himself with the thought that James would be back with his family within the next couple of hours. Meanwhile, the sun climbed in the east and the temperature began to rise. It was still quite comfortable, but gave the promise of being a warm afternoon. Pilate returned to his horse, tied behind the hut, and retrieved one of his most prized possessions from his saddle bag.

It was a Greek telescope, used by astronomers to study the stars and see places far off. Pilate did not fully understand how it worked, but it had been in the effects of his first commander, Flavius Sixtus, when he had died, and Tiberius had given it to him. It was a tapered bronze tube with two highly polished pieces of perfectly clear rock crystal mounted in either end. When viewed through the small end, it magnified far-off objects, making them appear only a few feet away. Pilate had carried it to every posting he had

169

been to for the last fifteen years. Now he lifted it to his eyes and watched the place where the western road left the confines of Nazareth. The town was too small to have a fortified wall, but there was a low stone curb that separated the road from the yards that the small, stone houses sat in. He was startled, as he always was, by how the lenses caused him to leap across a distance of two miles and seemingly stand a few feet from the dusty road.

A woman came out of the house on the edge of town, water pot on her shoulder, and headed toward the well near the town square. Even in her long Jewish robes, Pilate could tell that she was young and lovely. Several young men apparently agreed with the governor's judgment, for they paused on their morning errands to watch her pass. She rounded the corner of a house and passed out of his sight, and a few moments later the young men returned to their chores. He watched a few other locals going back and forth on their morning errands—gathering eggs, heading to the well for water, and getting ready for a day of agrarian toil.

A few moments later, the "merchant caravan" came into view. The men looked suitably bored and disreputable, and Longinus was scowling as he urged them to get moving. He was wearing a fairly expensive robe of good Tyrian cloth, and had a bulging moneybag at his belt. The mule was laden down with two large saddlebags that were obviously quite heavy. In short, to a bandit, the group of disguised Roman legionaries presented a very tempting target. Pilate watched as they made their way out of town and westward down the road.

"Why are you staring into a bronze tube?" asked James at his elbow.

"It is called a telescope. Some say Archimedes invented it, others say the ancient Egyptians came up with the idea," explained Pilate. "I am not entirely sure how it works, but it does make far off things look much closer." He invited the Jewish carpenter to take a look. James peeked through the small end and gasped at the closeness of the images, quickly handing it back to Pilate.

"It seems like sorcery to me!" he said.

"I do not know if it is magical, or simply something to do with the shape and spacing of the clear crystal lenses," said Pilate, "but it is one of the handiest things I have ever owned. Now, once our caravan hits that little bend in the road, I am going to allow you to walk back to Nazareth.

Understand that I will be able to watch you right to the city gates, so there had better be no attempt to warn anyone! You are to return to your shop and resume your work there. Speak to no one outside your family. I imagine this entire operation will be concluded by midafternoon. Be wise, young man, and you and yours will be unharmed. Try to betray my plans to my enemies, and I will see you and your whole family crucified for it!"

Pilate snarled the last bit pretty convincingly, and the young Jew blanched and retreated to the opposite side of the hut. Pilate watched the caravan as it trudged down the road, and once it was past the bend and out of sight of the gates of Nazareth, he turned and nodded. James wasted no time taking off for the village. Pilate monitored his progress and saw him cut a straight course for the point where the road entered the village, and then head toward the main square.

"Are you sure that was wise?" asked one of the legionaries. "If he warns the Zealots, our entire plan would go for naught."

"Sometimes you just have to take a chance with people," Pilate said. "I want them to see that Rome can offer them the extended hand of trade and friendship—or the iron fist clenching a gladius! It is up to them which it will be. We will know if he tries to send out a warning—no one can leave Nazareth and go westward without our seeing it from here."

They watched the caravan wend its way down the road for nearly an hour. Finally, as it drew so far away it could barely be distinguished, he ordered the men to begin quietly moving westward on the reverse slope of the ridge. He skirted the top, keeping his head just high enough to watch the caravan as it plodded down the road. About six miles from Nazareth, he saw a narrow defile full of rocks and scrub brush trailing off to the south of the road. It was just around a slight right-hand curve, which meant that it would be difficult to detect for anyone who was actually traveling along the road—only his considerable altitude advantage made it evident. *There*, he thought. *That is the most logical place I have seen yet for an ambush.*

He quietly gave word for his men to be prepared. They had brought six cavalry horses along with the mules that hauled their luggage, and Pilate and the six most senior warriors in the cohort mounted up. Then Pilate slowly directed the horse up the slope of the ridge until he could see over the top to where the caravan steadily marched westward. They were drawing nearer to the narrow defile by the moment.

The attack came so swiftly that Pilate simply watched it unfold for a moment, even though he had been expecting it at that precise spot. Suddenly the "mercenaries" were all sprouting arrows from their torsos and collapsing to the ground. Then about twenty figures came leaping down from the defile, blades flashing in the sun. He kicked his horse forward.

"Now, boys! Let's teach these Zealot dogs the power of Rome!" he cried, and he and the mounted men rode at the scene full tilt, with his legionaries jogging at double time behind him. Meanwhile the attackers suddenly found their hands full, as the six dead "mercenaries" leaped to their feet with blades in their hands. So focused were the Zealots on trying to put down this unexpected resistance that they did not see Pilate and his mounted escort until they were only a few yards away.

Pilate was holding his *pilum* high and launched it at a burly Zealot who was trying to kill Longinus with a wicked Persian scimitar. The spear caught the big man in the small of his back and he dropped to the ground screaming, clutching at the wound and trying to pull the spear out. Longinus silenced the screams by driving his gladius down the man's throat. Once Pilate was among the attackers, he leaped from his horse—the gladius was not a long enough blade to be effective from horseback—and launched himself at the first Zealot he saw. The man was wielding a pair of curved daggers, and obviously knew how to use them. Pilate's blade was longer, but the assassin could still parry his thrusts with one blade and counter with the other. The two of them fenced back and forth for a moment, and then Pilate managed to slash the man's left forearm so badly that he could no longer grasp the dagger with that hand. His enemy's dual wielding advantage gone, Pilate quickly overcame the Zealot and drove his blade through the man's chest. The Jewish rebels would not give up easily, however. They continued to press the attack against the caravan and Pilate's advance guard, and two legionaries were already down. Pilate managed to block a dagger thrust that would have disemboweled one of his men, and used his free hand to punch the Zealot in the face as hard as he could. The man staggered, dropped his guard, and Pilate gutted him with a slash of his gladius. Then suddenly the legionaries who had been approaching the scene on foot arrived and threw themselves into the fray, and it was over.

Fifteen Zealots lay dead, three managed to flee, and four were captured alive. Two of these were badly wounded, but the other two were only lightly hurt. Several legionaries had minor wounds, one was dead, and two were hurt badly. One of Pilate's men had taken an arrow through a joint in his armor, and it had penetrated into his chest. He was coughing up blood, but the wound did not bubble and froth, so Pilate thought his lungs had been spared. He might recover. The other, a veteran named Lucius Graccus, was not so fortunate. He had sustained a wide slash to the abdomen, and his lacerated bowels were protruding from the wound. Pilate had been on enough battlefields to know that even the best Greek physicians could do nothing for a stomach wound that severe. The man might live a few days, but he would die screaming in agony from blood poisoning. Pilate tried to figure out what to do as Longinus came up alongside him.

"We gave them a good walloping, didn't we, Prefect?" Graccus asked him.

"That we did, soldier," said Pilate. "You fought very well."

Graccus laughed grimly, blood running down his chin. "Not well enough, it seems. I'm a dead man and we both know it. I made the bastard pay for sending me to Hades, though!" He spat at his fallen foe, lying a few feet away. "Longinus, Governor, you know what needs doing. Make it quick, please, and Longinus"—he reached into his tunic and pulled out a coin purse—"give this to my girl Rebecca down in the village. Her folks disowned her when she took up with a Roman, and I don't know if they will take her back or not. Try to look after her as best you can. It's been an honor to serve under you—both of you."

"I'll add a little something to that purse to make sure your woman is taken care of," said Pilate, kneeling down and taking Graccus by the hand. He glanced at Longinus, who quietly got up and took position behind the mortally wounded legionary. "I will also see to it that you are properly burned in the Roman manner, with coin for Charon's passage. I am sorry to lose you, Lucius Graccus. Good soldiers are hard to come by."

The dying man took Pilate's hand in both of his, and Pilate nodded. Longinus drove his blade straight down into the juncture of the man's shoulder and neck, penetrating the heart and ending his life in a matter of seconds. Pilate watched the life drain from his eyes, regretting the grim necessity. But now it was time for some deaths he could enjoy!

"All right, men," he said. "I need four tall beams and four shorter ones for our prisoners here. Then gather enough wood for a pyre for our fallen comrades."

Longinus scowled. "There are not enough trees here to make proper crosses," he said. "This scrub brush will burn well enough, but we'll need some bigger beams than these trees can provide to take care of these dogs."

Pilate nodded. "Take two of my men and go back to the shepherd's huts where we spent the night. I left our supply wagon there. Get the wagons and go into Nazareth, and you will find a carpenter's shop where a Jew named James son of Joseph works. Buy the beams from him, and pay him well—he helped make our ambush a success by guiding us to a perfect vantage point. Try to get back here by the fourth hour." He turned to the rest of the men. "You fought bravely and well today, legionaries. We will camp for the night in that defile. But there are many hours till dark, so let's dispose of these bodies before they begin to smell, and build the pyre for our companions who fell. Get to work!"

That done, he went to survey their prisoners. One was a young man with a nasty bump on his forehead—Pilate suspected he had been bashed with the pommel of someone's gladius. The other was an older man, his beard shot with gray and his face scarred, who stared at the Roman Prefect with naked hatred in his eyes. Two were badly wounded—one had been stabbed through the gut and simply held the wound and groaned, the other had a ghastly slash across his throat that had severed his windpipe but missed the major blood vessels. None of them spoke a word as he interrogated them. He finally gave up and sat down on a nearby rock, taking a long pull of water from his leather canteen.

The men quickly despoiled the bodies of the enemy dead, dividing up the gold and weapons among themselves, and piling the bodies in a heap some distance off the road. They threw brush over them and then lit them up from the campfire that had already been started. It took a few minutes for the flames to catch hold, but soon the Zealot bodies were crackling and hissing, and the unmistakable aroma of cooking flesh filled the air. Under other circumstances such a smell might be appetizing, but the knowledge that the flesh was human made it nauseating instead.

The two fallen legionaries were placed on a pyre woven from several scrub trees. Pilate put two denarii in each mouth so that they could pay the oarsman's fee to enter the afterlife, and then arranged each man's clothes about them, laying the weapons and clothes of a fallen Zealot at their feet. He removed his helmet and bowed his head at the pyre for just a moment, in respect for their memories. Like most Romans, he did not believe in an individual survival after death—he thought of death as a long dreamless sleep for those who were accepted into Hades' realm. Only those who were deified by the Roman Senate, like the *Divus Julius* and the *Divus Augustus*, lived on in the individual sense of the word once they left the mortal world.

One legionary took a flaming brand from the campfire and thrust it into the pyre. The wood blazed up quickly in the afternoon heat, and the two bodies were mostly consumed within a couple of hours. The men would continue to throw wood on the fire all night, and in the morning the ashes of the two soldiers would be raked into urns and taken to Caesarea for burial.

About four hours after he had sent them off, Longinus came back with the supply wagon. Eight beams of wood lay across the top of the men's equipment.

"Any trouble?" asked Pilate.

"The young carpenter did not want to sell us the wood—something I figured on, since the Jews cannot stand to see any of their own nailed up. They believe it carries a curse," said Longinus. "I explained to him that it was a legal necessity, but he still wanted to refuse, so I had the men take the wood anyway. I thought he was going to attack us, but his older brother came out of the house and restrained him. Odd customer, that one. He said something to his brother I didn't understand, and James just went limp in his arms. Then he looked at me and said, 'We must render to Caesar the things that are Caesar's, even when we do not approve the use they will be put to. But we do not want your money.' I offered to give it to the synagogue, but he pointed out that it would still be blood money and tainted. So he suggested I give it to a poor widow and her son who lived in one of the houses nearby, and I did that."

Pilate shook his head. "Was there ever a stranger people in all the *gens humana* than the Jews?" he asked. "Well, let's put these beams to good use!"

In half an hour, the three surviving Zealots—the man with the stomach wound had died wordlessly during the afternoon—were hanging by the side of the road, their wrists and ankles nailed to the beams, all of them writhing and screaming except the one with the slashed windpipe. He had lost consciousness almost immediately, and Pilate figured he would be dead within the hour. The other two made up for his silence, though, as they split the air with their cries. He let them hang there for an hour or so before speaking to them.

"Now you see the price for defying Rome!" he said. "Let me tell you a thing or two about crucifixion. First of all, it is not quick. Most men last for about three or four days on the cross, depending on how hot the weather is. Dehydration will be your worst enemy at first. Then the birds will come. They generally arrive about the second day or so. Birds love living flesh, and they will probably go for your eyes first. You can thrash your head about for a while, but eventually you will wear out, and then you'll be blinded. After that they will take your lips and cheeks. You will think you are going to die then, but you won't. If you are lucky, by the third day you will be unconscious, and won't feel it when they start to pull out your bowels."

The men's cries fell silent as they began to soak in the truth of what Pilate was saying. The older fanatic simply stared at him with redoubled hatred, but the younger one's face was streaked with tears, and he was trembling in agony and fear. Pilate grinned internally. Time to make his play, he thought.

"One odd thing about crucifixion, though—if someone is cut down before the end of the second day, they usually survive and recover. The hands don't necessarily work as well as they once did, but a man can live a fairly normal life after being cut down from the cross, if he gets proper medical attention. So here is my offer. I make it but once. Tell me where your company of brigands hides out, and I will have you cut down from the cross and send you on your way. There is a stream here where you can get water and lay up for a couple of days till you are mobile again. Who knows? After we ride on, perhaps you can cut your companions down as well. That is my offer. It expires at sunset."

"Sheol and Gehenna take you, Roman swine!" shrieked the older man. "I will let the birds feast on my carcass for a week before I betray my companions."

Pilate gave the man a wry grin. "And so they will, my Jewish friend. I imagine you will be singing a different tune when it is too late to do you any good." He turned and gazed at the younger man. "Are you as stubborn and foolish as your companion?" he asked. "Or do you want to live?"

The young man's body racked with sobs. Finally he spoke. "I . . . want . . . to live!" he exclaimed.

"Samuel, you traitor! How dare you!" screamed the leader.

Pilate had two of his legionaries cut the young man down and bring him forward. He could not stand on his punctured ankles, but he was able to keep upright by leaning on the Roman soldiers.

"Now tell me," he said. "How many are in your company, and where do you hole up when you are not out murdering and pillaging?"

"There are about fifty of us," said the young man, still wincing in pain. "Thirty, after this disaster. If you follow this defile northward into the desert, you will see a tall, craggy hill on the right. On the far side of that hill is a cave that goes back several hundred feet. That is where we sleep and store our arms, and hold any prisoners we wish to have ransomed."

Pilate nodded and turned his back. "Thank you, Samuel the Zealot," he said. "Now, as I have promised, I will send you on your way!" He drew his gladius and whirled about, plunging it to the hilt in the man's chest. The Zealot sunk to the ground without a sound, and the two legionaries dragged him over to the fire where the other bodies were burning.

"You Roman dog!" shrieked the elder Zealot from his cross. "You said you would let him go!"

"I said I would send him on his way," said Pilate, "and that is what I did. Quickly and painlessly on his way to wherever it is you people go when you leave the land of the living. He really should have listened better. Did you honestly think I would let a murderer of Roman citizens live?"

"I curse you!" shrieked the rebel. "May you see the face of God and realize the full shame of what you have done! May your wife be a widow, and your children fatherless! May your teeth fall out and your eyes go blind!"

He kept going on in that vein for a good while, until Pilate finally had one of the soldiers climb the upright beam of the cross and cut his tongue out.

# CHAPTER FOURTEEN

A month later, Pilate was back in Caesarea. The remainder of his inspection tour had been a notable success. The same night that the Zealot survivors were crucified, he led his men into the wilderness and found the hideout that the young bandit had told him about. The rebels were in a frenzied preparation to leave, warned of the Roman ambush by the handful who had escaped it, but apparently none of them thought that the Romans would find their hideout and attack them that same night. Advancing under the light of the full moon, Pilate and his men stayed in the shadows until they were only a few hundred yards from the mouth of the cave, with faint torchlight flickering on its walls to mark the fact that it was occupied. The Roman cohort surged up the hillside and stormed in, killing all who resisted—which was just about everyone, except for a handful of women and children, and one terrified captive—a young Roman girl that had been kidnapped from her father's caravan outside Ptolemais a week before. The Jews had treated her roughly and threatened her with death, but she seemed to be physically unharmed.

Pilate had the captives sent to Caesarea, to be shipped from there to the slave markets of Rome. The fifteen of them would not fetch a fortune, but it would be more than enough for him to cover all the costs of the expedition, and pay each soldier that had accompanied him a bonus as well. "Take care of your soldiers and they will take care of you" was a dictum he had learned from Tiberius, who had in turn learned it from Augustus, and so on all the way back to Gaius Marius himself. The young girl was returned to her grateful father, and Pilate had to choke back his emotions as he watched the reunion, knowing he would never see his own daughter again.

After destroying the Zealot stronghold, Pilate and his men had turned southward and visited every other Roman garrison in the small province before returning to Caesarea. Every garrison but one—Pilate wanted to wait and go to Jerusalem with his full legion for the winter season, not with the small guard he had taken on his inspection tour. The season of the Jews' big festivals was coming up soon, and that would be a good time to let them know that they had a new governor.

It was late afternoon when he got back to the governor's residence and found a pile of correspondence waiting for him. A letter from Sullemius was at the top of the stack, so he picked it up first. Reclining on his couch, he opened the scroll and read it at his leisure.

*Old friend*, it began.

> *I cannot tell you how grieved I was to hear of your daughter's savage treatment at the hands of Gaius Caligula! The misery was compounded when the crew of the returning ship told us that she had ended her life on your voyage to that gods-forsaken hellhole that Tiberius has banished you to. There are no words to express my sorrow for one who has been both a partner in crime and a generous patron to me.*

> *If it is any comfort, young Gaius, according to my sources, has had a rough recovery. They say one of his arms may never be quite the same length as the other. It's a shame you did not kill the little worm when you had the chance! The Emperor has become more glum and morose than ever. It seems that he is resigned to accepting Gaius as his heir, but the episode apparently did serve the purpose of removing his illusions about the kind of man Caligula is becoming. He told one member of the Senate that he was raising up a viper for the people of Rome! Agrippina and her other two sons have fallen even further from his favor since you left—it is a matter of open speculation how long it will be before they are banished from Rome.*

> *As for the Emperor himself, he no longer leaves the Isle of Capri. Sejanus is in charge of the city now, and is showing himself to be a petty tyrant as well as a venal mercenary. He actively takes bribes from anyone and everyone, proscribes those who displease him, and is currently planning to marry his longtime lover Livilla. He is boasting that her children (notice I do NOT call them Drusus' children!) will inherit the purple rather than Gaius Caligula. I cannot think of anything he could possibly do that would further cement the wretched Caligula's succession in Tiberius' eyes. The Emperor truly hates his former daughter-in-law, and her brats!*

*None of this is good news for you, I know, but I figured you would rather hear it from a friend than from common gossip. I hope that you are finding Judea tolerable, at least. Your predecessor there, Valerius Gratus, is one of the worst specimens Rome has belched forth on her hapless subjects in our generation. You should be a welcome improvement to the men and to the people of Judea as well. Let me know if there is any way that I can advance your fortunes here in the city. And come home soon—Rome is a very boring place when you are not in it!*

*I remain your faithful client,*

*Quintus Sullemia.*

Pilate nodded at the letter, grateful for its thoughtfulness, but also for its matter-of-fact manner. Sullemius had been a good investment for him, indeed! Looking through the other scrolls, he was surprised to see one bearing the seal of the Emperor himself. He wondered what Tiberius would have to say in light of the circumstances of his departure, and opened it next.

*Lucius Pontius Pilate,*

*I was wrong, you know. I thought Caligula was young enough to retain some childlike innocence, but if it ever existed in him it has long since been slain by the dark spirit that lurks in his breast. It grieves me more than I can say that a loyal client and friend like you should have suffered so much misery at his hands. The death of young Porcia broke my heart when I was told of it.*

*Unfortunately, the young monster is still my heir. There simply is no one else. I know that this must grieve you even further, after what he did, but I am working on him as he recovers from the injuries you inflicted. I am trying to make him see that what he did was not only morally wrong but horrifically impolitic as well, and that the proper thing for a future ruler of Rome to do is make amends as best he can. Right now I do not think he fully understands, but I hope that before I die I can at least persuade him that vengeance against you and your family for his injuries would be against his self-interest. Since true compassion seems to be altogether absent from his breast, that may be the most you—and I—can hope for.*

*In the meantime, I hope that your assignment to Judea is not too unpleasant. Gods know that you can only be an improvement after the wretched Gratus—I only sent him there to get him out of Rome, where his disgusting habits were a constant embarrassment to his father, an old comrade from my youth who has since passed on. Clean the province up as I know you are capable of doing, and perhaps before I go to the land of shades we can look on each other once more. I regret my anger at our parting; in your place I would have done no differently than you.*

*Tiberius Caesar*

Pilate set it aside with a snort of disdain. Nice to know the old dodderer still had a heart, but the affection he once felt for Tiberius was gone. How any man could realize that he had adopted a monster as his heir and not find the moral courage to set him aside was beyond his understanding! He would not go out of his way to alienate Tiberius, and would compose an appropriate reply to the letter, but all eagerness to please the man had left him. From this time forward, Lucius Pontius Pilate would serve only his own interests.

The other letters were routine inquiries from clients, and a short note of sympathy from his brother. All things that could be dealt with later, as far as Pilate was concerned. He stacked the correspondence neatly on the side of his desk and weighted it down with a polished piece of onyx he had found in the Zealots' cave. He was anxious to see his wife.

She was waiting for him in the living quarters, and supper was laid on the table. He gave her a gentle kiss on the forehead and they reclined to dine together, exchanging pleasantries and catching each other up on the news. Porcia was like many wealthy Roman women—forbidden by centuries of custom from pursuing anything like a public career, she followed her husband's fortunes with keen interest, anxious to see him rise and worried that he would fall. The death of their daughter and Pilate's posting to one of the worst duty stations in the Empire had grieved her, but she was proud to see the difference his presence here had already made. She told him how the soldiers were now competing with one another to see who could complete their duties with the greatest thoroughness and alacrity, and described the respect she received when she left their quarters to visit the market or to take a stroll through the city. Pilate, in turn, described his inspection tour and his victory over the Zealots, leaving out the more grisly details.

After supper, the servants were dismissed and Pilate and his wife were alone at last. She came to his arms and he covered her face with kisses.

"I have missed you, husband," she said.

"It grieves me that you have been uprooted from all you know and love, and been sent into exile with me," he replied. "I wish I could have left you safely in Rome."

She held him close and returned his kisses. "I am glad to be where you are, Pilate," she said. "Wherever that may be. After all we have lost, I am just happy that we have never lost each other."

"So tell me," he said as they moved toward their bed, "were our previous efforts to conceive successful?"

"Sadly, no," she said.

"Well, then," he said, lifting her in his arms, "we shall just have to try again."

And so they did. More than once, this time, for good measure.

The next morning Pilate reviewed his troops and was pleased with what he saw. The scraggly bunch of failures and rejects he had met some eight weeks before still wore the same faces, but now they looked and acted like Roman legionaries. He was pleased to see the hulking form of Brutus Appius, cuirass gleaming in the sun, standing ramrod straight at the head of his century. The big man was a natural leader, it seemed, needing only discipline and direction to help him discover his talent for command.

Pilate spoke to them for a few moments, congratulating them on their military bearing, and praising the men who had accompanied him on his inspection tour of the province. The other legionaries regarded them with good-natured envy, jealous that they had been given the opportunity to strike at the hated Zealots. Pilate dismissed the men and met briefly with the centurions, outlining their assignments over the next week. When he was done, Longinus lingered behind for a private word.

"With your permission, Prefect, I should like to return to Capernaum for a short visit with my family," he said.

"By all means!" said Pilate. "But make it a month or so, no more—I will want you with me when I go to Jerusalem for the first time this winter, and there may be other duties to get out of the way before we depart."

"The Feast of Booths is a good time to see the city," said Longinus. "It is one of the more joyful Jewish festivals. I shall make sure I return in plenty of time. I do think that you taught the Zealots a lesson, though! I imagine the roads will be safer than they were earlier this year."

Pilate nodded. "That was my intent," he said. "I will not have it be said that Romans are not safe in my province while I am governor!"

Longinus regarded him quizzically. "If I may be so bold, sir—" he began.

"By all means, Centurion, go on," said Pilate.

"I noticed that when we broke up the ambush, and we put those Zealots to death, that you—well, you seemed to enjoy the process, for lack of a better word," said Longinus.

Pilate's defenses went up. Truth be told, he had enjoyed watching those men scream and squirm on the crosses a great deal. The thing within him that enjoyed inflicting suffering on others was not something he liked to acknowledge, however. Particularly not to a subordinate.

"I have no idea what you are talking about," he said. "I did my duty as a Prefect and an officer of Rome, no more. I enjoy combat, like many soldiers—crossing blades with an enemy is the ultimate way to prove one's mettle and skill. But putting condemned men to death? It is a necessity, a duty; but not one that I particularly relish."

Longinus looked at him sharply, but simply said, "Well, I guess I misunderstood what I saw then. Thank you for your leave, sir, and I look forward to our next mission together."

At this point Pilate returned to his offices. He found a line of people had formed, all anxious to meet with the governor now that he had returned from his inspection tour. He donned his formal toga and seated himself in the curule chair, ordered his lictors to show them in, and waited for them to state their business.

Pilate always prided himself on being courteous and efficient when it came to seeing clients, but he had learned during his time in Spain that the people who called on provincial governors were not the same sort of clientele that Roman Senators normally dealt with. Tax farmers, merchants, speculators, and local citizens or hopeful citizens, each with their own complaints and grievances—all eager to bend the governor's ear and win his favor. It did not take long for the cumulative satisfaction of his victory over the Zealots and successful inspection tour to dissipate into impatience and frustration.

First came two Roman citizens, merchants of the Third Class, each claiming the other had interfered in their business contracts with local winegrowers. Behind them followed a gaggle of Jewish locals, each one claiming the two merchants had threatened them with death and enslavement if they were not awarded exclusive contracts. Pilate listened to their complaints and accusations until he could stand it no more.

"Enough!" he snapped. "I did not come here from Rome to watch as the worst of her citizens plundered a country too poor and fearful to take legal recourse against you!" He looked at the Jews. There were ten of them, all gazing at him with fear, suspicion, and no small amount of loathing. "Each of you tell me how many acres your vineyards cover," he said.

"Forty acres, Your Excellency!" said the first in barely understandable Greek.

"Twenty, sir!" said the next.

Pilate listened to them as they each proclaimed the acreage they owned, and then nodded when they were done.

"Thank you, gentlemen," he said. "Now you, you, you, you, and you— stand behind Licinius here." He indicated the older merchant, a red-faced, gray-haired Roman from Arpinium. "The rest of you, go stand by Cato Quirinius." He gestured at the other merchant, who hailed from the Suburba district of Rome. The puzzled Jews took up their position.

"Now then, *Quirites*," he said, addressing the two citizens by their formal titles, "each of you has five clients whose total acreage is roughly equal. You should each be able to count on an equal harvest of grapes and equal wine production every year. It will be up to you to make your product more competitive than your competition's. "

"Prefect, this is unheard of!" snapped Licinius. "I had contracts with seven of these men, not five!"

185

"And I had contracts with six!" said Cato.

"AND I SAY YOU HAVE FIVE EACH!!" roared Pilate. "Now get out of my office, and do NOT let me hear you complain about each other again, or I will void all your contracts and set you on the first ship back to Rome!" He glared at each of the men intensely, and they scurried out of his office quickly, each followed by their new clients.

Whether it was his voice carrying through the walls, or the frightened expressions of Licinius and Cato, the next few clients finished their business quickly and without bickering. Several of them were the local *publicani*, come to deposit the taxes and tributes they had collected for the Senate with Rome's official representative. Pilate called in his accountant, Silvanus, whom he had barely had time to meet before setting out on his tour of the province, to make sure that their accounts were in order. It appeared that they were, so he ordered Silvanus to deposit the money in the local treasury to be transported to Rome at the end of the month. Next came two of his soldiers, looking hangdog and apologetic, explaining that they had borrowed money from one of the local lenders, who turned out to be charging a much higher interest rate than advertised. The moneylender had trailed them in, shouting that they had entered the contract in good faith and must pay to the last mite. Pilate ordered each soldier to receive ten lashes, and docked their pay by ten denarii a month until the debt was cleared. Then he ordered the moneylender given twenty lashes for extorting from the Emperor's men, and forbade him from loaning money to legionaries again.

So it went for the rest of the day, as the official representative of the Senate and People of Rome heard the complaints and requests of an unending stream of citizens and subjects. Pilate listened, nodded, sympathized, or chastised as the occasion called for. This was the dreariest part of the governor's job, but also one of the most profitable, both financially and politically. At least, it would have been profitable in a decent province, where there was money to spare. After hearing the financial state of both the Roman citizens and the native subjects of the province, he began to understand better why Valerius Gratus had let himself be bribed by the priests in Jerusalem. In a poor, agrarian province with no mineral wealth and few marketable resources other than produce and wool, there was simply not much wealth left for the taking, except for two sources.

186

The Temple was the greatest depository of wealth in the region. Even the poorest among the Jews paid a tithe of their incomes to the support of the Temple every year, and while the priests and acolytes—who were called Levites for some reason Pilate did not yet know—lived pretty well, they did not live extravagantly. No doubt that there was an enormous trove of gold buried there somewhere, from which the priests had brought forth the generous bribes they paid to various members of the Senate annually for the privilege of being allowed to run the province as they saw fit. Even the most venal Roman governor, however, had refused to touch the Temple treasury, knowing of the Jews' fanatical devotion to their religion.

Then there was Herod and his household. The old Herod, known as The Great by his family and retainers, and The Monster by his Jewish subjects, had been richer than Midas and crueler than Lucius Sulla on a bad day. He had put his favorite wife and several of his sons to death before dying of gangrene when Pilate was still a youth, but he had bought the title "King of the Jews" from the Roman Senate, and paid dearly to keep it when his patron Marc Antony was defeated by young Octavian. Herod was survived by four sons, but the Senate had split his empire up between them. The oldest, Herod Antipas, had been denied the authority of "King" although he insisted on using the title. He was entrusted with the tetrarchy of Galilee, which put him in the position of being Pilate's subordinate in the elaborate Roman colonial hierarchy, but as a client of Tiberius, he could still go over Pilate's head to the Senate if the two of them should clash. Rumor had it that Antipas had carefully invested his share of the fortune the old Herod had left him, and had made himself one of the richest men in the region. Pilate had not yet met him, and did not look forward to it particularly, but thought it would be wise to stay in the man's good graces if he could. The last thing Pontius Pilate needed was another enemy!

At the end of the day, Pilate was exhausted. Dealing with petitioners and clients all day was much more tiring than riding on a long patrol or fighting bandits. He left his office behind and headed toward the residence, where Porcia was weaving a tapestry on the loom she had bought a few days before. Unlike many Roman matrons, she enjoyed working with her hands and was quite crafty. She saw the look on his face and came to his side.

"It's a shame we don't have a proper bath here," she said. "But let me show you something!" She led him past their bedchamber to a small corridor that he had always assumed led down to the kitchen. However, when they followed it downstairs, there were two hallways branching from the landing—one indeed went toward the kitchen, but the other ended in a small doorway to the outside. The door opened onto a lovely beach, hidden from the busy seaport to the north by a long rock jetty and some jagged cliffs. Other than the back wall of the governor's palace, no buildings overlooked it, and the sand and boulders stretched south for miles with not a single sign of human habitation. The sand was dazzling in its whiteness and still quite warm, even though the sun was nearing the horizon in the west. It was hard to believe that the busiest seaport in Judea was just on the other side of the jetty and cliffs!

"Care to swim?" she said.

Pilate shrugged out of his tunic and hit the water running. He had always loved the sea, and the warm waters seemed to soak the fatigue right out of his body. He paddled and dove, amazed at how clear the water was. Porcia joined him, and they swam and played in the surf for nearly an hour. The sun was about to set when they both finally turned to the shore. One of the maids was waiting by the doorway with towels and several buckets of fresh water to rinse the salt from their bodies. They both donned clean tunics, and Porcia wrapped a light mantle over hers—the Prefect's wife could not be immodest! Supper was waiting for them in their chambers, and by the time they had finished dining Pilate was so tired he found himself nodding over his food. He kissed his wife an affectionate good night and fell into a deep and dreamless slumber almost as soon as his head hit the pillow.

The next few weeks passed in a similar routine, with the daily demands of the job absorbing much of Pilate's energy. Despite Porcia's best efforts to keep him happy and contented with his home life, he longed to get out of Caesarea and find some sort of task that would get him away from the endless demands of the army of petitioners that crowded his days and haunted his dreams. As the year dragged on toward fall, he began to look forward to traveling to Jerusalem for the festival season.

About eight weeks after he returned from his inspection tour, the military equipment he had ordered from Rome for his legion finally came in. So much of the men's gear was old, worn out, and battered that he had decided to order replacement uniforms and new equipment in an attempt to improve the legion's morale and preparedness. There was also a new set of standards, each equipped with a Roman eagle, a polished bronze shield with a golden profile of Tiberius on it, and the Judean Legion's banner and number, above the traditional "SPQR." Pilate turned the uniform items over to the legion's quartermasters, and took the legion's old standards and placed them in storage while setting the new ones up in the courtyard.

The next morning, he called the entire cohort out to the courtyard and addressed them. "Well, boys, you know that it is almost time to march to Jerusalem for winter quarters, and to keep an eye on the Jews during their various festivals," he said. "But I want us to march into Jerusalem looking like Rome's finest, not like the rejects of the other legions! If your gear is worn out or damaged, report to the quartermaster to receive replacement gear today! Each legionary must sign for whatever equipment he receives, and if any new equipment is damaged or comes up missing, its full price will be deducted from your pay."

The men looked at one another, nodding happily. Longinus had informed Pilate that Valerius Gratus had charged the men full price for damaged or lost gear, and then charged them again for replacements—which were usually worn-out discards that were no improvement on what they had lost. That was one reason there were so many unreported missing uniform pieces when Pilate arrived.

Pilate then nodded to his lictors, who unfurled the new standards and brought them forward. "We will march in under these new standards which I also ordered from Rome. The face of our Emperor will smile on us as we continue to clean up and improve this wretched province!"

The men cheered at the sight of the new standards, and Pilate called on the centurions to disperse the men to their day's work. He thought no more about the changes he had made until Cassius Longinus reported in for duty a few days later. The *Primus Pilus* was discussing the upcoming move to Jerusalem when he spotted the standards and froze in mid-sentence.

"Great gods, you are not taking those with us to Jerusalem, are you?" he asked Pilate.

"Of course," answered the Prefect. "Along with the new uniforms and gear, I thought that the new standards would help the men look and feel more like true representatives of Rome."

"Prefect, you cannot carry those into Jerusalem! The whole province will rise up in revolt!" gasped Longinus.

"What on earth do you mean, Cassius?" asked Pilate. "They are no different from the standards every other legion marches under!"

"In every province but this!" said Longinus. "The Jews have a horror of what they call 'graven images'—any carving or representation of any person or living creature. Look at their architecture and coins. There are geometric designs aplenty, and inscriptions, but no faces, or animals. Such things are absolutely forbidden to them. And to carry such images into their holy city—they will view it as a direct affront!"

Pilate scowled. He understood the diplomatic aspects of his job, but this was too much! Roman legions marching without their standards? Ridiculous! He answered Longinus angrily: "They can prepare to be affronted then! I paid for these out of my own salary to try and restore a little pride to a legion that has been neglected and badly managed for years. I have already shown them to the men, and to put them away now and restore the tattered old standards that do not even have Caesar's image on them would be an insult to the pride of these legionaries and to the Senate and People of Rome!"

Longinus sighed deeply. "Sir," he said, "you asked me to be your liaison with the locals, and to give you my candid opinions on your decisions. I mean no disrespect, but this is a mistake that will inflame the people against Rome, and against you."

Pilate thought for a moment. Surely the man was exaggerating. Finally, he thought of a compromise.

"The fortress in Jerusalem where the troops are posted is closed to locals, and enclosed with high walls, is it not?" he asked.

Longinus nodded. "It's not formally closed, but no religious Jew will set foot across the threshold of a Gentile's house, so it might as well be," he said. "The castle of Antonia is securely walled and hidden from the city's view."

"Then we will carry the standards furled and covered," said Pilate, "entering the city at night and not erecting them until we are inside the walls of our own compound. The men will have the new standards before them every time they muster in the morning, and the Jews will be none the wiser."

Longinus shook his head. "It might work," he said, "but I doubt it. Many Jews who are not as particular about the Law and customs still enter the fortress, and all they have to do is complain to the priests and your game is up."

Pilate shrugged. "We'll never know unless we try!" he said.

Two weeks later, the legion set out for its winter quarters in Jerusalem. Two hundred men were left in Caesarea to maintain the Roman presence there and keep law and order in the city and its environs, but fifteen hundred men set out with Pilate toward the holy city of the Jews. The Feast of Booths was coming up soon, followed by the Day of Atonement and then the wintertime Feast of Lights. Come springtime the Jews would celebrate their holiest day, Passover, at which time the population of Jerusalem would be increased almost fourfold above its normal levels, as Jews from all across the Roman world converged on the city to commemorate the Exodus from Egypt some fourteen hundred years before. After Passover, the concentration of troops in the city would be dispersed for the summer, leaving only the standing garrison of 500 men inside the capital. As for Pilate, even during the winter he would divide his time between Caesarea and Jerusalem, riding back and forth with an armed escort to take care of business, first in one place, and then in the next.

The legion was smartly turned out as Pilate mounted his horse and rode down their ranks. The new standards gleamed in the sun, as did the uniforms of the two decorated legionaries who bore them. Pilate addressed the men in formal terms, as befit a Prefect of Rome.

"Legionaries!" he shouted. "It is time to make our annual journey into the capital city of the Jews, where we will display the might of Rome and keep the peace during their festival season. I would remind each of you that you are a representative of Rome in their eyes. How you treat them is how

Rome treats them, and how they perceive you, they perceive Rome. This province is ours by right of treaty and by right of conquest, but our stay here can be made easier or more difficult by how we conduct ourselves. I would urge every man among you to show restraint and respect where it is warranted—but should it become necessary to remind the Jews who their masters are, to act with strength, honor, and the proper amount of force. We are here to prevent fights, not to start them—but if someone else starts a fight, we are also here to finish it—and make sure they have no appetite for another!"

The men were regarding him with a respect that made his breast swell with pride. He had been here for just a few months, but these troops were his now. It was a good feeling, one that he had missed since leaving Spain. As long as one led troops bravely and treated them with the right mixture of respect and paternal regard, Roman soldiers were as loyal a clientele as any politician could ask for. But keeping that loyalty meant showing enough respect for the men to explain what you wanted them to do and why—a secret of command that Gaius Marius had passed down to the Caesars, and Pilate had learned from Tiberius.

"So in the interest of keeping the peace, and not starting trouble with our Jewish subjects, we will furl our standards as we pass through their territory, and as we pass through their holy city. Even though these standards are ours by right to display as we march, nevertheless we shall show respect to these locals by not displaying images they find offensive. We shall unfurl them when we are inside the castle of Antonia, our little plot of Roman soil inside Jerusalem, where no Jew will see them. So shall we demonstrate Rome's tolerance and forbearance for the religious customs of our subject peoples! Now let us march—and conduct yourselves well!"

So they set out southward, moving steadily toward Joppa over the course of the day. The road connecting the two cities was smooth and well-maintained, and there was a light breeze rolling in from the sea. Although it was thirty-two miles from Caesarea, the men reached the city walls well before dark. Pilate directed them to a large plain just east of the city, where a small brook flowed toward the sea. There they pitched a light camp and bedded down for the night after the cooks produced a generous supper of lamb stew, salted fish, and local fruits and almonds. Pilate sipped a large goblet of watered wine and reflected on the next day's march. It was over forty miles from Joppa to Jerusalem, and the road was steeper than the previous day's route had been. But his men were in good spirits and excellent physical condition, and he figured with one good rest stop in the middle of the day, they should reach the walls of the city between the ninth hour and midnight—well after dark, in other words. It would be child's play to bring the furled and shrouded standards into the Fortress of Antonia without anyone noticing. Pleased with himself for coming up with a plan that preserved Rome's pride while honoring local custom, Pilate retired to his tent and fell asleep instantly.

# CHAPTER FIFTEEN

The first few days in Jerusalem were unremarkable enough. The city was thronged with Jews from all over the Roman world, come together to celebrate their Feast of Booths. They camped in small tents or huts all over the city and outside its walls, sang strange wailing tunes that they called Psalms, and threw festive dinners for one another. Above all, they sacrificed—goats, bulls, and rams were burned by the hundreds in their Temple every day in tribute to their invisible God. For the most part, they were well-behaved—Pilate kept his patrols out on the streets every day, and other than the routine apprehension of cutpurses and the occasional drunken brawl, there were no incidents.

On the third day there, he received a courtesy visit from Herod Antipas. Antipas was about fifty or so by this time, although it was hard to be sure of his age beneath his rich, black beard and long curly hair. Like most Eastern potentates, he set great store by appearances. And, like most Eastern potentates Pilate had dealt with in the past, he was also a condescending, arrogant blowhard. At least, he told Pilate, he had no objection to the Prefect patrolling his tetrarchy to put down the Zealots. Herod acknowledged that he had no luck in that department.

"The locals have no respect for my soldiers," he said. "The Samaritans are commendably loyal, but the Jews have always hated them."

Herod seemed to think himself absolutely indispensable to Rome's control of Judea, and did not mind saying so. In fact, he said so at every opportunity.

"My father united and pacified this province at a great cost of blood and treasure," Herod droned. "He was mad by the end of his rule, of course—the people hated him and he knew it! On his deathbed he gave an order to arrest the elders and rabbis in every village of Judea and put them to death as soon as word of his own demise was made known—that way, he thought, there would be genuine grief at his passing!" Herod took a drink of wine from his solid gold goblet, rings flashing on his hand as he did so. "I went along with everything he said at the end, knowing that he could have me put to death for the slightest misstep! He had one of his most loyal servants flogged to death the day before he died, and made me hold him upright so that he could watch. I was quite relieved when he breathed his last, I can tell you! My first act as his heir was to countermand the executions he had ordered. I began my rule by saving lives, hoping the people would get the idea that I was not my father."

"Were you successful?" asked Pilate.

"Yes and no," said Herod. "The people do not think of me as a monster, as they did my father, but frankly they don't fear me as much as they did him. My Idumean blood tells against me! They say that no true King of the Jews will ever be accepted by God unless he is of the line of David—a line that has long since fallen into obscurity. The scattered descendants of the kings of Israel live as humble peasants all across the region of Galilee, and are as devoid of political ambition as can be. So I rule as a client king, obedient to Rome, and keep the peace here as best I can."

"Until the Messiah comes?" asked Pilate.

"You've been talking to the common folk!" said Herod. "They still hold to the belief that a great deliverer of David's line will come someday. Every so often a pretender will spring up and claim a great following, but they all come to nothing sooner or later, accomplishing nothing but a disturbance of the peace. I remember near the end of my father's life, some astrologers came to his court with a claim that the "King of the Jews" had been born in some tiny village or other. My father listened patiently to their discussion, sent them on their way, and had them followed to the little village where this alleged king had been born. As soon as those magi returned to their homeland, he sent his soldiers into the village and they slaughtered every male infant there. I am not as bloodthirsty as my father was, but I have little patience for rabble-rousers who would plunge my kingdom into war!"

"Neither does Rome, King Herod!" said Pilate, and raised his glass. "To peace!" he said.

The King of the Jews departed not long after, and Pilate breathed a sigh of relief. The man was quite insufferable. But he was a charmer compared to old Annas, the former High Priest, who dropped by not long after.

This audience was different, because Annas would not lower himself to cross the threshold of Pilate's palace. Instead, the governor seated himself in the *bema* seat overlooking a paved courtyard that opened onto the street, and the High Priest stood on the edge of the street some twenty feet away, two servants holding a canopy over his balding head to keep the sun off of him.

"My son-in-law says that you refused the stipend we generously offered you upon your arrival," rasped the old man. His bushy eyebrows and glittering black eyes gave him an expression of perpetual irritation.

"I am an employee of Caesar, not of the Temple," Pilate said. "While I intended no offense, I did not want to give the impression that I was for sale, to you or anyone else."

Annas shrugged. "Everyone is for sale at some price, Prefect," he said. "Your price may not be in gold, but that does not mean you do not have one."

Pilate was offended, but kept his tone cool and diplomatic. "It seems to me, Annas, that we both want the same thing. Peace, order, and prosperity—those are the things that make a province easy to govern and religion easy to maintain. I think we can work together to make those things happen here in Judea without money changing hands between us."

"I hope it will be so," said Annas. "But remember one thing, Prefect— the Temple is the most powerful force in Judea. It commands the loyalty of the people, and we priests are the Temple. We are the custodians of the laws of God, and the people will do what we say. We have the ear of Caesar and of the Senate, so if you cross us, you will regret it!"

"I have known Tiberius Caesar for nearly thirty years, your holiness," said Pilate contemptuously. "Judea is nothing to him—just a festering, impoverished province that has historically been more trouble than it is worth! If I were you, I would not try his patience! Not if you value your precious temple as much as you seem to!"

The old priest harrumphed at that and departed. Pilate regretted ending the interview on such a negative note, but the old man's smugness infuriated him. He was not sure which he found the most objectionable— Annas' scarcely concealed hostility, or Herod's unctuous overestimation of his own worth. At any rate, Pilate's attitude was soured enough that he decided to leave Jerusalem and make a quick trip back to Caesarea. The festival was nearly over anyway. Leaving Longinus in charge of the legionaries in Jerusalem, Pilate rode with a small escort and reached Caesarea late in the evening. He had supper with his wife and spent the evening catching up on his correspondence. There was another letter from Sullemius, which he enjoyed reading, even though the news was mostly negative.

*Esteemed Prefect*, it began.

> *Things are on a melancholy path here in Rome. Sejanus continues to govern on behalf of Tiberius, but his rule has become less corrupt and more malevolent of late. Treason trials have started up again! Any man may be accused, and once accused, he is fair game for anyone in the city—even a slave!—to kill. His property is taken over by the State, with a percentage of its worth going to the person who killed him or turned him in. Wealthy senators are disappearing left and right—some have been killed, and some are fleeing to avoid the wrath of Tiberius' grasping regent. Sejanus is putting the confiscated properties up for public auction, but not before he helps himself to the finest villas and richest lands. He is also not even bothering to hide his affair with Livilla anymore. The old-timers are saying that Rome has not been so gripped with fear since the days of Sulla's proscriptions a hundred years ago.*

> *Tiberius sits on Capri with his adopted brat and grows more gloomy and paranoid every day. They say he has Caligula taste all of his food for him now, so great is his fear of poison. His temper is increasingly irascible too; he even struck one of the children who danced for him not long ago. I doubt he will ever return to Rome.*

> *I know that your family has had enough grief to deal with in the last year, Pilate, but I thought you would prefer to hear this news from a friend. Your father-in-law, Gaius Proculus Porcius, is dead. Two of his closest friends were tried for treason and all their lands confiscated several weeks ago; this news, along with the death of Porcia Minor, was too much for him. He climbed into a hot bath and opened a vein. He had been dead for several hours before the servants found him. I am sorry, Pilate. He was a good man, a rarity among politicians. I hope this finds you and your wife doing well.*

*You have had enough ill fortune for one year. Take care of yourself,
old friend.*

*Your client, Quintus Sullemia*

Pilate bowed his head in sorrow for a moment. Proculus had been his
friend long before he had become his father-in-law; he was a hard-working
and conscientious Senator and a credit to his class. After a lifetime of labor
and service, he deserved better than to slit his wrists open in despair because
of a corrupt, venal sycophant! He thought for just a moment about how
different things in Rome might have been had he not fallen from Tiberius'
favor and been banished to Judea. Surely he could have compassed Sejanus'
downfall by now—or, failing that, at least curbed his horrible excesses! But
there was no use recriminating. What was done was done. With a heavy
heart, Pilate went to bear the grim news to his wife.

She bore it stoically, although he could see the pain in her eyes. That
night he held her in his arms for a solid hour before she finally drifted off to
sleep, and although she did not sob once, he could feel the hot tears dripping
onto his chest. He wondered how much more grief the gods would put his
family through. But then he reflected on his own overweening pride, and
realized that he had been guilty of hubris. How much, he wondered, of his
family's suffering had he caused? It was not a comfortable line of thought,
and when he faded off to sleep he did not rest well.

It was a fish merchant, Pilate later found out, who caused his first serious
conflict with the Jewish people. The merchant had been delivering food to
the Fortress Antonia in Jerusalem when he saw the legion's standards
displayed above the courtyard. The man was not particularly religious, but
he mentioned it to one of the Galileans who had come to sacrifice at the
Temple. The Galilean was unwilling to cross the threshold of the fortress in
order to get a direct look, but he climbed a tree so that he could get a quick
peek over the wall. What he saw sent him scrambling to the Temple district,
and within an hour there was a furious, shouting mob of Jews congregated
outside the barracks.

Longinus discovered their grievance quickly enough, and some of the
Jews from the Galilean hill country recognized him as one who respected
their religion. He explained that he could not remove the standards on his
own authority, but told them to take their complaint to the governor in

Caesarea. It was a measure of their outrage that several thousand of them set out at once to make the forty-mile march. Longinus sent a courier on a fast horse to warn Pilate of their approach.

So it was that after one night back in Caesarea, Pilate was woken early the next morning by a dust-covered, breathless legionary who downed half a bucket of water from the well while Pilate read Longinus' letter. It was short and to the point:

*Prefect Pilate:*

*Remember that I warned you bringing the Emperor's image into Jerusalem was a disastrous idea! All it took was one half-Jewish merchant catching a glimpse of it, and the whole city was up in arms. The mob was big enough that if I had tried to subdue them, most of my men would have been killed and the effort might well have failed. I told the leaders of the crowd that I lacked the authority to remove the images, and that they must take their complaint directly to you. Several thousand of them set out immediately; I imagine the forty-mile walk through the desert regions west of Jerusalem will make about half of them turn back. Hopefully, when they get there, they will be exhausted, thirsty, and easier for you to deal with than they would have been for me. You probably do not want to hear my advice, but I offer it because I believe it is best for Rome, this province, and you—remove the standards from Jerusalem at once! Otherwise, there will be bloodshed.*

*Cassius Longinus*

Pilate cursed the Jews and their foolish superstitions as he read the letter. As much as it annoyed him to admit it, Longinus was probably right—he would have done better to leave the standards at Caesarea. But now the battle lines were drawn. The eagles and profiles of Tiberius were now more than just military symbols—they stood for Pilate's personal credibility as governor. To give in—to admit defeat and remove them—would deal a blow to the prestige and respect he had worked hard to build since coming to Judea. On the other hand, to leave them in Jerusalem would mean a continual inflammation of the already volatile population. What should he do?

He set his scouts out to watch for the arrival of the mob, and placed the two cohorts on alert, ordering them to don full combat uniform with weapons at the ready. They arrived at dawn the second day after he got the letter from Longinus, about two and a half thousand or so, looking tired and bedraggled but determined nonetheless. He was surprised to see the priest Caiaphas in the lead.

Forewarned, Pilate was ready for them. The gates of the fortress at Caesarea were closed, and archers were posted on the wall at either side. A small platform had been extended from the top of the wall above the gate, so that Pilate could stand in full view of the mob. He had donned his formal toga, the purple trim indicating his rank as a consular and prefect. He stepped out onto the platform, ramrod straight, right foot slightly in front of the other, his rod of office tucked neatly into the crook of his elbow, with six lictors standing like statues on either side of him. He waited till the crowd was 100 yards from the gate to reveal himself, and as they came to the looming, silent walls and silent barred gate, the crowd's eyes were drawn upward to Pilate.

"People of Judea, why do you come here in such numbers? What is your intent?" Pilate asked in a clear, firm voice.

Caiaphas stepped forward and spoke. "Governor, you have disdained our faith and defiled our holy city by bringing graven images within its walls. We ask most humbly that you remove the standards and embossed shields from the Fortress of Antonia, lest our God be stirred to wrath by such open contempt for His laws!"

Pilate listened as the mob muttered their agreement with the priest. He waited until their comments died down and attention was focused back on him, and then spoke out.

"No disrespect was intended to your God or your temple," he said. "Out of respect for your traditions, I kept the standards furled and the shields covered as we proceeded through your territory. Only when we were inside the fortress did I allow them to be displayed, in a place where only Romans would see them. The Fortress of Antonia is owned by the Senate and People of Rome, as part of the treaty we signed with Herod the Great. That piece of property is, for all practical purposes, a small plot of Roman soil, not a part of Jerusalem or Judea. What Rome chooses to display for her citizens to worship is none of your business!"

The crowd howled in protest. A few threw stones or dirt clods at the locked gate. Finally Caiaphas stepped forward and spoke again.

"It is true that the fortress is an outpost of Rome," he said. "But even if it is a small parcel of Roman soil, it is still within the walls of our sacred city. None of your noble predecessors ever displayed such contempt for our laws, Pontius Pilate! All we ask is that you honor the precedent set by previous governors and keep your graven images here in Caesarea. Do not profane the city where David and Solomon ruled, where our sacred Temple stands! Do not affront the God of Israel in the place where his seat on earth resides!"

The mob began crying out "Great is the God of Israel!" in a constant chant, and Pilate stood, still as a stone, listening as their voices swelled around him. Gradually the crowd fell silent, and he spoke again.

"People of Jerusalem," he said, and drew himself up to his full height. "GO HOME! The standards of my legion are placed where only my legion can see them. They are not meant to be an affront to you or to your God. I have respected your traditions by placing them where your eyes will never light upon them unless you trespass on Roman soil. You have no grievance. Depart!" With that he spun on his heel and returned to his quarters, even as the crowd took up their chant again. They kept it up for hours. He ordered his sentries to watch them and look for any threat or outbreak of violence, but the crowd of Jews remained camped outside the gate all day and into the evening.

Pilate was fuming. They were challenging his authority, and the authority of Rome. It was intolerable! He issued an order through his soldiers that no merchant was to sell food or deliver any water to the mob. Let them starve outside the gates!

The business of the city and its garrison continued more or less as usual that day, but everyone was aware of the drama unfolding outside the locked gate. The Jewish inhabitants of the city muttered among themselves and cast dark glances at the soldiers as they marched by on their daily rounds. A few defied Pilate's order and ran food out to the crowd as the day wore on, but Pilate ordered the sentries not to let them back into the city. His blood was up and he was frankly hoping for an outbreak of violence so that he could have the whole lot of them put to death. He had just begun to get his legion whipped into shape, and now this? His patience with the Jews was gone.

That night, as darkness fell, they took up their chant again. They had apparently found a well or cistern somewhere—or perhaps it was just the relief of the cooler night air on their parched throats—but the defiant cry: "Great is the God of Israel!" carried through the walls of the fortress and even into Pilate's bedchamber. Not even Porcia's attentions could drive the noise from his head, and long after they fell silent it echoed in his dreams.

The mob was still there the next morning, so Pilate donned his toga and stepped out once more. Caiaphas the priest cried up to Pilate: "We will remain here, Prefect, until the graven images are removed from our city! Do not think a night or two under the stars will change our minds. Our ancestors wandered the desert for forty years in order to reach this Holy Land!"

Pilate scowled. "People of Jerusalem, once more I ask of you: GO HOME! My patience is limited, and your provocations grow tiresome. No harm has been done to any of you. The standards stay where they are. If you are still here tomorrow, I will not ask you to leave. I will make you leave, or stain the sand with your blood. Now go!"

As the day progressed, it became more apparent that they were not going to leave. They stood outside the gates, periodically taking up their chant again. At sunset Pilate met with his centurions and told them his plan.

"Tomorrow," he said, "three of you—Titus, Brutus, and Marcus—will lead your centuries outside the city gate and surround the mob on three sides. They are tired, thirsty, and weak from exposure. Leave the eastern edge of the mob open, so they can only move toward Jerusalem. Upon my mark, your men will draw their blades and advance upon the Jews. Give them every chance to get moving and get out of your way. If they start toward Jerusalem, let them go. If they stand their ground, kill the ones in the front rank first. I imagine the sight of blood will motivate them to go home pretty quickly. I want no more deaths than are necessary, but don't hesitate to kill if they refuse to move!"

The next morning Pilate did not don his toga. Instead, he pulled on his helmet and cuirass and girded on his gladius. He wanted there to be no doubt about his intentions. The three centuries, and their officers, were waiting for him in the courtyard. He went over their orders one more time, and then sent them out. They exited the fortress by the north gate and marched in perfect formation to the mob of Jews. One century took its position in front of them, backs to the barred city gate. The other two flanked them on the north and south sides. Drawn up in battle array, blades glittering in hand, they stood stock-still as Pilate stepped out onto the platform.

He looked at the crowd. They were a sorry lot—fatigue and dehydration written into every line of their faces. All that was needed was that last push, he thought, and they would break.

"People of Jerusalem!" he said. "Twice I have told you to go home, and twice you have refused. Now I do not ask—I demand. My soldiers are prepared to kill every last one of you if you do not comply. I have told you repeatedly that our standards were not placed in the fortress to offend your god or your traditions. Your lives went on as they always had before you knew they were there. Return to those lives now, or see them spilled out on the sand before you. Legionaries—ADVANCE!"

Blades lowered, the Roman soldiers stepped toward the crowd. Every eye went to Caiaphas the priest. What would he do? Pilate had already told the soldiers that, if it came to bloodshed, the priest must be the first to die. He locked eyes with Caiaphas as a burly legionary stepped directly in front of the priest.

It was the moment of truth. Caiaphas looked at the naked steel, just a yard before him, and looked up at Pilate again. Then he slowly sank to his knees and bared his neck to the blade. Seconds later, the man next to him did the same. One by one, twenty-five hundred Jews fell to their knees and offered their bodies to Roman steel. Pilate's jaw dropped. This was the one outcome he had never expected!

His mind raced. The brute within him wanted to tell his men to strike—to cut down every man, woman, and child in the crowd. But he knew that such an action would blacken his name, and the name of Rome, for eternity. Not only that, it would probably spark a rebellion that would end Rome's rule over Judea. He had no choice.

"Sheathe your weapons!" he ordered. Caiaphas lifted his head and looked at the Roman prefect, his eyes dancing with victory. Pilate was furious, but he knew he was beaten. "Out of respect for your laws and traditions, I will return the standards to Caesarea. Do not try my patience again!"

The hateful cry resumed, and followed him as he stormed back into the fort.

"Great is the God of Israel! Great is the God of Israel! GREAT IS THE GOD OF ISRAEL!!!"

# CHAPTER SIXTEEN

Pilate kept a low profile for the next couple of months. He had been humiliated—a sensation he had not felt in a long, long time—and he did not want to give those who had beaten him a chance to gloat. He drilled his soldiers till they were exhausted, tended his correspondence and official duties, and avoided casual contact with everyone that he could. It was an unhappy existence, and it made him an unhappy man. To counter the depression that gripped him, he took to drinking more than he ever had before. However, he discovered that over-indulgence in alcohol made it much harder to control the savage creature that lurked within him—when he was in his cups, his natural instinct for cruelty tended to come to the fore, as a couple of his soldiers learned to their intense regret!

The only bright spot during that dreadful Judean autumn was the news that Porcia had conceived. Pilate's gloom was lifted for a few days, and he even threw a banquet for his officers and all Roman citizens visiting Caesarea. But, a week after the party, a letter from Tiberius arrived. It was short and to the point:

> *Gaius Julius Tiberius Caesar, Princeps and Imperator, to Prefect Lucius Pontius Pilate, Proconsul of Judea; greetings!*
>
> *My sources tell me, dear Pilate, that you have done an admirable job in whipping the Judean legion into shape and have led a successful campaign against the Zealots who have been plaguing the land. This, of course, is the kind of performance that I have come to expect from you in the past. What I had not expected, and what is most vexing to me, is your blatant disregard for the religious beliefs of the Jews I sent you to govern. I need not remind you that Judea is a most troubled province, prone to rebellion at the slightest provocation. Please endeavor to be more diplomatic in your future dealings with the Jews. NO GRAVEN IMAGES are to be displayed in Jerusalem at any time, under any circumstances.*
>
> *The High Priest is Rome's partner in governing the province, and is instrumental in keeping the peace. Please treat his wishes with*

*greater respect in the future. I do not expect to have to communicate with you again on this subject. It pains me to take this tone with an old friend. Do not pain me again.*

Pilate cursed Tiberius in three different languages as he rolled the scroll up and slid it into a small compartment of his desk. After all he had suffered at the Emperor's hands, the thought that Tiberius would take the side of the Jews against Pilate was infuriating. But there was nothing he could do—at this point, speaking in his own defense would merely exacerbate the matter. Pilate was bored—colossally, incredibly bored. After years of being at the epicenter of Roman politics, engaging in that drive to excel in all things that lay at the core of every Roman nobleman's being, finding himself exiled to this lonely backwater was the worst punishment he could imagine. He looked long and hard at the full wineskin sitting on the table nearby. It was not yet noon. Part of him longed to drain that bottle and then three more, but Pilate knew the fate that awaited him if he gave in to that temptation too often. He had seen too many good men destroyed by their fondness for the bottle. He got up, walked to the window, and hurled the wineskin out into the courtyard, where it burst apart on the flagstones. Two legionaries looked up, startled at the sudden noise.

Pilate forced himself to smile. "As you were, men," he said. Then he returned to his table and wrote a short letter to Tiberius, ignoring the contretemps over the standards and instead informing him of the state of the province, and of his wife's condition. Then he wrote a longer letter to Sullemius, pouring out more of his frustrations to the client who had become the closest friend he had.

*Lucius Pontius Pilate, Proconsul of Judea, to Quintus Sullemia, loyal client, pirate, and scoundrel –*

*I don't suppose you feel a hankering for travel, do you? My existence in this blighted province is driving me mad with boredom! But, upon reflection, I suppose that I need you to continue being my eyes and ears in Rome too much to have you come here for such a frivolous purpose as keeping me sane! Thank you for letting me know about events in Rome; keep your eye on Sejanus for me—it is a shame I am not there to try and rein him in. It seems that his power has utterly gone to his head. I wonder, though, how much of this reign of terror is his own doing, and how much of it is that of Tiberius himself? Caesar has always been resentful of the Senate, and it seems as if his current campaign is designed to stifle opposition within that body as much as anything.*

*I suppose you have heard that I am now in even worse graces with the Emperor than I was before my exile to this latrine of a province. The Jewish priests got all up in arms over my legion carrying an eagle standard and shields with Tiberius' image on them into Jerusalem, their "holy city." They threw up such a protest that I eventually had to remove the standards and shields. But, not content with that victory, someone—probably a sly priest named Caiaphas who is angling to replace his father-in-law as High Priest—reported my offense to the old man on Capri, who sent me a very curt letter urging me to be more sensitive to local concerns. So now my return to Rome seems more like a dream than ever.*

*On to more positive matters! Months after the death of our dear Porcia Minor, my wife has conceived again. Please take the enclosed gold and go to the Campus Martus, and have the priestesses offer prayers to Lucina and Vagitanus, and all the other gods and goddesses who protect expectant women, that she may be safely delivered of a son and heir, or at the least of a healthy daughter. The death of our only child has weighed very heavily on her, and I would see her smile again.*

*In the meantime, may Fortuna favor you in all you do, as she seems to have forgotten about me. Keep your daggers sharp, your eyes open, and your patron informed!*

Autumn gave way to winter—at least according to the calendar; Judea's climate altered little with the seasons. Pilate kept himself busy, ordering the troops about and occasionally leading a punitive raid after the bands of Zealots who occasionally attacked caravans and travelers. The Zealots, however, had become more cautious, and he was unable to duplicate the success of his initial encounter with them. When he did apprehend some of them, it was usually two or three at a time instead of an entire band.

In Jerusalem, the Sanhedrin voted to renew Caiaphas' authority as High Priest for the next five years. The Sanhedrin—the Jewish equivalent of

Rome's Senate—submitted his name to Pilate for token approval, but Pilate could not come up with a reason for refusing their choice that did not appear spiteful, so he signed off on the extension of his enemy's tenure in office, and even sent a curt letter of congratulations in an effort to seem at least somewhat more diplomatic.

Spring came early in Judea, and brought with it most of the region's annual rainfall. Pilate went on another inspection tour of the province, but this time no military opportunities presented themselves. Things seemed to have settled down somewhat, and while this boded well for Rome, Pilate found it depressing. He feared that he might well lose his martial edge if he were not allowed a chance to use his skills soon! So he drilled and trained with the soldiers in the courtyard and watched as his wife's belly swelled with the new life growing inside her, and prayed to the gods of Rome that he did not entirely believe in to spare her life and that of his child. He did not even bother to attend the Jews' greatest festival, Passover, unwilling to face the smirks and mocking glances that he was sure would come his way when he returned to Jerusalem.

It was in the first month of summer, named for Juno, that word came in from the southern frontier. The Skenite Arabs, long enemies of the sons of Israel, had come raiding up from the desert and burned and looted two towns in southern Judea. This was a crisis that demanded a forceful response, and Pilate led three cohorts in pursuit of the nomadic raiders, leaving Longinus in command of the garrison at Caesarea. The Arab tribesmen proved to be an elusive quarry, and the king of the Skenites, Aretas, steadfastly denied any knowledge of the attackers. It took a combination of bribery and dogged pursuit through the scorching sands of the Arabian Peninsula, but Pilate finally cornered the band of about 400 at a large oasis near the Red Sea. His men were tired and thirsty, and their enemies were between them and the water they craved. The sun was an hour from setting, and the raiders had already pitched their tents and tied their horses up for the evening.

Pilate sent his single squadron of cavalry to drive off the enemy's horses, and then launched his legionaries at their quarry. The Arabs realized quickly that they could not outride the Romans when half their horses were already gone, and instead they charged at Pilate's men, their curved scimitars flashing in the red sun of evening. It was the worst mistake they could have made—while they resembled whirling dervishes, the steady, disciplined formations of the Romans made their wild, flailing attacks ineffective. By the time it was fully dark, nearly 300 of them lay dead and 50 had been made captive.

Inside their tents, Pilate's men recovered a huge store of stolen loot and twelve terrified Jewish girls kidnapped during the raid. He made sure that the men kept their hands off the frightened girls, instead turning them on the unfortunate women who had been camp followers of the Arabs. The leader of the raiders, a hulking brute named Halijah, he ordered crucified in the midst of the burned-out camp, while the others—warriors, women, and children—were bound and tied together, destined for the slave pens in Caesarea. The treasure from the camp was divided up, with Pilate taking a quarter of it, another quarter going into the provincial treasury, and the rest being split among the men. It was not a fortune, but it was a tidy amount all the same, and he would keep another twenty percent from the sale of the slaves. All in all, he thought as they began the long march back to Judea, the province was nowhere near as rich as Spain, but it was not proving to be as impoverishing as he had feared it would.

The soldiers were in good spirits on the return journey—they were able to take a more subdued pace, since they were not in pursuit of a quick-moving enemy this time, and the men were thinking of how to spend their share of the spoils when they got back to camp. But he still made sure that they set up a proper fortified camp each night, and kept careful watch. The Skenites were not ones to let an assault on their territory go unpunished, any more than the Romans would. As they neared the southern border of Judea, he sent out small patrols of his Jewish auxiliaries to watch for any pursuit.

Sure enough, not far from the two burned-out villages, they were attacked a second time, by some two thousand Skenite warriors. Forewarned, Pilate had sent word ahead to the nearest Jewish settlements that a battle was in the offing, and the Jews, who hated the Skenites even more than they hated Rome, quickly assembled a militia force at least as big as Pilate's. Just as his soldiers fully engaged the enemy, the Jewish vigilantes attacked them in the rear, and the Skenites' counterattack was wiped out in less than an hour. Twelve hundred lay dead, and perhaps half that many were taken captive before the remainder fled back into the desert. Pilate left half of the captives to the tender mercies of their Jewish enemies, and also returned the captive girls he had rescued to their people, who thanked him profusely. The rest of the captives were shackled beside the other prisoners and led back to Caesarea, where Pilate was greeted by Jews and Romans alike as a conquering hero. As he returned the waves of the crowd outside the city gates, he felt better than he had since arriving in Judea. The grief, rage, and depression of the last year were lifted from his shoulders as if by magic.

But as he scanned the faces that greeted him, he grew alarmed. Porcia was not standing on the wall outside their quarters, nor was she anywhere among the Roman citizens that cheered him from just inside the gate. He spurred his horse into the courtyard and dismounted, ignoring the cheers and flowers that were being thrown at him. Had it been nine months already? He added the weeks up inside his head and realized that she had been due two weeks ago. Jupiter! What if she had lost the child? What if—?

Suddenly Longinus stood beside him, smiling and clapping him on the shoulder. "Welcome back, Prefect! Your son is anxious to meet you!" he said with a smile.

Pilate sagged with relief. "My son?" he asked. "What about—"

"She's fine," said the Primus Pilus Centurion. "The midwife said the delivery was difficult, and she bled a great deal. But her strength has been returning steadily, and she eats ravenously—as does your son. Adonai has been gracious to you."

Pilate almost wept with relief. "Adonai, Lucina, Vagitanus, or Persephone herself!" he laughed. "At this point, I will make offerings to them all! This is the best news I could have had, Cassius! See the slaves to the market and the men properly billeted in the barracks. I want to see my child!" He took the steps upstairs two at a time.

Porcia was sitting up in her bed, attended by a maidservant. A plump, healthy baby boy with a jet-black thatch of hair was nursing at her breast. She looked up at him and smiled with a genuine joy that he had not seen on her face in a year or more. He embraced her gently and kissed her forehead—while her face was radiating happiness and satisfaction, he could tell from her pallor and the lines under her eyes that the delivery had not been an easy one.

"Are you well, wife?" he asked when he could speak.

"I will be," she said. "He did not come into the world easily! But I was determined to bring him here, and to watch him grow up. I am getting stronger every day, but I did not feel able to stand long enough to watch your entrance. The scouts brought word of your victories to us yester eve. Well done, husband! Even old Tiberius will have nothing to complain of when he hears how you punished the Skenites."

Pilate nodded. He enjoyed hearing the pride in his wife's voice, but now was not the time for war or politics. He took his son in his arms and lifted him high. The boy squalled in lusty protest at having his meal interrupted, but Pilate swaddled him in a soft linen sheet and he quieted down. Then the proconsul took his infant son and walked out the door, onto the rampart overlooking the courtyard. His men were there, laughing and boasting of their feats in battle to anyone who would listen, while the legionaries who had not been assigned to the mission looked on in envy. He watched them in pride for a few moments, but then Brutus Appius saw him standing there and nudged his companions. Soon the men were all looking at their commander and the white-clad bundle in his arms, whispering and pointing. Pilate let the sheet fall aside and lifted the tiny child high above his head, raising his voice so they could all hear.

"LEGIONARIES!" he cried. "I present to you my son, Decimus Pontius Pilate! As *paterfamilias* of the house Pontii, I proclaim him to be my legitimate issue, my son and my heir, who shall carry our family name into the next generation. I call on all the gods of Rome to witness that this is my son!"

The men cheered themselves hoarse and little Decimus wailed in dismay. Pilate wrapped the cloth back around him and returned him to his mother. In a moment he was happily nursing again, and Procula was studying her husband's face and form as he looked down on them. It was a face and body familiar to her, but she never tired of watching this man she loved.

At forty-four, Pilate was just under six feet tall and very lean. His black hair was thinning somewhat, and his mouth was set in a stern expression much of the time. There was a hint of danger about him that she had never fully understood, a certain ruthlessness that she only caught glimpses of from time to time. It seemed to gleam forth most fully when he was describing a battle or a tense political victory. But when he smiled, that hint of danger receded, and there was a kindness to him that had attracted her since she was a young girl. His nose was a proper Roman beak, and his eyes a steely gray. His shoulders were broad and his arms muscular from constant practice with blade and shield, and his exposed skin a deep tan from years of exposure to the sun. In a culture that prized physical fitness and strength, Pilate would never have cause to be ashamed.

The birth of his son and his victory over the Skenites seemed to banish the cloud that had hung over him ever since his arrival in Judea, and especially since the embarrassing episode with the standards. The Jews, it seemed, would never love any Roman governor, but for a time, at least, Pilate had won their respect. A week after his return to Caesarea, he received a package from Caiaphas, the High Priest. It contained a talent of gold and a single pearl of great value. The letter accompanying it was almost friendly.

*Esteemed Proconsul*, it read.

> *Please accept this gift, not in token of any favors granted or expected, but in simple congratulations for the birth of your heir and your notable victory over the enemies of our people. I do not expect that we shall ever be friends, but perhaps we can become, at the very least, partners in the governance of the sons of Israel during your time here. May the God of Israel bless your son with good health and long life. Matthew Caiaphas of the House of Zadok, High Priest of the Israelites.*

Not long after, a similar gift came from Herod Antipas. The letter, however, was more verbose and not nearly as tactful.

> *Greetings, Prefect Pilate! Congratulations on the birth of your son and heir. We here in Israel are fond of large families—in fact, my father had so many sons that he was able to indulge himself in the luxury of killing half of them! But no man should go through life without leaving a son to carry on his name and family honor, and I am glad that you have finally been blessed with offspring. Given the uncertainty of life, however, I would encourage you to go at your wife again as soon as possible, because a single heir is a tenuous bridge to posterity at best! Please accept this gift as a token of my*

*good wishes. Herod Antipas, King of Judea and Procurator of Galilee.*

Pilate rolled his eyes as he read the ponderous prose to his wife. She could not bring herself to believe that Herod's father had actually killed five of his own sons, but Pilate assured her it was true.

"No wonder he wants you to have another son!" she said. "He probably thinks you need an extra in case you decide to lop this one's head off!"

"Herod's father was mad," said Pilate. "Do you know that Augustus once said he would rather be Herod's pig than Herod's son? As a proper Jew, Herod would never kill a pig!"

They laughed together, and then opened the bag that had accompanied the letter. Herod had sent them two talents of gold, one for Pilate, and one for his son. In addition, there was a lovely gold and emerald circlet for Porcia to slip around her arm. Little Decimus was fascinated by it, and kept trying to pull it into his mouth.

"You know," said Porcia, "as soon as we find an acceptable wet nurse for our son, I will welcome you back to our bed properly."

Pilate smiled at his wife with great fondness. Thrilled though he was to finally have an heir to his name, he did not want to put her through the perils of childbirth again when she was in her thirties. The thought that he might lose her was terrifying to him. But he kept those thoughts to himself.

"I will be glad when the time comes," he said, and curled up next to her to sleep.

When Decimus was nearly four months old, a letter arrived from the Emperor. Pilate had sent him a detailed report of the defeat of the Skenite invaders, and mentioned the birth of his son in a brief postscript. Although his anger had faded somewhat, the affection he once felt for Tiberius had still not returned. Nonetheless, his old patron's letter made him smile.

*Gaius Julius Tiberius Caesar, Princeps and Imperator, to Prefect Lucius Pontius Pilate, Proconsul of Judea; greetings!*

*Your report of the Skenite incursion and your forceful and effective response was received with gladness. I have long held that you were the most competent and loyal of all my legates, and it is good to be proven correct once more! But the news of your son's birth was a*

215

*far greater joy to this lonely old man. I am a cold and impersonal being, as many have remarked, Lucius Pontius. My glum demeanor leads many to believe that I am incapable of human warmth. But the one thing that has always had the power to lift my spirits is the laughter of little children. I had once thought that you and I could share the same grandchildren, but the young serpent I adopted scotched that dream forever, and in the process cost me the friendship of one I held dear. I cannot undo what has been done, as much as I might like to, but I can thank all the gods of Rome that the laughter of children has returned to the house of the Pontii. Please accept my sincerest congratulations, dear Pilate!*

*I must admit that I do miss your capable eyes and ears in Rome. Sejanus continues to run amok, but his days are drawing to a close, though he knows it not. Young Caligula tries to endear himself to me, but I find myself unable to forget what he did to your daughter. If only I had another heir! At least he has forgotten for a time the hurt you gave him. He has devoted himself to the pleasures of the flesh altogether these last few months, and I think the constant indulgence is beginning to wear off some of his sharp edges. Such at least is an old man's hope.*

*May this letter find you and your dear Porcia safe and well. Perhaps your return to Rome can be accomplished sooner than we hoped. Keep yourself safe, and keep the Jews in line!*

Pilate shook his head. In all the years of their association, this was the most candid and emotional letter Tiberius had ever written to him. What a shame, he thought, that it should come at a time when the relationship was damaged beyond repair. Still, the thought of a return to Rome was encouraging.

Of all the letters he received, though, the one that warmed his heart the most came from Quintus Sullemius. It was short, pointed, and hilarious.

*Quintus Sullemius, scoundrel, pirate, spy, and corrupter of the youth of Rome, to His Excellency, Proconsul and Prefect Lucius Pontius Pilate, sovereign protector of the armpit of the Roman Empire known as Judea —*

*Congratulations, you old dog! Be sure to wipe the cacat from the table before you unfold this to read it. Probably an exercise in futility, since infants are a never-ending fountain of the smelly stuff, but still worth trying at least. I was glad to see that the house of my old friend is not doomed to extinction, for this generation at least. Tell the brat his Uncle Quintus will have a nice wench lined up for him when he is ready to don his toga and become a man! In the meantime, keep wiping up the messes, and try not to go all silly every time you look at your little blanket-soiler!*

Pilate did not read that one to Porcia, but he laughed every time he thought about its contents for the next week. Even the men noticed the change in their commander. He was still tough as nails and drove them hard, whether in training or on patrol, but he laughed and joked more often than before, and even went out of his way to show courtesy to the Jews he encountered. Perhaps his term as prefect was going to be peaceful and uneventful after all.

# CHAPTER SEVENTEEN

It was autumn, and Pilate was preparing to return to Jerusalem for the first time since the fiasco over the standards the previous year. His three cohorts were prepared to escort him, and the shields they carried were polished to a mirror finish with no ornamentation at all. The eagle standards would remain in the barracks at Caesarea, where the shields with the Emperor's profile were also kept. There would be no fuss over "graven images" this time!

The messenger from Jerusalem arrived the day before Pilate had planned to depart, and the news was not good. Jerusalem was suffering under a plague of the bloody flux. Thousands of Jews and other residents of the city were afflicted with vomiting, diarrhea, and dehydration, and hundreds had already died. Pilgrims flocking to the city for the Feast of Booths seemed particularly vulnerable.

The armies of Rome had fought this particular malady for centuries, and while its precise cause was still a mystery, everyone knew how it was contracted: by drinking foul water, especially water that had been contaminated with sewage. That was why the Roman legions followed strict guidelines dating from the years of Scipio Africanus concerning the placement of latrines and wells within their camps, and why fouling a well was a flogging offense. Every Roman officer could cite the example of Pompey Strabo, the father of Pompey the Great. He had been negligent about proper drainage for his camp's latrines and had thus died of the flux, after hundreds of his soldiers had suffered a similar fate.

Pilate knew that the city of Jerusalem relied on a few ancient wells and spring-fed pools for its water supply, and that those sources frequently became brackish and foul during drought years. A shame, he thought, that the city's rulers had never built a decent aqueduct to carry clean water to its teeming masses. But as he turned the thought over in his head, he began to wonder: why not? What better way to do a genuine service for the people that he governed and build some goodwill for Rome than to provide the people of Jerusalem with a year-round source of clean, safe drinking water?

He went to his desk and unrolled a map of Judea. Mount Hermon, the tallest mountain in the province, was capped with snow year round and was the source of numerous springs, but it was about fifty miles from Jerusalem and would make for an enormous engineering project. There was a small aqueduct leading into the city from the south, near the ancient hamlet of Bethlehem, which had been constructed during the time of Herod the Great. Four huge reservoirs, known as Solomon's Pools, had been there for many years, but the small aqueduct already there simply did not channel enough water to supply the city's need. A proper Roman-style aqueduct built parallel to this one would more than meet the demand, Pilate thought, and the distance to be covered was only about seven or eight miles. But where to secure the funding? he wondered. The two biggest holders of wealth were Herod Antipas and the Temple, but Jerusalem proper fell more within the Temple's jurisdiction. As much as he disliked the thought, Pilate would have to deal with Caiaphas.

He drew up his plans carefully, and packed them in his saddlebags when he and his men set forth the next day. He had hoped to have Porcia and Decimus come along, but he did not want them anywhere near the city while the outbreak of disease continued. Bidding them a fond farewell, he saddled up and rode alongside his soldiers as they set out. Longinus and Ambrosius were with him, and so he pulled his horse up alongside theirs as they wound their way southeast toward Jerusalem. As the cohorts fell into the rhythm of the march, Pilate broached the subject with his senior centurion.

"Longinus, I have a mission for you when we reach the city. I need to meet in private with Caiaphas the High Priest as soon as possible after our arrival. Can you go and summon him for me?" he asked.

"The High Priest will not set foot in the fortress," said Longinus.

"I know," said Pilate. "And I cannot set foot inside their temple. I will let him choose a neutral location where we can talk."

Longinus nodded. "That is a wise and politic gesture," he said. "He may even invite you to come to the Court of the Gentiles, where those like me, who worship the God of Israel but are not circumcised, are allowed to offer their sacrifices. May I ask what you wish to confer with him about?"

Pilate explained his idea for building an aqueduct to supply water to the people of Jerusalem from Solomon's Pools. Longinus nodded as Pilate explained his reasoning.

"That is a good idea, and long overdue!" he said when the governor finished. "The Temple has more than enough in its treasury to fund such a project, but—if I may be so bold—I would offer to split the expenses with them. Perhaps an end to the flux and the addition of a source of good clean water would make the people think a bit more favorably of Rome—and you."

"Those were my thoughts exactly," said Pilate. "Do you think Caiaphas will go along with the idea?"

Longinus thought for a long time. "I really don't know," he said. "The Sadducees who control the Priesthood are a strange lot. They are really not very religious—not at all, compared to the Pharisees—but they do believe in trying to make this earth a better place, and they are superb politicians. If Caiaphas finds it politic to go along with your idea, he will. If he thinks the people will be against it, he won't. And he can change positions in a heartbeat. So I would make sure that, whatever agreement you come to, you get it from him in writing."

Pilate nodded. "Good advice, centurion!" he said. "I appreciate, as always, your understanding of these strange people." He looked at the grizzled veteran riding beside him for a long moment. "What will you do when your years in the legion are complete, Longinus?" he asked. "Will you take your Jewish wife and children back to Italy, or will you remain here in Judea?"

Longinus paused a moment before answering. "I do not know," he said. "I have had one foot in both worlds for so long I don't really belong in either of them anymore. But Asia Province is a big place. Somewhere there will be a place my family and I can settle and live in peace."

They camped near the old city of Ephraim that night, and the next day they pressed on toward Jerusalem. The pilgrims thronging the city for the festival gave way, grudgingly, as the three cohorts marched toward the castle of Antonia and the barracks that awaited them there. Pilate was struck by how subdued the crowds were this year compared to the year before. Smiles and laughter were not nearly as evident, and the stench of vomit, excrement, and death formed a faint, foul miasma that underlay all the normal smells of the crowd. There was the usual look of sullen resentment from some of the people, but now many of the expressions smacked of despair. Despite his dislike for these odd people he had been sent to govern, Pilate felt a certain sympathy for them. No one should have to die simply because their leaders refused to provide them with clean water to drink!

As they marched toward the barracks, the cohorts encountered no fewer than three funeral parties carrying victims of the flux outside the city walls for burial. Pilate ordered the column to halt each time as the dead were carried by. After they arrived, he assembled the legionaries for a quick talk.

"As you can see, men, the flux is taking a toll on the city. I do not want to lose any of you to it. Do not drink water from the public wells or cisterns. So far the well here inside the fort has proven safe, but if anyone gets sick after drinking from it, I will forbid it as well. Experience has shown that mixing about a small amount of wine with your water seems to prevent the flux from spreading. I do not want you drunk on duty, but the wine jars will be available for you to add to your canteens. Now be careful, and stay well. Dismissed!"

Inside the governor's quarters, he called for a scribe and dictated a short letter to the High Priest. He read it over carefully before calling on Longinus to deliver it.

> *Lucius Pontius Pilate, Proconsul and Prefect of Judea, to Joseph Matthew Caiaphas, High Priest of the Nation of Israel, greetings.*
>
> *I am distressed to see the people of Jerusalem so gravely afflicted with the bloody flux during this holiday season. While I am sure that you are offering all the necessary prayers and sacrifices to your God to summon His aid in this crisis, we in Rome believe, as I am sure you do too, that man was blessed with two hands and a mind for a reason. If you would be willing to meet with me, I would like to discuss with you how to best alleviate the suffering this plague has brought upon Jerusalem. I realize that your religious beliefs do not allow you to enter the Praetorium, so I will meet you at the time and place of your choosing — but I would like the meeting to be soon.*

Longinus donned civilian garb, including the headdress with its phylacteries that Jewish men and God-fearing Gentiles wore to the Temple,

222

and disappeared into the masses outside the fortress. He was back in two hours' time, bearing the High Priest's reply.

> *Joseph Matthew Caiaphas, High Priest of the House of Israel, to the Proconsul Pontius Pilate, may the blessings of Adonai rest upon you!*
>
> *For your concern on behalf of my people I thank you; and I am curious as to how you might be able to help arrest the spread of this dreadful flux in our city. For that reason I am more than willing to meet with you. There is a large colonnade along the edge of the Court of Gentiles at our Temple. At the south end of this colonnade is a guard tower. Meet me in the guardroom there an hour before noon tomorrow and we shall discuss how to overcome this crisis together.*

Longinus was encouraging in his report. "Caiaphas was surprised to see me—we have met before, but I do not think he knew that I was a God-fearer," he said to Pilate. "Once he realized that my dress was more than just a disguise, he spoke quite plainly. This flux has the priests worried. The people are angry and despairing, and looking for someone to blame. One thing you can say for the Sadducees, they hate disorder almost as much as Rome does! I think the two of you will be able to come to an agreement."

"Thank you, Centurion," said Pilate. "Now go get back in uniform!"

The next morning Pilate donned a plain white tunic and a simple robe trimmed with purple. He left his sword behind, but strapped on a dagger beneath the robe just in case a random Zealot chose him as a target. Escorted by four lictors—half his normal guard—he set out for the Temple. While the Fortress of Antonia actually had an adjoining wall to the Temple complex, to get to the gates that led to the Court of Gentiles Pilate had to walk down a parallel street for several hundred yards, then round a corner and up the steps to the portico. The double colonnade was most impressive, almost two hundred yards in length, and thousands of pilgrims were making their way up and down the steps as they entered and left the Temple complex. The Court of the Gentiles, which Pilate now saw for the first time, was the largest of the Temple's open-air courtyards, but it was thronged with vendors, merchants, and moneychangers. Many of the merchants were selling sacrificial animals, and the haggling and hectoring between them and their customers drowned out the chanting of the priests standing on the steps of the Inner Court.

Turning his back on the noisy crowd, Pilate walked down the colonnade to the guard tower. One of the black-clad Temple guards let him in, and there he saw the High Priest standing, looking out a window to the gardens outside the city walls. He turned and Pilate studied him at length.

Robed in black and white, with an impressive headdress, Caiaphas was about fifty years of age, as near as Pilate could tell, although his thick beard covered enough of his face to make his age uncertain. He had keen, piercing eyes and bushy brows, although his nose was not as long as that of most Jews. There was a keen intelligence behind those eyes, as well as a strong will. But for the moment, the voice that carried across the room could not have been more deferential.

"Most excellent Proconsul, I am glad to see you!" said the priest. "I feel that we got off to a poor start, and perhaps this meeting can give us a second chance to make good things happen. What do you wish to discuss?"

"The health of the people of Jerusalem," said Pilate. "The flux is ravaging the city, and many of the victims are women and children. People are frightened and angry, which is never a good thing for those of us who are charged with keeping the peace. Tell me, Caiaphas, what do you know of the flux?"

"I know that it is a perennial hazard to city dwellers," replied the priest. "It always seems to strike during the hottest and driest parts of the year, although it can occasionally break forth when we have had torrential rains as well. Those who contract it suffer greatly with nausea and loose bowels, and usually die or begin to recover by the end of a week's time. My brother's daughter died of it last week. Some say it is God's judgment on us for our sins; that I cannot state with any certainty. The purposes of the Almighty are His own."

Pilate nodded. "We Romans have dealt with the flux for centuries. During the wars with Gaul and Carthage, in the days of the Republic, it ravaged our armies, killing more men than the enemy did. It was a physician in the armies of Scipio Africanus who discovered that water fouled by sewage was the chief means by which the disease spread. Since then, our armies have been very careful to locate our latrines as far from our wells as possible, and only to dump sewage into rivers well downstream from our camps. Jerusalem's water is foul, especially now when the drought has lowered the water table. Sewage from the cesspits has seeped into many of your cisterns and wells. The city needs fresh, clean water in order to check the spread of the illness."

Caiaphas looked at him thoughtfully. "Rome is a great and resourceful power," he said, "as the current status of my people bears witness. There are those among us who argue that we should reject every aspect of Rome's culture and law in order to restore our nation to greatness, but I believe that true wisdom lies in adopting those practices which work, regardless of who originates them. Bringing in fresh water to the city sounds wonderful, but how are you going to do it? And who would pay for it?"

Pilate was pleased by the priest's candor. "As to how it can be done, there is already an aqueduct leading from the Pools of Solomon into the city. It was built in the days of the Great Herod, but it is small and inadequate to supply the great population of Jerusalem. I propose building a bigger, wider aqueduct parallel to the existing one. It will run for about eight miles, and will deliver a constant flow of fresh, uncontaminated water to the heart of the city, whence it can be distributed wherever it is needed. My engineers can begin it before the end of the year and complete it in less than a year, if given enough workers."

Caiaphas nodded. "And the funding?" he asked.

"Aqueducts are costly," replied Pilate. "But I am willing to pay for half the cost from the governor's provincial budget, if the Temple will fund the other half, and urge the people to support the project."

Caiaphas frowned. "The people do not like it when we publicly cooperate with Rome," he said. "It fuels the radical elements among us. The money is not as big a concern to me as the public support for the project that you require of us. I will need to confer with the Sanhedrin."

Pilate nodded. "I will await the results of your deliberations with interest," he said. "If a public pronouncement of support is too much to ask, then at the very least I would require a letter from the priests authorizing the use of Temple funds to help construct the aqueduct."

Caiaphas raised an eyebrow. "The Temple's gold is *corban*," he said. "Those who donate it do so with the understanding that it will be used only to defray the expenses of our religion."

"But does your law not also say that *corban* gold may also be used for works of charity, and projects to benefit the poor and the destitute of Jacob's house?" Pilate asked, mentally thanking Longinus for that bit of information.

The High Priest gave a short, barking laugh. "You have learned much about us during your year in Judea," he said. "You are correct, and I will point that out to the Sanhedrin. I believe that we may be able to help you build this aqueduct together." With that, he gave a polite bow and swept from the chamber.

Pilate waited a few moments, then left, picking up his lictors at the door. All the way back to the fortress, he reflected on the conversation. It looked as if he and the priestly hierarchy might actually be able to work together after all, he thought, and that was not necessarily a bad thing. As he walked through the city, he looked at the crowds in the streets. The clothing and facial hair were different from what you saw in most districts of Rome, but they were still members of the *gens humana*, after all. They deserved, at the very least, a chance to live their lives to their natural end.

Two days later he received word that the Sanhedrin had agreed to the use of Temple funds to defray half of the cost of building the aqueduct. Pilate sent word to Caesarea for three Imperial engineers, and they arrived by the end of the week. Plans were drawn up and the men began hiring laborers to quarry and shape the stone blocks. By the first of the New Year, construction would be underway. With no holdups in progress, the aqueduct might well be completed by the following autumn.

The festival ran its normal course and ended with less fanfare and public celebration than normal. The pilgrims made their way back to their scattered homes all over Judea and points even further away, but many of them left children and loved ones buried in the pauper's cemeteries outside Jerusalem, victims of the bloody flux. Finally, in December, clouds began blowing in from the sea and it rained for days on end, refilling the wells and cisterns and ending the outbreak. All totaled, some five thousand had died in Jerusalem and its environs, although many of them had not been locals.

226

It was still a devastating death toll, and Pilate was determined not to see such a plague strike the place again.

Construction got underway with the beginning of the New Year, and went quickly at first. Pilate decided, in March, that he would return to Jerusalem for the next great Festival of the Jews, the Feast of Passover. Since the city was relatively free of disease this time, Procula and Decimus accompanied him. As they approached the city, Longinus filled him in on the nature of the holiday.

"After the age of the patriarchs—the original forefathers of the Jews, named Abraham, Isaac, and Jacob—the sons of Israel were enslaved in Egypt for four hundred years. They prayed to Adonai, who sent a deliverer named Moses to persuade the Pharaoh to let the people go. Pharaoh refused, and so Egypt was smitten with one mighty plague after another. When the foolish king still refused to release the Jews from bondage, God sent an angel of death to destroy the firstborn son from every household in Egypt. But the Jews were warned in advance, and they sacrificed a lamb—one for each family—to take the place of their firstborn. They marked their doorposts with the lamb's blood, so that the Destroyer might pass over their households," the centurion told Pilate.

"Hence the term 'Passover'?" asked Pilate.

"Exactly! God commanded the Jews to sacrifice a lamb each year, and to read from the Torah the story of the deliverance from Egypt, so that they would never forget God's watchful care over them," said Longinus. "Passover is the one feast that all Jews everywhere celebrate, no matter what sect they belong to. It is the holiest day of their faith."

Pilate surveyed the road leading to Jerusalem, thronged with pilgrims already though the Feast was still a week away. Behind his cohorts, thousands more Jews came straggling up the road. "It looks as if every Jew in the world is coming to Jerusalem!" he said.

"Not quite all of them," said Longinus. "But every Jew who lives within traveling distance and is in good health tries to come to Jerusalem for this feast. Every Jew wants to be here at least once in his lifetime. There are many legends associated with Passover. The people believe, for instance, that the great prophet Elijah will return on Passover to announce the coming of

Messiah. Many Jews actually leave an empty seat at the table for him, to show that they long for the Hope of Israel to appear."

"Elijah?" asked Pilate. "I am unfamiliar with that name."

"Oh, he was a man of many miracles!" said Longinus. "Let me tell you the story of him and the wicked King Ahab . . . ." Pilate listened attentively as the God-fearing centurion described the improbable exploits of Jewish prophets and holy men for the next hour, then he got off his horse and strode up and down the ranks, visiting with the men and their officers.

Since he had his family with him, Pilate stayed in the palace of Herod, across the city from the Fortress of Antonia. It meant having to put up with the odious presence of Herod Antipas for a few days, but the living quarters at Antonia were simply too sparse for a woman with a baby. The city was so packed with people that travel through its narrow streets was almost impossible, but by late evening, the troops were properly quartered and Pilate was ensconced with his family. Herod insisted on having them to dinner, despite his religious views, so Pilate and Procula joined him, leaving the boy with a wet nurse for the evening.

Antipas was in rare form, regaling them with tales of his eventful thirty-year rule and the various rabble-rousers and charlatans he had been forced to deal with during his reign. The Jews, it seemed, were always looking for the Messiah, and the quickest way to get them riled up was to pose as the promised deliverer.

"Back during the days of the census ordered by Augustus, there was a character named Judas of Galilee who rose up and tried to say he was the deliverer of Israel," said the bejeweled king. "He claimed to be immune to weapons and all manner of poisons, and drew thousands to his cause—until a well-placed arrow showed his claim to be false! But his followers became the Zealots who plague us to this day."

"So are there any more recent developments that I, as governor, should be concerned about?" asked Pilate.

"There is one fellow who showed up in rural Galilee about a month or so ago and has been drawing huge crowds," the King said. "His name is Jehonan—or John, in its short form. He claims that Messiah is coming soon, and that he is the chosen herald of the new King of Israel. He commands all the people to be immersed in the Jordan to wash away their sins and prepare for the day of the Lord."

"From what I have seen," said Pilate, "the Jordan is too muddy to wash away much of anything! But is this John character someone to worry about?"

"Not yet at any rate," said Herod. "The Temple is keeping an eye on him for the moment. But so far he is urging the people to live lives of holiness, obey the law, and honor God rather than men. I find none of those demands particularly alarming."

The noise was faint enough at first that they did not particularly notice it, particularly since the overall clamor of the crowds outside covered it up. But soon it became apparent that there was a mob gathering outside the palace of Herod, clamoring for their notice. Pilate and the King of the Jews walked to the balcony together to see what was going on.

Several hundred Jews were gathered in the plaza outside the palace, with more arriving every moment. When they saw Pilate, they all began crying out at once, and he could not make out what it was they wanted. He called for order several times, and finally one of them, a burly Jew with thundering brows, stepped forward to speak for them all.

"Most Excellent Pilate, I am called Simon bin-Yosef of Galilee," he said. "We have come because of a rumor that is sweeping the city, so that you may set our minds to rest."

Pilate met his gaze with a steely glance. "And what is the nature of this rumor?" he asked.

"Great Proconsul, we have a tradition that the gold which we donate to the Temple becomes *corban*—that is, exclusively dedicated to our Great God, and that it may never be used for any purpose that is not related to our faith, nor may it ever be touched by the hand of an unbeliever," he said. "But the story says that you took the *corban* gold from the Temple, in order to construct the new aqueduct that is being built even now. Is this true? For it would constitute a grave offense against our law if it were!"

Pilate nodded. "I am aware of your tradition," he said. "Give me a few moments to finish my supper and gather my thoughts, and I shall answer you in full." He ducked back inside before the man could respond, and the crowd began roaring its disapproval. He knew that they would not like the delay, but he wanted to be prepared to deal with the unrest appropriately, and needed some time to prepare. He summoned four of his lictors.

"Go as quickly as you can," he said. "Bring two cohorts from the fortress, but tell them to doff their uniforms and cover their cuirasses with plain robes. They are to surround this unruly mob on all sides, but no blades are to be used! Tell them to arm themselves with cudgels, position themselves on the fringes of the crowd, and not attack unless I give the word." He turned to the last man. "You have a separate mission," he said. "Find Longinus and tell him to carry this message to the High Priest as quickly as he can."

The note he scribbled was short and blunt:

> Prefect Lucius Pontius Pilate to High Priest Joseph Matthew Caiaphas: Some of the Jews are protesting the building of the aqueduct with Temple funds. They have gathered outside Herod's palace. Send some priests to help calm and disperse them, or I will use force to do so. Send them quickly—I cannot delay for long.

With his messengers dispatched, he sat at the table very calmly and finished his dinner. Herod was eyeing him nervously, obviously uncomfortable with the huge numbers of people thronging the square below, but he did not second-guess Pilate's decision to delay the response. When they were done, Pilate sent his wife to stay with their son in the child's bedchamber while he conferred with the King.

"I know that your jurisdiction is in Galilee rather than Judea proper," he said, "but both of us have a vested interest in keeping the peace, and many in this crowd are Galileans. Any aid you could render at this point would be much appreciated."

Herod's face was pale beneath the rouge he wore on his cheeks, and the perfume that soaked his beard did not entirely mask the smell of the nervous sweat that beaded his brow. "Most excellent Pilate," he said, "there is very little I could do to calm this mob. They do not love me here in Jerusalem—or in Galilee, for that matter. I have done my best, for thirty years, to scrupulously adhere to the religious traditions of the Jews in order to win the small measure of trust and loyalty that I enjoy. If I try to plead Rome's case before an angry mob, I run the risk of losing all I have worked for. Were we in Galilee, I would do so regardless. My office would require it. Were I

King of all the Jews, like my father was, I would aid you. But with my diminished authority, and outside my own small jurisdiction, the risks outweigh the potential gains."

Pilate scowled. "The *Divus Julius* used to say that a coward dies a thousand deaths, while a brave man dies but once," he commented. "If I called myself a King, I would act with more courage and less fear. How many times, I wonder, have you died on the inside?"

Herod's eyes glittered with hostility. "If you were a King, Prefect, you would understand that fear is the most healthy and natural emotion to accompany that estate," he said, and swept from the room, his richly embroidered robes reflecting the lamplight as he waddled down the corridor to his chambers.

Moments later, one of the three lictors he had dispatched to the barracks returned, a bit winded but unharmed. "They are ready, Governor," he said. "Nearly four hundred of your men are in position with cudgels along the edges of the crowd, awaiting your signal."

"Very good," said Pilate. "Any word from Longinus or the priests?"

"Caiaphas refuses to send any aid," said the centurion, striding into the room behind the lictor. His robes were torn and there was a cut above his left eye. "The cowardly dog says he cannot squander the Temple's standing with the people to defend an engineering project that was purely Rome's idea," Longinus reported.

Pilate grimaced. "Well," he said, "it is a good thing that I secured his agreement in writing! By Jupiter, I will NOT back down this time! The project was undertaken purely for the good of these people, with the cooperation of the Temple and the priests! Hades take their sensibilities—I am tired of this!" He turned to Democles, his loyal steward, and snapped, "Bring me my military uniform, decorations and all! I want them to see that I mean business!"

He quickly dressed himself in his cuirass, grieves, *sagum*, and boots. He left off his helmet so that he could don his Civic Crown. He left his sword sheathed, but tightly gripped the rod that symbolized his office, tucking it into the crook of his arm, and then stepped out onto the balcony again.

Their numbers had swelled to two or three thousand, packing the square. Many of them were still leading their sacrificial lambs and goats on leashes, and all of them were shouting and furious. When they saw him their howls of rage intensified for a moment. Looking at the fringes of the crowd, he saw his men strategically placed every ten feet or so. Their faces were grim but unafraid, ready for battle if it proved necessary. Pilate held up his hands, and the crowd gradually quieted.

"People of Jerusalem," he said. "Rome is not your enemy—unless you make it such. I was not sent here to oppress, but to govern you. In my two years here, have I not done much to restore peace? Have I not pacified the Zealots and *sicarii*? Have I not shown myself amenable to persuasion? When the standards of my legion offended your religious sensibilities, did I not order them removed? There is no need for this insurrection I see brewing before me! In the words of your own prophet, 'Come, let us reason together.' Listen to me now."

The square fell silent as the people reflected on his words. He could tell that the quotation from their Scriptures had caught them by surprise and thrown them off guard. He spoke again quickly.

"Last fall when I came to Jerusalem to keep the peace during your holidays, I saw a city gripped by the bloody flux. I saw despair in the eyes of mothers and children. I heard the weeping as the bodies of the dead were carried outside the city walls, many to be buried in pauper's graves miles from their homes." He looked at the crowd as he spoke. Some of them were actually beginning to nod. "This is a disease that Rome has dealt with for centuries, and we know that it is caused by drinking water that has been contaminated with sewage. The city's water supply was clearly inadequate, especially for the great numbers who flock here to worship during your holy days. After conferring with your own High Priest, and receiving his pledge of cooperation, we agreed that the Temple would work with the Senate and People of Rome, as embodied in my office of Proconsul, to build an aqueduct that would supply the people of Jerusalem with clean, abundant water year round and keep the disease from devastating you again. Is it not written in your own law that the Temple's *corban* offerings may be used to benefit the poor and orphaned among you? What greater gift of charity could there be than to assure the poor and helpless that they will not fall victim to a disease that is preventable? Can you not see that I have acted, not for the enrichment of Rome, but for the health and welfare of the people of Jerusalem?"

He paused and looked over the crowd again, this time seeking out the face of Simon bin-Yosef. The Galilean was staring at him with unremitting hostility, and raised his voice to reply. "It is good that you wish to prevent disease among our people, Prefect," he said in a voice that dripped sarcasm. "After all, corpses cannot be leached of their life's earnings to pay tribute to Rome! But the Law remains the Law. That which is *corban* cannot be passed into the hands of Gentiles for any reason. You have defiled our offerings!"

The looks of understanding in the faces of the crowd faded, replaced again by outrage. Pilate spoke once more. "People of Jerusalem," he said. "I did not take holy relics from your Temple! I did not lay hands upon any of the items that are dedicated and used for the worship of your God! In fact, the High Priest even made sure that the Temple coins he donated from the treasury were traded in for Roman *sesterces* before they were passed into our hands. In every step of this project I have shown respect and restraint with regards to your religious beliefs. This protest is unlawful and unnecessary. I have listened to you with patience, and I have explained fully how our actions are both legal and respectful of your traditions. Now"—he raised his voice to his loudest barracks bellow—"GO HOME! This assembly is unlawful. Disperse, or I will disperse you! Go!"

Simon's face hardened with resolve. "Never!" he shouted back. "The money is *corban* and therefore sacred. *Corban* has been defiled. Down with Rome! Great is the God of Israel!!"

The mob began chanting "*CORBAN! CORBAN* HAS BEEN DEFILED!" at the top of their lungs. Pilate's temper, held in check for many months, boiled over at last. It was time to show these stubborn, irrational people who truly governed Judea. He dropped his emotional guard completely and let the beast that lived within him slip its cage and snarl with his voice.

"Let them have it!" he shouted. From every side of the square, Roman legionaries waded into the crowd with cudgels swinging. The shouts quickly gave way to screams as the terrified mob tried to flee.

The legionaries knew their business. Those who dropped all weapons and simply ran were spared, while those who continued to shout received sharp blows to the head and shoulders until they fell unconscious or joined the fleeing masses. Some of the most stubborn, though, armed themselves— a few had swords or daggers under their robes, while others grabbed anything they could lay their hands on and launched themselves at the hated Romans. But they were amateurs, for the most part—the legionaries quickly disarmed them, and those who had actually struck a soldier wound up getting their skulls bashed in. Terrified sacrificial animals ran this way and that, trying to flee, and some of Pilate's men killed them too. Their blood ran among the cobblestones with that of their owners.

Simon bin-Yosef stayed at the center of the fray, trying to organize the resistance, a curved sword drawn from under his cloak. Pilate pointed down from the balcony at the burly Galilean. "I want him alive!" he shouted. Six legionaries, led by Centurion Marcus Pullo, charged him. He screamed his resistance and swung his blade mightily, killing Pullo and two legionaries, but the rest disarmed him and then knocked him over the head, rendering him unconscious. When he fell, the last resistance crumbled and the survivors fled.

About thirty Jews lay dead, and a hundred more or so were wounded. Four legionaries and Marcus Pullo had been killed, and about a dozen or more were wounded badly enough to require medical attention. Pilate summoned the physicians to treat them, and told his men to allow the Jews to collect their dead and wounded, as long as they did so peacefully. He then walked over to the men who were guarding Simon of Galilee. The big Jew still slumped unconscious in their arms.

"Is he wounded badly?" asked Pilate.

"Shouldn't be," said the oldest legionary. "I just gave him a little love tap on the head—although I wanted to cave his skull in, seeing as he killed our Pullo. We lost a good officer today."

Pilate nodded. He looked at the veteran soldier, trying to remember his name. "You are Brutus Valentius, are you not?" he asked.

The man straightened up and saluted. "Aye, sir!" he said. "I've marched before the standards for twelve years now."

"I appreciate your restraint, Legionary," said Pilate. "I want to make an example of this one—the mob was ready to disperse if it were not for him. That blade tells me he was not a simple pilgrim. Tell me, Brutus, can you give orders as well as take them?"

"I've never been in a position to have to do so," he said, "but I suppose that I could learn. I've been in the legions long enough to know what needs doing in most situations."

Pilate nodded. "We shall find out, then," he said. "I am promoting you to centurion to take Pullo's place. Now take this scum to the dungeons at the fortress. I want to find out as much as I can from him before we nail him up."

The next day Pilate sent this letter to Tiberius Caesar:

> *Lucius Pontius Pilate, Proconsul of Rome and Prefect of Judea, to the most excellent Gaius Julius Tiberius Caesar, Greetings! Since I am sure that the High Priest is frantically scribbling his own account of yesterday's events to you as I write this, I thought I would inform you of what happened so that you would have a clear impression of the events.*
>
> *As I reported earlier, with the cooperation of the Temple and High Priest, I have begun constructing an aqueduct to relieve the notoriously unhealthy shortage of drinking water in Jerusalem. As you can see by the attached letter, the Temple donated money from their offerings to help fund this project, without protest or reservations. However, during the feast of Passover, a Zealot activist (for such he confessed to be after interrogation) worked the Jews up to a frenzy, claiming that sacred funds had been stolen from the Temple to fund the building of the aqueduct. I went out to reason with the crowd, and they were prepared to accept my words, had not this Simon the Zealot kept them stirred up. I ordered my men to disperse the mob, using cudgels only to avoid unnecessary bloodshed. Most of the Jews simply fled, but the Zealot agitators drew steel and had to be put down by force. Thirty were killed, and Simon hangs from a cross outside the city as a warning to his kindred and followers. The rest of the feast has passed thus far without incident. From the information gained by my interrogators, we should be able to burn out another Zealot nest or two in the next few weeks. Work on the aqueduct continues, and it should be finished within a year or so. Otherwise, the province is more peaceful and prosperous than it was when I arrived, and I*

doubt Rome's supremacy will be challenged again anytime soon. May the gods bless your noble person, and may Jupiter Best and Greatest continue to shine his favor upon Rome.

A few months later he received this reply:

*Gaius Julius Tiberius Caesar, Princeps and Imperator, to Prefect Lucius Pontius Pilate, Proconsul of Judea; greetings!*

*You did very well to send me the letter and your own version of the events that transpired in Jerusalem this spring, because a letter from Caiaphas followed it by only a day, in which he and the Jewish Senate tried to lay the entire blame for the affair upon you. I am afraid, dear Pilate, that they do not care much for you in the Temple! However, in this instance, I believe you acted with complete correctness. The Zealots are a danger that must be eradicated whenever encountered, even if it means occasionally ruffling a few feathers. But, if possible, strive to avoid confrontations that are unnecessary — a word of advice you probably do not need.*

*Moving on to other things, it might interest you to know that my mother Livia, having attained an age of eighty-six years, finally joined her husband in the afterlife this spring. While I never cared for her as much as she did for me, her absence will make it harder for me to keep up with the machinations of Sejanus, who continues to run Rome in my absence. Upon my orders, he has agreed to exile Agrippina and her two eldest sons from Rome once and for all. Their constant attempts to undermine my authority will be much more difficult from a thousand miles away! His own day will come sooner than he thinks. The spider may be motionless at the center of the web, but he always knows who is pulling the threads!*

*Gaius Caligula continues to grow and mature. I begin to see a more reasonable and temperate side of his personality, although how much of it is authentic and how much of it is dissembling I do not know. I heard a Greek philosopher once say that most people are governed as they deserve to be. It may be that Gaius will be the scourge that Rome has called down on itself for generations — or that he will be a peaceful and clement ruler that will bring out the best in her. See? You thought I was incapable of making a joke!*

*Jests aside, I continue to drum into him that what he did to your daughter was wrong, and that your response was perfectly justified under the mos maorum of Rome. I hope that this groundwork I am laying will make it possible for you to return to Rome sooner, rather than later. May Fortuna bless you with her favors!*

Pilate filed the letter away with the rest of his Imperial correspondence, and walked down to the parade ground where his legionaries were training. Someday, perhaps, he would be allowed to go home.

# CHAPTER EIGHTEEN

"So what do you think of this John the Baptizer?" asked Pilate as he and Longinus watched the troops march out of the barracks to begin a patrol of the district.

It was January again, and the New Year had begun in a quiet and peaceful fashion. Pilate had indeed led his men to attack and destroy two Zealot strongholds after the aqueduct riots in Jerusalem, and since then the native resistance movement had subsided. The autumn festivals had come and gone without incident, although Herod Antipas had treated Pilate with nothing but thinly veiled hostility since their exchange on the evening of the riot.

All the talk in Judea was of the Baptizer, the closest thing the Jews had seen to a real prophet of their God in hundreds of years. He wore a rough tunic of camel's hair, and carried a shepherd's rod in his hands. Years of roaming the wilderness had made his feet as hard as leather, and rumor had it that he fed on whatever wild things he could eat, most notably locusts and wild honey. Thousands of Jews flocked to the wilderness beyond the Jordan to see him, even though his message was not heartwarming or complimentary. He berated the people for their sinful hearts and wicked ways. When the priests sent a delegation from the Temple to find out what his message was, he called them a brood of vipers. But to one and all, he thundered a message that the time was short.

"Repent, for the kingdom of the Lord is at hand!" was the message that Pilate had heard repeated by everyone who had been to hear the fiery prophet. That was not the entirety of his message, but everything else seemed to stem from his belief that the God of Israel was about to do something astonishing. So far, however, he had not breathed a word against Rome, so Pilate was more curious than he was concerned—hence his casual question to Longinus.

"I am not sure what to make of him, since I have not heard him myself yet," was the centurion's reply.

239

"Why don't you take a few of your lads and go hear him out?" asked Pilate.

"I would enjoy that," said Longinus. "Should I go incognito, or as an officer of Rome?"

"Go in uniform, and your men, too," replied Pilate. "I want to see how he reacts to the representatives of the Empire."

The next morning Longinus and a dozen of his men set out for the Jordan wilderness, south of Jerusalem, where the prophet was preaching his message daily. Pilate, in the meantime, was enjoying his job more than he had since arriving in Judea. Although the military action he once craved was notable by its absence, he now found his off-duty hours absorbed in the raising of his son. Little Decimus was now nearly two, and he was the terror of Caesarea. His father had given him a small wooden practice sword for his first birthday, and after cutting several teeth on it, Decimus had discovered that, once he mastered the trick of walking upright, he could swing the practice blade and hit things with it. Nothing was safe from him—not his father's military equipment, not the shins of visitors to the governor's office, and certainly not the backside of any dog, cat, or other child that crossed his path. Procula Porcia had her hands full keeping up with him, and despite her firm discipline—occasionally shored up by a firm smack across the buttocks from his father—Decimus remained incorrigible.

"Perhaps if we had another child, it would give him a more appropriate channel for his energies," said Pilate one evening as he carried the limp toddler to the nursery.

"Do you want to kill me?" Porcia said with mock seriousness. "I do not think I could ever do this again! Are all boys such terrors?"

Pilate laughed. "Since this is the only boy I ever raised, I cannot give a definitive answer to that," he said. "But I do remember by the time I was six, most of my energies were directed towards keeping my brothers in line—or leading them to new mischief."

"No, thank you, husband!" she said. "Having one child in my thirties was hard enough. I do not wish to go through this again—although it is in Vesta's lap, not mine. But—let's not tempt her tonight, if you please."

Pilate sighed. Raising their hyperactive son had left his wife too tired to perform in bed very often, but honestly, as he approached fifty, he found

240

that his own libido had slowed down perceptibly. It was enough, he thought, that he had made a home in this forbidding foreign land, with a son who alternately delighted and infuriated him, and a wife who always loved him, no matter how exhausted the day left her. He poured her a cup of wine and she rubbed his tired shoulders before they fell asleep for the evening.

Two weeks after he had sent them out, Longinus and his legionaries returned from the Jordan. Pilate invited his senior centurion to share a cup of wine with him in his quarters, and then listened as Longinus gave his report.

"He was certainly not hard to find," he said. "Every half mile, it seemed, we passed another group walking or riding out to hear him. And the closer we got, the thicker they were. By the time we arrived at the Jordan, there were at least ten thousand people gathered there. We arrived early in the morning, and the people were quietly talking among themselves, waiting for him to put in an appearance. Sure enough, about the fourth hour, he showed up suddenly—there was a rocky promontory that the river wound around, and suddenly he was standing on top of it, facing the multitude. He chose the spot well, to be sure—everyone could see him, and hear him plainly."

"What sort of man is he?" asked Pilate.

"Big," said Longinus. "Not really tall, but broad-shouldered and built like a boulder, with massive arms and stout calf muscles. His voice is remarkable—trumpeting like a war elephant one moment, soft as a mother singing her babe to sleep the next—yet it carried perfectly over the sounds of the river and the crowd, like he was standing next to us the whole time. His eyes are the most surprising part of him—there is a strange gentleness about him, despite the harshness of his message."

"So what was his message?" asked Pilate.

"In one word—REPENT!" Longinus intoned the command in his best parade ground bellow. "He believes that the Messiah is at hand, and that the people of Israel—and us Gentiles too—have only a short time to get our house in order before the Promised One appears. He urges everyone to turn away from their sins and embrace a life of holiness, before God reaps away the evildoers from the earth and gathers His chosen ones unto Himself."

"A madman, you think?" asked Pilate.

Longinus hesitated a long time before answering. "You know, sir, that I am a believer in the God of Israel, even though I am a Roman. God has sent many prophets to speak to Israel in the past. I have read some of their writings. I have also seen a half dozen or so false prophets during my years here—vagabonds, charlatans, and at least one who was stark raving mad. False prophets tend to be interested in money or acclaim—which they win by telling the people what they want to hear. This man—he doesn't give a fig what the people think of him, and he certainly does not flatter them. I have yet to see or hear of him ask for as much as a single denarius. One woman tried to give him a purse full of gold, and he told her to give it to the poor instead. I don't believe that this man is a crook or a revolutionary, Prefect. He is either a madman, or a genuine prophet of God."

Pilate rolled his eyes at Longinus' gullibility where religion was concerned. How could any Roman of the Romans embrace such a bizarre set of beliefs? But then he asked the question that he had sent the man to discover John's answer for. "What did he say when he saw your uniforms? What does he say about Rome?"

Longinus answered: "He did not even blink when he saw me and my legionaries standing at the edge of the crowd; just kept right on preaching. The boys and I were pretty taken in by his message. Legionary Cornelius even called out at one point: 'Sir, what about us? How can we be considered righteous?' The Baptizer looked right back at him and said: 'Don't make false accusations against God's people, or anyone else! Don't extort money, and be content with your wages!' The crowd looked at us strangely, I can tell you!"

Pilate seemed surprised. "Anything else?" he said.

Longinus nodded. "There were two or three *publicani* among the crowd. One of them cried out 'What about us?' and John looked at him and said: 'Collect no more tribute than your orders require!' That surprised me, because if there is one group that the Jews hate even more than the Legions, it's the tax farmers."

Pilate nodded. "That is the truth," he said. "It certainly sounds as if this Baptizer is no threat to Rome. What does the Temple make of him?"

242

"They sent a delegation to interrogate him," said Longinus. "They asked him if he was the Messiah—and he said no. They asked him if he was Elijah, come again as the prophets foretold—he said no. They asked him if he was the great prophet foretold by Moses—he said no."

"Sounds like they don't know what to make of him either," commented Pilate.

"They were getting frustrated," said Longinus, "so one of them finally said, 'Please give us some sort of answer to return to those who sent us! If you are not the Messiah, and not Elijah, and not the great prophet foretold by Moses, then just who are you? Why are you here?'" He paused a moment, replaying the scene in his mind. "His answer was pretty interesting. He told them: 'I am the voice of one crying in the wilderness: Make the roads straight for the coming of the Lord! For I tell you, there is One coming after me whose sandals I am not worthy to untie! I baptize you with water, but He will baptize you with the Holy Spirit of God, and with fire!' I can tell you the crowd got really quiet at that point. Men were looking at each other, and watching the crowd, expecting this Chosen One to pop out from behind a bush at any moment."

"Interesting," said Pilate. "I think this man bears some watching."

"I agree, sir. In fact," said Longinus, "I left my chief servant—a Greek named Stychius—to stay over the next few weeks and listen to the Baptizer's message. He was eager to do it—in fact, he had already gone down to the river and asked to be baptized along with many others."

"Really?" said Pilate. "Did you join him in Jordan's muddy waters?"

Longinus looked a bit sheepish. "Well, sir, it was beastly hot, and if he is a genuine prophet of God, I figured a bit of damp hair would not hurt anything!"

Pilate laughed. "You might as well go ahead and circumcise yourself," he said. "You're a Jew at heart already!"

A few days later, Stychius came into Caesarea, breathless with fatigue after a very swift journey from the wilderness around Jordan. Longinus heard his story, and then brought him before Pilate immediately. The Prefect was busy hearing cases from local Roman citizens, as he did on the first day of every week, but he hustled them out quickly after listening to Longinus' whispered message.

Once the audience room was clear, Stychius came in, his face less flushed after a long drink from the well and a cup of watered wine. He was a slim, deeply tanned Greek of about forty years. Like many young men from his impoverished country, he had sold himself into slavery at a young age, knowing that he could build a better future for himself as a slave in Rome than he could as a free man in the ruins of Athens. Longinus' father, who had squandered most of the family's fortune on drink and women, had purchased the teenager as a gift for his only son when he joined the Legions. Longinus had told Pilate that Stychius was the only gift his father had ever given him. The slave was completely devoted to his master, and the two of them had saved each other's lives on numerous occasions. So Pilate regarded the man with a respect he might not have accorded another slave.

"My centurion tells me you have some news of interest," he said.

"Yes, Your Excellency, I do!" said the Greek. "I stayed behind after my master and his men returned to Caesarea last week, in order to hear more of what the Baptizer was preaching. For a while there it was more of the same message that he was proclaiming when we arrived—the day of the Lord is at hand, repent and be baptized, that sort of thing. It sounds repetitive when I describe it, but let me tell you, when you are standing there, it is something else entirely. There is so much fire and conviction in his words! But then, two days after master Longinus and his men departed, something altogether different happened. It started like any other day—a large crowd was gathering, and John was warning them of the wrath to come if they did not cease their sinful ways—but suddenly he fell dead silent. He was staring intently at the back of the crowd, at one man who was standing there among the people, listening. The people began to part, forming a corridor to where this very ordinary-looking Jew was standing, his eyes and John's eyes locked on each other. For what seemed like an hour the two of them stood there, although I suppose it was only a minute or two. No one dared say a word!"

Pilate nodded, intrigued. "So what happened next?" he said.

Stychius continued his tale. "John spoke first," he said. "He raised one knobby, massive finger and pointed directly at the man, and cried aloud: 'Behold the Lamb of God, who takes away the sins of the world!' When he said that, this young Jew began walking towards him, never saying a word

244

until he arrived at the bank of the river. Their eyes were locked on each other, and John's voice trembled when he spoke next: 'This is the one of whom I spoke, who is mightier than I, for He existed before me!' The crowd gasped out loud, and began murmuring to one another, so I lost what was said next. The young Jew said something to the Baptizer, I'm not sure what it was, but John shook his head. The crowd grew quiet, and I heard the newcomer's voice for the first time. It was a voice unlike any other I have ever heard, deep and rich and sad, but at the same time shot through with some sort of irresistible joyfulness. It was the most compelling voice I have ever heard in my life!" He fell silent, his eyes far away.

Pilate interrupted his reverie. "So what did this compelling voice say?" he asked sardonically.

"Sorry!" said Stychius. "He said, 'Permit it this once, that we may fulfill what is righteous.' I didn't know what he meant when he said it, but then it became clear. John walked out into the Jordan, and this stranger followed him. John laid his hands over the stranger's head and bowed his own head in prayer for a moment, then dipped him in the Jordan and raised him up again—he baptized him the same as he had done countless others in the previous days. But when he brought the young man up out of the water, that's when it suddenly became very, very different!"

"How so?" asked Pilate.

"It was a cloudy morning, but at the moment that he brought the young man up out of the water, the clouds split and a single, blinding ray of sunshine blazed down on the stranger. Everyone gasped at that moment, because he seemed to shine with a light beyond just the reflection of the sun's glory in that moment. And just then, a white dove flitted down out of nowhere and landed on his shoulder."

"A bizarre coincidence, surely!" said Pilate.

"Maybe so, maybe not—but I can tell you I fell to my knees, and so did nearly everyone there!" said Stychius. "And while we were kneeling, the heavens thundered with a deep booming sound, unlike anything I have ever heard before. It made the ground shake, sir! And not just that—there were words in that thunder, although I could not understand them."

Pilate stopped him. "Wait a minute!" he said. "Are you telling me that the sky actually spoke?"

Stychius nodded slowly. "Yes, sir. I know it sounds improbable, but I was there and that was what I heard."

Pilate shook his head. Like most educated Romans, he tended to take all religions, even the many gods of Rome, with a grain of salt—but at the same time, he was also deeply superstitious. Signs and portents were real, as any true Roman could attest. But surely some anonymous Jew should not attract the attention of the gods in such a manner!

"So what happened after that?" he finally asked.

"When the sky thundered out like that, most of us hid our heads or closed our eyes," said Stychius. "When I dared look up again, he was gone—the stranger, that is. John was still standing there in the river, the crowd was still gathered, and the clouds were slowly parting. But there was no sign of the young Jew—although I thought I saw someone disappearing into the wilderness on the other side of the river. It was just a glimpse, so I do not know if it was him or someone else, or just a wild beast retreating into the scrub. But that was the end of it. The crowds began to drift apart, and John the Baptizer was deep in conversation with some of his disciples."

"Did you at least get the name of this mysterious stranger?" asked Pilate.

"I did hear someone in the crowd say it," replied the Greek. "They called him Jesus of Nazareth."

Pilate tossed the slave two golden sesterces. "Thank you for your report, Stychius. Now please leave us."

Stychius caught the coins neatly, tucked them in his purse, and bowed as he left. Pilate turned to Longinus, who was regarding him silently.

"Well, First Spear Centurion, what on earth do you make of that?" he asked.

"As an officer of Rome, or as a believer in God?" Longinus asked in turn.

"As a Roman, first and foremost," replied Pilate. "Although if your faith gives you any insights, feel free to share them as well."

"It sounds as if John believes this Jesus is the promised Messiah," said the centurion.

"But why call him 'the Lamb of God'?" Pilate asked. "From all you have told me, shouldn't the Messiah be more of a lion than a lamb?"

"There you strike on one of the mysteries of Hebrew prophecy," Longinus answered. "Many of the prophesies do speak of a Messiah who shall be a conquering king, but there are others—especially the prophet Isaiah, who lived about seven centuries ago—who talk of a suffering servant, who shall bear in his own body the penalty for all the sins of Israel."

"What superstitious twaddle!" snorted Pilate. "What you see in this religion I will never know. But . . . Jesus of Nazareth. That name seems familiar to me somehow, but I cannot place it. No matter! I want you to keep eyes and ears open, and if this Nazarene becomes a public figure, let us keep an eye on him. John the Baptizer posed no discernible threat to Rome. But who knows what someone who thinks of himself as the Messiah of the Jews might do?"

But Jesus of Nazareth had dropped off the face of the earth after his baptism, it seemed. For the next month, no one saw or heard a sign of him, although John continued to preach that the kingdom of God was going to begin on earth any day, and huge crowds continued to go and hear him. Rumor had it that he was denouncing many of the high and mighty among the Jews for their opulent lifestyles, and that he had singled out Herod Antipas in particular for his most scathing denunciations. Herod had recently stolen his brother Philip's wife, a formidable beauty named Herodias, and John was publicly calling her a harlot and Herod an adulterer. The King of the Jews had been called much worse in his time, and seemed to be taking it in stride, but the Jewish gossip mill said that Herodias was furious and wanted to see the so-called prophet dead.

Finally, over a month after Jesus' baptism, word began to come down into Judea that the Nazarene had appeared in Galilee, first turning up at his sister's wedding, where he apparently turned seven large jars of water into wine of the finest vintage. Then he began preaching to large crowds up and down the villages that dotted the shores of Lake Gennesaret. The stories also attributed remarkable healing powers to Jesus, who, as it turned out, had lived the first thirty years of his life as a humble carpenter. But, as far as Pilate could tell, there was nothing revolutionary in the man's teachings, and certainly no hint of violence. Besides, Galilee was technically in Herod's bailiwick, and Pilate had no desire to deal with the King of the Jews unless it was absolutely necessary. The man revolted him.

Another issue claimed the governor's attention that fall. After more than a year of peace, Zealot activity was on the increase. It was autumn, and Pilate was preparing to return to Jerusalem for the annual festival season, when two auxiliaries came galloping in to Caesarea, with the body of a third draped over his horse. They reported to Brutus Appius, who was the duty officer that day. He immediately went and got Pilate.

"Sorry to disturb you, sir, but I think you are going to want to hear this," said the centurion. Pilate descended the steps to the courtyard, where the men were standing over the body of their comrade.

"What has happened? Who has done this?" he asked.

"Well, Your Excellency, we were part of the garrison stationed down at Joppa," said the nervous young cavalryman. "Things have been pretty quiet-like down our way of late, and several of us have been hiring ourselves out as armed escorts for merchants traveling inland to Jerusalem or Samaria."

Pilate glared. Such activities were not technically illegal, but they were not particularly professional either. "Go on," he said coldly.

"I know what you're thinkin', sir," said the soldier. "It's not something we would have done when things were so bad with the Zealots before you got here. But with the attacks down, instead of sending an entire patrol to escort a caravan of merchants, it made more sense for three or four of us to go and escort them individually. We've been doing it for a year or more without incident—until this!"

"Tell the Prefect what happened!" snapped Appius.

"Three of our mates had signed on to escort a seller of perfumes from Joppa to Jerusalem, and they left town five days ago. Two days later, one of their horses wandered back into the post without a rider. We sent out a full patrol, and about ten miles up the road from Joppa we found the bodies. The merchant's head was cut off and perched on a rock with a perfume jar in his mouth, and our three comrades were all lying dead in the middle of the road, stripped of their armor and gear. Rutilius here was the senior one among them, and I guess the *sicarii* must have tortured him into admitting it, because he's the one they left their signature on."

"Signature?" asked Pilate.

They rolled the body over. He had been dead for three days, and was already starting to stink, but it was not the stench, nor the ghastly wounds, that cause Pilate to scowl. Carved into the man's chest in crude Greek letters was a name. A Jewish name—BAR ABBAS. The fanatics had found a new leader, it seemed, who was determined to provoke the Romans to wrath. Very well, thought Pilate. If wrath was what they sought, he would deliver it.

# CHAPTER NINETEEN

The hunt for Bar Abbas consumed most of Pilate's time that fall and winter. The new Zealot leader was elusive and very wary; he struck infrequently, and always in the areas where Pilate was not looking for him. In fact, Pilate became increasingly certain that the man must have an informant in Caesarea who kept him posted as to where the patrols were searching. Unfortunately, there were so many travelers, traders, prostitutes, and merchants in the city that finding the culprit was almost impossible. Pilate began keeping his plans more and more secret, only trusting his centurions with their orders at the last minute, and keeping the men in the dark until they actually set out. But the bandit leader still eluded him.

Little Decimus was growing rapidly, and continuing to terrorize the town and soldiers with his antics. Concerned for his safety, Pilate detailed two legionaries to follow the boy around at all times. They immediately fell under the toddler's spell and could be seen at all hours giving him rides on their shoulders, and sparring with him using wooden swords. Of course, at two years of age, they let him win every battle. But Pilate made sure that the child did know some limits; he had no desire to raise a spoiled monster like Gaius Caligula in his own household.

Procula was less tired now that the boy was bigger and not quite so dependent on her, and at times she seemed almost like herself again. Only occasionally did the memory of the daughter that Caligula had destroyed erase the smile from her face, but the scars of that loss were still there for both of them. Pilate, in the private recesses of his mind, bounced back and forth between a stoic acceptance of his fate and a primal desire to bathe in Gaius Caligula's blood. But in front of his family, he was affectionate to his wife and amused by his son and generally presented an attitude of contentment. Still, he missed Rome. As he wrote in a letter to Sullemia that spring,

> *I know that the Senate will resume its meetings in a few weeks, and I miss the give and take of the debates. I miss the honors that my Civic Crown accorded me when I entered the chamber, and I miss*

*proposing and commenting on legislation. I even miss the things I never thought I would—the interminable speeches that set us younger Senators whispering among ourselves, and the droning voice of the Princeps Senatus as he called us "Conscript Fathers." Most of all, though—and I will say this to you because you know what I mean—I miss those special missions for the Emperor; those opportunities to clean up a messy situation or silence a dangerous voice. It's not that I miss Tiberius himself—the old curmudgeon can go rot for all I care—but I miss being important! I miss being a player in the great game of Roman politics. I don't know that I will ever return to that world, but I remember it and long for it with an aching heart sometimes.*

He received a reply from Quintus Sullemius as summer began:

*Old friend, rest assured that the Rome you remember so fondly is not the Rome that I live in now. In fact, I may be coming your way soon if things do not improve. Last week Sejanus, who had recently been elected Consul, was summoned to a meeting of the Senate, where a sealed letter from the Emperor was opened and read. In it, Tiberius ordered the Conscript Fathers to immediately arrest his longtime agent and fellow consul Sejanus and execute him for treason on the spot! For once, Sejanus had no clue what was coming, but oh! How eagerly the Senate carried out that order! He was dragged screaming from the Forum and locked in the ancient Latumnia prison, and tried the next morning for treason. The trial lasted an hour; the Senate unanimously voted Condemno and he was strangled shortly thereafter. They rolled his body down the Gemonian stairs, and the crowd tore his carcass to pieces. There was rioting in the city all evening as the people tore down every statue and bust of Sejanus that they could find. His longtime lover Livilla is under arrest, along with both her children. Macro is now Prefect of the Praetorian Guard, and he seems like a much more reasonable fellow—for the moment, at least.*

*Now everyone is waiting in anticipation to see what Tiberius will do next. The problem is, the people of Rome have not seen their Emperor for nearly five years! There are all sorts of rumors about him that swirl about—many claim that he has degenerated into a disgusting pedophile who has boatloads of children brought to Capri for his pleasure, and that he executes those who do not please him. Although my sources in Neapolis tell me that this is not true, the fact that the mob is willing to believe it shows how little they think of their Emperor now. We do not know what to expect with Sejanus gone, but no one I know thinks that things will get better.*

Pilate put the letter aside with a sigh. Now that he was three years removed from his close acquaintance with the Emperor, he was more objective than he had been while acting as Tiberius' confidential agent and client. It seemed to him that Tiberius' problem was that he simply did not like himself very much, and being perpetually disappointed with himself had made him disappointed with everyone else. He wondered sometimes if Tiberius had ever been truly happy.

As for his own feelings about Tiberius, Pilate's anger had faded since the birth of his son, although it was never gone completely. He blamed Caligula for the death of Porcia Minor, and would till the day he died, but his feelings for the Emperor were more of a detached pity than the rage that had consumed him. He would never be fond of Tiberius, but he could at least understand the man more now than he once did. He decided that he would write a personal letter to the Emperor soon, something more friendly than the professional reports on the province that he had been sending out.

The day after his missive from Sullemius arrived, Longinus returned from an extended patrol in pursuit of Bar Abbas. He had managed to capture a couple of Zealots alive, but even under torture they had refused to betray their leader's location—in fact, they would not even admit knowing where he hid out. But the unknown bandit leader was growing bolder—as Longinus could testify.

"Right there in Capernaum, where my family lives, he set fire to the synagogue and burned it to the ground—and his men killed the local rabbi who was a good friend to me and my wife. He left his name carved on poor Samuel's chest, so that we would know who was responsible," said the centurion.

"Horrible!" said Pilate. "Bad enough they attack the soldiers of Rome, but when they start murdering all who are friendly to us, things can get ugly very quick. What about your family? Are they safe?"

Longinus nodded. "I am bringing them to Caesarea until this plays out," he said. "Too many Roman citizens and sympathetic Jews are being targeted by this scum."

"Do we know anything about him yet?" asked Pilate. "What sort of man is he? Does his name give us any clues?"

"Bar Abbas just means 'son of my father' in Hebrew," said Longinus. "It's commonly used by the sons of prostitutes or adulteresses who have no idea who their true father was. I did get a bit of a description from one of the Zealots we interrogated. We had to remove most of his toes before he started talking, but when he finally broke he gave us some details." He unrolled a small scroll and read aloud: "'A man of less than average height, but broad shouldered and powerfully built. He has a large scar down one side of his neck, and a chunk of his left ear is gone.' According to the man we interrogated, he is incredibly strong. When one of the *sicarii* flinched at killing the Jewish children of a Roman citizen, he picked the man up and strangled him barehanded while holding him in the air. I'm a strong man, Prefect, but I doubt I could do that to the smallest member of our legion. This fellow is a brute!"

Pilate sighed. "All the more reason we need to find him and nail him up!" he said. "If we cannot protect the people, or our own men, we will be held in contempt, and our governance of the province will be threatened. Continue to use all our resources to locate this man and his followers. Now, any other news of note?"

"Herod finally arrested John the Baptizer at the insistence of his wife Herodias," said Longinus. "Fat lot of good it did her, though. The king goes down to the dungeon to hear John preach and steadfastly refuses to lay a hand on him—apparently he either fears the wrath of God or the wrath of the mob."

"Herod!" said Pilate. "I got an invitation from him this week—he is throwing a celebration of his birthday in a fortnight. As much as I despise the man, I suppose I will have to go. Sorry, Centurion. What else?"

"This Jesus of Nazareth is drawing a wide following," Longinus continued. "He now has thousands flocking to hear him, and they say that he is cleansing lepers."

"Lepers!" said Pilate, his face wrinkling in disgust. "Everyone knows leprosy is incurable, and highly contagious! Does he actually touch them?"

"That's what they say!" said Longinus. "In fact, he cured ten of them a couple of weeks back, all at once."

Pilate shook his head. "More than likely he'll contract the disease himself if he persists," he commented. "If the search for this Bar Abbas were not so demanding, I would have you go and listen to him. I am curious to see what kind of threat he might pose."

"None so far," said Longinus. "One thing that all my sources agree on is that he avoids politics altogether, and only encourages his listeners to live their lives in honesty and purity. He says God cares more about the heart than he does about the Law."

"Then why have laws at all?" asked Pilate.

"That's why the Pharisees hate him so much," replied Longinus. "Their devotion to the ancient laws of Moses is passionate to the point of fanaticism, and they seem to think this Jesus is going to set aside all those laws."

"Interesting," said Pilate. "What does the Temple faction think about him?"

"This is truly odd," said Longinus. "The Sadducees and Pharisees have hated each other since I have been here—and long before that, from what everyone says. Yet both factions are united in their hatred of this Jesus of Nazareth. The Temple clique thinks that he will upset their cozy arrangement with Rome, and break their hold on the people's religious loyalties. The Pharisees think of him as a dangerous heretic out to abrogate the laws of Moses. But the common people adore him, flock to hear him, and apparently believe him capable of all manner of miraculous deeds."

"And what do you think, my compass of all things Jewish?" asked Pilate.

"I think I would like to hear him for myself," said the centurion. "I am very curious about him."

"Maybe soon," Pilate said.

Over the next couple of weeks there were no further attacks, and no clues emerged as to the location of the Zealot leader. Pilate decided to honor the invitation of Herod Antipas and attend the tetrarch's birthday party with his wife. He brought young Decimus along, but included the child's guards and nurse along with the entourage so that Porcia would be free to accompany him to the banquet. Given the events of the previous six months, they traveled with an escort of fifty legionaries and twenty-five mounted auxiliaries. They traveled quickly, and reached Herod's impressive fortress at Machaerus. The massive hilltop fort also included a luxurious castle in which the king could enjoy a respite from the oppressive summer heat, and it was here that Herod invited his family, friends, and the leading citizens of Judea as he celebrated his fifty-fifth birthday.

Pilate did not care much for Herod—the self-styled king (his official Roman title remained "Tetrarch," which irritated Antipas no end, since his father had been recognized by the Senate as "King of the Jews" throughout his reign) was a pompous ass whose long-winded, self-promoting monologues bored the Prefect to tears. But, being a politician, Pilate was aware that good relations with the native ruler were part of his responsibilities as governor, regardless of his personal feelings.

Perhaps attempting to atone for their previous argument, Herod made sure that Pilate and his wife were accommodated in a luxurious suite, with an adjoining room for their son. Little Decimus squealed with delight when he saw the carved wooden elephant with movable joints that had been deposited on his bed as a gift. Leaving the boy and his nurse to explore the elaborate nursery, Pilate and his wife bathed and donned clean garments for the evening's festivities.

Pilate wore his formal toga, bordered in purple to mark his *imperium* as Prefect, with purple stripes on the sleeves denoting his Proconsular status. Porcia wore a beautiful, sky-blue gown trimmed in pearls, with a single diamond solitaire around her neck and a woven net of pearls in her hair. Shortly before sunset, they were escorted to an elaborate dining hall, where the couches were piled high with cushions and the tables groaning with food.

The guest list was impressive. As High Priest, Caiaphas could not dine with Gentiles, but he had sent his father-in-law, Annas, the former High Priest, along with several other retired priests, to represent the Temple. A number of wealthy merchants and Roman citizens were also in attendance, as was Pilate's nominal superior, Aelius Lamia, the Proconsul of Syria, who had been in Rome for most of Pilate's term thus far and was conducting a brief tour of the provinces under his command before returning to the capital. All told, somewhere between fifty and a hundred people reclined at the dining couches as the servants prepared to begin filling their plates.

Herod was thoroughly enjoying himself—seated next to his wife Herodias at an elevated couch near one end of the room, he rose and greeted the guests in his usual florid fashion, then drained a cup of wine and wished for continued good relations between Rome and the people of Judea and Galilee. Herodias simpered and smirked next to him. Pilate had no doubt that she had been a beauty in her own time, but that time was clearly passing. Heavy applications of *stibium* could not erase the wrinkles that were beginning to line her face, and there was a hardness to her eyes that belied the giggling, girlish attitude she affected. No one knew her precise age; some said she was only forty, while others said she was almost her husband's age. By all accounts, she was not a woman to cross.

The food was rich, varied, and delicious. Pilate enjoyed good food, but always tried to eat in moderation, since he tried to keep his body in top condition. This evening, however, he made an exception and tried to sample a bit of every delicacy that was offered—everything from roast crocodile to glazed hummingbird tongues to the exquisite flounders that Romans prized above every other marine fish.

After the courses were served, the opening of birthday presents began. Pilate had gifted Herod with a beautiful, ornate shortsword modeled on the gladius carried by legionaries, but encrusted with jewels and a golden hilt. Lamia the Proconsul gave him a proclamation from the Roman Senate, allowing him to officially refer to himself as a client king, although his actual rank remained that of tetrarch. Herod humbly thanked the Roman Legate, although his eyes betrayed his contempt for the paltriness of the gift. Other, richer gifts followed—a tame ostrich with a golden collar, six comely Macedonian slave girls (whom Antipas leered over, while Herodias regarded them with a venomous glare—Pilate did not envy the lot of those hapless slaves!), a pair of golden goblets encrusted with rubies and emeralds from the High Priest, and on and on it went. Finally, when the last gift had been presented, Herodias stood up and spoke.

"In tribute to her father's generosity and grace, my daughter Salome will now dance for the king!" she said, and clapped her hands. A beautiful, lissome young female pranced into the room, accompanied by three slaves playing the flute, lyre, and timbrel. She swirled about the room with consummate grace, pirouetting and leaping in time to the music. The long, silken scarves that covered her nubile form were shed one by one, and as the tempo of the music sped up, so did the rate of her disrobing. By the time the final note was sounded and she knelt at her stepfather's feet, Salome was wearing only the golden slippers she had danced in, and a few gems scattered in her luxurious black hair.

Pilate was no prude, but he was somewhat scandalized nevertheless. It was one thing to have a slave perform a titillating dance at a birthday banquet, but one's own stepdaughter? It crossed all bounds of propriety!

Herod was enthralled, however! He had ogled every moment of the dance, and when it was done, he stood and applauded loudly, joined by most of the sycophants and merchants in the room. Pilate followed the lead of Aelius Lamia and gave a few polite claps of his hand, then resumed his seat. As the banquet hall fell silent, Herod spoke.

"Lovely daughter, your performance was most incredible! What a beautiful flower you have become, fit to adorn the garden of a king!" Porcia looked at Pilate and raised an eyebrow. The man was laying it on thick, her glance said. "In gratitude for your skill and grace, and your oft-shown willingness to make an old man happy," Herod continued with a leer, "I reward you with any request that you may desire! Indeed, up to half my kingdom is yours if you request it!"

Salome leaped to her feet, deftly wrapped one of the silks lying on the ground around her waist, and ran to her mother. Pilate could not hear what took place between them, but the girl's excited smile faded at what her mother said. She shook her head vehemently, but Herodias fixed her with a glare so fearsome she hung her head and returned to her place before the king.

"For your generous offer, Father, I thank you," she said. "After consultation with my beloved mother, the one thing I request of you is simple and plain. Bring me the head of John the Baptizer upon a platter!"

King Herod paled and sank back onto his couch. He shot a desperate glance at his wife, who returned it with a look of pure triumph. No one in the banquet hall said a word. Finally, Herod turned to one of the guards and whispered something. The man nodded, and taking two others with him, disappeared from the chamber. People began to whisper, and then Herod stood once more.

"Musicians!" he cried. "Give us something merry!"

The three-piece ensemble struck up a sprightly tune, and life began to return to the party as Herod weakly sank back down onto his couch and drained another glass of wine, his face still pale. Some of the guests began talking and laughing loudly, but most were still trying to process what had just happened. Salome managed to wrap herself in enough silks to restore a measure of decency and stood to one side, nibbling fruit off of a tray. Pilate looked at the succulent morsels on his plate and pushed them away—the whole tawdry exchange had taken his appetite. Lamia glared at the Jewish potentate with raw contempt.

Perhaps ten minutes passed before the large doors behind Herod's couch opened again, and one of the guards entered bearing a grisly trophy. There on a golden platter was the bearded head of the hapless prophet, eyes serenely closed, blood soaking his dark hair and beard. Whatever else could be said for him, thought Pilate, John's face was that of a man who faced his end with courage, leaving his *dignitas* intact.

The soldier carried the tray to Salome, who swallowed hard, looking sick, and carried it to her mother. The minute she handed it off she ran from the banquet hall, and the sound of her retching was clearly audible moments later.

Herodias lifted the prophet's head by the hair and looked at the dead face with a gaze of intense satisfaction, then spat upon it and tossed it back onto the platter. Herod glared at her. "You have your trophy, woman! Now get out of my sight!" he snapped.

She hesitated, and the Jewish king raised his hand as if to strike her. She froze him with a vicious look, then gathered up the tray and swept from the chamber. Herod turned to his guests and found himself met with looks that ranged from anger to contempt to amusement.

"I must apologize for this horrible interlude," he said. "But once I had given my word to the girl, I was bound to honor it—"

"SHAME!!" thundered a voice from the end of the room. Rheumy old Annas stood there, fixing the Tetrarch of Galilee with a look of pure contempt. "You have brought shame upon your father's name tonight, King of the Jews! You who were never worthy to pull up your father's bootstrap! The old king killed many men, some for good reasons, and some for bad, but he would never have murdered a holy man simply because a pubescent girl shook her bosom in his face! You are a thrall of strumpets, a king of whores, a disgrace to your family! I may have despised the Baptizer as an Essene extremist, but he had more honor in his camel's hair robe than you possess in your entire plump carcass!"

The man who had been High Priest for years, and who still controlled most of the Temple faction, stood and swept from the chamber, bristling with indignation. Most of the guests from Jerusalem who had come with him followed suit, whispering their outrage as they left the party.

Aelius Lamia stood next. As Rome's senior representative present, his voice was the voice of the Emperor, and the Senate and People of Rome. "You have indeed debased yourself here tonight, Tetrarch!" he snapped. "The Senate may have given you the honorary title of king, but I will not address you as such. You Easterners wonder why we see you as barbarians? You need look no further than these disgraceful goings-on to see why. I am returning to Antioch this very hour. Good night!"

Now all eyes turned to Pilate. He too rose, and Porcia stood beside him. "Well, Tetrarch," he said, "I had a low opinion of you before tonight—and you have done nothing to raise it. My wife and I must return to Caesarea, and please do not invite us to your next birthday party. I'll simply send you a present. I know a girl named Fatimah who would be a perfect addition to your lovely household!" He turned on his heel and departed, ordering the servants to wake Decimus and prepare to leave immediately.

As they donned their traveling clothes, Porcia gave him a kiss on the cheek. "You made me proud tonight, husband!" she said. "I do believe that Fat Fatimah would make a fitting tutor for young Salome, don't you?"

Pilate's laughter echoed down the hall as they walked down to the stables to retrieve their horses. He decided that they would not travel too far; it was late in the evening and the legionaries had not been expecting to set out again so soon. They rode in the dark until they reached the nearest town, where Pilate commandeered the inn while his soldiers pitched their camp around it. By then it was nearly midnight; he stayed awake long enough to pen a quick letter for Longinus and send it by way of three mounted auxiliaries. His message read:

> *Pontius Pilate, Prefect of Judea, to Primus Pilus Centurion Gaius Cassius Longinus: Herod ordered the execution of John the Baptizer this evening, on a drunken whim, at his birthday banquet. I am wondering what the reaction of Jesus of Nazareth and his followers will be when they get the news. If it is possible, please go with a small, unobtrusive escort and observe him and his followers for the next few days. Let me know if there is any danger of violence or insurrection. Also, alert your men and all the scattered garrisons to keep a watch out for Bar Abbas and his band of thugs — this seems like the kind of thing that they would exploit in order to work more harm on our people. Be careful, and report back soon!*

After dispatching the letter, he lay awake for a long time, pondering the evening's events. He wondered how the common folk would react to the murder of a man they considered to be a prophet, and whether Herod would be able to keep peace in the province after killing such a popular figure. Time would tell, he thought before finally fading off to sleep.

# CHAPTER TWENTY

Pilate arrived back in Caesarea two days later, after a quick stop at Jerusalem to place the garrison there on high alert. As word of the Baptizer's death spread across the countryside, the local mood turned bitter and ugly. At least for once, he thought, the anger was not directed at Rome! Herod, it was said, had barricaded himself inside the fortress at Machaerus and was not seeing anyone except his most loyal servants. Pilate tried to imagine the life of the king, locked in a castle with Herodias and her strumpet of a daughter, and could not suppress a smile. It couldn't happen to a more splendid fellow, he thought.

A week after that, he got a letter back from Longinus. The centurion's report was much lengthier than he expected:

> *Gaius Cassius Longinus, Primus Pilus Centurion, to Prefect Lucius Pontius Pilate, Greetings! Forgive the length of this epistle, but I think you will find it worth the time it takes to read it. Upon receipt of your letter I took three of my trusty lads and my servant, Stychius, and we went together to see the response of Jesus of Nazareth once he learned of the death of John the Baptizer—not a difficult assignment, because this Jesus seems to have taken up temporary residence here in Capernaum. He has hundreds of followers, but there are a dozen or so that he has named his "Apostles," and four of them live here—two sets of brothers named Simon and Andrew and James and John. He seems to enjoy speaking to the people along the shores of the Sea of Galilee, where the water can amplify his words to the point that those furthest back in the crowd can hear him plainly.*
>
> *He was standing up in the bow of a fishing boat when we arrived, telling a rather complex story about a farmer and some seeds that he sowed, when word began to filter through the crowd about the Baptizer's execution. Incidentally, I heard from no fewer than three people that John the Baptist was in fact a second cousin of Jesus! Be that as it may, the word of John's death spread through the crowd*

*like wildfire, and the mood turned ugly and resentful in a hurry. It was near the end of the day, and when Jesus finished his story, the crowd began shouting out to him about John's death, and asking what he was going to do about it. I don't think he was surprised to hear it—he certainly did not act shocked. He simply bowed his head in absolute silence for two or three minutes, then told the people that he was done teaching for the day, and lay down in the boat so that he could not be seen at all from the shore.*

*We waited as the crowd dispersed, hoping to speak to him when he came ashore. But as the people went home, the boat's oars deployed, and it headed to the other side of the lake. We went back to my home in Capernaum and ate a late supper, and then we slept for a few hours, making a point to be back at the lakeshore by dawn. The crowd began to gather again at first light, even bigger than the previous day. However, there was no sign of Jesus. The boat he had been in was beached on the far side of the lake, a tiny dot in the distance.*

*I don't know who first proposed the idea, but somehow the people got it in their head that they would walk around the northern end of the lake, ford the Jordan, and find Jesus wherever he was on the other side. Within an hour they had all set out—well over ten thousand, perhaps closer to fifteen. Men, women, little children, and oldsters, all still angry and outraged at the death of their old prophet, and longing for a guiding word from their new one.*

*My lads and I followed the group, trying to mix in with the crowds. Our shaven faces marked us as non-Jews, but there are many Greeks and Syrians now following Jesus also, so I don't know that anyone actually marked us as soldiers. It took several hours to cover the distance around the lake, and a bit of wandering through the hills on the far side before we finally sighted the small gaggle of men who were Jesus' closest followers—his apostles, whatever that designation means. The crowd gathered around them and began asking them where the Galilean had gone, but before they could answer, Jesus appeared at the brow of the hill and took a seat on a rock. The crowd pressed in as close as they could and everyone sank to the ground, exhausted.*

264

*I find it interesting that Jesus was now ready to teach, and they were now ready to listen. The day before they had been angry, outraged, and ready to march wherever anyone directed them. Now they were still upset by the death of the prophet, but they were not looking so much for someone to blame or punish as they were just seeking answers. By forcing them to march several hot, wearisome miles to find him, Jesus had sucked the fury right out of the crowd.*

*What did he say to them? Well, he started out by telling stories—a series of short tales that all had some applicable moral lesson. They say he calls them parabolas, because they lay a spiritual meaning into a story of earthly things. He spoke of landlords and tenants, of laborers and harvests, of shepherds and their sheep. Then he abandoned symbolic language and spoke straight and clear about the importance of forgiveness. He said that God cannot forgive our trespasses unless we forgive those who trespass against us. He also said that God will judge the souls of all men one day, and that the wicked will be held accountable for all the evil that they have done— but in the meantime, it is not our place to exact revenge, for that is God's prerogative. In short, Prefect, if you or I had written a message for him designed to calm the crowd and keep the peace, we could have done no better.*

*But this is not the end of the tale. As sunset drew near, his disciples approached him. I was too far out to hear what was said, but from their gestures and tone they appeared to be asking him to send the crowd away before dark. His reply drew several dismayed stares and negative looks, but finally one of the men—I think his name was Andrew—approached the crowd and asked if anyone had brought any food with them. Everyone looked at one another and no one said a word. Finally, one little boy, about ten years old, stepped forward with a basket. Andrew took him and his basket to Jesus, who reached into the basket and drew out some fish and bread. He hushed the crowd and raised the food up to the sky, thanking God for providing sustenance for his people, and blessing it for their consumption. Then he began to break the bread into pieces and distribute it to his disciples.*

*What happened next defies description, even though I have had a day or two to reflect on it now. Jesus kept reaching into that tiny basket and pulling out more bread! Each of his disciples had a larger basket, and I swear he filled each of them to the top with pieces of bread and fish! Then they began passing it through the crowd, and no matter how many people reached in to help themselves, the bread never ran out! Now I have no doubt that some people in the crowd had brought food with them, and seeing the child's willingness to share probably shamed them into sharing what they had with their neighbors—but the baskets the disciples were passing around never ran out, no matter how many people reached in and took out loaves and fish. I actually looked into the basket when it came to us, and it was nearly full! I took out three pieces of fish and a loaf, and each of my men took about the same—but it was still seemingly full when we passed it on.*

*Sir, I am a practical man in most ways, although I know that you scoff at my religion. But what I saw today can be termed nothing less than a miracle. Make of it what you will, and feel free to ask the men who were with me—but I know what I saw and have no other explanation for it.*

*We camped in the field that night and made our way back to Capernaum the next day. A terrific storm swept over the water shortly before dawn, and by the time we got back to town Jesus had already arrived with his followers. He was in the door of Simon the fisherman's house, and people were coming from far and wide to be healed by him of various sicknesses and diseases. How he does it I do not know, but I do not think it is by deception—the hardest reputation to maintain is that of a faith healer. I saw one young lad I have known personally, who has been lame in his ankles since birth, skipping down the street and yelling for joy. Whatever the source, this Galilean does seem to have some truly miraculous powers.*

*Well, this has rambled on for far too long. If I have bored you, I apologize, but I figured you would want to know what was going on. I am going to set my house in order here and do a sweeping patrol of the area before I return to Caesarea. Long live Rome!*

Pilate set the lengthy scroll down with a thoughtful expression. Feeding the multitudes, pretending to heal the sick? What was this Jesus up to? What did he hope to gain by such activities? Could he truly have miraculous powers of some sort? Pilate was skeptical of such things, but at the same time, like all Romans, he did believe in omens and auguries and the like. Could the gods actually be trying to communicate something to mankind through a Galilean carpenter?

Not bloody likely, he thought. Even if it was the invisible God of the Jews carrying out some plan for his people, why would he choose such a humble vessel? More than likely this Jesus was building a following so that he could make some sort of political move in the near future. Or perhaps, he thought, this Jesus was simply a madman, utterly convinced that he was some sort of divine agent. But how did that explain the "miracles" Longinus described? Surely the carpenter had learned some sleight-of-hand tricks, and planted a few actors in the crowd to mimic the sick. Pilate resolved to continue following the actions of Jesus from a distance, ready to intervene if the man posed a threat to Rome.

The rest of the summer passed quickly, with Pilate and his legionaries on the lookout for Zealot activity. Bar Abbas struck twice, once ambushing a patrol of six legionaries and leaving their gutted bodies beside the road, and then murdering a Roman citizen and his family as they traveled from Joppa to Caesarea. Pilate was furious at the loss of his soldiers, but their bodies were not discovered until three days after the attack. The second set of murders, however, was discovered almost right away by a squad of cavalry, and they sent word back to Caesarea while immediately following the trail.

Pilate personally led 200 mounted auxiliaries on the chase, and caught up to the band of scouts within three days. They were following a barely discernible trail through the wilderness between Jerusalem and the ancient city of Jericho. The countryside was wild and jumbled, with fallen boulders, rocky crags, and hills everywhere. It was one of the most dangerous parts of Judea, home to bandits and highway robbers that no amount of patrols could fully suppress. Pilate and his men followed the scouts at a distance of a half mile or so, not wanting to alert the enemy prematurely or do anything that might destroy the trail of barely discernible footprints that they were picking out of the rocky soil.

After a day and a half of this, the lead scout, a wiry, jet-black Numidian named Scarsus, called Pilate to the fore. "They knows about us, sir!" he said in his thick African accent. "See here, how the tracks completely disappear? They send troops back to erase them with hyssop branches. That can only mean we getting close."

Pilate knelt down in the clearing. Sure enough, the hoof tracks and footprints that entered the clearing disappeared without a trace in the center. Only a couple of fragments of the small leaves betrayed the use of the bushy hyssop branches used to erase the tracks. Looking closely, Pilate could see the tiny lines the leaves had left in the dust as it was swept back and forth. He eased forward, surveying the three rocky gullies that led out of the clearing into the hills.

"They take the middle one, Excellency," said Scarsus. "I already see two hyssop leaves near where it starts. We still finds them, no worries. Just be a little slower."

Pilate nodded slowly. He did not doubt the tracking skills of his Numidians, but if the enemy knew they were being tracked, he did not doubt that they were capable of mounting a response. Returning to the main body of his force, he called the senior officers in and spoke to them quickly and quietly, urging them to be on the lookout for an ambush at any time.

It came just after noon the next day, during the hottest weather they had encountered yet. The barely discernible trail of hyssop fragments and swept dust had led past a small, spring-fed water hole, so Pilate had ordered his men to dismount and fill their canteens while the scouts tried to see where their elusive quarry had gone from there. Suddenly the Numidian scouts came racing back, their startled cries causing the horses to rear and plunge. Pilate noted that three of them were missing, and as that realization dawned on him, he saw Scarsus fall face first into the ground, a feathered shaft protruding from between his shoulder blades.

"They are on us, boys!" he shouted. "Form turtle!"

Even though they primarily fought from horseback, Pilate had trained all his auxiliaries in basic infantry tactics, and issued each of them shields and blades as well as the lances and bows they preferred. In a trice they formed into a defensive circle, shields covering their bodies as arrows rained down into the clearing by the spring. The arrows seemed to be coming from the slope of two hills in front of them.

He ordered his archers to ready their bows beneath the cover of the shields their companions were holding, and then had them fire a volley in the direction the arrows had come from. The Zealots were shooting from well-chosen cover, and only one or two arrows found their mark, but the volleys forced them to duck back, and Pilate used the opportunity to maneuver his own forces.

"Divide!" he shouted, and the one turtle formation became two, each group about 120 strong. He heard the familiar *thunk* of arrows striking wood and leather, and ordered his archers to prepare another volley.

"When I give the word," he said to Marcus Quirinius, the senior centurion present, "we will launch a second hail of arrows, and then one century will charge up each hill. Don't slow, don't stop, and kill anything that shows its head. Once we are on top of them they won't be able to pick us off with bows. If we do not do this quickly, they will pin us down and send for reinforcements. If you can, try to take Bar Abbas alive."

He waited until each century had received his orders, then raised his gladius and gave the command. "FIRE!!" he roared, and half a hundred arrows streaked toward each slope. As soon as the bows twanged, the men let loose a battle cry and charged for the two hills. Pilate led the way, gladius in one hand and pilum in the other, waiting for a Zealot to show himself. There! Fifteen yards in front of him, a bearded archer stood, taking aim at the oncoming Romans. Pilate launched his spear with grim accuracy, and it caught the bandit in the head, sinking deep into his eye and piercing his brain. The man dropped without a groan, and Pilate looked for another target.

The Zealots had obviously not expected the Romans to go on the offensive quite so quickly. Many of them were still trying to aim their bows, but the Roman pilum, a four-foot-long spear with a sharpened iron tip, was deadly at this range, and these Romans were well trained—and angry. One by one, the Zealots who were not skewered dropped their bows, drew their swords, and charged at the hated occupation forces. Soon two sharp skirmishes were being fought, one on each slope. Quarter was neither asked nor given by either side, and several legionaries fell with arrows piercing their torsos, or guts spilled by the curved blades of the *sicarii*.

Pilate was in his element. Combat made him feel alive as nothing else could, and his blade sang in his hand as he cut down one Jewish bandit after another. Suddenly a pain like he had never felt before shot up his leg, and he looked down to see a feathered shaft protruding from his knee. The injured limb buckled beneath him, and he pulled himself onto a boulder so that the men would not see him on the ground. He waved the gladius over his head and shouted: "Don't stop, men! They are breaking! Keep at them!"

Indeed they were. Accustomed to ambush and stealth, the Zealots were not very good at pitched battles. Dozens of them had been cut down in the initial charge, and the others were wavering. One by one, they dropped their weapons and began to run for their lives. Pilate's auxiliaries launched arrows and pila after them, and several went down shrieking. For just a moment, at the crest of the hill, he caught a glimpse of a scarred neck topped by a swarthy face twisted with rage, before its stocky owner mounted his horse and took off at a gallop, with several others riding in his wake.

"That's Bar Abbas!" Pilate snapped. "After him, men! Mount up and bring him back to me alive!"

About thirty auxiliaries, led by Quirinius, leaped on their horses and took off after the fleeing Zealot leaders, while the remainder, still on foot, focused on killing those who still resisted. Now that the heat of the battle had passed, any who threw down their weapons, or were too badly wounded to fight, were taken into custody and bound hand and foot. The cavalrymen herded them into the clearing about halfway up the slope where Pilate still sat on a boulder, covering his wounded leg with a shield. It still hurt, but he would not let himself show pain in front of his own men, much less before these captured enemies.

He took a long drink from his water skin and wiped the sweat from his eyes with the sleeve of his tunic. Finally the senior cavalryman present, a Gaul named Silas Hirtius, approached with a scrap of parchment.

"Here is the tally of our losses and the enemy's casualties, pending the return of Centurion Quirinius, Prefect," he said.

Pilate glanced at the crudely lettered list. Sixteen auxiliaries and twelve horses killed, another twenty wounded—with six not expected to live long.

Over fifty Zealots were dead, with men still dragging bodies up from the brush. Eleven of the enemy had been taken alive, eight of them unwounded or only lightly wounded. It had been a bloody affair, and he disliked taking that many losses—but considering that they had been ambushed, things could have gone far worse.

"Let's head back down to the spring and make camp for the night," he said. "Chain these dogs up and make sure they get neither food nor water this evening. Those two are likely too far gone to be anything but a burden, so go ahead and finish them off now. Set the men to gathering wood so that we can burn our dead—and stack the enemy's bodies up on top of the hill. Let their bleached bones be a warning to their companions!"

The cavalryman nodded, and before he walked off to carry out his orders, Pilate said: "After the prisoners are out of my sight and the men are set to work, come back here and bring our physician with you!"

Not long after that—at least, it didn't feel very long, although the shadows were lengthening by the time Hirtius returned—the Greek doctor, Aristarchus, was able to examine Pilate's injured knee.

"It's a bad wound, Governor, and no mistake," he said after poking and prodding the already swollen joint and gently wiggling the arrow—which nearly caused Pilate to pass out with pain. "This thing has to come out, but pulling it will only aggravate the injury. The best way to deal with it is to push it all the way through, cut off the barbed point, and then pull the shaft out. I have some milk of poppy in my kit, and it will numb the pain a bit— but you cannot ride or walk until it begins to heal."

"A commander must be able to ride!" Pilate snapped.

The Greek looked at him patiently. "Sir, with all due respect, if you do not allow this injury to heal properly, you could very well lose your leg—or your life. In time, perhaps, you can ride again. But you must allow me to treat you now."

Pilate nodded, and several strong arms lifted him gently and carried him back toward the spring. A command tent had already been erected, and a cot was waiting for him. He drank a long swig of water and chased it down with some wine. His vision was clearing a bit, and he could see that the entire lower half of his leg was soaked with blood, some drying and some still wet. The shaft of the arrow pointed up at an angle, but its head was buried several inches deep into his knee joint. The slightest movements made him want to scream.

"Drink this, sir," said the Greek, and held a small bronze ladle to his lips. Pilate drank, and immediately he felt a deep sense of relief as his senses were blunted. He lay back against the rough cushions, and Aristarchus nodded. Three large cavalrymen, probably the same ones who had carried him into the tent, came in. "I am going to have to push the arrow all the way through your knee," said the physician. "If it were not so deep, I could use an arrow extractor, but it is so far through that letting it push out the back of your knee is the easiest course. You may lose consciousness from the pain, but you need to bite down on this so that you do not injure your tongue." He handed Pilate a short stick, about the diameter of his thumb, wrapped in leather. "Make all the noise you wish, but try not to move your leg. These men will immobilize you as much as they can. Remember, the more you thrash, the longer this will take and the more it will hurt."

Pilate nodded and took the wooden stick in his mouth. One large Gallic cavalryman held his shoulders down firmly, while the other two held his legs still. The physician carefully put both his hands on the arrow and studied its angle for a moment, then suddenly and sharply pushed with one hand while striking the butt of the arrow with the other. There was a ripping sensation, and white-hot pain shot from Pilate's wound to every nerve ending in his body. He arched his back and bit down so hard he felt the stick break in his mouth—or was it his teeth? He could not tell. Pain was his world, the dark, laughing god of his universe, a sea into which he had plunged, determined to find the bottom.

He barely heard Aristarchus as the Greek looked at the arrowhead protruding from the back of his leg. "No doubt this was the best course," the little man said. "This is a double barbed point and would have done more damage coming out than going in." He brought over a pair of iron shears and there was a loud snap as he cut the point off the arrow. "This should be nothing compared to what you have already felt," he said, and with a brisk tug pulled the shaft out of Pilate's insulted joint. Despite his words, Pilate felt as if his leg were being torn off by a crocodile. He reached the bottom of the sea of agony, and lost consciousness.

When he came to, he saw sunlight rippling across canvas over his head. There was a sensation of motion, but he was lying on a linen blanket. His leg was swathed in a huge bandage. He raised himself slightly, and a warning tremor of pain shot up from his knee, so he lowered himself again with a groan.

"You're awake!" said Aristarchus. "Good!"

"Where am I, and how long was I out?" asked Pilate.

"Only a day and a half," said the Greek. "Your wound bled extensively—the arrow must have nicked a blood vessel—and I had to alternate a tourniquet with spiderweb bandages to keep you from bleeding to death. The men commandeered this merchant's wagon from Jericho, and I rigged up this hammock to spare you the bumps and jostles of the road. We are on our way back to Caesarea with the prisoners, and our wounded."

Pilate nodded. "How are the men?" he asked.

"Three of the wounded have died, and one I do not expect to last the day. The rest will recover, but two of them will never swing a blade again," the Greek said matter-of-factly.

"Has Quirinius reported in?" he asked.

"Not yet," said the doctor. "But Silas Hirtius has sent word to him that we are returning to Caesarea. Everything is in hand at the moment, Prefect. The best thing you can do is sleep and let your body heal itself. Sip a bit of this, and I will change your bandage and wash your wound."

Pilate tasted the familiar flavor of milk of poppy, and then watched with some detached interest as the bandage was deftly unwound from his injured joint. The wound was ghastly—swollen and red and leaking blood and pus. But there was no blackness, and no angry red streaks running up his leg. He had seen enough battlefield injuries to know that he was very fortunate to have avoided infection thus far. With gentle hands, the Greek began washing the wound with vinegar and warm water. There was some pain, but the opium blocked it sufficiently that Pilate dozed back off before Aristarchus was done.

Sometime the next day Quirinius and his men caught up with the slow-moving caravan. Pilate was more alert, and listened with interest as the centurion reported the result of the chase. "There were about a dozen or more of them, sir, that mounted up and took off with Bar Abbas leading them," he said. "They led us on a merry chase all the way from the Jericho Road to Mount Ebal. We were closing in and I could tell their horses were about to drop. Suddenly all but one of them dismounted, and turned to face us. They were heavily armed, and we had to stop and give combat. Turns out that they were all of Bar Abbas' top lieutenants, and they had agreed together to sacrifice themselves in order to let him get away. Two of my boys took off after him while we attacked the rest. They fought like lions, I will give them that. We only took three of them alive, but the battle lasted an hour and cost me four men killed and six wounded. Once they were dead or subdued, we went after Bar Abbas and found the bodies of the two men who had chased him down. But he took all three horses then and disappeared towards Salim and Aenon. We lost his trail in the wilderness there, and decided to bring his officers back with us so you could question them."

Pilate swore. "I hate that the ring leader eluded us," he said, "but I think we have crushed his insurrection. We will put these prisoners to interrogation when we get back to Caesarea—the officers at least. Go ahead and nail the others up outside the city gate as soon as we get there. Send word to Cassius Longinus to report for duty directly to me as soon as possible." He shifted on his hammock and groaned as the pain shot upwards from his knee. "And tell that Greek to bring me some wine!"

They arrived back in Caesarea two days later, and Pilate was handed off to the loving ministrations of his wife. The leg still throbbed like mad but was growing more tolerable. It was the forced sedentary lifestyle that drove Pilate half mad with frustration. For the first three days, he was unable to move from his bed at all. Longinus took over the day to day command of the legionaries, and reported in every afternoon.

Bar Abbas' lieutenants held out for almost two days of brutal interrogation, but Pilate's men were very good at extracting information. Eventually they broke two of the men, although the third managed to strangle himself with his own long, shaggy locks in the dungeon cell where he was being held. Longinus summarized the confessions for Pilate late that afternoon.

"Bar Abbas had a total of one hundred fifty men under his command," he said. "Of that total, we have now killed or captured some one hundred forty. They had a large network of caves in the wilderness, not far from where you engaged them near the Jericho road. I have already dispatched troops to search the caves, seize all weapons and loot, and burn what they cannot transport back here. Bar Abbas had sent a few men into Galilee to scout for a new hideout; he has probably joined them. But with such a pitiful force at his command, I would say we have eliminated him as a threat for the time being."

Pilate nodded and carefully sat up, swinging his injured leg over the side of the bed but careful not to allow it to touch the ground. "What about the remaining two Zealot lieutenants?" he asked.

"We crucified them this morning," Longinus said. "They are hanging outside the gates, near where we nailed the others up—the last one of them died yesterday morning, and I ordered them all cut down because they were beginning to stink."

Pilate gritted his teeth. "I want you to help me stand and get dressed," he said. "It's been a week since I was hurt, and I want to see those barbarians on their crosses. There is a crutch in the corner—Aristarchus brought it for me yesterday, and said I could try it when I was ready."

With great difficulty, he donned his uniform and cloak, omitting only the boot that would have gone on his injured foot. With the help of Longinus and his sturdy cedar wood crutch, he made his way down to the courtyard. The legionaries cheered when they saw their commander on his feet again. He acknowledged their support with a wave and a nod, and stumped his way toward the city gate. His leg was throbbing already, but his face was a stoic mask. He acknowledged the greetings of Caesarea's loyal citizens with a curt nod, and finally came to a halt in front of two fresh crosses.

The men who hung there, heads lolling, did not notice him at first. One of them finally regarded him with a vacant stare, but the other managed to speak through a mouthful of broken teeth. "Think you've won, Roman pig?" he asked in a voice thick with blood and exhaustion. "Bar Abbas lives, and as long as he lives, loyal sons of Israel will rally to his cause! You will never subdue our homeland!"

Pilate looked at him with scorn. "When I am where you are, and you stand before my cross, you can gloat, you simpleton!" he snapped. "Your beloved master bandit will hang on a cross next to you soon enough. He is hiding like a cornered rat in a barn full of cats. Your insurrection is over." He turned and started to limp away.

"Too bad it's left you a cripple," shouted the man on the cross. "A crippled leg for a crippled soul!"

A thin haze of red covered Pilate's vision, and the beast within him, which had been in a pain-numbed sleep, woke up and howled for blood. He kept his voice very calm as he walked up to the legionary who was standing his post at the city gate. "Bring me a bow, please," he said.

Longinus looked at him with concern. "What are you going to do?" he asked. "And are you sure you can do it?"

"Shut up and hold me upright!" snapped Pilate. Moments later the bow was in his hand, and Longinus propped him up as he took careful aim and skewered the mocking bandit's knee with an arrow. The man's cursing imprecations disappeared in a howl of pain.

"That was for my knee," said Pilate. He drew a second arrow from the quiver, sighted the bow again, and sent a second arrow through the man's other knee. The *sicarii*'s voice hit a new octave of pain. "And that," said Pilate, "was because I felt like it."

The man looked at the Roman prefect, moaning in agony. Pilate nearly forgot his own pain as he watched his enemy suffer. Finally the bandit captain spoke, his voice trembling. "Kill me," he begged. "Kill me, you Roman bastard!"

Pilate gave him a sweet smile. "No," he replied, and limped back through the city gates.

# CHAPTER TWENTY-ONE

Pilate never really remembered how he got back up to his bed afterwards. He knew he had pushed himself too far, and when he forgot, his leg reminded him. He stayed in bed all that day; and for the week after that Pilate contented himself with moving from his bedchamber to his office, and occasionally to the dining room. The pain was ferocious whenever he tried to put any weight on the leg, and after the first week, Aristarchus refused to give him any more of the painkilling poppy milk.

"It is a powerful drug, Prefect, and I have seen too many become addicted to its effects," he explained.

Pilate nodded in agreement, but the pain was still unbearable at times. He found himself drinking more than he ever had before. His body proved tough and resilient, and gradually the torn tissues knitted back together. By the end of a month he could put a little bit of weight on the leg, and graduated from a crutch to a cane. His wife's constant support helped his recovery, but over time the frustration at his limited mobility became a greater source of stress than the pain itself. Simply put, Pilate was not used to being hobbled, and it angered him.

His soldiers quickly learned that the spare, muscular figure limping about Caesarea on a cane had less tolerance for failure than ever before, or else they paid the price in docked pay and corporal punishment. They still respected Pilate, but many of them began to lose the affection they had developed for him. Only the veterans and officers, who understood his frustration, still treated him as the commander that they had learned to admire over the last few years.

A couple of months after his injury, Pilate received a letter from the Emperor. Tiberius' handwriting was shakier than ever, but his tone was friendlier than it had been since Pilate was banished to Judea. It read:

*Gaius Julius Tiberius Caesar, Princeps and Imperator, to Prefect Lucius Pontius Pilate, Proconsul of Judea; greetings!*

*I am sorry to hear of your injury, and hope that your recovery is quick and complete. One thing a life on the battlefield has taught me is that no part of the human body seems capable of generating as much pain as the knee joint. I have seen grown men, strong and brave warriors, scream like little girls from the sort of injury you describe.*

*On the other hand, I am glad to see that the Zealot forces have been trounced once again, thanks to your leadership. I am sorry their leader Bar Abbas eluded you, but I have no doubt you will bring him to justice soon enough. Perhaps the gods have allowed you to suffer this hurt as a warning that you are past the age when you should lead from the front! You are as brave a soldier as I have ever commanded, but you have proven all you can as far as physical courage goes. Don't continue to risk yourself after this!*

*I miss your competent leadership in Rome. Since arranging the fall of Sejanus, I have begun to purge the Senate of its worst elements. They call me a tyrant and a second Sulla, but the Republic has become a travesty of its former self, and I am determined to set it right again before I die! Cutting off gangrenous members is an odious task for a physician, but sometimes it is the only option in order for the body to heal itself. Although I suppose this might not be an appropriate time to mention the subject of gangrene, eh?*

*Gaius Caligula is a man now, and I like him less and less as the years go by. I should never have made him my heir, but he is the last of the Julian line except for my grandson Tiberius Gemellus, and Gemellus is still a youth. If I live long enough, perhaps I can dispose of Gaius and elevate Gemellus in my place—but I am not sure I will be spared that long. You tried to warn me, and I was foolish not to listen. Now Agrippina and her other sons are dead, and this youth I thought would be the savior of Rome has grown into a serpent. I should have died a decade ago, when my son might have succeeded me. Longevity is a terrible burden.*

*I wish I could order you back to Rome, but I fear that the moment I breathed my last, Gaius would have you and your entire family murdered. The only thing that restrains him now is the fear of my ill will, and once I am gone, he will have no brakes at all. May the gods help poor Rome then! In the meantime, Lucius Pontius, keep the peace in Judea and continue to cherish your family. If you can find it in your heart, forgive the sad old man who once called you friend.*

Perhaps it was the wine he had drunk that evening, or maybe it was the lingering pain and frustration from his debilitating injury, but when Pilate put that letter down, he put his head in his hands and wept—for himself, for his lost daughter, for his wife's pain, and even for the pitiful old man who ruled the known world. He found himself hoping that his own end would come swiftly and before his body had begun to wear out. At forty-seven, he wondered how many years he would have before he began to fail physically. Ten? Fifteen? Much would depend on how completely he was able to recover from his wound, he realized. With that in mind, he levered himself up and began climbing up and down the stairs, relying on his cane as little as possible. His healing joint screamed in outrage, but he kept it up until he was soaked in sweat and could not lift his leg up one more time. Then he collapsed onto a couch and fell asleep in his office.

Little Decimus did not exactly understand why his *tata* had become so grumpy, but he did quickly pick up on the idea that it was no longer a good idea to climb into Pilate's lap. Still, he ran around the family's living quarters and his father's office, destroying crockery with cheerful indifference, and generally provoking smiles and groans in his wake. Pilate found that he was incapable of remaining angry at the toddler, even when the boy bumped his injured leg.

Meanwhile, Cassius Longinus had returned his family to Capernaum, since the Zealot threat was greatly reduced. With Pilate's permission, he had stayed there for a couple of weeks before returning to Caesarea to escort Pilate and his cohorts to Jerusalem for the autumn festivals. He had been away from Caesarea for a couple of weeks when Pilate got a letter from the centurion that caught him by surprise.

*Gaius Cassius Longinus to Prefect Lucius Pontius Pilate:*

*In the wake of recent events, I have been remiss in not reporting on the activities of Jesus of Nazareth. However, what happened yesterday was remarkable enough that I feel I have to share it with you. I know your skepticism well by now, but if you have a rational explanation for this, I would really like to hear it when I get back!*

*We had only been in Capernaum for a day when my servant Stychius began to run a fever. The sickness grew steadily worse over the next three days, and by the end of the week it was obvious he was dying. His face was gray, his breathing labored, and his lungs rattled with each exhalation.*

*Stychius was a gift from my father, and served me as my slave for years. Even when I freed him five years ago, he chose to remain with me as a paid servant. We have been in countless battles together, and he has saved my life on more than one occasion. Despite the way our relationship began, he is more of a brother to me than my real brothers ever were. Needless to say, I was deeply distressed at the thought that he might perish.*

*About that time, one of my men said that Jesus was returning to Capernaum after preaching and healing at Bethsaida and Chorazin. Knowing his reputation as a healer, I decided to ask if he could help Stychius. I set out alone, and by the time I spotted the crowd approaching town, I was running, soaked in sweat and out of breath. Several of the locals knew me, and they helped me push through the ring of supplicants and curiosity seekers that surround Jesus everywhere he goes.*

*So it was that I found myself speaking to the itinerant from Nazareth for the first time. I addressed him as Rabbi, and explained my servant's plight to him. He looked at me with the most piercing eyes I have ever encountered, and said nothing for a moment.*

*"Please, rabbi, do this for him," said my friend Jacob, a rabbi from Capernaum. "He is the one who paid to rebuild our synagogue when the Zealots burned it." Several other locals who know me also spoke up, urging him to help poor Stychius for my sake. He nodded his assent, and gestured for me to lead him to my home.*

*I am not sure why I said what I said next, but the words came out of me before I knew what I was saying: "Lord, you do not have to come with me. I am a man under orders, but I also have a hundred men under my command. All I have to do is tell them what I want done, and they do it. If you will speak the word, I believe my servant will be made well."*

*Jesus looked at me, and his eyes widened with astonishment—and pure joy. I got the sense that there was enough merriment bottled up inside him to set all of Rome to laughter, were it let loose.*

*"Did you hear this?" he said in that wonderfully mellow voice. "I tell you, not in all of Israel have I found such faith! Go your way, my friend. Your servant is healed."*

*I turned and walked slowly back to Capernaum—realizing as I did so that I must have run several miles in my desperation to find Jesus. When I got back to the house, I found Stychius sitting up and sipping some broth. His color had returned and his breathing was normal. When I asked them at what time he had begun to improve, they told me that the fever had broken an hour ago—which, by my reckoning, was at the moment Jesus told me 'Your servant is healed.'*

*What can I say? I have no explanation, except that this man's powers of healing are real. The stories I have heard about him are remarkable, and I had discounted most of them—till now. If he could recall Stychius from the threshold of Hades, I have no doubt that he can cure lepers, give sight to the blind, and do all the other things they say of him. I can imagine your face as you read this, Prefect, but if you had been here, you too would believe.*

Pilate put the letter down with a frown. Longinus was so reliable in so many ways that it befuddled him to think that the man could be so gullible when it came to religion. So a man's fever broke when he seemed at death's door? Stranger things happened all the time. It did not mean that a carpenter had suddenly become Apollo incarnate! At least, he thought, this Galilean still showed no sign of urging his followers to revolutionary activity.

A month later, Pilate set out with two cohorts for his fall visit to Jerusalem. Herod was returning to the city for the first time since the death of John the Baptist, and had invited Pilate to stay in his palace again—along with "as many soldiers as you care to bring with you," the letter said. Pilate smirked—apparently Antipas was not very certain of his welcome in the city! Well, despite Pilate's scorn for him, Herod was a tetrarch appointed by the Roman Senate, so Pilate figured it would not hurt to post a century of legionaries around his palace to keep his plump hide safe.

His leg was definitely improving, but he still had to carry a cane, and riding on horseback was an exercise in misery. Wine dulled the ache a bit, but Pilate was trying to cut back on his drinking now that his recovery was near complete. So he gritted his teeth like a true Stoic and endured the misery as the three-day, fifty-mile journey dragged on. When they finally arrived in the city, Pilate ordered the main body of the troops to the Antonia Fortress, and took Quirinius and his century with him to Herod's palace.

The king was a bit slimmer and grayer than he had been, and the lines around his eyes had deepened. Herodias and Salome had remained at Machaerus—"for their own safety," was how Herod put it, although it was obvious he was delighted to leave them behind for a while. His hostility to Pilate was still there, but veiled for the moment behind a mask of artificial charm. Pilate endured his greetings, then limped to his room and ordered the servants not to disturb him until noon the next day. He drank one glass of strong, costly wine from Herod's extensive cellar, then removed his cuirass and boots and collapsed onto the bed.

It was about mid-morning when he finally got up. He used the chamber pot and stretched, his injured knee still throbbing. He pulled up his tunic and studied the damage done by the Zealot arrow. The sharpened iron head had gone clean through the bone of his kneecap, splitting it in two, and there was still a divot in the center where it had not fully healed, as well as an ugly, inch-wide scar. The point had then passed between the bones of his upper and lower leg, shearing through some of the tendons, and finally come to rest just under the skin behind his knee. There was a second scar, which felt identical to the first one, behind his knee, where the arrow had been pushed through so the barbed point could be removed. The major damage had been within the knee joint itself—the top and bottom bones of his leg had been forced apart, and probably chipped and damaged, by the arrow's passage. The damage to his sinews was such that the leg had less than half the strength of the other, and his knee was liable to buckle without warning if he put his full weight on it. But as long as he used his cane, he could now limp along at a decent pace. Aristarchus had told him that the sinews might heal further in time, but that the knee would never be the same as before. He looked at the iron arrowhead, which he had kept after it was removed, and wondered that such a small thing could cause him so much misery.

Pilate went to the door and called for bread, olive oil, and some grilled fish. As he was breaking his fast, a servant appeared, bearing a letter. Pilate set it aside until he was done eating, and then broke the seal and read it.

> *Joseph Matthew Caiaphas, High Priest of the Temple, to Lucius Pontius Pilate, Prefect of Judea: Greetings, noble governor, and I pray that your recent injury is healing cleanly. I realize that you do not care much for me or for the Temple, but I know that you do care for the peace and order of our province, as we do. There is a matter which threatens that peace, which I would discuss with you at your earliest convenience. You can meet me at the guard house where we met before. Please let me know the most convenient time by letter.*

Pilate sent a short note back, offering to meet the High Priest the next morning. He then sent word through one of his soldiers to have Longinus report to him as soon as possible. The senior officer of the Judean legions responded with alacrity.

"Good morning, Longinus," Pilate greeted him. "How fares your servant Stychius?"

"Most well, sir," said the centurion. "He was fully recovered by the next day and is performing his duties as if he were never even sick."

"Now that you have had time to think about it, do you really think this Galilean healed him from miles away?" asked Pilate.

"Sir, he was dying. I have no doubt that if I had not sought out Jesus, Stychius would not have lasted the rest of the day. I have no explanation for it, but I am convinced Jesus did it," explained Longinus.

"Most peculiar," said Pilate. "But there are other matters to attend to. How goes the search for Bar Abbas?"

"We have put a reward of five hundred denarii out on him," said Longinus, "and we have also posted warnings throughout Galilee and the other provinces that anyone caught harboring him should be crucified alongside him."

"Has anyone come forward?" Pilate asked.

"One young Greek, traveling through Galilee selling fabrics, said that he saw a man resembling Bar Abbas traveling through the hills north of Chorazin," said the veteran soldier. "But we sent three patrols through the country, and all we found were a few cold campfires. A week later, a retired legionary named Milo Lammius and his Jewish wife were found stabbed to death in their beds at their home near Cana. The killer took every coin they had, as well as clothes and horses—and left the name Bar Abbas painted on the wall in their blood."

"Double the reward!" snapped Pilate. "And amend the earlier notice to read that anyone caught aiding or harboring Bar Abbas will be crucified, along with their entire family! I want this man caught!"

Longinus nodded. "I think that it is only a matter of time now," he said. "There was some popular support for Bar Abbas early on, but as he has become more violent and less discriminating in his targets, the people have become more and more resentful of him. Sooner or later, someone is going to bring him in, dead or alive."

"Let's hope so," said Pilate. "Now, take a look at this." He pushed the High Priest's note from that morning across the table, and Longinus read it carefully. "Do you have any idea what is bothering him this time?"

"I can guess," said Longinus. "I imagine he wants you to arrest or kill Jesus of Nazareth."

"Whatever for?" said Pilate. "The Galilean has harmed no one, he does not preach insurrection, and the people are mad for him!"

"You touched on the reason right there," said the senior centurion. "Jesus has become enormously popular, and he has become increasingly scathing in his comments about the Temple cult, and about the Pharisees as well."

"Don't the priests and the Pharisees hate each other?" asked the Prefect.

"Normally yes," replied Longinus. "But they are now united in their opposition to Jesus, and are working together to discredit him. He draws crowds in the thousands wherever he goes, and they are afraid he will spark an insurrection that will cause Judea to lose the small measure of independence it retains—which, of course, would also destroy the Temple's political standing with the Empire."

284

Pilate nodded. "If I thought he was a danger to Rome, I would have dealt with him already," he said.

"I know that," said Longinus, "but they do not know you as I do. They probably assume you to be completely ignorant about the matter."

Pilate shook his head. "Was there ever a race in all the *gens humana* as mad as the Jews?" he said. "I have bitterly atoned for my misdeeds by being sent to govern them! No matter, I suppose I will meet with old Caiaphas tomorrow and hear his side of the story. So what is it that Jesus says about the religious leaders that has them so upset?"

Longinus laughed. "He compared the Pharisees to whitewashed tombs the other day—shining white on the outside, but full of corruption and rot within!"

Pilate grunted: "Are you sure he was not talking about the Roman Senate?"

Longinus said: "You would know the truth of that better than me, sir. He has repeatedly condemned the corruption and wickedness of the Temple, and said on more than one occasion that if the Temple was destroyed, he could rebuild it in three days!"

Pilate shook his head. "No danger of testing that hypothesis!" he commented. "It would take an army with many siege engines to pull that massive thing down! But that is an odd comment. Didn't the Temple take fifty years to build?"

"It did that, sir," replied the centurion, "and they are still working on the north tower."

"Is Jesus mad then?" asked Pilate.

"I don't think so," said Longinus. "I think it may have been some sort of figure of speech."

"I guess we'll find out tomorrow," he said, rising with a groan as his knee protested.

"So how are you healing, Prefect?" Longinus asked him.

"Slowly and painfully, Centurion," replied Pilate. "I never knew anything could hurt so much."

"Perhaps Jesus could heal it for you," Longinus said with a smile.

"Perhaps he could give you a mouth that knows when to shut!" Pilate jibed back at him.

The next morning Pilate and Longinus walked across town to the long colonnade where Caiaphas was waiting. Pilate dismissed his lictors and sat down at the guard's table while Caiaphas explained his reason for requesting the meeting.

"Prefect, I must ask that you arrest this teacher named Jesus, from Nazareth, immediately. He should be jailed at the very least, or sold into slavery, or put to death!" exclaimed the priest. "Whatever the means, he must be silenced!"

"If he has committed a crime, Caiaphas, then you should arrest him and judge him under your own laws!" Pilate responded.

The angry Caiaphas glared at the Roman governor. "We cannot!" he replied. "He has too huge a following. If we move against him openly, the people will rise up and stone us to death."

"So you want Rome to do your dirty work for you?" asked Pilate. "Why should I allow that?"

"Because the man is as big a threat to Rome as he is to the Temple!" snapped Caiaphas.

"Even if I believed that to be true, primary jurisdiction would still rest with the Sanhedrin," said Pilate. "And the fact is that this Jesus has not preached rebellion or resistance to Rome. It seems to me that you simply are jealous of the man's popularity."

Caiaphas scowled as if he had been confronted with a piece of roasted pork. "That is NOT the case at all!" he snapped. "It is his teachings that flout our laws and traditions. They threaten the Temple's hold on the hearts of the people. Even the muleheaded Pharisees can see that his contempt for traditional values and our interpretations of the law are a danger to our nation and our people!"

Pilate rose and took his cane. "Unless I can be persuaded that this Jesus is a political threat to Rome's control of the province, then I cannot help you," he said. "We do not generally persecute civilians because their religious beliefs differ from those of their countrymen.

Lewis Ben Smith

Caiaphas glared at Pilate with raw hatred. "I shall not forget this, Pontius Pilate!" he said, and swept out.

After he left, Pilate and Longinus followed him through the door. Pilate kept his silence until they were back at the Fortress of Antonia—he did not want to have this conversation in Herod's palace, where the walls had ears. Once they were safely sequestered in the sparely furnished commander's office, Pilate spoke.

"So what did you make of that?" he asked Longinus.

"Not a great deal," said the *Primus Pilus* centurion. "But if I am not mistaken, you, my dear commander, made a new enemy!"

Pilate made a wry expression. "I'll have to add him to my collection," he quipped. "He'll look lovely on the shelf between Bar Abbas and Gaius Caligula!"

Longinus looked at his commander with interest. "Caligula?" he asked. "What have you done to make Gaius Little Boots your enemy? Isn't he just a boy?"

Pilate looked at his senior centurion for a long moment. He knew that there was gossip around the barracks as to how he had gone from being a rising political star in Rome to governing the Empire's least desirable province, but the details of his fall from favor were known only to a small handful of family and friends, and the reclusive Tiberius discouraged inquiries into family matters. At the same time, he genuinely liked Longinus, and the centurion had shown himself to be a man of discretion. Perhaps it would be good to let someone else know his story. Perhaps sharing his pain might even diminish it in some degree. Pilate decided it was worth a chance.

"Pour yourself a glass of wine," he said. "While you're at it, pour me one too. This is a long story."

When he was done telling it, Gaius Cassius Longinus looked at him in astonishment. Pilate had held back very little, other than the nature of some of the confidential work he had done for the Emperor. The actual story of his daughter's rape, Pilate's attack on Caligula, and the response of Tiberius he laid out in raw, short sentences. The words ripped out of him almost involuntarily at times. After the tale was told, Pilate felt as if a weight had been lifted from his shoulders. Longinus, on the other hand, looked as if he had taken a hard blow to the midsection.

"By Jupiter!" he said, reverting to the common Roman invocation in his shock. "I always figured you were sent here for angering the Emperor, but I had no idea you nearly killed the heir to the purple!"

Pilate nodded. "If I hadn't been knocked out cold, I would have finished the job, regardless of the consequences. Now my family and I live in fear every day of what will happen when that abomination succeeds the Emperor." He looked Longinus dead in the eye with his coldest gaze. "Needless to say, Centurion, you must never speak of this!"

Longinus nodded. "By the God of Israel I swear it!" he said with fervor. "I would not dream of betraying your confidence. And I am honored that you chose to share it with me."

"The only other person besides my wife and steward who knows the full story is a longtime friend in Rome," said Pilate. "I prefer to keep it that way."

# CHAPTER TWENTY-TWO

The autumn festival season went by without any major incidents. Jesus and his followers came to town for the Feast of Booths and stayed for two weeks. A delegation from the Temple and Sanhedrin followed him around the whole time, trying to pin him down on controversial statements he had made, or to provoke him into saying or doing something that would dampen the people's affections for the Galilean rabbi. Jesus answered every challenge carefully and creatively, healed several gravely ill people, and then told a series of parables that were pointedly aimed at the religious establishment. About the time that the High Priest had made up his mind that he needed to arrest Jesus, the Galilean holy man retreated back to his native province, along with all of his followers. Jerusalem buzzed with gossip about him for a week or two, then things calmed down and Pilate returned to Caesarea.

His leg was gradually regaining some of its strength, and over the winter Pilate tried to train with the troops again. Although he could still wield a sword quite well, the injured leg was simply not dependable. The slightest wrong move or turn would cause it to buckle, and excruciating pain would shoot up his leg. As much as he regretted it, he found that the Emperor's advice about not leading men in direct combat any more was the best policy. But that did not keep him from training two or three times a week in the courtyard, and as he regained his strength, the men became more sympathetic of his plight, and he regained the affections of some who had come to dislike him during his painful recovery.

Bar Abbas was nowhere to be found. After the murder of Milo Lammius, he disappeared without a trace for three months, and Pilate began to hope that perhaps the Zealot leader had fled the province, or—gods willing!— met with a well-deserved death in the desert wastes. The reward notices were posted in every village, along with Pilate's warning proclamation against harboring the dangerous fugitive.

At the end of the year, Pilate received a letter from the Emperor. It was short and businesslike, for the most part—Pilate found himself wondering if the emotional missive from that fall had been written when Tiberius was drinking. Near the end of the letter, the Emperor said this:

> *I received yet another angry, outraged letter from the High Priest recently about your disrespect for the Temple and for his own religious authority. Oddly enough, however, he declined to give any details about whatever it was you said or did that set him off this time. I am certainly not going to chide you for some unspecified, undescribed offense, but do try to show proper respect to the local religious establishment when it is practical to do so! That being said, it is Rome and not the Temple that rules Judea, and if Caiaphas needs to be reminded of that, I will always back up your authority.*

Pilate read the paragraph with a sigh, and set the letter down. Confound the High Priest and his connections in Rome! He had no doubt this was about his refusal to cooperate with regard to Jesus of Nazareth. Pilate was not going to arrest an innocent, harmless man just to satisfy the malice of a corrupt, jaded religious potentate. Still, he supposed at some point he might need to make a gesture of conciliation to the Temple.

A week after the letter arrived, one of Pilate's patrols came thundering into Caesarea, horses puffing and soaked with sweat, bearing news. Bar Abbas had struck again!

"He was in a public marketplace in Damascus," said Lucius Scribonia, the senior legionary of the group. "Apparently he and his handful of followers were in the hills outside town, starving for lack of food, and he decided to take the chance of purchasing it himself. He pulled a shawl over his head and went looking for bread and fish, and a young girl in the crowd recognized him and called his name out loud. That was when Bar Abbas made what may prove a fatal mistake. Instead of turning and running, he grabbed the girl, clapped his hand over her mouth, pulled her into an alley, and cut her throat. But she had been heard by several, and when Bar Abbas came out of the alley covered with blood, an angry mob took out after him. He killed two more and slashed several others cutting his way to the gate, but was wounded himself in the process."

Pilate spoke sharply. "Why are you here telling me this?" he asked. "You and the others should be in pursuit, instead of riding here to inform me!"

"Longinus sent us," he said. "He has an entire century out beating the bushes, trying to find him. But here is the thing, Your Excellency—every person from the village is out looking too! The girl Bar Abbas killed was the daughter of a local rabbi, and they are outraged—furious even—at her death. The entire countryside is inflamed against the Zealots now, and Longinus thinks it is only a matter of days—perhaps even hours—before Bar Abbas is dead or captured."

Pilate broke into a grin. "Well done, then, soldier! You and your men have a rest and a drink, and be ready to set out with me in the morning. I want to be in Damascus when this wretch is captured!"

Before they could set out the next day, another rider came into Caesarea, bearing a note from Longinus. Pilate broke the seal and read it greedily.

> *Gaius Cassius Longinus, Primus Pilus Centurion, to Prefect Lucius Pontius Pilate, Governor of Judea, greetings. They got him! A volunteer patrol from Damascus found the Zealot murderer Bar Abbas in the wilderness west of the town, holed up in a small cave. They beat him pretty severely before my men showed up to take him into custody, and he is still bleeding from a stab wound sustained during his escape from town. The locals insist on bringing him to you in person, but I am coming along with a squad of my lads just to make sure he does not meet with a fatal accident en route. We should arrive a day or two after you receive this letter.*
>
> *Ironically, for all his revolutionary fervor, this bandit may have done more to build positive feelings for Rome than anything you or I have done. His cruelty, disregard for innocent life, and brutal guerrilla tactics have made him the most hated man in Judea. My men and I were cheered when we brought him back into Damascus in chains! I look forward to turning him over to your authority.*

Pilate shared the news with all the cohorts in Caesarea, and sent riders to carry the news to every other Roman garrison in the province. The joyful mood was not only shared by every Roman legionary and citizen in Judea; in many towns the locals came out and celebrated as well. Only in a few Zealot strongholds was the capture of Bar Abbas not openly celebrated. About noon the next day, excited guards from the tower reported a large group approaching along the north road. Pilate had already donned his formal toga and ordered his curule chair brought out into the courtyard, where a raised dais had been prepared. Flanked by his lictors and an honor guard, he waited as the crowd was ushered in through the city gates.

The procession was an interesting one to say the least. A group of prominent citizens of Damascus led the way, flanked by mounted legionaries commanded by Longinus. Behind them, dragged on a chain, was the bleeding and bedraggled form of the guerrilla leader who had complicated Pilate's life for the last year. Behind Bar Abbas was a lengthy parade of Judean country folk, all of them in a jolly mood, some singing, others shaking their shovels and pitchforks at the bound bandit. All told, Pilate estimated that nearly a thousand people had come to witness Bar Abbas being handed over to the Roman government. He let them fill the courtyard and held up his hand for silence. Gradually, the crowd complied.

"First things first," he said. "Who actually captured this thug?"

Two young men stood forth, looking so much alike Pilate thought he was seeing double. "We did, Your Excellency," they said at the same time.

"And who might you two be?" he asked.

"Elijah and Elisha, sons of Eleazar ben Matthias," one of them answered. "We are brothers, and Tamar, the young girl who was killed, was our cousin. We were leading a search party of a dozen men from our village, but it was the two of us who entered the cave and subdued Bar Abbas."

"Well," said Pilate, "this is now yours." He reached into the sinus of his toga and pulled forth a purse heavy with coin—a thousand denarii, as promised, to which he had added another four hundred from his own funds. "In addition, in the name of the Senate and People of Rome, I will offer you and your family full citizenship in token of gratitude for your courage."

One of the twins stepped forward and accepted the bag of coins. "I humbly thank you, sir, but no reward will bring back the life we lost. Tamar was her father's only daughter, the jewel of his old age. The only thing we really want is to see justice done."

"You need have no fear on that account," said Pilate. "Bar Abbas, for your foul murder of Roman citizens and your own countrymen, I sentence you to flogging and crucifixion. Given the extent of your injuries, I am postponing your flogging until your wounds have healed. Then you will receive forty lashes every two weeks until the time of Passover, when you will be publicly crucified at Jerusalem, where all the citizens of Judea can witness your well-deserved demise."

The battered head lifted and the eyes focused on Pilate. "Just kill me now and get it over with, you Roman dog!" growled the murderer.

"Oh no," said Pilate. "For all the suffering and misery you have inflicted, I will make sure your spirit dies long before I allow life to leave your body. I will see to it that you are not just killed, Bar Abbas. I will see you broken!" As he uttered those words, he glared at the bandit leader with all the ferocity he could muster. Bar Abbas tried to meet his gaze, but the sight of the slavering beast that dwelt inside the heart of Pontius Pilate was too much for him—he dropped his eyes, and the legionaries hustled him off to the prison cells. Several of the onlookers caught Pilate's glare and averted their eyes as well. He let his expression return to normal, and looked out at the crowd.

"It has been several years now since I came to serve as your governor," he said. "During that time, it has been my primary goal to keep the peace in this province and hold the enemies of Rome and Judea at bay. I know that many of you will never love Rome as do we who were born on her fair hills, but I hope that all of you have come to realize that Rome is not your enemy unless you make her so. What the Senate and People of Rome want is not that far from what you want. You wish for peace, prosperity, and the right to worship your God according to your law. All these things Rome is willing to grant, in exchange for your submission to her authority and her laws. Freedom and independence are fine concepts, but freedom is messy and divisive. Independence leaves Judea open to invasion and war at any time. Rome's yoke is not heavy unless you make it so. With the capture of Bar Abbas and the end of Zealotry as a political cause, let us together create a new era of harmony, where Roman and Jew can live side by side in peace, under the wise leadership of the Senate and People of Rome, and of our beloved Emperor Tiberius Caesar." The crowd was silent, but the raw hostility that might have met such a speech a few years before was not there. Pilate even saw some of the older Jews nodding as he spoke.

"Now, in celebration of the capture of Bar Abbas and the destruction of his band of brigands, I declare today to be a feast day! The merchants of

Caesarea have been paid out of my purse to provide you with all the food and wine you desire for the rest of the day. Enjoy this occasion, and may your journey home be safe and uneventful!"

The crowds cheered at the news of the feast, and Pilate stepped down off the dais and made his way to the steps that led to the governor's quarters. Longinus followed him up a few minutes later, after making sure that Bar Abbas was securely chained in a heavily guarded cell. Pilate was seated behind his desk, rubbing his throbbing knee.

"Well done, sir," said Longinus. "I think you handled the crowd quite well—they hate Bar Abbas so much that I didn't even hear any grumblings about him being crucified. I would make one suggestion, however, if I may."

"What would that be?" asked Pilate.

"Don't crucify him right before Passover," said Longinus. "The Jews don't want bodies hanging on the cross on their holiest of days. Wait and nail him up when Passover ends Saturday evening, or even first thing Sunday morning. That way they will all see him as they leave the city."

Pilate nodded. "Or," he suggested, "we could nail him up first thing Friday morning and break his legs an hour or two before sunset. He'd be dead before the Passover actually began that way. I hate to cut short his time on the cross, but after multiple floggings he'll be half dead anyway."

Longinus shuddered. He could not imagine having your whip scars healing and scabbed over, only to be torn open again—and again, every two weeks. Bar Abbas would truly be broken long before he went to the cross. But, he reflected, it was still a better end than the murdering thug deserved! He fixed the images of Bar Abbas' victims in his mind, and all trace of sympathy for the Zealot vanished.

"Do you think that Judea will ever truly become a peaceful province?" Pilate asked. "The more I learn about the people, the more I doubt it. Everything about the Jews' culture and religion is so alien to Rome; I don't see how the two can ever co-exist. But then, Caesar's men probably said that about Gaul eighty years ago, and look how thoroughly Romanized Gaul is now."

Longinus looked thoughtful for a moment. "I fear you may be right," he said. "Much of that will depend on the direction the Empire takes when Tiberius is no more. It seems to me, from my perspective way down at the

294

bottom of the political dung heap, that the Empire has been drifting for many years now. If the new Emperor governs wisely and respects the culture and religion of Judea and the other provinces, we may actually see long-term peace. But if he should prove to be reckless and dangerous—and what you have told me of Gaius Caligula makes me fear that is his nature— I doubt Judea will ever be free of rebellion."

"One thing is for sure," said Pilate. "Once Tiberius is gone, this province will not be my responsibility for long."

"What will you do when Caligula succeeds to the purple?" asked the centurion.

"I only wish I knew," said Pilate.

For the next couple of months things remained peaceful. The Zealots, their warriors dead and their leadership languishing in the dungeons, were a spent force for the time being. Jesus of Nazareth remained in Galilee, preaching and teaching to enormous crowds, but did not venture into Judea. According to Pilate's sources, Herod Antipas had tried repeatedly to see Jesus in person, only to be brushed off by the Galilean rabbi.

For Pilate, these months were to be the last truly happy times he had as governor of Judea. His son, now four and half years old, was proving to be a highly intelligent lad, speaking in complete sentences and asking questions about the world and the people that he encountered on a constant basis. His thirst for knowledge was insatiable, and Pilate usually enjoyed explaining things to him. Occasionally, however, the boy would ask about things that Pilate would have preferred he not bring up. One day he saw the guards dragging Bar Abbas from his cell to be flogged and came running up to his father's office.

"*Tata*," he said in a very serious tone. "Why are they whipping that man?"

"Because he is a murdering thug," said Pilate.

"What is a thug?" asked Decimus.

"A person who kills the innocent," answered his father. "One who kills men, women, and children for his own amusement."

"But hasn't he already been whipped? His back has red lines all over it," insisted the boy.

"His sentence was to be whipped every two weeks, then nailed to a cross next month," Pilate explained wearily.

"That sounds mean," said Decimus.

Pilate lifted his son up onto his good knee. He looked at that earnest young face and tried to explain the world in terms a four-year-old could grasp.

"There are some very bad people in the world, my son," he began. "Sometimes the only way to keep bad people from taking control and hurting all the good people is to make such a terrible example of them that no one else wants to be bad. That man, Bar Abbas, did terrible things to many, many people. By making him suffer so harshly, a warning message is sent to any who would be like him that they should change their ways."

The little boy nodded. "Can Romans ever be thugs?" he asked.

Pilate thought of Gaius Caligula, heir to the Imperial throne. "Yes, my son, they can," he replied.

"Then we should flog them too!" said Decimus, and ran off. Pilate looked after him, and then envisioned Caligula wailing and flailing as a cat-o-nine-tails flayed the skin from his back. He smiled and returned to his work.

That evening, after Porcia had put his son to bed, Pilate pulled her to the couch for a talk.

"It is time, my dear, that we decided what we are going to do when Tiberius dies," he said. "The man is seventy-four, and any day could possibly be his last. When he is gone, Caligula will become Emperor, barring some miracle. I know that he must want to even the score with me—maybe by killing me outright, or it may be by striking down my family."

She shuddered. "That horrible, horrible brute!" she finally said. "He stole our little girl from us, but that is not enough for him."

Pilate shook his head sadly. "I do not know that the whole world contains enough misery to slake his thirst for suffering," he said. "I am a hard man—partly due to the path the gods have laid before me, and partly due to my own nature. You rarely see that side of me, but I am sure you know it is there."

She nodded. "I know you better than you think," she said. "All men have a beast that lives within them, I believe. Yours is just hungrier than most. But the thing is, my dear, you control your beast. It does not control you. That is what sets you, and all decent men, apart from creatures like Gaius Caligula. You are a man that has a beast lurking inside. He is a beast, wearing a man's clothing."

Pilate looked at his wife in amazement. All these years, he thought he had hidden the brutal side of himself from her! But looking into her clear gray eyes, he realized that she knew him just as well, if not better, than he knew himself. And yet, she still chose to love him. It was a revelation he had not sought, but would never forget.

"You know my client, Quintus Sullemia?" he asked, changing the subject.

"That rather seedy-looking fellow that used to come around our old place in Rome?" she said. "I never liked the look of him."

"Don't let his scruffy appearance deceive you," said Pilate. "He has been a faithful friend through all our trials. He keeps me posted on everything that happens in Rome, and makes sure his letters arrive well before the latest imperial decrees. I have already told him to inform us the instant word gets out that Tiberius is failing. I have about twenty talents of silver and gold invested with Greek bankers that I can pick up anywhere within the Empire. When Caligula becomes Caesar, Lucius Pontius Pilate and his family will disappear forever. But somewhere within the Empire, a Greek merchant named Lentulus, who has a wife and a young son, will settle down in a small village and melt into the local population. It will be hard—we will have to say goodbye to all we have known and loved—but we will live on, and Decimus will grow up to be a man without living in constant fear of his life."

Porcia nodded. "You seem to have put a great deal of thought into it," she said. "Where do you wish to settle?"

"That I do not know," said Pilate. "But I want to live somewhere that has actual seasons, where I can see snow in winter and real rains in the fall and spring. Perhaps Gaul, in the country of the Belgae? It is quite lovely up there, and the region is remote, but civilized."

"I will go where you go, my husband," she said. "But for now, let that be to our bedchamber. Our son is sleeping, and we are both awake. That is a rare occasion, and not to be wasted!"

As the month of Martius passed, Pilate and his family began to prepare to travel to Jerusalem for the annual Passover feast. In addition to moving his headquarters from Caesarea, Pilate also made preparations for Bar Abbas to meet his date with the crossbeam. A large cage was mounted on a wagon, and the Zealot leader, his back a mass of half-healed scar tissue and his mind a seething, broken mess of pain and hate, was placed in it for the journey.

All along the way, the crowds gathered around Pilate's procession to see the famous outlaw. The governor was happy to see that despite Bar Abbas' wretched condition, very few faces showed any sympathy for the man's fate. For once, it seemed, Pilate's actions met with the approval of the citizens of Judea. He was even greeted with cheers by the people as they drew near to the city.

Longinus met him a few miles out with a mounted escort of legionaries. They took custody of Bar Abbas and brought his wagon into Jerusalem ahead of the rest of the procession. Pilate dismissed his soldiers to the Fortress of Antonia, and took up residence with his family in the upper tower—Herod's antipathy for Pilate had returned as the memory of John the Baptizer's death faded from the minds of the people. He had sent word to Pilate that his guest rooms were being repainted, so the Prefect and his family would have to stay in the fort with the soldiers this time.

After seeing Porcia and Decimus settled in, Pilate walked to his office with Longinus right behind. When they were behind closed doors, he turned to his senior centurion.

"Anything of note to report, Longinus?" he asked.

"Only one thing is on everybody's mind at the moment, sir," replied the soldier. "Jesus of Nazareth is coming to Jerusalem for Passover."

"Jupiter!" said Pilate. "Didn't Caiaphas try to arrest him last time?"

"Yes sir," Longinus answered. "And he has a reward of thirty silver sesterces for anyone who can lead him to the Galilean when he is not surrounded by crowds. But there is more than that."

"What else then?" Pilate demanded.

"A few days ago, Jesus visited a house in Bethany, a small village not far from here. He is friends with a man named Lazarus, who lives there with his two spinster sisters. Lazarus had fallen ill, and died before Jesus arrived. Four days before he arrived, in fact," explained the centurion.

"Go on," Pilate said.

"When Jesus arrived, he demanded that the stone be removed from the entrance of the tomb," Longinus continued. "People thought he wanted to see Lazarus' face one last time, as is the custom of the Jews. They warned him the body would be rotten and discolored after that long a time, but Jesus insisted. So they removed the stone, and the stench of dead flesh filled the air. Jesus bowed his head, prayed, and then called out for Lazarus to come out of the tomb."

"That's ridiculous!" said Pilate.

"It would have been, sir, except for one small detail. Lazarus came."

"Preposterous!" snapped Pilate. "Dead men stay dead! Either it was an actor, or else Lazarus faked his own death. What you are describing is an impossibility."

Longinus nodded. "Sir, my mind agrees with you fully. This is not a healing, it is a resurrection! But I have talked to three different people from the town, and all of them agree on two things: first, that Lazarus was dead. Secondly, that he now lives. The High Priest takes it seriously enough that he has put a price on Lazarus' head too."

Pilate looked at Longinus carefully. "You said your mind agrees, Centurion. What does that mean?"

Longinus looked at him ruefully. "My heart tells me that something miraculous is going on among us," he said. "I don't know what it means, or why it is happening now, but this is just the last in a long train of events that Jesus has set in motion. The people believe it, too. Many of them are saying that Jesus may publicly declare himself as Messiah when he enters Jerusalem this time."

"And when will that be?" asked Pilate.

"Later this afternoon," said Longinus.

"Get us some hooded cloaks," said Pilate. "I want to see this. If this man declares himself king, we will arrest him at once."

There was a guard tower that overlooked the plaza just inside the main gate of Jerusalem, where tens of thousands of pilgrims entered every day to celebrate the Passover. Pilate and Longinus positioned themselves at a window overlooking the plaza. Disguised legionaries were posted all around, ready to spring into action if things turned ugly. There was a growing roar in the air as the Galilean's entourage approached the main gate. The sounds grew louder as more Jews packed into the square to see the miracle worker arrive.

"Hosanna!" they shouted. "Hail to the Son of David! Blessed is he who comes in the name of the Lord!" Longinus stiffened at the words.

"What is it?" Pilate asked.

"Those words have not been sung in Jerusalem for six hundred years!" said the centurion. "That is a coronation psalm, sung when a new king takes the throne of David."

Pilate scowled. "Where is this king, then?" he asked.

"Right there!" said Longinus.

The man was so nondescript Pilate would not have been able to pick him out from the crowd, were it not for the palm fronds and cloaks being thrown into his path. Medium height, medium build, with reddish-brown hair worn long, as was the Jewish custom, Jesus of Nazareth was not a particularly commanding figure. His choice of mounts did not improve that impression—he was seated on a fat young donkey, its mother tethered beside it. He was surrounded by a small group of rustics who tried to keep the crowd at bay. But the singing and shouting rose all the louder when they caught sight of him. A small group of children, off to one side, began singing the coronation psalm again.

"Silence!" a voice roared. Clad in black, a small group of priests had worked their way through the crowd to the front. Their spokesman was glaring at Jesus. "Rabbi, tell these brats to be quiet!"

A clear, mellow voice that reached to the furthest corner of the plaza answered the irate priest. "I tell you in truth," Jesus said, "that if these be silent the very stones will cry out!"

Silence fell across the crowd. Jesus raised himself up and looked at the eager faces, every eye upon him. It was hard to see across the distance, but Pilate could have sworn that the rough carpenter's face was seamed with tears.

"Oh Jerusalem, Jerusalem!" cried Jesus, his voice breaking with grief. "How often I would have gathered you to myself, as a hen gathers her chicks under her wings. But you would not have it," he continued, his voice growing softer but still audible. "And now your house is left to you desolate, because you did not recognize the hour of your visitation." With that, Jesus suddenly slipped from the donkey's back and vanished into the crowd, leaving every mouth agape. The murmur became a roar as the people asked one another what had just happened, and where Jesus had gone.

"Well," said Longinus. "So much for him wanting to be a king!"

They did not say a word all the way back to the Praetorium.

Over the next few days, Jesus taught in the Temple daily. The Pharisees and Sadducees sent delegation after delegation, trying to trick him or provoke him into some statement that they could use against him. Jesus mastered each challenge effortlessly, turning their own words against them and answering their questions with unanswerable questions of his own. The crowds flocked daily to see the rabbi from Galilee stump the teachers of the law, and cheered when Jesus did so again and again.

"I just wonder what he is getting at?" Pilate asked, but no one could give a satisfactory answer.

# CHAPTER TWENTY-THREE

A week after Passover, an exhausted, emotionally wrung-out Pontius Pilate dictated a letter to Tiberius Caesar. It was as formal in tone as he could make it, trying to outline for the Emperor the fantastic events of that bizarre week.

> *Lucius Pontius Pilate, Senior Legate, Prefect, and Proconsul of Judea, to Tiberius Julius Caesar Augustus, Princeps and Imperator of Rome, Greetings.*
>
> *Your Excellency, you know that it is the duty of every governor to keep you informed of events in the provinces that may in some way affect the well-being of the Empire. While I am loath to disturb your important daily work with a matter that may seem trivial at first, upon further reflection, and especially in light of subsequent developments, I find myself convinced that recent events in Judea merit your attention. And I would be telling an untruth if I said that I am not concerned that other accounts of these happenings may reach your ears which are not just unfavorable but frankly slanderous of my actions and motives. The situation was one of unusual difficulty and complexity, and hard decisions were called for. As always, I tried to make the decisions that I felt would most lend themselves to a peaceful and harmonious outcome for the citizens of the Republic and the people of Judea. But local passions in this case were so strong, and so diametrically opposed to each other, that it may be there simply was no completely correct choice to make. I leave that to your judgment.*
>
> *To help you understand the choices that were thrust upon me during the Jewish festival of Passover this year, Caesar, I will have to summarize the events over the last three years that led up to it. As I am sure you are aware, the Jews' rather odd religion has for centuries prophesied about the coming of a savior they call the Messiah—Christos in Greek—who would redeem them from slavery and restore the great kingdom that was theirs at one time. This belief makes them particularly vulnerable to various*

*charlatans and lunatics who pop up from time to time claiming to be this Messiah. Such men invariably spell trouble for whoever is currently holding the Jews on a leash—be it the Assyrians, the Greeks, or we Romans.*

*However, most of these men in the past were quickly exposed as the frauds that they were. For all their protestations of holiness and religious fervor, the House of Zadok which controls the Jewish high priesthood is quite comfortable with the mutual arrangement they enjoy with Rome. Indeed, since Pompey the Great added this troublesome province to the Empire nearly a hundred years ago, the Priests have been Rome's staunchest allies, and an invaluable aid in keeping the peace. So when rumors began to circulate of a new would-be Messiah rising up in Galilee, I figured they would take care of him soon enough.*

*This particular would-be Messiah of the Jews was a former carpenter who apparently claimed descent from their ancient King David—founder of a dynasty that was toppled by the Babylonians over five centuries ago! I first heard the stories and asked the centurions whom I have stationed in the various cities of Judea to keep me informed if this fellow gave signs of making trouble. However, he seemed to have no interest whatsoever in politics. He wandered about with a small band of farmers and fishermen—and, oddly enough, one Jewish publicani who chose to renounce tax farming and join him for some reason. His activities seemed to focus on long, rambling sermons commanding people to love one another, and describing a "kingdom of God" that would rule over men's hearts rather than their bodies. Harmless mystical nonsense, it seemed to me. The other stories about him were so incredible that I ignored them at first, but they continued over so long a period that I eventually began to pay them heed. This man, Jesus of Nazareth, apparently had a remarkable power of healing that was widely witnessed. Indeed, one of my senior centurions told me that Jesus had healed a servant of his by merely saying a few words from miles away! I scoffed at that account, but he swore that it was true. But, as you will (I hope) agree, I saw nothing in this man that caused me any concern for the Empire or its control of Judea. However, the religious leaders of the Jews were adamantly opposed to this man's teachings—he claimed some sort of direct relationship to their God that they said was blasphemous. As governor, I saw no reason to involve myself in a minor religious dispute.*

*By the time of the most recent Passover, this Jesus of Nazareth had acquired a huge following, and the stories about him were becoming fanciful to the extreme. They said, just before Passover, that he had actually brought a man back to life that had been dead for FOUR days! It was after this story began circulating in the city that the Jewish leadership decided that Jesus must die. His followers now numbered in the thousands, and the Priests feared an armed revolution. When he came to the city for the Passover feast, their plans for his demise were already cemented into place—even though he refused the offering of a crown that the enthusiastic mob made when he entered the city.*

*You may be wondering why I did not step in at this point. While I do have several informants who are seated on the Jewish Grand Council, the Sanhedrin, at this time, the high priest and his cronies only met with a select few that did not include my agents. This small group bought off one of Jesus' disciples (that man has subsequently disappeared; rumors abound that he hung himself after the events that followed) and sent a large mob, accompanied by the Temple guard (and a single cohort of legionaries whose centurion wisely saw the commotion and followed along to see what was going on and keep the peace if necessary). They proceeded to a quiet garden outside the city walls where the Nazarene was known to meet with his disciples. Jesus was arrested without any major incident—apparently he was with only a small group of followers, and only one of them even tried to defend him. He was then interrogated before both the former High Priest, that evil old serpent named Annas, and the current holder of that office, Caiaphas, whom you and I know all too well. Finally, in the third hour past midnight, the enormous mob showed up, with a bloodied and battered Jesus, at the Praetorium, angrily demanding that I sentence him to death.*

*This I was reluctant to do. First and foremost, I believed and still believe that the man was innocent of any offense against Roman law. The second reason is more personal, but you of all people should understand it. For each of the three previous nights, my wife had woken me with her screams. She was not entirely coherent, but one thing she said on each occasion was, 'Do not kill the Galilean! He is innocent! You will be damned forever if you do!' These statements troubled me deeply. Every Roman knows the story of how the noble Calpurnia sought to dissuade the Divus Julius from going to the Forum on the Ides of March. Dreams are powerful things, and sometimes the gods use them to speak to us. Even as I stood before this angry mob, trying to make sense of their accusations, she sent me a note that read 'Have nothing to do with the death of this innocent man.' At this moment, I remembered that Jesus was actually a subject of King Herod Antipas, since he was from Galilee rather than Judea, so I sent him to stand trial before Herod. Unfortunately, Herod was unwilling to pronounce judgment on him, and two hours later Jesus was brought before me once more. The only positive development from this incident was that Herod, who had been quite hostile to me for some time, has become friendlier ever since—although given his mercurial nature, I have no confidence the improvement in our relations will be permanent.*

*At this point, most excellent Tiberius, I felt that I could not proceed any further without at least trying to find out what this Galilean holy man had to say for himself. My Aramaic is not the best, so I sent one of my centurions into the crowd to find an interpreter. He returned a few moments later with a terrified-looking youth of about 20 years of age, whom he described as one of Jesus' disciples. I found myself admiring his courage, following a screaming mob that was howling for his master's blood! The young fellow did not speak Latin very well, but his Greek was quite passable. Although the mob outside and their religious leaders had voiced many charges against the bloodied figure before me, I asked him about the only one that really mattered to me as a Roman magistrate. "Are you the King of the Jews?" I demanded, nodding at the youth to translate.*

*My interpreter proved unnecessary. Jesus looked at me with a deep and curious gaze that I found quite unnerving, then spoke in clear, excellent Latin without a trace of an accent. "Do you say this of your own accord?" he asked. "Or did someone else tell you this about me?"*

*"Am I a Jew?" I asked, more harshly than I intended. His intense stare was throwing me off balance. "Your own people—your own priests!—have delivered you up to me as an evildoer. What do you say for yourself?"*

*He was silent for a long moment, his lips moving as if he was speaking to someone I could not see. Finally, his eyes met mine again, and he spoke with incredible force and clarity. "My kingdom," he said, "is not of this world!"*

*Caesar, I have stood in the presence of majesty on many occasions. I can remember your noble father, the Imperator Augustus, speaking before his armies and the Senate, and you know that I fought as a legate under you in Germania as well, and saw the honor your legionaries rightly accorded you there. I have stood in the presence of many foreign potentates as well, from Herod to King Juba. As you know, most Eastern monarchs are grasping, venal creatures whose only nobility is in the trappings they cover themselves with. Trust me when I say that this bloodied and battered Galilean itinerant radiated as much honor and dignitas as any Roman patrician. But there was also something . . . alien about him. Otherworldly. His statement, as ridiculous as it no doubt sounds when I recount it, made perfect sense to me as I stood there looking into his eyes. But he was not done—he continued: "If my kingdom was of this world, my servants would be fighting to rescue me as we speak. As it is, my kingdom is not of this realm."*

*I asked the question more directly. "So you are a king, then?"*

*He nodded, and replied: "You say correctly that I am a king. For this purpose I have been born, and come into this world, that I might testify to the truth. Everyone who welcomes truth will hear my voice."*

*I pondered his statement a moment, and I said out loud the thought that leaped into my mind. "Quid est veritas?" But I had heard all I needed for the moment, and did not wait for his answer. This man was no threat to Rome, I was convinced of that. I stepped out onto the balcony and addressed the mob below.*

*"Absolvo!" I cried. "I find no guilt in this man!"*

*The crowd exploded with rage.*

*Noble Caesar, anyone who has lived in Rome for any time has seen a Roman mob in action at some point or other. But I have never seen such raw hatred for any human being expressed so loudly and strongly as this crowd of Jews screamed its hate at Jesus. Ironic, since a few days before, half the city had been ready to crown him as their king. Now for the first time, they took up that awful cry: "CRUCIFY! CRUCIFY!!"*

*"Why?" I shouted. "What evil has he done?"*

*One of the priests stepped forward—although not so far as to step past the threshold of the Praetorium. Hounding an innocent man to his death was apparently fine according to his religious convictions, but setting foot in the home of a pagan like me would have made him unclean! "We have a law," he shouted. "And by that law he ought to die, for being a man, he made himself out to be a god!"*

*The situation was deteriorating, so I removed Jesus from their sight—as well as myself. They were determined to see blood, it seemed. Very well, I would give them blood. But not as much as they wanted. I turned to Brutus Appius, the centurion who led my household guard. "Take him and flog him," I said. "But don't kill him!"*

*The young Jew that had been brought in to interpret leaped to his feet in protest. I had forgotten he was there, but I looked at him now and saw his raw fear, barely held at bay in his concern for his master. "I am trying to save his life," I said, as gently as I could, and retreated to my quarters until the deed was done.*

*I was not pleased when my legionaries brought the Galilean back to me. As I had ordered, they had not killed him, but they had come very close. His back was scored to the bone in places, and they had placed an old purple robe over his shoulders and a crown of poisonous Galilean thorn branches upon his head. Most legionaries hate the Jews, of course—this is not a choice posting for a hard-drinking, hard-fighting Roman man—and given a chance to humiliate one of them, the men had taken full advantage of it. But, I thought, perhaps I could play Jesus' pitiful condition to my own advantage. I led him back out onto the porch of the Praetorium and shoved him in front of me, giving the mob a good view. "Ecce homo!" I shouted. Some of the crowd cried out in pity, but the priests once again took up that hateful cry: "Crucify! Crucify!"*

*I held up my hands for silence. For the life of me I did not know what to do. This man had an enormous following. If I put him to death, would the common people who loved him rise up in open revolt? But if I spared him, the ruling class, whose cooperation is so vital to our government here, would be turned against me, perhaps permanently. What to do?*

*I thought of something. Raising my hands for silence, I cried out, "People of Jerusalem, you know that it is my custom to release one prisoner to you during your Passover each year. This year, I give you a choice. Shall I release this Jesus of Nazareth, your king?" I laced my voice with sarcasm, trying to throw scorn on the very idea that this wretched figure could ever be considered royalty. "Or shall I release to you the murderer Bar Abbas?"*

*Once more the crowd roared. "Bar Abbas! Bar Abbas!!" they cried.*

*By this time, Your Excellency, I was rapidly running out of options. I pulled Jesus back into the Praetorium and looked at him in frustration. Those remarkable eyes stared into mine through the blood, bruises, and grime without a trace of fear, which began to anger me. "Where are you really from?" I demanded. He gave no answer. "Why will you not speak to me?" I shouted. "Don't you know that I have the authority to crucify you, or to set you free?"*

*He answered softly, "You would have no authority over me at all except for that which is given you from Heaven," he said. "You do* not understand what you are doing; therefore the ones who delivered me up to you have the greater guilt."

Caesar, I am not a superstitious man, and I am certainly no coward. But I will tell you in truth that his words shook me to the core. I felt as if I was the one on trial, and that this strange figure before me had somehow found me wanting. I led him back out before the mob. They were still screaming for the Galilean's blood.

"Behold, I bring him forth to tell you that I find no guilt in him!" I cried for the last time.

Then the former High Priest, Annas, lifted his voice to be heard. "If you release this man, you are no friend of Caesar! Everyone who proclaims himself a king is Caesar's enemy!" The threat was very clear—he would report me to you unless I did his bidding.

I had done everything in my power, Caesar, to prevent the execution of an innocent man. But at this point the continued government of this troublesome province seemed to be hanging by a hair. Personally, I have never been more revolted by the hypocrisy of the Jewish leadership. I called for a basin of water, and sat down in the judgment seat overlooking the crowd. I dipped my hands in the water three times and carefully dried them, then spoke.

"I am innocent of this man's blood!" I cried. "I wash my hands of this whole affair!"

Old Annas spoke again. "Let his blood be on us and on our children!" he shouted back. Even his son-in-law Caiaphas scowled at this remark, and many in the crowd howled their opposition, but the old man glared at them and refused to retract his ridiculous statement. But then that hateful cry of "Crucify, Crucify!" drowned out their argument.

I had had enough. "Take him then, and crucify him!" I snapped to the legionaries. "But I find no guilt in him," I muttered as they left. There was one duty left to attend—listing the formal charge against Jesus, to be posted on the cross above his head. I took a broad-tipped quill and wrote in bold letters: "This is Jesus of Nazareth, King of the Jews!" and ordered my scribe to copy it in Greek and Hebrew. I would accord the strange man this much honor, at least. For in my heart, I think he may have been a king of some sort.

As I returned to my quarters, I found the young disciple of Jesus, whom I had quite forgotten, staring at me with tears streaming down his face. "Get him out of here!" I snapped.

Even after I had granted them their wish, Caesar, the Jewish priests were still not happy with my handling of the Galilean. I had just sat down to my noontide meal when I got word that one of Caiaphas' secretaries wanted to see me. Once more I had to leave the Praetorium, since their ridiculous religion would not allow them to cross the threshold of a Roman. "What is it now?" I snapped.

"The inscription," he said. "You wrote 'This is the King of the Jews.' It should read that he called himself the King of the Jews."

I had had just about enough from these fools at this point. "I have written what I have written!" I snapped. "I will hear no more of this!"

It was a strange day after that. Within the next hour, the sky grew black as night, even though there was not a cloud in view. The light of the sun simply faded—not blotted out gradually, as in an eclipse, but all at once, and did not return to normal for three hours. At the third hour past noon, a huge earthquake shook the city. My centurion told me that it happened at the exact moment that Jesus died, and he was much shaken, babbling that we had murdered a living god—although he was quite drunk when he said it.

Not long after that, a very different sort of Jew came to see me. His name was Joseph, and he ignored protocol and entered the Praetorium to speak with me. He explained that, while he was a Pharisee and a member of the Jewish Senate, he had not even been informed of the charges against Jesus, nor was he present at the trial. He asked me for Jesus' body, that he might give the Galilean a decent burial. I instructed my soldiers that he could take custody of the body as soon as they had made sure that Jesus was truly dead. The least I could do for this harmless man I had failed to save was *let those who loved him bury him according to their own religious rituals.*

*I am sorry to have troubled you for so long about this matter, Caesar, but I am afraid that the story does not yet end. The sun had not yet set on that endless Friday when emissaries from the High Priest came to see me yet again. As you can imagine, they found me in no good mood. Why could they not return to their sacrificial Passover lambs and leave me be?*

*"Noble procurator," purred old Annas. "While he was alive, this troublemaker repeatedly said that if he was killed, he would return to life on the third day. Could we trouble you for some guards to watch over the tomb until after the first day of the week? We fear his disciples may try to steal his body and proclaim him alive again, and then the deception will only grow worse!"*

*"You have your Temple guards," I growled. "Guard the bloody tomb yourselves!"*

*They bowed and scurried out, anxious to return to their families before sunset, when their religious observance actually began. After they left, I called in primus pilus centurion, Gaius Cassius Longinus, who had headed the crucifixion detail. He had sobered up some, but was obviously still deeply troubled over his afternoon's work.*

*"The Jews think someone may attempt to disturb the Galilean's grave," I told him. "First of all, are you sure that he was dead when his family cut him down from the cross?" I asked.*

*"Absolutely," he said. "He had quit breathing a half hour before, but I still had one of my boys skewer his heart with a spear before I allowed them to cut him down. I have never seen anyone die so bravely, sir. Not a curse! In fact, he even prayed for us as he hung there. Asked his father to forgive us! I've never heard the like!"*

*"Never mind that," I said. "Just make sure a couple of your legionaries keep an eye on that tomb for the next few days."*

*That Saturday, Caesar, was one of the quietest days during my entire tenure here in Judea. The Jewish leaders, having gotten their way, were quiescent the whole time, absorbed in their Passover rituals. The Galilean's followers were in hiding, no doubt in shock and grief at his death. After that incredibly long and difficult Friday, I began to feel I could breathe again.*

*But Sunday morning, shortly before the noontide meal, Longinus came to see me. He saluted crisply, but his countenance was grim. Not just grim, either. He was afraid.*

*"He's gone," he said.*

*"Who is gone?" I asked.*

*"That bloody Galilean! Jesus of Nazareth! His tomb is empty, his shroud an empty shell, and his body is missing!"*

*Rage filled me. "How could this happen?" I demanded.*

*"My three legionaries were camped some distance away," he said. "But there were twenty of those Jewish Temple guards watching the tomb, and the stone across the entrance would have taken a dozen men to move! They had even sealed it with a big wax seal, proclaiming death to any who violated the tomb."*

*"Then what happened?" I demanded.*

*"Just before dawn, they heard the ground shake, and the Jewish Temple guards shrieking. My two boys started towards the tomb, and saw the Jews lying on the grass as if dead. The huge stone was moved several yards away from the entrance. Decius Carmella approached the opening, and then a blinding flash of light knocked both of them out cold. When they woke up, the Jews had fled, and there was a group of women at the tomb wondering what had happened. That is when they came and reported to me!"*

*Caesar, I write these last pages with my own hand, because I am not sure that I trust even my faithful scribe with the words that follow. As soon as Longinus made his report, I ordered him to arrest some of the Temple guards and bring them to me immediately. It took a couple of hours, as they were closeted with the priests in some secret meeting. My legionaries discreetly nabbed two of them as soon as they left, and dragged them to the Praetorium.*

*At first they tried to pass off the story that the disciples of Jesus had stolen the body as they slept near the tomb. This tale was obviously a concoction—a guard detachment of twenty all asleep at the same time? The band of frightened rabbits that was too afraid to rescue their beloved rabbi, suddenly risking life and limb to retrieve his ravaged corpse? Ridiculous! I ordered them scourged, and their story soon changed.*

*What they told us was that before dawn Sunday morning, about half the detachment was asleep as the other half stood in front of the tomb, bored and talking among themselves. Suddenly there was a blinding flash of light and a great earthquake that knocked them all to their knees, and the stone in front of the tomb was flung about ten yards away, nearly crushing one of them. As they stared at the entrance of the tomb, two glowing balls of light descended from the sky and assumed human form at the entrance. They turned and looked at the guards, and every one of them fell down as if dead. When they came to, the tomb was empty, and three Roman soldiers were there unconscious as well. They fled to the Temple to report what they had seen to the High Priest, leaving my men stretched out on the grass.*

*The story sounds unbelievable, but even after another dose of the cat-o-nine-tails, they refused to change it. I ordered them both put to death and buried outside the city walls, so that no one would know what they had told me. Then I summoned the High Priest and met him outside the Temple District.*

*"What has happened?" I demanded.*

*"Exactly what I warned you of!" he snapped. "The Galileans came at night and stole the body of the Nazarene!"*

*"You mean all of your Temple guards let themselves be overpowered by a dozen frightened fishermen?" I sneered.*

*"There were nearly a hundred of them!" he said, obviously shaken that I refused to believe him.*

*"So how many did your guards kill?" I asked.*

*"None!" he said. "The blackguards overwhelmed them as they slept!"*

*His lies were so preposterous I did not want to listen any more. I turned on my heel and called over my shoulder: "It sounds like your guards were derelict in their duty. Let me know if you want them crucified, too!"*

*By evening the city was abuzz with rumors that the crucified Galilean had been seen again, by several of his disciples and by a group of women as well. There were also stories that the earthquake had torn the veil of the Temple, that several long-dead holy men had been seen wandering the streets preaching about the Messiah, and that the disciple who betrayed Jesus had hung himself. The priests were strangely silent, and I did not know what to believe myself.*

*The next morning, I walked down to the tomb where the crucified Jesus had been interred four days before. The heavy stone that had been rolled across the entrance was indeed several yards away, and one side of it was strangely scorched. The seal that had been placed on it was a half molten blob of wax. I looked into the tomb, but there was only the lingering scent of myrrh and some empty linen wrappings lying where the body of the Nazarene prophet had been placed. I sat down on the stone outside, lost in thought.*

*"Why do you seek the living one among the dead?" a voice asked me.*

*I looked up to see the young disciple of Jesus whom I had recruited to act as my interpreter at the trial. He was alone and unarmed, and I motioned my legionaries to let him approach. He looked to be just out of his teens, and his expression was one of confidence and . . . for lack of a better word, joy.*

*"What happened here?" I demanded.*

*"Here the man you killed returned to life," he said simply.*

*"That is impossible!" I snapped.*

*"All things are possible with God," he calmly replied. "Our prophets have long predicted that the Lord's Messiah would be betrayed, tormented, and killed, and then rise again from the dead. I watched it happen. I saw him tried, I saw him nailed to the cross, and I saw your soldiers drive a spear through his heart. I wrapped*

315

his body in the shroud, and I stepped into the tomb yesterday morning to see the same empty cloths you just did."

"An empty tomb and an abandoned shroud don't mean a corpse came back to life!" I snapped. "They mean a grave was robbed, and I intend to find out who did it!"

His eyes softened. "Noble Governor," he said. "I saw that you did your best to spare him, and I am grateful. As long as I live to tell the story, I will tell that you did your best to save his life. But there is more to the story than the empty tomb. I know that he lives because I have seen him myself! Alive, healthy, eating supper, the wounds of his ordeal healed! I have touched the nail scars in his hands! If you had seen what I have seen since yesterday morning, you too would believe in him!"

The audacity of this peasant stunned me! That he would dare to _forgive_ me for simply carrying out my duties as governor! I raised my hand to strike him, and then lowered it again, unnerved by his unwavering stare. Whatever he had seen, I realized that it had left him utterly without fear. As quickly as my dignitas would allow, I turned on my heel and left that accursed place.

And that is the end of my tale, Caesar. I have tried to conduct myself as a Roman prefect and nobleman should. I still do not know what it is I have done. Have I been the victim of an incredibly elaborate fraud? Have I lost my mind? Or was I the unwitting accomplice in the murder of a god? I do not know. So I leave judgment of this matter in your hands. Mine are too stained with blood to deal with it any further. I beg you, Caesar, recall me from this benighted place and let me return to Rome! I know that it was my own actions that drove you to send me here, but surely I have paid for them by now. Please let me come home! I remain, respectfully yours, Lucius Pontius Pilate, Governor of Judea.

316

# CHAPTER TWENTY-FOUR

Forty days, thought Pilate. What a horrific forty days they had been! First, the reports that had kept pouring in that the man he crucified was somehow alive again, no matter how impossible that seemed to be. Jesus had been seen by eleven of his surviving disciples. Jesus had been seen by his own brothers in Nazareth. Jesus had appeared inside a locked room in Jerusalem. Jesus had cooked breakfast for some fishermen on the shores of Lake Gennesaret. Finally, Jesus had appeared to a gathering of some five hundred of his followers in the hills outside Jerusalem. Manifestly impossible, yet the tales kept coming!

Then Pilate had lost the services of a man he had come to depend on greatly during his years in Judea. Cassius Longinus had come in to see him about a month after the crucifixion of Jesus, carrying his sword and armor, clad in a simple tunic and a homespun robe.

"I'm done, sir," he said quietly when Pilate looked up at him curiously.

"What do you mean, Centurion?" asked the prefect.

"I've been a soldier over twenty years, Pilate. I've killed more men than I care to remember and seen horrors I can't forget," said Longinus. "I've always been able to live with myself until now. I've told myself that my service to Rome was for the greater good. There were times it was hard for me to keep thinking that, but serving with you had made it easier—till now."

"So what has changed?" Pilate asked.

"Jesus of Nazareth," Longinus said simply. "First and foremost, the fact that our Roman legal system could send a completely innocent man to the cross. That was hard enough for me witness. But now"—he bowed his head and actually sobbed—"sir, he was no ordinary man. He was not even an extraordinary man. We have killed the Son of God!"

Pilate's temper snapped. "You think I don't know it?" he snarled. "I see his blood on my hands every night! You may have driven the nails, but you were following orders, Centurion! Your obedience to me, to the Senate and

317

People of Rome, wipes the stain from you. Nothing can expiate my guilt in this matter. I don't know about this 'Son of God' business, really—I don't know what this Jesus was! But he was no ordinary man, as you say. There was something supernatural about him, and I sent him to his death. I've never believed in the immortality of the soul, Longinus. That's something the Greeks cooked up to alleviate their fear of dying. But if any part of us lives on after we die, I am hopelessly damned!"

Silence fell in the room. For the first time, Pilate had articulated the fear that paralyzed him, that haunted his dreams. The murder of a god was a crime of cosmic proportions, and every time this Jesus appeared yet again, he was reminded of his own guilt.

"It is not hopeless, sir," said Longinus. "He can forgive you—just as he forgave me."

"What are you talking about?" Pilate demanded. "Do you mean that nonsense he was spouting as he hung on the cross?"

"No, sir," replied the centurion. "I have seen him since then. He appeared to me ten days ago."

Pilate sunk into his chair. "You, too, Longinus?" he finally said. "I refused to believe these tales at first, but they would not die. Just like this Jesus would not die! Tell me, sir, how can a man whom we thoroughly killed be up and walking around?"

Longinus smiled—a wonderful smile full of deep joy and abiding confidence. "Because he is more than a man, sir. He is exactly what his disciples called him—the Son of God. He still bears the scars in his hands and feet—the scars I put there. I was like you, sir. Nightmares every night, guilt overwhelming me. I finally decided to fall on my sword and end it like a good Roman. I sent Stychius and Abigail away, along with the children. They didn't want to leave me—Stychius knew what I intended, I'm sure. I was drunk and surly, and had to chase them out of the house. I drained another flagon of wine, then braced the sword against my bed and prepared to skewer myself through the chest."

"Isn't suicide against your religion?" asked Pilate.

"What does that matter when you are already in hell?" asked Longinus. "But what happened next showed me the way out. The room suddenly filled with light, and a sweet scent like nothing I have ever smelt before. A strong

318

hand grasped my shoulder and spun me around, and there he was, looking me straight in the eye."

Pilate shook his head. "Impossible!" he snapped.

"The Jews say all things are possible with God," the centurion replied. "Jesus looked at me, and said, 'You did not take my life from me, Cassius Longinus. I laid it down, and I took it up again.' I fell on my knees and wept like a child, sir. He lifted me up and asked if I would like to atone for all I had done, and I said there was nothing I would like more. He looked at me with those eyes that are as deep as the oceans, and simply said: 'Be my disciple.' So now I am going to meet with one of his apostles, a man named John, and ask to join their new faith—they call it The Way."

"Longinus, you were drunk and had a hallucination!" Pilate said. "You wanted a way out from your guilt, so your mind manufactured one!"

The senior centurion laid his gear on Pilate's desk. "You know that is not true, sir. I am not the only one who has seen him—you told me that yourself. You are angry because of your own sense of guilt. He can forgive you too, sir. All you have to do is ask!"

"I DON'T WANT TO BE FORGIVEN!!" roared Pilate. "Forgiveness is for weaklings, and no one has ever been able to call me weak! If guilt is my lot, I will live with it." Then the anger leeched out of him as quickly as it had come. He sat down and buried his face in his hands. "You are a good man, Longinus, and you have served Rome—and me—very well. I regret your leaving, but will not try to stop you." Standing up, Pilate walked around the desk and put his hands on Longinus' shoulder. "You are the only true friend I have made here, you know. I will miss your wise counsel."

Longinus embraced him. "I am still your friend," he said, "and always will be. But a soldier I can be no more. May God bless you, Lucius Pontius Pilate. You are a bigger man than the demons that beset you. I pray you find peace."

So Pilate lost his best officer and closest friend. He promoted Titus Ambrosius to *Primus Pilus* of the Judean Legion, but even though the big veteran was completely competent, he and Pilate had never become friends the way Pilate and Longinus had. The nightmares continued, though— almost without change. Every night he relived that horrid, humiliating trial, and every night he was unable to wash the blood of Jesus from his hands.

He tried drinking himself into a stupor before going to bed, but the dreams kept coming—and he always found himself stone cold sober when he woke. His weight began to drop, but food held no interest for him. Porcia was deeply concerned, but could do nothing to help him.

Fifty-three days after the crucifixion, he was sitting in his office, trying to focus his brain on the pile of petitions and requests before him—his clients and supplicants were too frightened of his mood swings to appear before him in person—when a cheerful voice boomed across the room in greeting.

"*Ave*, Lucius Pontius Pilate!"

Pilate raised his head and glared at the cheerful young man who grinned at him from the door of the prefect's office. "Who in Jupiter's name are you?" he snarled.

Undaunted, the youth, clad in a junior officer's uniform, crossed the room and sat down across from Pilate. "I am *Quaestor* Marcus Balbus Phillipus, your new junior legate! Tiberius Caesar sends his greetings!"

Pilate shook his head. Seven years in this thankless job without a single officer from Rome to assist him, and now they send him a junior legate? It made no sense. But what did, these days? He stood and poured his guest a glass of wine.

"Welcome to the armpit of the Empire, Marcus Balbus Phillipus," he said. "So what disgrace did you commit to earn this punishment?"

"Punishment?" the young man asked. "No punishment at all, Prefect Pilate! The Emperor's friend Sergius Paulus asked me to come here in person in order to investigate the remarkable tale of the carpenter who returned from the dead."

Pilate's attention snapped around to the *Quaestor*. "You know about that?" he asked.

"Paulus allowed me to read your report to Tiberius," he said, "so that I would know what it was I was sent to investigate. The Emperor is fascinated and curious about the whole thing. Here, I was told to give you this." He tossed a scroll from his satchel to Pilate. It was sealed with Tiberius' familiar signet. "I'll step out and let you read it in private," he said before leaving.

Pilate broke the seal and opened the letter. Tiberius' handwriting seemed to grow shakier with each missive he sent, but he still wrote every message himself, refusing to use an *amanuensis* for even routine correspondence.

*Gaius Julius Tiberius Caesar, Princeps and Imperator, to Prefect Lucius Pontius Pilate, Proconsul of Judea; greetings!*

*I read your lengthy and fascinating report on the events of Passover week in Jerusalem with great interest. As you know, I am a deeply religious man—I believe in the gods of Rome, but I am not so foolish as to think that our gods are the only gods that exist. The God of the Jews is far older than our deities, and although his laws make little sense to us dwelling on the Tiber, they were laid down hundreds of years before Romulus laid the foundation stones of Rome.*

*This Jesus of Nazareth seems to be linked to the God of the Jews somehow, although the nature of that link is unclear to me. But the events you describe are fraught with all kinds of remarkable portents that need to be investigated. I asked Sergius Paulus, who serves as one of my confidential agents in matters I do not wish for Macro or Gaius Caligula to know about, to send a trustworthy person to gather information and report back to us about what you described. Please understand, dear Pilate, that this is not because I doubt your word! But in matters this important, more than one set of eyes is needed to verify the truth. Frankly, I have also been remiss in not sending you some help any sooner. Judea is a difficult province to govern, as you above all Romans should know, but due to the unfortunate circumstances I sent you to govern it without a single legate, tribune, or even a conterburnalis to help you! Marcus Phillipus is an able and intelligent young man of good family; he should be of great assistance to you once his investigation is concluded. You may consider him absolutely trustworthy; he has no reason to love Macro or Caligula.*

*As far as your request to return to Rome, it grieves me to say no, but I must. For the time being, your return is neither safe nor politic. But when I do recall you, it may well be that I need you to come home quickly and quietly. Hold yourself in readiness for that day. Send my greetings to your family.*

Pilate read the note twice, and gave a low whistle. Why on earth would the ruler of the world concern himself with such a matter? Jesus' refusal to stay dead was an enigma, but was Tiberius truly thinking that the Nazarene was some sort of god? Of course, his reports from Sullemius said that Tiberius had become more and more superstitious as well as more paranoid in his old age. Perhaps he was mad enough to add a Galilean carpenter to the Roman pantheon? Pilate stifled a chuckle as he imagined the Senate's reaction to that!

He called Phillipus back into his office and looked him over again. "So tell me, Balbus," he said, "a little bit more about yourself."

"Not a lot to tell," the young man said. "My family is linked with the Emperor's for many generations, and when I was about fourteen I was sent to Capri at the request of Tiberius. He said that young Gaius Caesar—he truly hates to be called 'Caligula' these days!—needed the company of young men from his own social class, rather than the children from the rural tribes around Neapolis. This was perhaps a year after your last"—he winked at Pilate—"encounter with Gaius. His bones had knit and his face was mended, but his temper was foul! My job was to help him train with blade and shield, to prepare him for his military duties. I'd been training on the Campus Martius since I was ten, and was reckoned to be handy with a gladius. Oh, how he hated it! The brat could not stand that anyone was better than him at anything, but he was too lazy and sloppy to ever be any good with a blade. Every time I disarmed him or whacked him over the head with my *rudis* for dropping his guard, there was murder in his eyes. But Tiberius made a point of attending all the training sessions, leaning on his cane and watching us practice, so my young companion had to disguise his true feelings and laugh, congratulating me on a good move. He was biding his time and waiting, but I figured his revenge would come in the form of a brawl or practical joke of some sort. I didn't really know Caligula very well at that point." He paused and took a sip of wine; his face grew grim.

"After several months of training with the *rudii*, we graduated to metal blades and real shields. Little by little, despite himself, Caligula was getting better at fighting, and it was more rarely that I disarmed him or got through his guard. So those murderous looks became fewer and further between, and I began to think that maybe the little monster had forgiven me for being a better warrior than he will ever be. Then one day Tiberius was in bed with a cough during our normal training session. It was cold and damp, and we were not going at it that hard—just the standard circling, parrying, and blocking that soldiers do every day. He seemed unusually cheerful that day, but it made him careless. I must have gotten past his guard a half dozen times, but all I did was tap him with the flat of the blade to show him his mistakes. But he would not correct himself, and I got a little tired of it. So the next time he let his guard down, I made sure that I scratched his arm with the blade. That's all it was, I swear! Just a little scratch. He got that nasty expression, and I turned to walk away. Suddenly I felt a sharp pain and looked down to see the tip of Caligula's gladius sticking out of my chest, just below my right shoulder. The *mentula* ran me through—for trying to make him a better swordsman!"

He pulled his tunic off his shoulder, and Pilate saw the angry red scar just below his collarbone. Marcus turned around and showed him the corresponding scar on his back.

"What happened after that?" Pilate asked him.

"I slowly turned around, and there was Gaius Little Boots, grinning at me with the most cheerful expression imaginable," Phillipus continued. "All I remember thinking was that I could not let myself fall backward, because it would drive even more of the blade into me. So I watched that evil grin as I slowly fell forward onto my face."

"Jupiter!" said Pilate. "An inch or two lower and that thrust would have killed you."

"If several servants had not come running up, I'm sure he would have finished me off," said Marcus. "As it was, Tiberius' physician dressed my wound and I was bundled back to my parents with a generous gift of gold to purchase my silence. Like you, I live in fear of the day that maggot becomes Emperor."

Pilate nodded. "So how did all of that bring you here?"

"Like you once did, my patron, Sergius Paulus, runs confidential errands for Tiberius, and helps him hear what is happening in Rome," explained Phillipus. "Your testimony about the trial of this Jesus character has the Emperor aflame with curiosity. He thinks it may be a significant omen of some sort, this man who refuses to stay dead. So he sent me to gather information and report back to him, after which he wants me to stay and help you govern the province."

Pilate wasn't sure how much he wanted the young man's help, but he saw no harm in helping him fulfill his mission. "The man you really want to talk to is Gaius Cassius Longinus," he said. "He was my *Primus Pilus* Centurion until a week or so ago. He has left the legion in order to join the followers of this Jesus. He lives in a village called Capernaum, where Jesus often taught."

The next morning Phillipus took off, bearing a letter of introduction from Pilate, who was somewhat relieved to see him go. However, his relief was short-lived. A week after Phillipus rode off in search of information about Jesus, yet another irate delegation from the High Priest showed up, led by his eldest son Alexander. Pilate's head was splitting with the cumulative effects of sleep deprivation and too much wine, but he donned his toga with its purple borders, symbolizing his Proconsular rank, and went out to hear their grievance.

"Well, what brings the Temple leadership all the way out to Caesarea?" Pilate asked as charitably as his mood allowed.

"Governor, you must intervene!" snapped Alexander. "Ever since the Feast of Pentecost three days ago, the followers of this Galilean have been running amok!"

"Are they murdering Roman citizens, destroying public property, and flouting the laws of the Republic?" asked Pilate, knowing the answer already.

"They are flouting the Laws of Moses! They are flouting the traditions of our Elders! They are undermining the authority of the Temple!" shouted Alexander, a younger and less restrained duplicate of his father.

Pilate yawned. "None of those are an offense under Roman law," he said.

"They blame us for the death of their leader, the Nazarene!" snapped the priest.

"So do I, when it comes down to it," said Pilate. "Your father manipulated me into crucifying him!"

"These men must be put to death! Or at the very least, sold into slavery far from Judea!" snapped Alexander.

Pilate allowed the beast within him to stare out through his eyes. "Listen to me, you self-righteous fraud, and listen well! We tried that! We put the Galilean to death, and guess what? Three days later he was up and walking again! I don't know how he did it, and I don't care, but I will NOT be manipulated into killing his followers too! First of all, it did not achieve the desired end of getting rid of the man's teachings. He seemingly has more followers now than ever. Secondly, it seems to me that this is a religious problem of the Jews, and unless and until the followers of Jesus pose a clear and present danger to Rome's rule in this province, I will not lift a finger to harm a one of them! Tell your father and the Sanhedrin he commands that from now on they do their own dirty work. I will not act as their executioner again!"

The delegation was utterly quailed, and they turned and made their way back to Jerusalem. Pilate wondered if they would report him to Tiberius again, but apparently word of Marcus Phillipus' mission had got back to them, and they kept their silence this time. Evidently something remarkable had happened at Pentecost; the disciples of Jesus, who had been relatively quiet since the events of Passover, suddenly stepped forth boldly and began preaching their new faith, The Way, on the very steps of the Temple, publicly charging the Sanhedrin and the priesthood with conniving to murder the Messiah of Israel, one of the names they were now calling Jesus.

Converts flocked to hear them, especially the three fishermen who led the group—Peter, James, and John. When Pilate came to Jerusalem that fall for the annual festival season, he passed by the Temple steps on the way to the Fortress of Antonia. On each side of the Temple, the long porticos were covered with hundreds of men, women, and children, quietly seated, listening as the followers of Jesus repeated his teachings from memory. As he and his lictors walked by, trailing two centuries of legionaries, a bearded man rose from where he sat and greeted Pilate by name. It took him a moment to recognize Cassius Longinus.

"Jupiter!" he said, taking his former officer by the hand. "You look like a Jew!"

Longinus laughed. "So many of the brothers were nervous at having a former Roman officer join The Way that Andrew told me I should let my beard grow out, and find a new name to go by. So now I am simply Brother Gideon to most of them. It makes it easier for me to fit in; the Apostles know that I was part of the crucifixion detail, but the others do not. If they asked, I would tell them—but I am not volunteering that information right now."

Pilate nodded. "Then you probably do not want to stand here talking to me for long," he said. "I'll be staying at Herod's palace for the season. Come by and visit with me; I know someone who is anxious to meet you."

"I shall do that," said Longinus, and returned to the lovely Jewish woman and three small children who waited for him on the Temple steps. Pilate realized it was the first time he had ever seen Longinus' entire family. They all seemed so happy there, hanging on the words of the tall, rugged Galilean who was speaking to them. Pilate's Aramaic was not the best, but nearly seven years in Judea had enabled him to understand most of what he heard, even if he could not repeat it. The big fisherman was repeating some form of verse, each stanza beginning with the same phrase: "Blessed are." Pilate heard something about hungering and thirsting after righteousness, and wondered what that would be like.

After settling the guards in, Pilate walked across Jerusalem to Herod's palace. Ever since the trial of Jesus, the Tetrarch of Galilee had bent over backward to accommodate the Roman Proconsul, although Pilate did not understand why. He found the king pacing back and forth in his audience room, the lines on his face deeper than ever. He seemed glad to see the Roman prefect.

"Lucius Pontius!" he said. "It is good to see you again, sir! What do you make of this time of wonders?"

"What wonders do you refer to, King Herod?" asked Pilate.

"The Nazarene, of course!" Herod said. "How many men have you crucified that have actually returned from the dead?"

Pilate paused for a moment. He was not sure he wanted to share what he really thought with the slippery tetrarch, but on the other hand, the man

326

was well disposed toward him and he had no interest in provoking his ill will, either.

"It is inexplicable to me," he finally said. "If only one or two had seen him, it would be easier to discount it. But between the empty tomb, the stunned guards, and the multiple eyewitnesses, it is very difficult to write this off as a fraud or a case of mistaken identity."

"So you don't believe his disciples stole the body?" asked Herod.

Pilate snorted. "Do you really think that a rag-tag band of frightened rabbits who wouldn't even fight for the man while he was still alive would risk life and limb to retrieve a broken, battered corpse?" he asked derisively. "And that they could be so effective that not a single one of them perished, nor a single one of the guards? Believe me, Herod, the story of the stolen body was a desperate ploy by the High Priest to try and detract from something he could not explain."

Herod nodded slowly. "Do you think that he really was—well, that he really was what his disciples are now claiming him to be?"

Pilate paused for a long while. "I don't know," he finally said. "Did you speak to him when I sent him to you that night?"

"I questioned him for an hour, but he never said a word to me," replied Herod. "He would not even look me in the eye."

"He spoke to me only a little," said Pilate, "but his words shook me to my core. He said that he was indeed a king, but that his kingdom—how did he put it? He said his kingdom 'is not of this world.' He said that those who turned him over to me were guiltier than I was. In all honesty, King Herod, he made me feel like I was on trial—more than that, he made me feel like I had been weighed in the balance and found wanting! I have sent many men to the cross in my lifetime, and most of them richly deserved it. But I have never wanted to set someone free as badly as I wanted to release the Galilean."

Herod looked at him curiously. "Then why didn't you?" he asked.

Pilate sighed. "They had me betwixt Scylla and Charybdis," he said. "The High Priest was threatening to report me to Caesar for supporting insurrection if I didn't give him what he wanted. My position here is somewhat precarious, and after being reported to Rome several times already over different matters, I simply didn't have it in me to fight them anymore."

Herod nodded. About that time the steward announced that Marcus Balbus had arrived. Pilate introduced him to the King and then the young legate settled on a couch between them as food was brought in. Pilate explained to Herod why Marcus was there, and then asked the young man to discuss his findings.

"At first I thought that it would be very difficult to get Jesus' disciples to talk to me," he said. "But when I explained my mission they were delighted to tell me everything I wanted to know! One of them—a huge, grizzled fisherman named Simon, although the others call him Petros—he could recite many of the Galilean's teachings by heart. I found that there was much wisdom there, although there were many ideas and concepts that were very foreign to me. Another one, a former *publicanus* named Matthew Levi, cited one Scripture after another from the Jewish holy books that he said were direct prophecies of this Nazarene. Apparently Jesus was descended directly from some ancient Hebrew King named David."

Herod shuddered. "It was always said that the Messiah would be born of David's line," he said. "My father, about thirty-five years ago, heard some Babylonian astrologers say that the Messiah had been born in David's ancestral village of Bethlehem. He was so fearful of a potential rival that he had every male child in the village slaughtered!"

Balbus raised an eyebrow. "Remarkable! Matthew told me that Jesus was actually born in Bethlehem about that time, but that his parents were warned in a dream of Herod's actions, and fled with the baby to Egypt for a year or so," he explained.

"So what are you going to tell the Emperor?" Herod asked.

"I am simply going to document everything that happened for him," said Balbus. "But I am going to let him make his own decision about what to do with the information."

Pilate nodded. "But what does Marcus Balbus Phillipus think about the whole thing?" he asked.

The young legate squirmed, not comfortable being put on the spot. "I think that every bit of evidence I have uncovered indicates that something supernatural happened," he said. "What it was, what it meant, I do not know."

"The Galilean's followers certainly seem to know," commented Herod. "Or at least, they think they know. For the moment, I am content to wait and watch. But if I perceive a threat in them, I will silence them one way or another!"

Pilate nodded. "If I thought they were any kind of threat to Rome, I would be more concerned," he said. "But for the moment, what I see is a large group of people devoting themselves to a religion whose chief teaching is love and obedience. Such men should be good citizens."

Later that evening, after Herod had retired, Longinus was shown up by Pilate's faithful steward Democles. Pilate introduced him to Phillipus and then sat and listened as Longinus gave a detailed description of his own role in the execution of the Nazarene. When he was done, Phillipus grilled him for details on what had happened on that Sunday morning. It was long after midnight when he finished, and Longinus slipped out the door and returned to his family.

Marcus Phillipus sequestered himself at the Fortress of Antonia for several days thereafter, drafting a lengthy report for Tiberius on everything his investigation had revealed. Once he was done, he and Pilate sealed the document together and sent it off to Rome. Pilate remained in Jerusalem for an unusually long time that summer, partly because his poor sleep and wounded leg did not let him move about comfortably, and partly to see what would happen next with the followers of Jesus.

He did not have to wait long on that count. Early in the fall, Centurion Brutus Appius reported that a major confrontation had taken place after Peter and John had healed a lame man on the very steps of the Temple. Caiaphas had ordered the two fishermen arrested and beaten, sternly warning them to stop preaching in the name of Jesus. But the big fisherman, Simon Peter, threw the charges right back in the High Priest's face.

"Let it be known to all of you, and all the people of Israel, that by the name of Jesus Christos, the Nazarene, whom you crucified and God raised from the dead—by this name this cripple stands before you able to walk again!" thundered the Galilean.

The High Priest and his cronies huddled for a few minutes and warned the fishermen a second time against continuing to preach, but Peter simply said that he and his friends would have to obey God rather than men, and turned on their heels and walked out. Within the hour, backs still bleeding from the beating they had been given, he and John were standing on the steps of the Temple preaching—with the once lame man standing beside them and dancing a happy jig whenever they spoke about his healing.

"It was the best show I've seen since the last time I was in Rome, sir," said the big centurion, who had wound up making a fine officer. "Old Caiaphas was opening and shutting his mouth like a fish out of water, but the crowd outside the Sanhedrin's chambers was so huge he was afraid to do anything!"

"So what do you make of all this, Brutus?" asked Pilate.

The burly officer sighed. "I don't hold much with the Jews' religion, to be honest," he said. "Those priests are as slick and oily a bunch as I have ever encountered, living high on the hog while the common people scrabble for a living. But these fishermen—every penny anyone gives them they use to buy food for the crowds who come to hear them preach. They all live together in an upper room that someone donated to them, but I don't think any of them have two denarii to rub together. Say what you like about their teachings, those fellows at least practice what they preach."

"Did they really heal a lame man, though?" asked Pilate.

"That old beggar has been lying on his cot outside the Temple for as long as I've been coming to Jerusalem," said Appius. "His legs were no bigger than sticks, but now his calves are as big as mine! I don't think he's quit running and leaping since he was healed yesterday."

A few weeks later, Pilate returned to Caesarea to take care of business and see all of his clients. His nightmares were gradually lessening in intensity, although he still found himself unconsciously rubbing his hands together at odd times, trying to wash away a stain only he could see. Near the turn of the year he and his family journeyed to Jerusalem, since the Jews were gathering to celebrate the Feast of Lights. Longinus had explained this particular festival to Pilate long ago—something to do with lamps in the Temple burning for eight days on one day's worth of oil—but Pilate really only cared to see that the city remained calm and peaceful despite the arrival of thousands of pilgrims.

A few days after his arrival, little Decimus fell sick. His fever spiked dangerously high, and neither water nor food would stay in his stomach. Porcia and Pilate took turns staying up with him, and Pilate watched helplessly as the hope slowly drained from his wife's face. Aristarchus the physician was called in, and his diagnosis was bleak.

"There is no easy way to tell you this, Prefect, so I will be blunt," the Greek told him. "The boy has the flux. It is nearly always fatal in children. The disease is halfway through its course; it will be another three days to a week before he becomes too weak to endure it any longer. I am deeply sorry. Some of the milk of poppy will ease his pain, but that is the most we can do for him."

Pilate bowed his head and waved the man out. Porcia came storming into the room, grief and fury etched into her features.

"Did I not tell you?" she shrieked. "Did I not warn you to have nothing to do with his death?"

Pilate looked at her numbly. "You would send me away from our son's sickbed?" he asked in bewilderment.

"Not Decimus!" she snapped. "The Nazarene! This is your punishment for killing an innocent man, Proconsul Pontius Pilate! My dream told me that our son's life would be forfeit if you did not save him!"

"Save him?" Pilate said. "I could not save him. I could not . . . save him!" Suddenly an idea flared in his head. He shoved his wife aside as gently as his haste allowed and ran downstairs in his tunic, barefoot, not even worried about the appearance he was presenting to his men.

"Brutus Appius!" he roared. The big centurion emerged from the barracks moments later, rubbing the sleep out of his eyes.

"Yes, Governor?" he asked.

"Do you know how to find Cassius Longinus?" he asked.

"He and his family have taken rooms over by the weaver's market," said Appius.

"In the name of all the gods, man, go and find him. Tell him that he must bring one of the Nazarene's apostles to me right away. Perhaps the one named John—he at least knows me. Go, centurion, and quickly!"

"What if he won't come?" asked Appius.

"Tell him—" Pilate paused a moment and swallowed hard. "Tell him that I am begging him to."

The big officer pulled on a cloak and disappeared into the night. Pilate went back up to his quarters and took up his place by the boy's bed. Decimus was now five and a half years old, and big for his age, but the disease made him look shrunken and lifeless, like a porcelain doll. Beads of sweat glittered on his forehead, and the room stank of vomit and diarrhea. Porcia had wetted a cloth and was letting him suck moisture out of it, trying to slake his thirst without triggering the retching that would dehydrate him further. Pilate took his son's hand and looked his wife in the eye. Her raw grief and anger had made a wasteland of her beauty; accusation radiated out of her countenance like the raw cold of a winter storm in the mountains.

They sat there like that, neither saying a word, with the unconscious, whimpering child between them. Finally, after the changing of the midnight guard outside, they heard voices in the courtyard, and the outer door of the apartment opened. Pilate, now decently clad in a robe and sandals, stepped out of the sick room to see if his desperate summons had been answered.

There in his office stood Brutus Appius and Cassius Longinus. Between them stood a young man that Pilate had last seen outside the empty tomb of Jesus of Nazareth. He extended his hand.

"Your name is John, is it not?" he asked.

"Yes, Governor," said the young Jew. "The others were afraid, but I know that you are no threat to us."

"And I will not be, unless you become a threat to Rome," said Pilate. "I regret the outcome of that trial more than anything I have ever done. But that is not why I have brought you here. My son is deathly ill; the doctors give no hope for him. I have heard that you and the others have been given the gift of healing your master once had. Can you help him?"

"Can I help him?" asked John. "No. But God can help anyone. Do you believe that?"

Pilate hung his head. "I don't know what I believe," he finally said. "Except that I know your master was more than a normal man. I believe that he would have healed my son if I asked, and I believe that you can, too—whether it be by the power of God, or the power of the man I crucified."

John nodded. "Take me to the boy," he said.

Pilate led him into the sick room, where Porcia looked more grief-stricken than ever. She stared at the young Jew as he followed Pilate into the room. Finally she spoke.

"Are you one of the disciples of the Galilean?" she asked.

John nodded. "I am a follower of Jesus," he said.

"Do you come here to behold your master's vengeance on my husband?" she said bitterly.

John gave her a look full of compassion. "My master did not believe in vengeance," he said. "He taught us to love our enemies and do good to those who hate us."

She gave him a desperate look of hope. "Can this be true?" she said.

John bent over Decimus' tiny form. He took in the pale face, the drawn expression, the tortured breathing, and a single tear ran down his cheek. He gently laid his hand across the boy's forehead and bowed his head. His lips moved in silent prayer.

For a few moments nothing changed. Then, gradually, the ambiance of the room began to subtly shift. The aroma of sickness was replaced by a much more subtle scent—the hint of flowers, of springtime, of sunshine on green meadows. The shadows crept back into the corners, and the oil lamp seemed to burn brighter. Finally, the Galilean leaned forward and kissed the boy's forehead, and then he sat back, exhausted.

Pilate was astonished. Decimus' face color was normal; his breathing was even, his cheeks full and ruddy. As Porcia took him in her arms, he opened one eye.

"Mama, I'm hungry," he said.

Pilate hugged his son and called for broth, then kissed his wife on the forehead. By the time he turned around to thank John, the apostle of Jesus had quietly slipped out the door and was gone.

# CHAPTER TWENTY-FIVE

"Wait!" Pilate yelled, limping across the courtyard after John's retreating form. The disciple of Jesus paused at the gate and allowed Pilate to catch up. Pilate got within a few feet and paused, his old injury throbbing.

"What else may I do for you, Governor?" John asked calmly.

"I just wanted to thank you," said Pilate, "and give you whatever reward you ask."

"Thank God, and his Son, Jesus," said the Galilean. "I did nothing but act as an instrument of their power."

"But it was you that answered my summons," said Pilate.

"A sick child needed healing, so I came." said John. "But I perceive that your need for healing is just as great as his."

"Me?" asked Pilate. "No, this injury is over a year old. It is as healed as it is going to get, at my age."

"I do not speak of your knee," said John. "I speak of your spirit. You are a tortured soul, in the agony of perdition."

Pilate stopped, stunned that this stranger could know so well what he was feeling. "I don't know who told you this—" he began.

"No one told me," said John. "It is written in every line of your face. The guilt of sending the Son of Man to the cross is more than anyone can bear. But He offers you His forgiveness, even now!"

Pilate's face darkened. "I neither want nor deserve his forgiveness, or anyone else's. You do not know me, Jew. My life's path has been stained with much blood—your master's was just the latest."

"You speak out of pride, Governor. All men need forgiveness," said John. "That is why the Master came into the world—so that the forgiveness of all the sins of man could be purchased once and for all. Would you not find peace?"

"Peace?" Pilate asked. "I don't even know what that means. But I owe you a debt for my son's life. What can I do to repay you?"

John shrugged. "I want nothing for myself," he said. "The only thing I ask is this, because I know you did your best to spare my Master. You believed in his innocence. My brothers and I are likewise innocent of any crime, as Rome reckons such things. Will you continue to let us speak of The Way without interference?"

Pilate nodded. "As long as I am convinced that you and your fellow disciples pose no threat to Rome, I see no reason to interfere with you. I do not think that the religious leaders of the Jews share my sentiment, however."

John smiled. "How could they?" he said. "To acknowledge the merits of our Gospel is to acknowledge their own guilt towards our Master. But we will bear their hostility and resistance as a badge of honor, and rejoice that we have been found worthy to suffer in the name of Jesus."

With that, the young man smiled beatifically at Pilate. "When the burden of your sin becomes so heavy you can no longer bear it, my Master will lift it from your shoulders. All you need to do is ask. *Shalom*, Prefect Pontius Pilate!"

Then John turned and was gone, leaving Pilate staring after him. He felt drained of all energy, and yet the gnawing anger and frustration that had defined his life since the death of his daughter nearly eight years before was lightened. He slowly climbed the steps back to the room, where Porcia cradled their sleeping son in her arms. Her face was still streaked with tears.

"Forgive me, husband," she said. "I said things in my grief that I would recall, if I could."

Pilate looked at her and saw the young girl he had fallen in love with so long before, looking so aged and careworn that his heart broke for her. He limped across the room and kissed her furrowed brow. "You said nothing to me that I had not already said to myself many times over," he said. "The Galilean holds no grudge, it seems. So how can I?"

He took Decimus' sleeping form in his arms and looked at the calm, untroubled face of the child, seeing in its planes the faces of his beloved wife, his lost daughter, his distant brothers, and even his own youthful self. He wondered what this child of the Pontii would grow up to be one day. He kissed the tiny, ruddy face, and the boy opened one eye and gave an enormous yawn.

"Hello, *tata*," he said. "Have I been asleep long?"

"Only a little while," Pilate answered. "You can go back to sleep if you want."

"I think I will," said the boy. "I was dreaming of the kindest man. He had a beard and funny scars on his hands, and he gave me a tiny little lamb to play with. Do you think I could have a pet lamb?"

Pilate nodded gravely. "I believe that the governor of Judea can procure one for you," he said.

"That's silly," said Decimus. "You are the governor!" Then he let out another yawn and closed his eyes. Pilate watched him fade back off to sleep, and then laid him back on his bed. He took his wife by the hand and led her to their own bedchamber, which they had not shared since the boy first grew sick days before. They held each other tightly until sleep claimed them both, and for once, Pilate did not dream of the blood on his hands.

The next few years were eventful. The followers of The Way continued to increase in numbers, boldly preaching the "gospel" of Jesus on the steps of the Temple, until finally the Sanhedrin felt forced to act. About a year after the healing of Decimus, one of the leaders of the new sect, a Greek proselyte named Stephen, was accused of blasphemy and dragged before the Jew's religious tribunal. When the charges against him were read out, he responded with a lengthy diatribe, accusing the Pharisees and priests of perverting and distorting the laws of Moses, and of murdering the Messiah of Israel. Unable to refute his soaring eloquence, the Temple supporters stopped up their ears and mobbed him, dragging him into the streets of Jerusalem and stoning him to death just outside the city walls. Even in death, Stephen conducted himself with grace and dignity, asking Jesus to forgive the men who slew him. Bleeding from a dozen cuts and gashes, Stephen exclaimed that he could see the Messiah standing in heaven at the right hand of God—and then he collapsed beneath the barrage of deadly rocks.

Stephen's murder broke the strange paralysis that had kept the priests from acting against the followers of Jesus for the two years since the death of the Galilean. Suddenly the open-air meetings were targets of violent attacks by the Temple priests, and many of the converts fled the city to avoid arrest. But they were not silenced; instead, they continued to preach the message of Jesus—which they had learned from his Apostles—wherever they went.

Pilate was angry at the flouting of Roman law—the Temple had no authority to execute anyone without his consent—and summoned Caiaphas before him at Herod's palace, charging him with breaking the peace. Caiaphas was not in the least repentant.

"We have repeatedly asked you, Prefect, to arrest these troublemakers!" he said. "But you have refused to do so, and their blasphemy finally angered the people so much that a spontaneous demonstration of outrage was necessary."

"Spontaneous!" roared Pilate. "That event was about as spontaneous as a Greek mime! You even had your oily little clerk, Saul, on hand to hold the cloaks of those who threw the stones! Understand me clearly, High Priest— there will be no more unauthorized executions! Roman law forbids it!"

Caiaphas spread his hands with an unctuous smile. "My dear governor, I cannot control the passions of the people!"

Pilate allowed the beast within to glare out of his eyes for a moment. "No more of Jesus' disciples will die in 'spontaneous demonstrations,' priest, or I may arrange for a spontaneous demonstration of Rome's displeasure—on one of your sons! Am I clear?"

Caiaphas blanched in fear. "You would not dare!" he said.

"I nearly killed Caesar's heir with my bare hands," said Pilate. "You think an obnoxious priestly brat would give me a moment's pause?"

"Fine!" snapped the High Priest. "We won't kill any more—but we will imprison as many as we see fit!"

"That is within the law," said Pilate. "But know that I will be watching you, Joseph Caiaphas."

Over the next year, dozens of followers of the Galilean were snatched from their homes and thrown into dank prisons, to be held without charges or trial. But the "apostles" remained in Jerusalem, occasionally roughed up by the Temple guards, but otherwise unharmed. The High Priest himself seemed reluctant to lay hands on them. However, the arrests continued, and Saul of Tarsus, the young clerk of the Sanhedrin, was sent to the ᵒ

surrounding area with orders to arrest any followers of The Way he might find, regardless of age or gender, and bring them to Jerusalem for trial.

Suddenly, a remarkable interruption stopped the march of persecution in its tracks. On the way to Damascus to arrest a group of believers, Saul was struck down by some sort of apoplexy and blinded. Then he suddenly showed up a few weeks later in the synagogue at Damascus, renouncing his allegiance to the Sanhedrin and boldly proclaiming that Jesus of Nazareth was indeed the Son of God and the Messiah of Israel. The Jewish leaders were thunderstruck at this defection, and then tried to have the apostate Pharisee seized and killed. But Saul slipped over the city wall and eluded them, vanishing from sight for the next three years.

But even as the Sanhedrin paused in its oppression of The Way, Herod the Tetrarch stepped up. He had been watching with alarm and hostility the remarkable numbers of those who followed Jesus, and was not at all convinced by Pilate's assertions that they were harmless. However, he waited until Pilate was in Caesarea to make his move against the Apostles of Jesus.

Armed with his authority as Tetrarch of Galilee, he sent a group of soldiers to arrest any of the original followers of Jesus they could find. The unfortunate disciple that they happened across was none other than James, the brother of John the Healer. After a trial that lasted less than an hour, James was hustled outside the city walls and beheaded, according to Titus Ambrosius, who had witnessed the whole thing.

Pilate was furious, but Herod was within his rights as Tetrarch, since all the original followers of Jesus were from his province of Galilee. Pilate nonetheless sent him an angry letter.

*Lucius Pontius Pilate, Proconsul of Rome and Prefect of Judea, to Herod Antipas, Tetrarch of Galilee and King of the Jews by decree of the Senate and People of Rome –*

*My dear Herod, I am deeply distressed to see you doing the dirty work of the Priests and Sanhedrin, who bear you neither love nor respect. The followers of the Galilean, Jesus of Nazareth, are a harmless lot who have done nothing to earn the abuse the Temple faction heaps upon them. They do not break the law, commit acts of violence, or seek to undermine the authority of Rome. I would ask you as a friend to reconsider this course of action; we have seen from experience that persecution does nothing to silence this sect, but only increases their devotion to their founder. Killing the Galilean's disciples will not earn you respect but the enmity of the common people of this region, who regard them as holy men and prophets.*

Pilate received a rather brusque message in return:

*Herod Antipas, Tetrarch of Galilee and King of the Jews, to Lucius Pontius Pilate, Prefect of Judea and Proconsul of Rome –*

*My dear Pilate, I am not in the habit of giving you advice about how to govern Judea, so please refrain from telling me how to run my own affairs. I know that one of the Galileans healed your son, accounting for your unusually tolerant attitude towards them. But the High Priest is right on this issue: the Nazarenes seek to overturn the ancient traditions of the Jews and destroy all respect for the religious and civil authorities of the land. I have arrested their chief, the fisherman called Simon son of Jonas, also known as Cephas. By the time you read this, his head will have parted company with his shoulders, and this pernicious sect will be on the path to extinction. I am sorry your sentimentality has blinded you to the seriousness of this situation, but out of respect and in memory of our friendship, I will refrain from mentioning this to Caesar.*

Pilate furiously balled the scroll up and threw it into his brazier, then began preparing to head to Jerusalem. He was unsure of how he would proceed when he got there, but he hoped that perhaps the big fisherman could be saved. However, a letter from Titus Ambrosius arrived by courier only a few hours behind Herod's missive.

*Titus Ambrosius, Centurion of the Jerusalem Cohort, to Lucius Pontius Pilate, Prefect of Judea, greetings!*

*You have asked me, Governor, to keep you informed of any events pertaining to the sect of the Nazarenes, or The Way, as they call themselves. The events of the last two days certainly merit a full report! First, Herod ordered the arrest of Simon Peter after seeing how pleased the Sanhedrin was with him for killing the Galilean James. The leader of the Nazarenes was dragged to prison and flogged, then informed that he would be put to death the next morning. The other disciples of Jesus were gathered at a house where they frequently meet, praying for the deliverance of their beloved leader. (In case you are wondering, my source is none other than our former Primus Pilus Centurion, Cassius Longinus! He has risen quite high in the leadership of the Jesus cult.)*

*While they were praying away, someone came knocking at the door of the house. A servant girl went down and answered and was stunned to see none other than Peter himself standing there, asking to be let in! She was so shocked she left him there and ran upstairs to tell the others. They thought she was hallucinating, but finally agreed to go to the gate and see for themselves. They were stunned to see Peter standing there alive and well! According to what he told them, he was praying and singing in his cell when he fell asleep and dreamed that an angel was urging him to stand up. He stood and found his chains were loosed, and the gates opened before him as he walked past the sleeping guards into the street. It wasn't until he was several blocks from Herod's palace that he realized it was not a dream, and went to the house where the disciples were accustomed to meet.*

*Herod was furious the next morning, I can tell you! He did find a use for his headsman, though—all six of the guards who were watching Peter's cell were executed before the day was out. Then Herod packed up his bags and headed for Sepphora in disgust. For the moment, at least, the followers of The Way are free of the fear of arrest, although the Temple guards are still under orders to rough them up any time they are seen in public, and to disrupt any attempts to proclaim their message about the Galilean they worship.*

*I don't know what to make of all this, sir, but you ordered regular reports, and I figured you would want to know about these events. I will keep you informed if anything else happens.*

Pilate shook his head in wonder. Someone was definitely looking after the followers of The Way—he wondered if it was their risen Master. His own feelings on the matter remained complex. The guilt of having murdered a god, or demigod, or whatever this Jesus had been, remained a heavy burden on his conscience. The dreams of the blood on his hands recurred fairly often, and he always woke up shaking and sweating from them.

He also began to notice a change in his wife. He and Porcia had never had secrets from each other, even during their long separations. Unlike most Roman men, Pilate did not feel the need to take on lovers when he was away from his wife, and Porcia had never given him reason to suspect her fidelity. But now he found her gone at odd hours of the day, and none of the servants seemed to know where she was. She glossed over these absences glibly at first—claiming she had gone to the market to fetch this or that item, or down to the docks to purchase some fresh fish—but her answers seemed somewhat contrived to him. Finally, one day, he saw her slipping out the door that led down to their secret beach. Wistfully, he realized they had not gone swimming together since right after his injury, when the exercise had helped his leg to heal. On impulse, he decided to follow her.

Standing at the door, he saw her slipping past the rocks that separated the small beach from the coast south of town. She seemed furtive in her manner, so he ducked back in and donned a hooded cloak. It was time, he decided, to get to the bottom of her mysterious absences. He slipped through the gap in the rocks just in time to see her disappear over the hillside on a road that led to a small spring a mile or two out of town. It was a popular watering hole for local shepherds to bring their flocks, and there were several stone sheep pens around it. Pilate's heart was aching—surely, after all they had been through, Porcia had not decided to stray!

He eased toward the sheepfolds, listening intently. From inside one of them, low voices came. He crept toward the door, trying to make out their words. One of the voices was definitely that of a man.

"Then Jesus told us, what does it profit a man to gain the whole world, and lose his own soul? What shall any man give in exchange for his soul?" said a familiar voice. "That young ruler had everything that the world could offer—but he left us that day a broken and empty man, because he chose the riches of this world over the kingdom of God."

"John?" exclaimed Pilate, stepping into the sheepfold. A circle of perhaps a dozen men and women were seated at the feet of the apostle, and one of them was his own wife, Porcia. The Jews shrieked at the sight of him and huddled together against the far wall, but Porcia and John stood their ground, facing him calmly.

"Greetings, Prefect," said the Apostle. "Your wife tells me young Decimus is doing very well."

"He is the same little terror that he was before he fell ill," said Pilate with a reluctant smile. "But I am curious—what is the meaning of this?"

"Please do not be angry, husband," said Porcia. "I have been searching for a way to tell you. Ever since John healed Decimus—I'm sorry, rabbi, I mean, ever since Jesus healed Decimus through John—I have been consumed with curiosity about this Galilean and his followers. I asked some of the members of The Way in Caesarea to tell me more, but they were afraid of me because you were my husband. When I heard that the man who healed our son was coming to speak here in Caesarea, I could not contain my curiosity. I have been coming out here every day to hear the stories of Jesus for two weeks now." She lowered her eyes. "I was baptized three days ago. I am a follower of The Way myself, now."

Pilate sat down on one of the stone benches and let out a long sigh. This was an unexpected development! After a moment, he looked up at the group. The local Jews were still pressed against the far wall, regarding him with anticipation and dread. John seemed completely calm, as if the possibility of physical danger had lost all fear for him. Porcia looked at him with the same loving gaze she had always borne for him, but he could see now that there was something else shining in her eyes—a fervor that had nothing to do with the passion between husband and wife. Finally he shrugged.

"You may believe what you wish, my wife," he said. "However, it is awkward for me as governor and a representative of the Senate and People of Rome to have my own family involved with such a controversial cult. I must ask—no, I must order each one of you"—he glared at the assembled circle—"to let no one know that my wife is among your number. Especially not in Jerusalem, where the priests would almost certainly use such information against me. I have withheld my hand from you people out of gratitude for what this man John did for my son. But do not presume that I will continue to withhold it if you cross me! Am I clear?"

343

The Jews nodded, their faces pale, while John the Apostle regarded him with a smile that was almost fond.

"Will you return to Caesarea with me now, wife, or would you like to listen to the end of this story?" Pilate asked.

Porcia blushed slightly. "With your leave, dear, I should very much like to hear a little more. But if you wait for me at our beach, I will join you there shortly."

The Apostle John spoke. "Prefect, I would be honored if you, too, would stay," he said softly.

Pilate looked at him. The invitation was obviously sincere. He thought a moment, and shook his head. "Another time, perhaps. I think that if I stayed, the rest of your audience might not enjoy the story as much."

With that, he turned on his heel and slowly walked back to the grounds of the governor's palace. His own wife, a follower of the Nazarene! He did not know what to think.

This uncertainty lasted for a good while longer. Porcia continued to be as loving and affectionate toward him as ever, but he could see in her eyes and hear in her voice that something was different. There was a strange otherness about her that had not been there before—Pilate did not understand it, and it made him uncomfortable. It reminded him too much of the eyes that haunted him in his dreams—the eyes of a man who had been a simple Galilean carpenter, and yet something more.

Over the next two years, Pilate's attitude changed. Whatever it was that weighed down his soul, he found himself becoming accustomed to the burden. The idea of forgiveness, redemption even, that had appealed to him at first now seemed like an elusive dream. His old nastiness began to surface—never toward his wife and child, but more and more toward the people he governed. True to his word, he did not lift his hand against the followers of Jesus, but he ceased interfering with the Temple when they continued their persecution of The Way. It was as if his heart was growing harder by the day.

Four years after Jesus was crucified, the Zealot movement, temporarily scotched by the capture of Bar Abbas, began to stir again—but without its former leader. Somehow the notorious brigand had been changed by the circumstances of his release, and after several lengthy conversations with

344

Peter and John, Bar Abbas had departed Judea forever. Some said he had gone to carry the teachings of Jesus to Gaul, others said that his guilt had driven him to suicide. But the new Zealot movement was centered in the district of Samaria, north of Jerusalem, and led by yet another Galilean, who called himself Moses ben Judah. This Moses claimed to be a direct descendant of the Jewish lawgiver from over a thousand years before, and he began preaching to the multitudes that he knew the location of a rod and sword that the great hero had buried near Mount Gerizim in Samaria. He quickly drew a large following, although he did not commit direct attacks on Romans as Bar Abbas had done.

Pilate was deeply concerned about this new movement. He summoned Longinus from his new home in Jerusalem to see if his old friend could tell him anything about this new Galilean cult, and whether or not it was related to the followers of Jesus. The former centurion, now beginning to show white in his beard and at his temples, was a bit reluctant to appear before his old commander.

"Nothing to do with you, sir," he said, "but many of the disciples who have joined The Way since the events of Pentecost have no idea who I am. When I am summoned to appear before the governor, it makes them nervous."

Pilate nodded. "I understand, old friend," he replied, "but your religious scruples must sometimes take second place to the needs of Rome. What do you know about this Moses character, and is he related to The Way?"

Longinus sighed. "No," he said. "He followed us for a brief while, but he was preaching that what Jesus wanted was an armed assault on Rome to usher in the Day of the Lord. Peter and John finally expelled him from our midst for his disruptive nature and unwillingness to submit to the leadership of the Apostles. Since then, he has been going all through Samaria and Galilee, saying that if the disciples of Jesus will not challenge Rome, then he will—using the very sword of Moses to drive the Empire into the sea. He has called all his disciples to follow him to Mount Gerizim today."

Pilate snorted. "Where do these people get their delusions?" he said. "I suppose that I will have to pay a visit to Mount Gerizim and put a stop to this nonsense once and for all."

Longinus winced. "Be gentle, Prefect," he said. "I understand your responsibilities, and the needs of Rome. But these are simple country folk who have been misled by a charlatan. Imprisoning Moses will be enough to disperse them back to their farms."

Pilate's face hardened. "I am tired of being gentle!" he snapped. "I have sent the humble folk back to their farms again and again, and every time they jump back up to follow whatever terrorist waves a sword and screams 'Death to Rome!' I am tired of insurrection and rebellion in this damnable province! I wish I had never seen Judea, or heard of Moses, or Caiaphas, or Galilean carpenters who won't stay dead when you kill them!"

Longinus looked at Pilate sadly. "Your anger is misplaced, my friend," he said. "Your deepest loathing is for yourself. You can lay down that burden of sin and misery any time you choose—and I wish for your sake that it would be soon! You are too good a man to punish yourself thus."

Pilate snarled: "I am also sick and tired of good Romans forgetting who they are! I have lost you and now my wife to this gentle Galilean who saps the mettle from warriors and turns them into women! Even my son says this Jesus talks to him in his dreams! When my wife makes love to me, I see in her eyes that she loves this foreign god more than she does me! I am sick to death of Jesus!!"

Longinus bowed and left the room, and Pilate took a deep drink of wine, and then called for Brutus Appius. The burly centurion appeared promptly, and Pilate thought to himself again what an excellent soldier the former troublemaker had become.

"What do you need, Governor?" he asked.

"Tell the cohort to saddle up," he said. "We are taking a little ride."

"Where to, Excellency?" asked Appius.

"Mount Gerizim," said Pilate. "We are going to dig up a sword and kill some Jews with it!"

He mounted the stairs to his quarters to don his cuirass and helmet. Procula Porcia was there, with Decimus, now nearly nine years old. She watched him strap on his sword with trepidation in her eyes.

"Where are you going, husband?" she said.

"To put down a rebellion before it gets started, my dear," replied Pilate.

She nodded. "I never really liked you going into battle," she said, "but now I positively hate it! Jesus said those who take up the sword will perish by the sword, and I live in fear that those words will prove true of you."

Pilate bit his lip before replying. "I am a servant of the Empire, my love. My job is to keep the peace, whatever the cost. I cannot let the Zealots rise up yet again."

She sighed and kissed his cheek. 'Come home safe to me," she said.

Mount Gerizim was only a couple hours' brisk ride from Caesarea, and Pilate was relieved to find it unoccupied when he and his men arrived. It was the highest point for miles around, and using his Greek telescope, he could see a mob of people about five miles off, slowly coming in the direction of the mountain.

"Looks like good timing, sir," said Appius.

"Indeed," said Pilate, handing him the bronze tube. "How many are there, do you reckon?"

Appius stared at the oncoming mass for several minutes before speaking. "I'd make it three or four thousand, sir, but about half the numbers are women and children."

Pilate shook his head. "These rustics are so inept," he said. "What do they hope to accomplish?"

"They probably expect their god to fight for them, like in the old tales," said the centurion.

"Well, if he shows up, we fight him too!" Pilate said. "Now put the men in that ravine over there, and you and I will take cover in those boulders. Let's see what they are up to, and then scatter them good and proper. The leader—this Moses ben Judah—I want him for myself, but keep an eye on the fight. My leg has not bothered me in a while, but if it goes out from under me, I may need you to keep me alive!"

The men quickly followed orders, and from a cleft between two boulders, Pilate watched as the mob grew closer. Leading them was a tall, white-bearded Jew with strong shoulders and a wild-eyed look about him, leading them in a song about horses and riders being cast into the sea. When the congregation had climbed the slopes of the mountain, he hopped on a rock and addressed them.

"Children of Judah and Samaria!" he said. "Too long have you let the Temple priests teach you to hate one another, while they grovel to the true enemies of God—the dreadful minions of Rome! The spirit of my great ancestor Moses appeared to me and told me where to find his rod and his sword, and the God of Abraham promises that with them, we will drive the Romans into the sea and restore the Kingdom of David forever! Oh, I know many of you thought that Jesus of Nazareth was the Messiah—but Jesus was weak! He tried to tell you to love your enemies! God has commanded me to hate the enemies of Israel with hatred never-ending, until the soil of Judea has drunk the last drop of their pagan blood. In the name of Elijah and Elisha, of Moses and of Judas Maccabee, I command you to fight until you can fight no more. Behold the sword and staff of Moses!"

He nodded at four young men and hopped off the boulder he had stood on. They levered it out of the way, revealing a stone box buried in the ground. From within, Moses ben Judah retrieved a long wooden rod and a blade, and then held them aloft. Pilate suppressed a snort of contempt. The sword had probably been in the ground no more than a month, and it looked for all the world like a legionary's gladius given a new hilt, with the Star of David etched on each side of the pommel. As Moses held the blade aloft, Pilate put a small horn to his lips and blew a note.

Roman legionaries poured from the gully and launched themselves at the crowd, cutting down the armed men in the front ranks before they could even draw their blades. Pilate drew his own gladius and swiftly moved toward Moses ben Judah, who was watching his revolution die before his eyes.

"Defend yourself, Jew!" snapped Pilate as he raised his weapon.

The shock on the Zealot's face twisted into rage, and he flew at Pilate, screaming as he did. If he had any skill to match his passion, it might have been an interesting fight, but the man had apparently never wielded a weapon before in his life. He made great, sloppy swings as if he were trying to cut down a tree, signaling his every move in advance. Pilate laughed at the pitiable quality of his opponent, angering him even more.

"Die, Roman pig!" shrieked Moses ben Judah, taking a massive swing at Pilate's head.

"Not today, I think," Pilate said evenly, parrying the blow with such force that Judah's blade buried itself in the ground. As the Zealot leader tried to yank it free, Pilate drove his own blade through the man's chest. Moses' eyes widened for a moment, and then he went limp, slowly sliding to the ground.

Pilate wiped the blood from his blade, using his enemy's robe, and looked around. Several dozen Jews lay dead, and the rest were running away in terror. A half dozen of the men had been rounded up and disarmed, while their wives and daughters shrieked and begged for their lives. Not a single Roman had been killed, although two legionaries had been lightly wounded.

Brutus Appius came over and saluted. "Too easy, sir!" he said.

"Indeed," replied Pilate. "This man was the most incompetent leader the Zealots have thrown up yet. Throw him in the stone box and put the boulder back over it, but remove his head first and bring it back to Caesarea and display it on the battlements. Crucify the men, let the children go, and do as you please with the women. I am going home."

He retrieved his horse from the valley where he had tethered it, and looked over the battlefield, such as it was. He noticed that some of the slain were hardly more than children; and one or two were actual children, probably trampled in the crush. He let out a long sigh. When would the Jews learn that Rome was not to be defied?

# CHAPTER TWENTY-SIX

Reaction to Pilate's crushing of the Samaritan rebellion was widespread and very negative. Caiaphas had been deposed by the new governor of Syria, Vitellius, but the new High Priest, Jonathan ben Ananias, led a delegation to Caesarea to protest the "excessive brutality," and Roman legionaries were hissed at and jeered in the streets. Angry letters were sent to the proconsul of Syria and to the Emperor himself. One Roman patrol was bombarded with the contents of chamber pots in the Merchants' Quarter of Jerusalem. Pilate was secretly amused—he doubted that the High Priest and his associates would spit on a Samaritan who was on fire, but now the despised half-breeds were being idolized as martyrs to the brutality of Rome. Just to be safe, Pilate fired off a quick, accurate report to Tiberius on the event and then ignored the storm. By midsummer it seemed as if the tempest had passed. The routines of governance and trade continued, and the outrage of the Judean people began to fade.

But on the Ides of the month of Julii, Pilate received a letter with the familiar seal of the Emperor, delivered by a swift courier ship. The captain informed Pilate that he had been ordered to stand by while Pilate read the letter, prepared to sail instantly with a reply. Puzzled, Pilate retreated immediately to his office, where he broke the seals and unrolled the letters. There were two sheets of papyrus, one nearly covered with the spidery, tremulous handwriting of the elderly Emperor, the other shorter and more official-looking, in the clear writing of a professional scribe. He read the scribe's letter first.

> *Gaius Julius Tiberius Caesar, Princeps and Imperator of Rome, to Lucius Pontius Pilate, Proconsul and Prefect of Judea, Greetings!*
>
> *You are recalled to Rome immediately to face a disciplinary hearing before the Emperor on charges of corruption, unnecessary use of force, misappropriation of state funds, and for generally failing to honor the customs, traditions, and laws of the Jewish people, whose homeland has been committed to your care for the last ten years. Your Proconsular imperium is revoked. Report to the Emperor on*

*Capri as soon as possible. Your family is commanded to remain in Caesarea until your case is heard and your sentence pronounced. This letter is to be forwarded to your superior offer, Lucius Vitellius, and recorded in the official annals of the province.*

Pilate shook his head as he read the letter. Nothing about it sounded right—the cold, impersonal tone, his abrupt relief of command, and the utter lack of interest in the circumstances which had led to the complaint. He turned then to the letter in the Emperor's own shaky hand and began to read. After the first three sentences, he turned pale and sat down slowly, read the rest of the letter and then reread it three times.

*My dear Pilate,* it began, dispensing with the usual ceremonies.

*First of all, I must command you to burn this letter as soon as you have read it and memorized it. Not a word of its contents can be revealed to anyone in Caesarea, not even your wife! You see, old friend, I require one last favor from you before I can restore to you the honor and dignitas that I wrongly stripped from you ten years ago—you must kill Gaius Caligula.*

*He has suborned most of my servants. I wrote this letter alone in my writing nook in the middle of the night, and now carry it inside my tunic, waiting for a chance to send it to you without being detected. The High Priest's whining letter about your very effective action against the Samaritan rebels gave me a perfect opportunity. I told Caligula I was going to relieve you of your command and try you for treason and corruption before the Senate. How he smiled! After the scribe takes my dictation, I shall carefully slip this letter inside the other and seal it.*

*I was more wrong than I could possibly realize about Caligula. He is a monster of the first order, a filthy creature addicted to cruelty and perversion, with no redeeming qualities whatsoever. His charm is considerable, but it is a mask for a soul that is utterly corrupted. I fear for my life every day, knowing that he wishes me dead so he can rule Rome. Only the faithful Macro stands between us, and I see Caligula constantly wheedling and cajoling him whenever he thinks I cannot hear. I trust no one in my own household now.*

*I do not care how he dies, but Caligula must never be allowed to become Emperor. He would sweep away the last vestiges of the Republic and become a despot far worse than any Eastern potentate. Do this for me, Lucius Pontius Pilate, and I will raise you higher than you ever stood before. The fate of the Republic is in your hands. If there is someone you trust implicitly, you may enlist their aid. But be careful! Caligula's spies are everywhere. The captain of the vessel bringing you this communication is his creature, I think. I certainly would not trust him. Act quickly, and with your usual competence. May all the Gods of Rome, and any other gods there may be, watch over you!*

Pilate quickly destroyed the letter, his mind still reeling from its message. At long last, a chance to avenge the death of his murdered child! But how to proceed? He summoned the captain of the courier ship and began pacing around his quarters as he waited. The man came along very shortly, and Pilate rounded on him immediately.

"Have you opened this letter?" he roared as the man stepped in.

"No, Prefect!" the main exclaimed. "It is sure death to break the Emperor's seal!"

"Do you know what that old man has done to me?" Pilate demanded. "He is relieving me of my command as governor because of the puling complaints of the local priests! This is an outrage!"

The captain looked very uncomfortable. "I am sorry to hear that, Prefect Pilate," he said unconvincingly.

Pilate resumed pacing. "I may have been gone from Rome for ten years, but I am not without friends in the Senate. I am going to demand a full and proper trial, but first I will report to Vitellius, my superior, as any proconsul should do before surrendering his office. I am going to send a letter back to Rome with you right now, and I will follow hard on its heels. Tell the Emperor I will not be summoned to a drumhead tribunal on Capri! I will stand before the entire Senate and refute every one of these charges. Corruption, indeed!"

He took a blank piece of papyrus from his desk and began scribbling furiously. The captain edged closer, trying to read over his shoulder, but

Pilate kept writing, then when he was finished and had blotted the letter, he read it out loud to the captain.

> *Lucius Pontius Pilate, Proconsul and Prefect of Judea, to Gaius Julius Tiberius Caesar, Princeps and Imperator of Rome;*
>
> *I must protest most strongly my unjust and unfair relief from the office you entrusted to me. I utterly reject and deny all the charges you have listed against me, and insist upon the right of a trial before the full Senate of Rome, not a private hearing on Capri with you and the odious creature who is your heir. I am sending this to you straightaway, while I will take all the official records of my term of office to Antioch, where I shall see them read out in the presence of my superior officer, Lucius Vitellius. Then, with his seal on my records, I shall set sail for Rome to formally stand trial before the Senate. If you wish to lodge the charges against me in person, then I shall see you there. This injustice against me will not be allowed to stand, when I have served you and the Republic faithfully and well for a decade in this gods-forsaken posting.*

The captain raised an eyebrow. "Far be it from me to tell you your business, Governor, but I would never dream of taking such a tone with Emperor Tiberius! I don't know what he was like when you knew him, but he is an irritable and deeply suspicious old man. A letter like that is a sure appointment with the headsman!" he told Pilate.

Pilate smiled grimly as he sealed the letter. He knew that Tiberius would be able to read between the lines, but hopefully the angry protest would blow some smoke into the eyes of Gaius Caligula long enough for him to arrive in Italy and make his way to Rome stealthily. He escorted the ship's captain down to the docks and ordered him to set sail for Capri by the end of the day. The sailors, already dispersed among the fleshpots and taverns of Caesarea, protested mightily, but they were rounded up and the ship set sail by sunset. Pilate stood and watched the sails shrink on the horizon before returning to the governor's palace. Porcia was pacing the floor in anxiety.

"Oh, Lucius!" she said. "Relieved of command? Charged with treason? Hasn't that dreadful old man hurt us enough already?"

Pilate hugged her close. "There is more to this than I can tell you," he said, "But I can promise you that things are going to be all right. Take care of my child, dear wife, and know that I love you beyond all reason! Now please leave me. I have much to do before dawn, when I ride to Antioch."

Once she had left the governor's office, he wrote a quick letter to Quintus Sullemius and then disappeared into a small cloakroom where he kept all his extra garments. He found a wrinkled, hooded robe and a gnarled staff that he had used before when he wished to walk unseen among the people, and pulled it over his head before disappearing into the growing darkness, hunched over and leaning heavily on the staff. The letter, rolled up and sealed, was tucked into an inner pocket of his robe. It said:

> *Lucius Pontius Pilate, former Prefect of Judea, to Quintus Sullemius, Scoundrel, Confidential Agent, and generally useful soul,*
>
> *Old friend—if all your talk about longing for bloody adventures is sincere, then you might be interested in the offer I have for you. I have been assigned to bring down my biggest quarry yet, and could use a trusted pair of hands and a sharp blade to assist me! I should be in Brundisium in about a month, traveling incognito. Ask for an historian named Lucius Scaveola, or leave a letter for me at the local tavern owned by Valerius Postumus. We are going to right an old wrong, my friend, and perhaps restore me to a position where I can remember with gratitude those who stood by me during my years of disgrace and exile. I hope to see you soon.*

About an hour later, Pilate came to the doors of the seediest tavern in Caesarea, which catered to smugglers, pirates, and fugitives. He already had a pretty good idea of who would be the best candidate to deliver his message quickly and discreetly to Rome, and the man was there, swilling down wine with a giggling barmaid on his lap—Diomyrus, who had brought him to Judea ten years before and acted as the occasional courier for his communications with Sullemia and other friends in Rome. Pilate walked over to the table, dropped a bagful of gold coins in the captain's lap, and stumped to a deserted corner of the tavern. Moments later, Diomyrus joined him.

"You're awfully free with your coin, old man," he said.

"Who are you calling old?" Pilate asked, raising the hood ever so slightly.

"Prefect!" exclaimed the sailor. "What are you doing here?"

"I'm not here," said Pilate. "I never was. But this letter needs to go to Quintus Sullemius in Rome, and it needs to be there in three weeks if you can do so. He will have another purse of this size for you if you deliver it within the appointed time. Don't dawdle, Diomyrus. This is important. Now enjoy your doxie, and then gather your crew. You'll need to sail tomorrow morning." Pilate rose and slipped out the door into the night.

A hard ride through the night and the next day took him to Tyre, where he caught a ship to Antioch, the provincial capital of Syria Province. Four days after the Emperor's letter arrived in Caesarea, he strolled into the office of Lucius Vitellius, the governor of Syria.

"Prefect Pilate!" he said. "How good to see you!" Vitellius was a genuinely likable man, a young, loyal functionary of the Empire who had been in place for a little over a year. He was class-conscious and knew that Pilate should have been his superior by virtue of birth, rank, and seniority. But rather than let his elevation go to his head, he had gone out of his way to be friendly and deferential to Pilate during his time as Proconsul of Syria.

Pilate smiled ruefully. "It may not be good to be seen with me anymore, sir," he said. "I have been relieved by order of the Emperor himself, and remanded to Rome for trial."

"Trial? Whatever for? You are a consummate professional when it comes to your duties in Judea!" protested Pilate's superior.

Pilate handed him the letter, then handed over the account books of his tenure in Judea. He knew that, if Caligula read his angry letter to Tiberius, the scheming heir to the throne would be suspicious and would check to see that Pilate had actually reported to Vitellius as he had threatened to. Following through on the written promise was the best way to keep Little Boots in the dark, Pilate thought.

"This is simply terrible," said Vitellius. "You have been occasionally harsh, Pilate, but in dealing with the Jews, Zealots, Nazarenes, and other troublemakers in your province, harshness is an absolute necessity! I will have my clerk go over your books, but I am sure everything will be found in order, and I plan to write a glowing reference to the Senate for you. This is a disgrace!"

Pilate offered his gratitude and then retired to the guest quarters for the evening. The next morning, he was summoned to Vitellius' chambers, and the Proconsul of Syria handed him a sealed scroll.

"Not a single irregularity!" he told Pilate with a smile. "You have made some money for yourself, but all in a perfectly legal and honorable fashion, altogether in keeping with Rome's *mos maorum* for provincial governors. I don't know who accused you, Lucius, but their charges will be very hard to prove with the report I just gave you."

"You have my gratitude," said Pilate. "Now I must depart for Rome quickly, and take advantage of the summer winds." He took the scroll and tucked it into his trunk full of confidential papers, then went down to the docks and found a swift trireme bound for Crete. The winds were favorable, and the voyage uneventful. Ten days later, he strolled down the gangplank, ducked into a seedy tavern, and changed into the hooded robe he had disguised himself with earlier. He had not shaved during the entire voyage, allowing his iron-gray whiskers to grow to a length they had never attained before. Glancing at himself in a burnished bronze mirror, he did not like what he saw. The gray beard made him look like some sort of religious fanatic. But it did a good job of masking his rather distinct face, so he let it keep growing.

The confidential papers he burned in the brazier that night, and the next morning a hooded, bearded man booked passage under the name Lucius Scaveola on a ship bound for Italy. It was nearly three weeks later that he arrived in Brundisium. By now the whiskers had become a full beard, and Pilate was confident that he could have walked by his own brother in the street without being recognized. The hood was now left pulled back, as he walked through the streets of the ancient Italian seaport to the tavern where he had told Sullemius to meet him. There had been some civil disturbance of some sort, he saw—several figures hung on crosses just outside the gates, shivering and moaning in agony. For some reason the sight unnerved Pilate slightly, even though he had seen many men die on the cross before. For a moment, the haunting gaze of Jesus of Nazareth floated before his eyes, and he swallowed hard and then shook his head. There was no time for such vain imaginings—he had a monster to slay!

"Is there a letter for Lucius Scaveola?" he said.

The innkeeper nodded knowingly. "Aye, master, a fellow left it for you yesterday! Seemed rather nervous, he did. Said you were an historian when he left it for you. Did you know that Gaius Marius himself stayed in this inn, back in my grandfather's day?"

Pilate forced himself to smile and listen to the story of Rome's great general and his time at the inn, and then excused himself to his chambers where he broke the seal and began to read. Sullemius' handwriting was unusually shaky, and Pilate had to strain to make out the words. His face grew pale as he read.

> *Lucius—RUN!*
>
> *I do not know who ordered you to Rome, but the wrong you suffered cannot be righted now. Tiberius is dead, smothered in his bed by Macro, and Caligula is the Emperor of Rome. He conducts himself with graciousness and generosity towards the people for now, but already his agents are scouring the Empire looking for you. Both your surviving brothers have been arrested, and I suspect I was followed here. Rumor has it that Praetorians have already been dispatched to Judea to collect your family. Hurry and save them if you can! I am about to disappear, and see if I am as good a fugitive as I once was. You're a good man, Pilate, and you deserve better than this. I'm sorry. Get out of Italy while you can!*

Pilate pulled the cloak over his head and slipped out the back door of the inn. He looked outside the city gates at the four crosses again, and suddenly a sinking feeling came over him. He slowly sidled toward the gate and the nearest cross. The man had only been nailed up for a few hours, from the look of him—he was still conscious and turning his head back and forth. It was Quintus Sullemia. The other two crosses held two men and a woman, and as Pilate stared at them, he realized he was seeing his two brothers for the first time in more than a decade. The woman it took him a moment longer to recognize, but then he saw that she was his sister Pontia— an inoffensive, middle-aged Roman matron. Rage seized him, and his face flushed scarlet. That Caligula would take out his rage against Pilate upon a

358

family that he had not even seen for years! He was filled with fury—if the Emperor had stood in front of him at that moment, he could have ripped Caligula's heart out with his bare hands.

He must have made some sound, because the bloody, battered head of Quintus Sullemia turned his way. The old smuggler's eyes widened as he recognized his former patron, and his mouth formed a single word—"Run!" It was good advice, so Pilate turned to go back through the gate, but bumped right into a burly legionary.

"Not so fast, old salt!" the man said. "We are looking for a dangerous fugitive who is supposed to be arriving here in Brundisium in the next day or so. How long have you been in the city?"

"About a month now," said Pilate. "Came south from Gaul with a slave caravan."

"Well, now, that's most odd, because the innkeeper told us you just arrived this morning, and collected a letter that was left for our fugitive!" the soldier drawled.

Pilate had kept his hand on the hilt of a wicked, sharp dagger inside his robes from the moment he turned to re-enter the city, and in a lightning-fast motion, he drove it through the man's neck and deep into the carotid artery. A second legionary was following the man Pilate stabbed; Pilate shoved the dying soldier at him, and then took advantage of the man's attempt to catch his mortally wounded comrade to drive the dagger through his neck as well. Then he ran as fast as his bad leg would let him into the slums of Brundisium.

He wandered through the narrow alleys and dives of the port city for an hour, until he was sure he was no longer being followed, then ducked into a small tavern and sat down to catch his breath and plan his next move. His mind was racing. The Emperor dead, Caligula seemingly as determined as ever to seek revenge for Pilate's savage beating of him so many years before, his family now threatened—all the plans of revenge that Pilate had nursed in his breast from Caesarea to Brundisium now lay in ashes at his feet. All that remained to him was to somehow save his wife and son—yet he knew the ships leaving Brundisium would be watched. Now that two legionaries were dead, Caligula would know that his quarry was nearby. What move would he least expect from Pilate?

After a half an hour in which he rested and nourished his body, Pilate's plan was formulated. He snuck over the city wall, avoiding the gates, and found his way to a small tavern a mile or two down the Appian Way. It was nearly dark, and he watched as a group of travelers turned their horses over to the groom to be stabled for the night before going inside to eat and spend the evening. He waited in the gathering gloom till it was fully dark, then slowly eased into the barn behind the inn. The groom had fed the horses and was bustling about, humming to himself. After a half hour or so, he ambled off to the inn, leaving the horses in the dark. Pilate had already picked the one he wanted, a long-legged, deep-chested roan that looked fast but not too wild. He saddled the beast and led it out of the paddock, taking it about a half mile down the road before mounting up and spurring it onward. By dawn he was in Tarentum, and he found a fast ship headed for Antioch, whose captain was not averse to taking on an anonymous passenger. Less than twenty-four hours after reading the letter from Sullemia, Pilate was at sea again, heading back to Syria and thence to Judea. He prayed he would not be too late.

The first strong nor'wester of fall struck just as the ship hit the open waters, and for days the vessel pitched and rolled in rough seas—but the wind was also pushing them steadily toward the eastern end of *Mare Nostrum*. It was three weeks and one day after rounding the heel of the Italian boot when the coastline of Syria came into sight, and Pilate disembarked as soon as the ship tied up to the pier, thanking the captain for the swift voyage and saving just enough gold to purchase a swift horse. Within an hour of landing, he was galloping southward toward Caesarea.

But now that the need for speed was greater than ever, so was the need for caution. Pilate did not know if Caligula's Praetorian Guard had arrived yet or not, nor what kind of welcome he would find in Caesarea when he got there. His long beard would prevent immediate recognition, but he had no doubt that the men who had served under him for so many years would know him despite the change in his appearance. Which one of them could he trust enough to give him an accurate report? Was there a reward on his head already?

He stopped in Tyre long enough to purchase and don a traditional Jewish robe and cloak, then traded out his horse for a less conspicuous mule. Listening to the gossip in the stalls, he was chilled by what he heard. The stories of Tiberius' death were already in circulation, and had grown in the telling. They said the old man was returning to Rome for the first time in a decade, throwing his entire entourage into a panic. Quintus Macro, the head of the Praetorians, was particularly concerned because he had been buying up the properties of proscribed Senators on the cheap and then reselling them at a huge markup. Somewhere between Neapolis and Rome the old Emperor had caught a chill, the story went, and been racked with a high fever. Caligula had gone mad with anticipation, strutting about and barking orders as if he were already ruling Rome. When it seemed Tiberius had come to the final throes of his illness, the young heir to the purple had entered the sick room and tried to remove the Emperor's signet ring. This attempted usurpation had rallied the old man, who regained consciousness long enough to cry for help. Caligula fled in panic, and Macro had entered the bedchamber to see what was upsetting Tiberius. When he emerged moments later, the Emperor was dead, and Macro handed the signet ring to Caligula, bowing deeply before the new ruler of Rome.

But that was not the only rumor that upset Pilate. A group of traders from Caesarea confirmed his worst fear: the Praetorian Guard had already arrived there, and had put out a reward for the arrest of Pilate's wife and son. The only comfort was that no one seemed to know where Porcia and Decimus were. Moving more cautiously, Pilate rode the big mule he had purchased toward the city that had been his home for the last decade.

He arrived on the outskirts of Caesarea and found a small tavern just outside the city walls that catered to Jewish travelers who did not wish to enter the thoroughly Romanized city. Pilate had purchased a small phylactery from a rabbi in Tyre, and bound it to his forehead. Living among the Jews for so long had taught him enough about them to pass for one, he hoped. He rented a room from the gloomy, taciturn innkeeper and sent his mule to the stables. Buying a hunk of bread and some salted fish, Pilate munched on them as he walked toward the city gate.

As he approached, he saw a Roman patrol preparing to ride out from the city gates. It was led by Brutus Appius, the huge centurion Pilate had promoted after beating the stuffing out of him on his very first day as governor. The former barracks bully had made an excellent officer, and more importantly, he was absolutely loyal to Pilate. Or at least, that was how

Pilate thought of him. Now it was time to find out where the centurion's loyalties lay.

Appius was chatting with the gate guard for a moment, letting his men ride on ahead, affording a window of opportunity. As the big man turned away, Pilate threw a small pebble which bounced off the man's cuirass. Brutus Appius looked to see where the missile had come from, and his eyes locked with Pilate's for just a moment. Pilate put a finger to his lips, while beckoning with his other hand.

"Ride on ahead, boys, while I see what this merchant wants," said Appius, turning to follow Pilate. He waited until they were a stone's throw from the road, and then turned to Pilate, his voice low.

"Jupiter, sir! You are taking a huge risk coming back here! The Praetorians have been looking for you and yours for the last week or more, and they are offering a huge reward to the one who brings you in alive!" he told Pilate.

"I won't be here long," Pilate responded. "I just need to find my wife and son."

Appius looked puzzled. "I figured they were with you," he said. "They have been gone for almost as long as you have."

Pilate was stumped. Where could they have gone? Then an idea occurred to him.

"What about the family slaves?" he asked.

"The Praetorians rounded them all up and questioned them pretty harshly," said Appius. "I don't think they got anything out of them, though. Most of them were sent to the slave markets, but your steward, Democles, was spared since you freed him last year. He is staying at that seedy inn down by the waterfront."

Pilate nodded. "You had best get on your way, then," he said. "I'll slip into the city once it's dark and try to find him."

Appius looked troubled, but nodded. "Sir, I was nothing till you gave me a chance. As far as I am concerned, you are Rome—not these strutting fools in black armor. If you get in a tight spot, I'll do what I can for you— even if it costs me everything you gave me a chance to become. I owe you that much."

Pilate found himself unable to reply. The "trick" of commanding loyalty, which he had struggled so hard to master in his youth, was no trick at all. Men of honor would give back what you had given to them, no matter the cost. Finally, he gave a gruff nod. "I hope to be here and gone before anyone else realizes it," he said. "I probably won't need you. But your offer—is appreciated. More than you can know. Now join your men before they start to wonder why you are spending so long chatting to a Jewish merchant!"

# CHAPTER TWENTY-SEVEN

About two hours after dark, a middle-aged, unkempt-looking Jew straggled in through the gates of Caesarea. He was a bit taller than average height, with a long, scraggly beard and an ornately carved phylactery bound around his forehead, where it occasionally snagged on the hood of the long cloak he wore. He was stooped slightly, and leaned on a heavy staff. The gate guards waved him through, and as he headed toward the waterfront, he was nearly knocked over by two burly Praetorians swaggering back toward the governor's palace. He shrieked curses at them in Hebrew and spat upon the ground; they laughed at his vehemence and returned to the barracks.

Once they were out of sight, the scraggly Jew let out a sigh and continued to his destination. He sidled into the tavern and took a seat in its darkest corner, ordering a jar of the cheapest wine they had. From his vantage point, he saw a sad-looking, middle-aged Greek sitting close to the bar. The man poured one cup of wine after another down his throat for an hour, then staggered upstairs to a room where long-term guests could rent a private bed for a week at a time.

The Jew watched and waited as the customers drank themselves into a stupor. Some headed to back rooms in the company of the tavern's three overweight, bored-looking prostitutes, others staggered out into the night when they had drunk their fill or spent all their coin, and a few others retired to upstairs rooms as the Greek had. Finally, when everyone in the bar was either passed out or staring senselessly into space, the slender, bearded man got up and stealthily crept up the stairs. He surveyed the scene to make sure no one was following his progress, and then slipped into the room that the old Greek freedman had entered.

Democles was lying on his side, staring at the wall, but wide awake. He started to cry out when the bearded stranger entered the room, but the man was at his side with a hand over his mouth before he could make a sound.

"Not a word, old friend. I am sorry I had to startle you like this, but I can't strut through the streets of Caesarea like I used to!" said Pilate.

"By Zeus and Hera!" exclaimed the startled servant. "That beard! I would have walked right by you on the street, master! Thank all the gods you are safe! They flogged me, but I could tell them nothing—not about you, anyway. You disappeared so fast no one knew exactly where you had gone or what you were doing!"

"That was my intent when I left, but unfortunately I was not able to achieve what I set out to do," said Pilate. "Do you know where my wife and son have gone?"

"A group of the Nazarenes left the area some time ago, returning toward Jerusalem," said Democles. "Lady Porcia suddenly decided to accompany them—I don't know why. She seemed adamant about it, though. She said that Cassius Longinus would know where she was. There was fear in her eyes, sir. It was as if she had some premonition of what was to come."

"It would not be the first time she has been granted the gift of foresight," said Pilate. "Now tell me, Democles—are you provided for? You have served me well for twenty years, and I would not see you left destitute."

The old man smiled. "You were a good and benevolent master," he said. "I have enough laid by to stay here as long as I wish and drink as much as I can. But, knowing you are safe, and that the lady Porcia will see you again, I don't see the need to drink quite as much. I may buy a small house away from the city and settle here. I did not like this place when we came here, but it has grown on me."

"Marry yourself a nice young Jewish girl so you will have someone to care for you in your old age," said Pilate. "This should help you purchase that house." He dropped a purse full of gold coins on his former steward's bed.

"Are you sure you can spare this?" asked Democles. "I do not know how far you will have to run to get away from the Praetorians."

Pilate smiled. "I have enough coin laid by to flee this region forever, and set up housekeeping wherever I choose," he said. "There wasn't really much to spend it on in this dreadful place, and my wife has always been a woman of simple tastes. Good luck, old friend! Now if you will excuse me, I am going to exit through the window—I don't think anyone saw me enter, and I want to be sure no one sees me leave."

Before dawn, the disreputable Jewish traveler had left Caesarea behind, never to return.

Four days later, in Jerusalem, a group of Nazarenes were meeting in the upper room of a wealthy merchant's home. This upper room had special significance to the inner circle, known as the Apostles, because it was there they had shared their last Passover with their beloved Master. Now it was a site where they brought the most promising converts to instruct them in the teachings of Jesus, so that these men could then spread the message of the Son of God wherever they went. On this particular night, three of the best-known Apostles were there: Simon Peter, commonly called the Big Fisherman; his friend and former business partner John, the Son of Zebedee; and one man who had known Jesus longer than any of them—James, the son of Joseph, or, as many were already calling him, James the Lord's Brother.

About two dozen acolytes surrounded the Apostles, as James told them the story he had heard from his father about Jesus' miraculous birth, and then Peter and John explained how they had been called away from their nets by the mysterious rabbi from Nazareth. One of the believers in the group looked a little different than the others—his olive skin and Roman nose marked him as Italian by birth, and the beard and robes he wore could not disguise the ramrod-straight bearing that twenty years in the Legions had drilled into him. Brother Gideon, as he was known these days, had heard the stories before, but could never get enough of them. He was one of the most effective preachers of the Gospel in the Jerusalem church, and he helped the Apostles choose those who would be trained as missionaries and pastors.

John had started describing the lengthy discourse Jesus had shared with the Apostles on the night of his betrayal, and everyone in the room was hanging on his words, when the door came crashing open and a bearded stranger entered the room, looking exhausted and bedraggled. He did not look at the startled Apostles, or at the faces of any of their acolytes save one. He crossed the room directly to Brother Gideon and said: "Longinus, where is my wife? Where is my son?"

James flushed pale as he stared at the face of the stranger. "It's Pilate!" he exclaimed. "This is the man who crucified my brother!"

John shushed him as Longinus looked his former commander in the eye.

"They are safe, sir," he said. "The Apostles have given them shelter. Lady Porcia is staying at the house of John and his wife, Miriam."

Pilate looked at John with an expression of mixed relief and guilt. "After all I have done, you would still shelter my wife and son?" he said.

"The lady Porcia shares our faith," said John. "And your son is an innocent child. We would never turn such away. Also, one of our number, a man named Agabus, who is occasionally gifted with prophecy, told me that I must warn her to flee Caesarea. He said that her fate was bound up with mine, and that if she perished there would be great harm to the advancement of the Gospel."

James interrupted. "This man is not to be trusted! He is a ruthless agent of the Roman government, here to betray us all!"

Pilate stood and faced him. "It is true that I was an agent of Rome for my entire life, until three months ago," he said. "It is true that I have inflicted great suffering on many in the name of Rome. I tried to make sure that it was the guilty who suffered most, but I also have shed innocent blood—most notably, that of your brother Jesus. I could have saved him—I wanted to save him—but when the crisis came, I was weak. I bowed to pressure from the High Priest and his cronies." He dropped to his knees and held his arms out to the Galilean. "From the bottom of my heart, I am sorry. I have not known a night of peace since I sent your brother to the cross. Can you forgive me, James of Nazareth?"

The entire room was frozen in shock at the sight of Judea's former governor, the scourge of the Zealots, on his knees before a carpenter from Galilee. James stared at Pilate for a long time, and his gaze slowly softened.

"I bear my own guilt, Prefect," he said. "When my brother claimed to be the Messiah of Israel, I did not believe him. When he performed miracles, I scoffed at them. When these men proclaimed him the Son of God, I cursed them for encouraging his delusions. When the High Priest wanted to kill Jesus, I dared him to go and confront Caiaphas and the Sanhedrin. I thought he was insane, an embarrassment to the family, and most of all I hated him because my mother and father always treated him differently. When I heard he had been sentenced to the cross, I left Jerusalem and refused to stand by him at the end. That is why my mother now lives with John and not me. You did not know my brother, yet these men tell me you acquitted him seven times of any crime. I knew him longer than any of them, and I was willing to see him die. I forgive you, Pontius Pilate, because despite my meanness and jealousy, He forgave me. How could I do less?"

Pilate looked at the young Galilean in wonder. Jesus' own brother had rejected him? He could not help but ask the question that crossed his mind.

"What made you become a believer?" he asked.

James smiled. "A week after he died on the cross, Jesus appeared to me," he said. "He came to me in Nazareth, walking through the door without ever opening it! When I saw him, I broke down and wept. He embraced me, just as he did when I was little and had hurt myself. I cried until I could weep no more, and he just held me as all the jealousy, misery, and guilt went pouring out of me. I felt them leave! It was as if my very soul had become lighter. When I finally looked up at him, he was staring at me with that same fond smile he always regarded me with. Then he simply said: 'Follow me, my brother—and believe!' Since then I have made my home with these men. I am the bond-servant of my Lord Jesus, and no longer his angry little brother."

John stepped up beside Pilate. "You are weary, Governor, and have journeyed far. Shall I take you to your wife and son?"

Pilate nodded, blinking back tears. Something inside him was shifting, changing—he could not grasp it, or perceive it, but he could feel a part of himself stretching, tearing, and separating itself from the rest of him. He had the feeling that some transformation was about to take place, but he could not tell what he was about to become. However, he found himself caring little. If he could hold his wife again, he was prepared to become whatever this strange new God wanted him to be.

John led him through the dark alleys of Jerusalem. The Jewish capital never went fully asleep, but the noises that would be cacophonous during the day were muted, murmuring all around him as those whose business took them out after midnight moved about, trying not to disturb those who slept. Pilate still felt strange, and found himself wanting to talk to John.

"I didn't know you were married," he finally said.

John looked back over his shoulder and smiled. "I married a girl from Nazareth that I met at the market one day," he said. "Miriam is beautiful and glad-hearted, and when I saw her smile I knew that she would be my wife. When I proposed, her mother and brothers told me that I would need to establish myself and prepare a home for her before they would give their consent. I fished harder and longer than ever and sold our catches all over Judea—even delivering to the High Priest's household in Jerusalem! It took me a year, but I saved enough money to build a small house in Capernaum and buy three boats in partnership with my brother and Simon. Miriam's mother gave her consent, and our wedding became the talk of the district."

"How so?" asked Pilate.

"We held the ceremony at the synagogue in Cana, since it was between her hometown and mine," he said. "The wedding party was at a friend's house. I had spent so much money purchasing our house and the fleet that I could not afford as much wine as I should have. The party had only been going two hours when the steward informed me that the wine was giving out."

"Wait a minute!" Pilate said. "I heard about this! You mean to say that it was your wedding where Jesus—?"

"Yes," said John. "Miriam was his sister. He and the others—he had already begun calling some of us as his apostles, even then—were all in attendance. He transformed the water in the big storage pots into the finest, sweetest wine that any of us had ever tasted."

"So it really was a miracle," Pilate said.

"Indeed it was," said John. "I followed Jesus for many reasons after that, but not least among them was the fact that, on my wedding day, he saved my bride and me from embarrassment and shame."

Pilate processed that information for the rest of their walk. Sometime later, they came to a small, narrow house, sandwiched between several other small dwellings in the merchants' quarter of Jerusalem. A slender, lovely young woman greeted them at the door, and stared in astonishment at the gray-bearded stranger who had accompanied her husband home. But she bowed courteously and bade Pilate enter their home in peace.

"Have our guests gone to bed already?" John asked.

"About an hour ago," Miriam replied. "The lady Porcia was very weary, and little Decimus had worn himself out playing with the children of the neighborhood."

"Your family is upstairs," said John. "Go and see them, my friend."

Pilate took the stairs softly and opened the door. Decimus was curled into a tight ball on one side of the bed, while Porcia lay on her back, eyes closed, her countenance calm but still showing the lines of worry and stress from the events of recent years. All Pilate could see when he looked at her, though, was the beautiful seventeen-year-old he had fallen in love with when he returned from Germania all those years before. He crossed the room and leaned forward, kissing her brow.

She opened her eyes and stared at his face for a long moment, then wrapped her arms around him in a tight embrace. Decimus, woken by the noise, sat up and saw his mother hugging a bearded stranger. He gave a startled squawk, but then when Pilate looked at him and smiled, his face lit up.

"*Tata!!*" he cried, and threw his arms around Pilate.

The governor of Judea, with his wife and son in his arms, broke down and wept as if his heart would break. The tears were a flood that swept through his troubled soul and washed away the pain of the last three months, leaving him as clean and untroubled as a child, innocent of the world's evils. Finally he fell asleep with one arm around his wife and the other around his son, and rested as he had not in many years.

Early the next morning, he woke up and sought out John the Apostle.

"So what do I do now?" he asked.

"I beg your pardon?" asked John.

"What must I do to be redeemed, or saved, or whatever it is you call it?" Pilate asked. "Whatever it is that my wife has gained since she became a follower of the Nazarene is what I want for myself."

John guided him to the small table where some writing materials were set up. He scooted the papyrus aside and sat across from the former governor of Judea.

371

"What you ask is both simple and difficult," he said. "Salvation is free to all who seek it, but you must seek it for yourself, not on behalf of another, or because you see it in another."

Pilate nodded. "I do," he said. "I once believed in Rome, but the Rome I served is gone. My service has only earned me the status of a fugitive, and the wrath of a madman. All my old life is dust and ashes, and I need something to take its place—a reason to live and go on."

John looked at him. "Then you must repent of all your sins," he said. "You must turn your back on anger, lust, hatred, and all the destructive impulses that weigh you down. You must let go of your old self and ask the Lord Jesus to save you from your sins. It means forgiving those who have hurt you, and abandoning all thoughts of vengeance, trusting in the justice of God to take care of those things."

Pilate swallowed hard. "I do not think I can forgive the Emperor for what he did to my family. I want to be saved—I want this new life that seems to make you people so happy and fulfilled—but your God is asking too much!"

"In our weakness, He is strong," said John. "Ask forgiveness for your sins, and invite Him to rule your life, and He may give you the strength to do the things which you thought you never could."

Pilate bowed his head. He had said the formal prayers to Jupiter Optimus Maximus and the other gods of Rome, and even called upon the *Divus Julius* from time to time, but praying to Jesus was something new and different. He knew no ritual or invocation to gain this man-god's attention, so he simply spoke the name of the Galilean.

"Jesus of Nazareth," he said, "Son of God, Messiah of the Jews—I know not how to address you properly. I know that you remember me, and I know you remember that I failed you. I knew you were an innocent man, and I let you be condemned. But I know now that you were more than a man. I believe that you are indeed the one sent to save mankind. You know that I have done great wickedness—that I have shed innocent blood and rejoiced in the deaths of my enemies. I have been cruel and ruthless, and my life has been marred by *hubris* and vain ambition. I don't want that life anymore. I don't want to be that Pontius Pilate anymore. If you can forgive me for all my wickedness, and find it in your heart to redeem a man so unredeemable, I beseech you to save me. I have finally realized that I cannot save myself."

Pilate felt the same sensation that he had experienced the night before — a seismic shifting of the soul, a rending and tearing as something was rooted out of him and cast aside once and for all. It was so powerful and overwhelming that he cried out and buried his face in his hands. A flood of tears poured down his face, but something shining and new was being unveiled within him. When he looked up again, he was smiling.

"Tell me everything you know about Jesus," he said. "I want to hear it all. I want to understand Him."

John smiled. "Then you will need to come with me. Ask the lady Porcia if she would like to go as well. It is time for the daily teaching session to begin."

The next few months were the happiest days that Pilate had ever known. His thirst for the words of the Christ was insatiable — he asked Peter, James, and John to repeat the stories over and over again, until he committed them to memory. The believers were stunned at first to find the man who had sent Jesus to the cross as one of their number, but Pilate's transformation was so complete that they came to accept him. All he asked was that not a single word of his presence among them be breathed to anyone. The Praetorians were still making inquiries throughout Judea, trying to find Pilate or his missing family. Through a disciple of Christ named Matthias, Pilate purchased a small home in a back alley of the Merchants' Quarter, and spent most of his time going from there to the Upper Room to meet with the Apostles.

This new Pilate was a different man in many ways. He was more patient and less proud, more happy and less angry, and quick to ask forgiveness if he felt he had given offense. Porcia was radiant, knowing that her husband now shared the faith she had embraced so passionately. Young Decimus, now ten years old, was still immature in his faith, but he had come to love the God who made his parents so happy together, and frequently came and sat with his father to hear the tales about the man from Nazareth who had come to save the world.

It took Pilate a while to realize the biggest change in himself, but one day he realized what it was. On the way back to their small house from the upper room, a burly Greek sailor bumped into them and swore, then gave Porcia a lascivious glance. Pilate put himself between the offensive stranger and his wife, and the man moved on. As they walked on home, Pilate realized what was different. The angry beast that had lived inside him for so many years would have been envisioning a dozen different ways to make the sailor scream and beg before ending his life—but all Pilate felt, after the initial flash of anger, was a certain sympathy for a man who was so consumed by his sins that he did not even realize how lost he was. The vicious, cruel side of Pilate's personality that had urged him to bathe in his enemies' blood was simply gone, and Pilate found he did not miss it at all.

He and Porcia talked at length about what to do once the Emperor's search for them faded away. Pilate still had a tidy sum tucked away, and thought that they might yet escape to a faraway land where the Emperor's arm could not reach them. The idea appealed to both of them, but neither wanted to leave the warm embrace of the Jerusalem church yet. Perhaps, sometime next year, they could take the Gospel to Gaul or Egypt. But for the moment, they were content.

By the Feast of Lights, the Praetorians had left Jerusalem, although the reward for Pilate's capture was still out there. By all accounts, Caligula, after an initial show of generosity and kindness to the people of Rome, was letting his true nature show. His behavior was becoming more erratic, cruel, and bizarre at every turn. Even in far-off Judea some of the stories about him caused people to shudder. According to one tale, he invited a wealthy Senator to a dinner party at his palace, along with a number of other prominent men and their wives. This Senator had recently married a lovely young girl from an ancient and honorable family, and Caligula took notice of her. Halfway from the meal, he grabbed her by the arm and abruptly hustled her out of the room. The Praetorian guards kept anyone from leaving the table, commanding them to continue eating, even though the young bride's cries for help were echoing from the room next door. After a half hour, Caligula came back, smug and smiling, and complimented the girl's husband on his excellent taste in women. The man's wife crept into the room moments later, her clothes torn and face bloodied. When the Senator tried to leave, the Emperor refused to let him, instead pouring him a cup of rich wine and thanking him for bringing such lovely entertainment to the party.

Pilate was deeply affected by this story, because it so closely echoed his own experience with the wretched man now ruling Rome. How could a just God let such a vile man control the fate of millions? Finally, he went to John, who was teaching at the Temple, and asked if he could speak to him alone. As always, the young apostle was gracious and kind, and walked away in deep conversation with the troubled Pilate.

So intent were they on trying to understand God's willingness to tolerate evil that neither of them saw a black-robed figure emerge from the Temple and follow them for several blocks. The mysterious observer was stooped with age now, his beard nearly solid white, but he kept the two Nazarenes in sight until he finally got a good look at Pilate's face. His mouth thinned to a grim line, and he scurried back toward the Temple as fast as he could without drawing too much attention to himself. Once there, he asked to be shown to the High Priest, Jonathan. The Temple guards escorted him in after a brief delay.

The High Priest was hunched over a scroll, attended by two scribes. He looked up from the passage he was reading and smiled.

"Uncle Caiaphas," he said. "What can I do for you?"

# CHAPTER TWENTY-EIGHT

It was nearly time for Passover again. Five years had passed since Jesus came to Jerusalem to celebrate the feast with his Apostles; five years since the turbulent trial that had seen the Son of God sent to the cross. Now the man who had uttered that death sentence was an accepted member of the Jerusalem church, and a passionate follower of The Way. Pilate preferred to be called Levi now; his old name, like his old life, had been left behind when he chose to follow Christ—partly to protect him and his family from the ongoing search ordered by Gaius Caligula, and partly because many newer believers would not have been comfortable worshipping with the man who had sent Jesus to the cross. But all the Apostles and their inner circle knew who the quiet, taciturn Brother Levi was, and were sometimes saddened that they could not share the story of his remarkable conversion with the world.

Pilgrims from all over the world were coming to Jerusalem for the Passover, as they did every year. But many of them were coming not only for the traditional Seder feast, but also to hear the teachings of the Apostles of Jesus. No one knew exactly how many followers The Way claimed at this time, but all knew that number increased daily. The Apostles baptized every week at the Pool of Siloam, and sometimes it took several hours to immerse all those who had proclaimed faith in the name of Jesus. Pilate had been baptized only a day or two after his prayer for salvation had been answered, and now he came each week to see the new believers welcomed into the fellowship of The Way.

That evening, Pilate and his family had retreated to their small home in the merchants' quarter, and shared a hot meal of soup, bread, and broiled fish together, after thanking God for providing another day of safety and sustenance. Little Decimus was yawning, and the family was thinking about bedtime when suddenly a loud pounding sounded on the door.

Some of Pilate's old instincts came flooding back. He told Porcia to take Decimus into the bedroom, next to the window, while he slipped toward the sturdy wooden door. "Who is there so late?" he demanded.

"It is John, Lucius," came a familiar voice. "Let me in, please!"

Pilate raised the bar and opened the door. John stood there with his wife Miriam by his side. She looked frightened, and the normally serene Apostle was a bit paler than usual.

"What on earth is the matter?" asked Pilate.

"Praetorians are on their way from Caesarea," said John. "The High Priest found out where you were and sent a letter to the Emperor, reporting your presence in Jerusalem—and that it was my family that had sheltered you and yours. They are coming for us all. We have a day at the most!"

Pilate stiffened. He had feared this day might come, but every week that had gone by without discovery had cause him to relax that fear ever so slightly. He had begun to think that he had avoided the Emperor's dragnet altogether. As he pondered possibilities, something occurred to him.

"How do you know this?" he asked.

"I once delivered fish to the High Priest's palace every week for nearly a year," said John. "I knew most of his household, and several of the servants became good friends of mine. One of them, Eleazar ben Simeon, is a follower of The Way—although he has kept his faith a secret from the priests. He told me some time ago that Caiaphas had asked for an audience with the High Priest Jonathan, his nephew. He has been trying for some time to find out what that conversation was about—he said that the expression on Caiaphas' face right before the two of them shut the doors and ran the servants out was positively frightening! Finally, this afternoon, he overheard the High Priest telling his uncle that the Praetorians should be in the city to arrest Pilate and all those who sheltered him first thing tomorrow morning. My friend, we must escape the city! James and Peter are safe, I think—their names are not associated with yours as mine has become. But for my wife's sake, and for the sake of the Gospel, we must avoid being apprehended if we can."

Pilate nodded. "Let us flee towards Ephesus," he said. "I have a large sum of money on deposit there under a false name. That will give us sufficient funds to flee wherever we wish to go, until the Emperor grows bored with trying to avenge an ancient grudge."

John looked at his friend curiously. "Why does the new Emperor hate you so?" he asked.

"I broke both his arms and nearly beat him to death," said Pilate.

John's mouth opened so wide that Pilate was forced to laugh, despite the urgency of the moment.

"It's a long story," he said, "and perhaps on the road I will tell it to you. But now, we need to prepare for our flight."

Porcia and Decimus had been listening from the bedchamber, and Pilate's ever-efficient wife was already throwing garments into a traveling bag. Pilate gathered the few possessions he wanted from his old life, tossing them in the pack. Last of all he picked up his battered, much-used legate's gladius. He drew it from its scabbard and studied it for a long moment.

"You know that is not our way," said a soft voice from behind him. He turned and saw John standing in the doorway watching him.

"That may be true, but can a man not defend his family?" Pilate asked.

John thought a long moment. "Jesus did tell us, just before he was crucified, that everyone who did not own a sword should sell his cloak and buy one, because dark and difficult days lay ahead for us all," he finally said. "Three of us had swords—and yes, I was one of them! When we showed them to him, he told us that would be enough. Yet later that night, when Simon tried to attack those who arrested our Master, Jesus told him to put his blade away—that those who took up the sword should perish by the sword. Is that what you want, Pilate? To die as you lived in your former life?"

Pilate swallowed hard. "What I want is to raise my wife and son in peace, and to share the words of Jesus with enough people to atone for the guilt I still feel for sending Him to the cross," he said. "But if I can save my family, or yours, by letting a blade take my life—then that is what I will do." He placed the sword in the bag and stuffed it under some of his clothes.

The city was going to bed, the rattle and clatter of the daily crowds giving way to the more muffled sounds of night. John led them to the Sheep Gate along the city's north wall. There was a small stable not far from the gates, whose owner was a recent follower of The Way. He had several horses saddled and waiting for them. The owner conferred with John for a few moments, and then Pilate walked over. He reached into his cloak for his bag of coin, but the man shook his head.

"I am glad to give you all a chance to escape the city," he said. "Don't take away my true reward by sullying the deed with money."

"I thank you, sir," said Pilate. "If we can, I will send these horses back to you from Ephesus." He threw his bags across the animal's back, and then Pilate lifted his son up to ride in front of him. John rode beside him on a large sturdy mule, while the two women were mounted on small ponies. Miriam started to ride side-saddle, but Porcia shook her head.

"When speed is required, maidenly modesty must give way to necessity," she told John's wife. "It is dark, and no one will care if your calves are showing."

Moments later, they spurred their mounts and disappeared into the moonless Judean night. They rode hard all through the night, and stopped briefly in Galilee late the next morning. John knew a tavern owner who was also a follower of Jesus; he directed them to a quiet back room where all five of them slept the daylight hours away. They woke as the sun was setting; eating a brief meal, they slipped out of the inn and were on the road again by full dark. They rode hard northward, towards the snow-capped peak of Mt. Hermon, and then on to the southern parts of Lebanon before stopping at midday near a sparkling, clear stream that flowed down from the mountain that now loomed to their east.

The horses, worn out from two days' hard riding, drank deeply. Pilate expertly hobbled them in the midst of a good stand of rich grass to let them graze for a while. His son joined him as he removed the saddles and rubbed down their tired mounts.

Decimus looked up at him curiously. The boy was now ten years old, and as Pilate watched the anxious young face, he could see in its lines the man his son would become someday—if he survived the current crisis. He had Pilate's steady gray eyes and aquiline nose, but the gentle lines of his mouth and slightly upturned brow reminded Pilate of Porcia—and, he suddenly realized, of her father, his old friend Proculus. But the troubled child was none of these, Pilate thought—he was his own, unique person, and was obviously unhappy with their current situation.

"*Pater,*" he said—using the more mature term for father was something he had just recently begun to do—"why did we have to leave Jerusalem? I miss Peter and Andrew and the boys I used to play with."

"My son, many years ago I made a very powerful person very angry with me," said Pilate.

"The Emperor?" Decimus asked.

"Yes, son," said Pilate. "He was not Emperor then—in fact, he was only a few years older than you. But he did a very wicked thing, and I hurt him for it."

"Did he deserve to be hurt?" asked the boy.

"By all rights, he deserved to die!" said Pilate. "I know that vengeance is the territory of God, but by the laws of Rome and of all civilized men, what he did was deserving of severe punishment. I certainly intended to kill him."

"Is he the one that killed my sister?" Decimus asked.

Pilate's jaw dropped. He and Porcia had never told their son about their lost daughter—partly because he was so young, at first, and partly because they feared the knowledge might fill the boy with thoughts of vengeance as he grew older. But Decimus merely smiled at his father's expression.

"I'm not blind, or deaf, you know," he said. "You and mama talk about her all the time when you think I am asleep or out of earshot. I know that she was named after mama, and that she died in a way that hurt you both very badly. Was it the Emperor that killed her?"

Pilate sat down on a flat rock and pulled his son up on his lap. He watched the horses for a few moments before he finally spoke.

"He did not kill her body," he finally told his son. "Oh, he abused her cruelly, and hurt her physically, but in a way, I think it might have been kinder if he had killed her outright."

"Why did he do it?" asked Decimus.

"Your sister was engaged to marry Gaius Caesar," said Pilate. "The old Emperor Tiberius and I were good friends, and he had proposed the marriage alliance some time before. She was twelve, and Gaius Caligula was fourteen, when we went to see the Emperor on Capri. The lad acted very kind towards her back then, and she was flattered by his attention, and had fallen quite in love with him. I had been suspicious of him earlier—I knew he had a cruel streak in him—but I thought that your sister's innocent love had conquered it. Your mother and I let them go off together, with some other children." He paused a moment. How could he tell someone so innocent of such a barbaric act without destroying that innocence? But Decimus obviously wanted to know, and Pilate did not know when he would have another opportunity to tell him.

"Do you know of the act that men and women do together to make children?" he asked his son.

"The thing that you and mama do when you think I am asleep?" he said. "I don't know how it works, but I know what it is."

Pilate smiled at the precocious answer, and vowed to himself never to believe his son was really asleep again without checking. "My son, the desire for that act is the strongest urge that God placed within man. You will understand that soon enough. That desire drives some men mad with passion, but in others, it becomes warped and twisted somehow. That which God made to be an expression of love instead becomes a desire to humiliate and hurt. Gaius Caligula was—and is—one who can derive no pleasure from anything unless it hurts someone else. He raped your sister—that is the term for when the act is forced, rather than given willingly. Not only did he rape her—he beat her in the process, breaking her arm and battering her face. When I saw her, I went mad with rage and tried to kill Caligula. One of the Emperor's guards knocked me unconscious, or I would have killed him."

Decimus nodded, his face strained from the mental effort of absorbing such cruelty. "I understand why you did what you did now," he said. "But what I don't understand is how did my sister die?"

A single tear coursed down Pilate's cheek. Decimus reached up and touched it as if it were something precious. Finally his father spoke again.

"Being so savagely assaulted by one whom she had fallen in love with broke something in her," he said. "Her spirit never recovered. The Emperor was both angry at me for nearly killing his heir, and fearful for what would happen to me when Caligula grew older. He sent us to Judea in order to punish me, and to protect us at the same time, I think. But Porcia Minor was convinced that I was being punished because she had failed me in some way. I could not dissuade her, and I could not heal what he had destroyed inside her. One night on the voyage to Judea she threw herself overboard. Your mother and I—" His voice broke for a moment, and then he continued.

"We never even got a chance to tell her goodbye, or to burn her body, according to Roman custom."

Decimus stood and looked his father in the eye. His small face had matured a decade in the course of a single conversation, but after that glance, he embraced his father like a man. His voice was hoarse with emotion as he spoke.

"You did nothing wrong, then," he said.

"Not as the world of men sees such things, no," said Pilate. "I am still trying to sort out what God would think of such violence—even if it was done to avenge a hideous wrong."

"Why does God allow us to be punished for something you did that was not wrong in itself?" asked Decimus.

"It is the way of the world," said Pilate. "The innocent suffer and the weak are abused by the strong. It is a reminder that this world we live in is utterly lost. Even Jesus did no wrong to any man, and yet I sent him to the cross. Perhaps my present suffering is a form of atonement for that wrong."

"I do not know," said the boy. "But I think I want to go find mama now."

Pilate watched his son leave with a mixture of sorrow and pride. He had such maturity for such tender years! As he finished tethering the horses, he saw John standing in the edge of the trees. He nodded at him, and the Apostle stepped out and sat on the rock Pilate and his son had just vacated.

"You heard?" asked Pilate.

John nodded. "I did not mean to eavesdrop, but you had just started speaking as I approached, and I did not want to disturb your time with your son by interrupting."

Pilate nodded. "Saves me the trouble of having to tell it twice, I suppose," he said.

John sat there for a long time. Finally he stood and placed a hand on Pilate's shoulder. "I am an Apostle of Jesus the Christ," he said. "I have sworn my life to spreading His Gospel of peace." He paused, and his grip tightened for a moment. "But if Gaius Caligula stood before me right now, I would have a hard time staying my hand."

Two weeks later they rode to Ephesus at the first light of dawn. There had been no sign of pursuit, although there were rumors that Caligula's hated Praetorians had been seen throughout the province. Pilate found a seedy inn near the south gate and rented two adjoining rooms for the two families, and then left John in charge while he went to take care of business. He was decked out in his Jewish garb—stooping over a staff, stroking his long beard with his free hand, and pulling his hood up over his head. As he strode through the streets of the capital of Rome's Syrian province, he saw a few legionaries ambling through the streets on patrol. They took no notice of him. The city's banks were near the governor's palace, and that was a high-traffic area that Pilate was loath to enter. Too many people in this part of the world knew his face, and he would not be able to wear his Jewish costume when he went to retrieve the money of a Greek businessman named Lentulus.

Near the business district was a public latrine. Pilate ducked inside and found it deserted. Quickly he doffed the long cloak and headdress of an orthodox Jew; in its place he pulled on a simple, blue mantle over the solid white tunic he had been wearing beneath his Jewish robes. He ran a comb through his hair and put a drop of sweet-smelling balsam oil in his beard. Last of all, he donned a simple, gold-colored headband with a small sapphire mounted in front. He had gone from being a wandering Jewish peasant to a sleek-looking Greek merchant in a matter of moments.

He wandered into the banking firm of Lucullus and Caepio, one of the oldest and best-established banking firms in the Empire. A pudgy clerk greeted him with an unctuous smile.

"Good day, sir, how may we be of service?" he asked.

Pilate produced a letter of credit from within his bag. "My name is Lentulus Aristophanes," he said. "I have over twenty talents on deposit with your firm. I need to withdraw one gold talent and two silver ones."

The clerk nodded, and waddled back to a shelf where hundreds of scrolls were filed in alphabetical order. He picked his way through them and found the proper one after a few moments. He compared the signature on the record with the one in Pilate's letter and gave a nod.

"Give me just a moment," he said. "Such a large sum will take a short time to count out."

Pilate waited, studying the frescoes on the wall, and listened to the chatter of customers around him. Two Jewish merchants were talking at the next table over as they waited for the bankers to bring them their withdrawal.

"So what happened to the old governor?" said one.

"I tell you, Daniel, no one knows!" said the other. "He just disappeared without a trace from Caesarea one day, and then there were rumors flying all over that the old Emperor had called him on the carpet for corruption, cruelty, and incompetence. Not long after that his family disappeared, and then, the next thing you know, Tiberius is dead, and Praetorians from Rome are scouring the province looking for Pontius Pilate!"

"That is a bizarre tale, Joseph!" his companion said. "So what is the new governor like?"

"Marullus? Ha! He is lazy, corrupt, and incompetent!" replied Joseph. "Pilate, for all his faults, had crushed the Zealots once and for all. I have the feeling that they will enjoy a real rebirth under this new fellow. So far all he has done is try to curry favor with the priests and squeeze the merchants for all the bribes and tax money he can get."

"You really think Pilate was any better?" Daniel said in disbelief.

"I tell you, old friend, Pontius Pilate was a hard man with a mean streak a mile wide," said Joseph, "but he was competent. He was a reminder of why the Romans rule the world—he was ruthless, cruel, and tough as old boot leather. But there wasn't a hint of corruption about him, and those legionaries under his command were never allowed to forget that they were soldiers of Rome!"

In another lifetime, Pilate might have felt a surge of pride at this praise coming from his enemies. But now he was just anxious for his banker to return with the money he needed to finance his flight to parts unknown. Fortunately, the clerk returned moments later with three heavy bags of coin. He opened each, so that Pilate could see the contents, and then weighed them on the scales to show that he had indeed produced the required amount.

"Can I have someone carry this for you?" he asked. "It is a considerable amount of coin!"

Pilate shook his head. "It's not that heavy," he said, "and I have pack mules waiting."

It was a statement he came to regret, as the coins were a good deal heavier than he had thought they would be. Once clear of the bank, he stepped into the same latrine to don his Jewish robes for the walk across town to the Jewish quarter where the other four were waiting for him. He had just pulled off the blue mantle and was about to put his Jewish robes back on when a man walked in.

"Jupiter!" a familiar voice exclaimed. "Pontius Pilate! Is that you?"

It was Lucius Vitellius, the governor of Syria. Pilate heaved a sigh and looked up at his former superior.

"Hello, Proconsul!" he said.

"The Praetorians showed up at my palace yesterday looking for you," he said. "I told them that I had no idea where you were, and that was the truth. Now if I see them again I am going to have to actually lie, I suppose."

Pilate surveyed the young bureaucrat curiously. He did not know Vitellius well, but he had no idea the fellow had that much spine. Still, he was grateful.

"If you can keep my secret for another day, sir, I will be gone from this quarter of the world forever," he said.

Vitellius lowered his voice. "Do not charter a ship here, Pilate!" he said. "The Praetorians are watching the docks very closely—apparently someone tipped them off that you might bolt here."

Pilate frowned. The bustling docks of Ephesus had played a prominent role in his escape plans all along; not being able to visit them would be a huge inconvenience. Vitellius noticed his expression.

"Listen," he said. "I don't know why Caligula wants you, but after watching the Praetorians crucify poor Marcus Phillipus for no good reason, I have no desire to help them apprehend you, regardless of what you may have done. This new Emperor is a monster! There is a smaller seaport about a half day's ride south of here called Miletus. A few dozen boats sail from there, mostly fishermen and low-level wine merchants. Many of them are dirt poor and would gladly take a high-paying commission. If you can charter a boat from there, you can escape Syria and find your way to someplace where no one has ever heard the name of Pontius Pilate. I would suggest you do so quickly!"

Pilate winced when he heard of the death of his young junior legate. Apparently Caligula truly never forgot or forgave any slight. He thanked the governor for his discretion and good advice, then walked as briskly as the considerable load of gold and silver would allow across town to where his family, John, and Miriam were staying.

They were ensconced in their rooms, nervously awaiting his return. He quickly related the conversation he had with Vitellius, and John's brow furrowed.

"Are you sure you can trust him?" he asked.

"It would have been very easy for him to apprehend me," Pilate replied. "He had eight lictors waiting for him outside. I don't know him well, but he strikes me as a good, honest man. I have an idea, though, on how to proceed."

"What would that be?" asked John.

"Let me ride down to Miletus alone," he said. "I will conduct a reconnaissance, find a ship's captain willing to take on a charter, and pay him half in advance. Then I will return for you all and we will ride down together, board a ship, and be gone from this part of the Empire forever."

Porcia nodded. "It is the safest way, but the danger to you frightens me. What if the Praetorians are there ahead of you?"

"There aren't that many of them, and they can't be everywhere," said Pilate. "I think this is our best chance to get free once and for all. Let us break bread together, and I will sleep for a few hours, and then set out when it is fully dark."

Together they went down to the tavern's common room and purchased roast chicken and fish, mixed in a broth with onions and olive oil, and a good-sized loaf of reasonably fresh bread. They ate quickly—the tavern had few customers at this hour of the day, but the supper crowd would be in soon and they wanted to be back in their rooms before more people arrived. As they finished the meal, John spoke to Decimus.

"Why don't you come to our room and let me tell you some stories about Jesus and the children that knew him?" he asked.

Decimus, who loved listening to John, nodded eagerly, and Pilate shot his friend a grateful glance. After they retired to their room, he took Porcia in his arms and held her for a long time.

"Are you afraid you might not see me again?" she asked.

"It is the only thing I fear," he said. "Death holds no terror for me—it never did, really, but now that I have pledged myself to one who conquered it, death is a passing inconvenience. But not seeing you—not having a chance to say goodbye—that would hurt. I know that we will meet again on the other side, but I still want to grow old with you, Porcia. I want to see our son attain his manhood and marry, and live well. Listen to me!"

He shifted so he could look her in the eye better. "No matter what happens, take my boy to safety! Do not squander your life, or his, in an attempt to save mine. I will die happy knowing that the two of you are safe."

"How about if you do not die at all?" she said, and kissed him passionately. "How about we abandon this dreadful conversation and take advantage of these precious moments we have been given before our son returns?" For the next hour, Pontius Pilate did not think once about Caligula, Praetorian guards, or ships sailing from Miletus.

An hour after dark, dressed once more as a Greek merchant, Pilate spurred his horse southward. The moon was nearly full, the night cool, and the roads deserted. Pilate carried half a talent of gold under his robes—he had split the rest of his treasure between the adults in the group, for safer carrying, and to make sure they were provided for in case something happened to him. It took him only four hours to cover the distance riding alone; mentally he calculated that it would take another hour or more with the entire group. It was well before dawn when he rode into Miletus. The city guard waved him through with a bored look; certainly it did not appear that there was a manhunt on. He left his horse at a stable outside the city walls and then walked down to the waterfront. Perhaps fifteen ships were tied up there; most were small fishing vessels that did not look as if they could weather a long sea voyage. But there was one larger vessel, obviously a merchant ship of some sort. Its crew was beginning to stir; some of them were transferring amphorae full of wine from a waiting wagon to the hold of the vessel. Pilate waited until the first rays of the sun rose behind the town, and then saw a tall, well-groomed man emerge from the small cabin in the front of the ship. The man spoke to the oldest member of the crew, who gestured at the wagons, showing that the wine was nearly all loaded. The man nodded and made a check on a small scroll he pulled from his robes.

Pilate stepped forward onto the dock. "Ahoy!" he addressed the tall fellow. "Is this your vessel?"

"Indeed it is," said the man. "I am Antigonus Philo, and this is my ship. We leave first thing tomorrow morning, bearing wine to Narbo in Spain."

Pilate nodded. Narbo was a long way from Judea, and not far from his old haunts in Spain. It should be easy for him to find a place for his wife and family to settle down and wait out what he hoped would be Caligula's brief reign.

"I would like to speak to you, Antigonus," he said. "I think I might be able to make this voyage much more profitable for you."

The ship's owner walked down the gangplank, and Pilate took him to the end of the pier to avoid being overheard. In a matter of moments, the deal was struck. Pilate would pay half a talent of gold now and the other half when his family arrived in Narbo. In exchange, Antigonus guaranteed them a swift and confidential voyage through the length of the Mediterranean, with no stops in Italy or Sicily. It was an outrageous fee, but one that would be irresistible to any merchant with a lick of fiscal sense. He told Antigonus that he and his family, as well as two Jewish servants, would board the ship at dawn the next morning.

As soon as the deal was made, Pilate returned to the stables and claimed his horse. He was nervous of traveling during the day, but willing to take the chance this once. All the way to Ephesus, he kept an eye out for any suspicious parties. There were no Praetorians or legionaries patrolling the road, and the few travelers he saw were humble country folk or busy merchants—not a single familiar face presented itself. By mid-afternoon he had returned to Ephesus and rejoined John and the others.

Once more the family was able to enjoy supper together, and afterward, they retired to their rooms. This time all five of them congregated in Pilate's slightly larger chamber and went over their travel plans one last time. Afterward, they rested and talked of light things—of some of the more amusing moments that Pilate had experienced in his years in the legions, and John's tales of the ups and downs of fishing the Sea of Galilee. As the evening drew later, John related a long story about Jesus and a little girl whom he had called back from death at the village of Capernaum. She had succumbed to a high fever and a racking cough, and was being washed and dressed for burial when Jesus had chased all the mourners out of the room, leaving only her parents and the three closest disciples—Peter, James, and John. Then He had taken her by the hand and gently told her to wake up— and she did! Her breath resumed, she opened her eyes, and the flush of life returned to her cheeks. Pilate listened in wonder, and wished that Jesus could have healed the broken heart and spirit of his own daughter before her tragic end.

Shortly after midnight they set out. The streets were largely empty except for a few drunks and prostitutes, but just outside the gate they passed a squad of Roman legionaries led by a centurion in his thirties. Pilate reflexively ducked his head, but the torches they carried still illuminated his face for a moment. No one called his name, however, and by the time they cleared the city walls and spurred their horses southward, he thought that once more he had avoided detection.

The leader of the patrol was a man Pilate should have known. Antonius Hadrian was the ranker who had been promoted to centurion ten years before for securing the services of Fatimah the prostitute for Valerius Gratus. Pilate had tried hard to make a good officer of the man, but he tended to be lazy and liked drinking too much, so after two years Pilate had demoted him back to legionary and sent him packing. It had taken Hadrian several years and lots of favors for various superiors to regain his centurion's rank, but he had never forgotten the man who took that rank away from him.

He did not recognize Pilate right away, but that half-glimpsed face in the torchlight lingered in the back of his mind for a couple of hours as he finished his patrol and returned his soldiers to their barracks. But as he poured himself a cup of wine, and reflected with bitterness on his career and the man who had nearly ruined it, the realization of who he had seen leaving the city hit him as forcefully as a charging bull. Leaving the wine untasted, he ran as fast as he could to the governor's palace, where a half dozen Praetorian guards had been staying all week, looking for Pontius Pilate, former Prefect of Judea.

Meanwhile, Pilate and his group rode leisurely through the night, southwards toward Miletus. Pilate was looking forward already to a leisurely summer sea voyage, and to seeing the mountains of Spain once more. Land was cheap north of Narbo, cheap and fertile. A small farm, perhaps a chance to raise horses, and the opportunity to carry the Gospel of Jesus to a place where it had never yet been heard—all these things were flitting through his mind as he rode along, with his son dozing in front of him.

Dawn was breaking in the east as they spied the city in the distance. He had told Antigonus that they would be ready to board ship within two hours of sunrise, so he spurred the horse along a bit faster. The trotting gait woke young Decimus, who stretched and turned around to give his father a hug. The group stopped to let the youngster empty his bladder, and Pilate and John dismounted, as did their ladies, to stretch and pace a moment. They were less than a half hour from the ship, and safety.

"*Pater*, there are riders coming up behind us in the distance!" his son said.

Pilate turned and saw six horses crest the horizon about a mile or more behind them, riding swiftly. He pulled his bronze telescope from his saddle bags and looked through it, the blood draining from his face as he recognized the black uniforms.

"Praetorians!" he said. "We are detected!"

"Can we get to Miletus ahead of them?" John asked.

"Barely," said Pilate. "But I don't think the ship would be able to get underway before they caught up to us."

"Oh, Lucius, what shall we do?" Porcia asked.

"You will take my son to Spain and raise him to be an honorable man, and a follower of Christ," said Pilate. "I shall purchase the time you need." The decision had required little thought—he had made his mind up the moment he recognized the black uniforms of his pursuers. He drew his gladius from the bottom of his sack of worldly goods.

John shook his head. "Let me stay," he said. "You and the others can escape."

Pilate laughed grimly. "My dear friend, you are an apostle of Jesus and a man of peace. You barely know one end of a sword from the other! The Praetorians would eat you alive and barely be slowed for a moment. I can buy you a half hour or more. You have the money to pay passage to Spain—now go!"

John swallowed hard. "I will never forget this, and I will make sure the world remembers that you sacrificed yourself to save us!" he said.

"No!" said Pilate. "Don't sully my sacrifice by glorifying it. In fact, forget I ever became a believer. Let the world remember me only as the man who crucified Jesus."

"I don't understand," said the Apostle.

Pilate shook his head. "There is no time to explain," he said. "But please honor my wishes." He turned to his wife, who was watching him with tears streaming down her cheeks. "My Porcia," he said, his voice catching for just a moment. "I have never deserved a love as pure as yours, but I have never ceased to be grateful for it. Ride like the wind, and save our son!"

Last of all, he looked at Decimus. "My son," he said, "take care of your mother, and never forget me—but I would suggest you leave the name Pilate behind forever. It is too dangerous a name to carry."

"What should I call myself then, *tata*?" asked his son, tears streaming down his face.

"Use a name no one would ever suspect Pilate's son of choosing," he said. "Call yourself Gaius. Now go! All of you! I don't want this to be in vain!" The five followers of Jesus spurred their horses down the road. Pilate called after them, "I'll try not to kill any more than I have to!"

With that, he said a short prayer to Jesus of Nazareth, and then positioned himself in the middle of the road. Moments after his companions disappeared over the edge of the hill, the six riders topped the ridge to the north, descending upon the former Governor of Judea like a swift-moving storm cloud. When they saw Pilate, they reined in their horses and trotted toward him, stopping a few paces away.

"Whom do you seek?" Pilate asked in a loud clear voice.

"We are looking for Pontius Pilate, the former Prefect of Judea, and traitor to Rome!" said their centurion, a lanky youth with a jaded look in his eyes. "The Emperor wishes to see him punished for his many crimes!"

"I am Pilate! Does your master think so little of me as to send only a half dozen men? I figured I should merit a cohort at least!" Pilate said.

The centurion glared at him. "The Emperor has many scores to settle!" he said. "But there were over a century of us—twenty remain in Caesarea, and another score or more in Jerusalem. The rest rode to every port in the region, hoping to catch you as you fled. But it appears we have won the prize. Surrender yourself, old man, and perhaps I can persuade Gaius Caesar to make your end quick!"

"I know Gaius Little Boots better than that," said Pilate. "He gives a quick, clean end to no one. I will not make it easy for you, centurion! Achieve me if you can, but I shall make you work for it!"

The six men spurred their horses toward him, but Pilate stood his ground. He knew the beasts would get in each other's way, and would shy to the right or left, leaving him only one to deal with. The centurion's mount was a spirited animal, surging ahead of the others, so Pilate made it his target. As he thought, the others swerved aside at the last moment, and he ducked low just as the horse gathered its strength to hurl itself over him. When it did, he thrust upward hard and felt a gush of warm blood spray his arm. The screaming animal plunged hard to the earth, snapping its neck and throwing its rider. The centurion landed head first and lay there, dazed. The other five wheeled their mounts about.

"Is that all you've got?" asked Pilate. "I was gutting war horses in Germania when you whelps weren't even thought of!"

Alarmed by his skill, the five men dismounted and drew their blades, as Pilate had hoped. He prayed his bad knee would not choose this moment to give out on him, and waited for them to charge. In his experience, the Praetorians, although drawn from the ranks of the regular legions, tended to be spoiled, arrogant boors who quickly forgot the discipline and skill that had earned them their appointment. Sure enough, all five of them charged him at once, getting in each other's way and slowing their reaction time. Pilate waited till they were a couple of paces away, then lowered his body, lunged wide to the left, and with a strong swing of his blade, severed the calf muscle of one of the men trying to kill him. The man fell to the ground, dropping his blade and screaming as he held his injured leg. Two down, thought Pilate. He could have finished the man with a quick thrust, but he had sworn not to kill unless it was absolutely necessary.

Now the four remaining Praetorians charged him again. They were more wary this time, and Pilate was forced to drive his blade through one man's throat to avoid being skewered. But the force of the Praetorian's charge tore Pilate's blade out of his hand. He lunged for the twitching corpse and grabbed the hilt of his gladius, but as he yanked it free he felt the sting of a deep, slashing cut to his left arm. He spun away and counter-thrust, grazing his opponent's ribs. As he raised the weapon for another attack, he felt a searing pain in his middle and looked down to see the point of a sword sticking out of his belly. He tried to swing his blade at the man behind him, but it was growing heavy. He saw the point that was impaling him pulled free, and turned, swaying on his feet, to see a burly Praetorian drawing back for another swing. With one last surge of strength, he stuck his sword deep in under the man's arm, puncturing a lung. But then his grip loosened, and he could not pull his blade free. He fell to his knees, and then slowly collapsed backward. He put his hand to his stomach, and it came away bloody.

He closed his eyes for a moment, and said a prayer for the souls of the men he had killed. He asked Jesus to forgive him this final foray into violence, and to his great satisfaction, he found that the beast that had once lived within him, which would have rejoiced in this carnage, was still gone. Die he might, but he would die as a follower of Jesus, not a bloodthirsty madman.

Pilate felt a hand on his shoulder, rolling him over. Opening his eyes, he saw that the centurion who had been knocked senseless was sitting up, glaring at Pilate and the three men lying on the ground, one dead, one mortally injured, and the other most likely crippled for life.

The centurion stood and looked at the remaining two men. "Is he alive?" he asked.

"I . . . live," Pilate said.

The man walked over and looked down at him. "Not for long, from the look of that wound," he said. "A pox on you, old fool! Our orders were to bring you alive to Rome."

"What do you want us to do?" asked one of the remaining Praetorians.

"Get me some timbers from that old barn on the hill," the centurion said. "We'll nail him up, like he killed that Galilean everyone talks about."

"Isn't he still a citizen?" asked one of them.

"Do you think the laws of the old Republic still matter?" asked the centurion. "Caesar wants him killed as painfully as possible, and crucifixion will fill the bill nicely."

"He won't last an hour on the cross," said the man Pilate had hamstrung. "That gut wound will bleed out in no time."

He crawled over to Pilate and looked at him. "You could have killed me easily, old man. Why didn't you?"

Pilate tried to focus his eyes on the young soldier. His mouth was dry, but he could still form words. "I didn't want to kill any of you," he said. "It is not our way. The others . . . I had to. You were out of the fight, so I spared you."

The man angrily punched Pilate in the face. "Not before crippling me!" he snapped. "I'd rather be dead than useless."

Pilate nearly lost consciousness from the force of the blow, but he looked the man steadily in the eye. "No life is useless to God," he said. Then he blacked out for a few moments.

He came to as the spikes were driven into his wrists, and vaguely wondered who was screaming for a full minute before he realized it was himself. When the crossbeam was hoisted up and tied to the upright, he felt as if he was being torn in half. He looked down and saw the blood sluicing from his wound, and could feel the life ebbing out of him. At the foot of his cross, three men stood looking up at him, while the other was sitting up, his leg wrapped in a bloody bandage.

"I forgive you," said Pilate, "as Christ forgave me."

He raised his eyes and looked southward, at the bright blue waters of the Mediterranean stretching away from Miletus. He could see the sails of the vessel carrying his wife and son to safety pulling away from the port, heading westward to freedom. A spasm of pain gripped his body, and he prayed to Jesus one last time for strength before his spirit left his body.

Pontius Pilate died trusting his soul to the Christ, but also with the knowledge that, in his own eyes, at least, he had redeemed himself.

# EPILOGUE

Gaius Caligula ruled Rome for nearly four years, and his name has become a synonym for madness and debauchery. Of his end, the historian Suetonius recorded:

> *In the covered passage through which he had to pass, some boys of good birth, who had been summoned from Asia to appear on the stage, were rehearsing their parts, and he stopped to watch and to encourage them; and had not the leader of the troop complained that he had a chill, he would have returned and had the performance given at once. From this point there are two versions of the story: some say that as he was talking with the boys, Chaerea came up behind and gave him a deep cut in the neck, having first cried, "Take that," and then the tribune Cornelius Sabinus, who was the other conspirator and faced Gaius, stabbed him in the breast. Others say that Sabinus, after getting rid of the crowd through centurions who were in the plot, asked for the watchword, as soldiers do, and that when Gaius gave him "Jupiter," he cried, "So be it," and as Gaius looked around, he split his jawbone with a blow of his sword. As he lay upon the ground and with writhing limbs called out that he still lived, the others dispatched him with thirty wounds; for the general signal was "Strike again." Some even thrust their swords through his privates. At the beginning of the disturbance his bearers ran to his aid with their poles, and presently the Germans of his bodyguard, and they slew several of his assassins, as well as some inoffensive senators.*
>
> *He lived twenty-nine years and ruled three years, ten months and eight days. His body was conveyed secretly to the gardens of the Lamian family, where it was partly consumed on a hastily erected pyre and buried beneath a light covering of turf; later his sisters on their return from exile dug it up, cremated it, and consigned it to the tomb. Before this was done, it is well known that the caretakers of the gardens were disturbed by ghosts, and that in the house where*

*he was slain not a night passed without some fearsome apparition, until at last the house itself was destroyed by fire. With him died his wife Caesonia, stabbed with a sword by a centurion, while his daughter's brains were dashed out against a wall.*

As for Pilate's wife and child, the only clue to their later life is found in the text of the Third Epistle of Saint John:

*The Elder to the beloved Gaius, whom I love in truth. Beloved, I pray in all respects that you might prosper and be in good health, as your soul prospers. For I was very glad when brethren came and testified to your truth, that is, that you were walking in the truth. I have no greater joy than this, to hear of my children walking in truth.*

# CAST OF CHARACTERS

## HISTORICAL CHARACTERS

**LUCIUS PONTIUS PILATE**—Roman soldier and statesman, protagonist

**JULIUS TIBERIUS CAESAR**—Roman general and second Emperor of Rome

**GAIUS OCTAVIUS JULIUS CAESAR AUGUSTUS**—First True Emperor of Rome

**ARMINIUS**—Tribal leader from Germania; defeated Roman General Varus and took his Legions' eagle standards

**CAIAPHAS**—Jewish high priest, ordered the arrest of Jesus of Nazareth

**ANNAS**—Father-in-law of Caiaphas, former High Priest, powerful Jewish political leader

**HEROD ANTIPAS**—Son of Herod the Great, tetrarch of Galilee, honorary "King of the Jews"

**PROCULA PORCIA**—Wife of Pontius Pilate

**GNAEUS POMPEIIUS MAGNUS**—AKA "Pompey the Great," Roman general, consul, and statesman; political enemy of Julius Caesar

**MARCUS ANTONIUS**—also "Marc Antony," cousin and would-be successor of Julius Caesar, defeated by Octavian in 31 BC; committed suicide

**GAIUS JULIUS CAESAR**—aka "Divus Julius"; Roman general, statesman, and dictator, adoptive father of Augustus, "the greatest Roman of them all"

**CLEOPATRA**—Last of the Ptolemies to rule Egypt; lover of Julius Caesar and Marc Antony; committed suicide following their defeat in 31 BC

**MARCUS AGRIPPA**—Roman General and statesman; right-hand man and closest friend of Caesar Augustus; married to Julia, the daughter of Augustus

399

**QUINCTILIUS VARUS**—Roman general, defeated and killed by the Cheruscii in Germania; lost all three of his legions

**GAIUS MARIUS**—Seven-time Consul of Rome, uncle of Julius Caesar, famous reformer and leader of the Roman army

**GAIUS JULIUS CAESAR GERMANICUS**—Nephew of Tiberius, brilliant general, potential rival for the Imperial throne

**LIVIA DRUSILLA JULIA AUGUSTA**—Mother of Tiberius and wife of Caesar Augustus

**JULIA CAESARUS FILIA**—Daughter of Caesar Augustus and widow of Marcus Agrippa; married to Tiberius after her husband's death

**AELIUS LAMIA**—Roman legate and Proconsul of Syria; Pilate's nominal superior

**CLAUDIUS CAESAR GERMANICUS**—Stuttering younger brother of Germanicus, later Emperor of Rome

**GNAEUS CALPURNIUS PISO**—Governor of Syria, accused murderer of Germanicus

**GAIUS CAESAR GERMANICUS**—Germanicus' son, Tiberius' successor as Emperor of Rome

**LUCIUS AELIUS SEJANUS**—Commander of the Praetorian Guard and confidant of Tiberius; ruled Rome while the Emperor was on Capri

**DRUSUS JULIUS CAESAR**—Natural son of Tiberius and his first wife Vipsania, poisoned by his own wife Livilla in 23 AD

**LIVILLA JULIA**—Sister of Claudius and Germanicus, wife of Tiberius' son Drusus, and his alleged murderess

**QUINTUS SUTORIUS MACRO**—Second in command of the Praetorians under Sejanus, later commanded the Praetorians after supplanting him

**VALERIUS GRATUS**—Governor of Judea before Pilate

**JAMES OF GALILEE**—Carpenter, half-brother of Jesus, later emerges as church leader

**JOSEPH CAIAPHAS**—Jewish priest who led protests against Pilate; later emerges as High Priest and leads the conspiracy against Jesus

**LUCIUS VITELLIUS**—Governor of Syria in 36-40 AD, Pilate's superior

# FICTIONAL CHARACTERS

**DEMOCLES**—Pilate's Greek slave during his time as governor of Judea

**DECIMUS PONTIUS PILATE**—Roman senator and businessman, father of Lucius Pontius Pilate

**FLAVIUS SIXTUS**—Veteran Roman general, Pilate's commander

**SEXTUS DIVIDICUS**—First Spear Centurion of Pilate's Legion in Germany

**SOSTHENES**—Greek slave badly beaten by Pilate in Germania

**DECIMUS TULLIUS**—Roman legate who succeeded Pilate in command of his legion

**GAIUS PROCULUS PORCIUS**—Pilate's longtime friend and father-in-law

**MARCIA PROCULUS SCRIBONIA**—Wife of Proculus, Pilate's mother-in-law

**CORNELIUS SEPTIMUS PILATE**—Brother of Pontius Pilate, military officer

**CORNELIA CLAUDIA PILATE**—Pilate's sister, died in childbirth

**PONTIA PILATE APPIUS**—Pilate's sister, married to Appius Claudius Sempronius

**MENCIUS MARCELLUS**—Chief steward of the Villa Jovis, Tiberius' palace on Capri

**QUINTUS SULLEMIUS**—Smuggler, ship's captain, and Pilate's lackey

**PORCIA MINOR**—Pilate's daughter

**LINTUS ANTONINUS**—Roman proconsul, Pilate's successor as Governor of Spain

**ARISTION**—Pilate's household steward

**DIOMYRUS**—Captain of the ship that took Pilate to Judea

**BRUTUS APPIUS**—Roman legionary known for his strength; promoted to centurion by Pilate

**CASSIUS LONGINUS**—Senior centurion of Rome's Judean Legion, later known as Brother Gideon

**TITUS AMBROSIUS**—Centurion of the Judean Legion

**MARCUS QUIRINIUS**—Centurion of the Judean Legion

**LUCIUS ANDRONICUS, MARCUS PULLO, and METELLIUS MACRO**—more Centurions of the Judean Legion (Pullo later killed by Zealots)

**SIMON BIN-YOSEF**—Galilean peasant, led the protest against the Jerusalem aqueduct

**BRUTUS VALENTIUS**—Legionary promoted to Centurion after the death of Pullo

**CORNELIUS**—Legionary who went to hear John the Baptist, later converted by Peter's preaching

**STYCHIUS**—Longinus' chief slave, later healed by Jesus

**SCARSUS**—Numidian scout employed by the Romans to track Zealots

**SILAS HIRTIUS**—Gallic cavalryman in the Judean legion

**ARISTARCHUS**—Physician of the Judean legion

**MILO LAMMIUS**—retired Roman legionary murdered by Bar Abbas

**LUCIUS SCRIBONIUS**—Roman legionary of the Judean legion

**MARCUS BALBUS PHILLIPUS**—Pilate's junior legate after 33 AD

# TIMELINE OF EVENTS

**42 BC** — Future Emperor Tiberius Caesar is born

**31 BC** — Caesar Octavian Augustus becomes Emperor of Rome

**16 BC** - Lucius Pontius Pilate is

**1 BC** — Young Pilate is assigned to Tiberius as junior lieutenant

**9 AD** — Quintcilius Varus and three Roman legions killed by the Cherusci

**10 AD** — Pilate joins Tiberius on punitive expedition to Germania

**11 AD** — Pilate wins the Civic Crown for valor defending his camp

**12 AD** — Pilate returns to Rome with Tiberius, becomes Tribune of the Plebs, and marries 18-year-old Procula Porcia

**14 AD** — Death of Augustus, Tiberius becomes Emperor

**19 AD** — Death of Germanicus, Pilate deals with Calpurnius Piso

**20 AD** — Pilate elected as Consul of Rome

**21-24 AD** — Pilate serves as Governor of Further Spain

**23 AD** — Death of Drusus Julius Caesar

**24 AD** — Pilate returns to Rome; Tiberius proposes a marriage alliance

**26 AD** — Tiberius takes up permanent residence on Capri; Pilate sent to Judea as governor; death of Porcia

**27 AD** — Pilate serves as governor; stirs controversy over funding for a new aqueduct; Sejanus' reign of terror in Rome continues

**28 AD** — Pilate's son Decimus is born; Pilate begins constructing Jerusalem aqueduct

**29 AD** — Pilate orders dispersal of aqueduct protestors; John the Baptist begins preaching

**30 AD** — John's ministry at its height; Jesus begins preaching in Galilee

**31 AD**—Bar Abbas becomes a nuisance to Rome; John the Baptist killed by Herod, Jesus' public ministry gains a huge following

**32 AD**—Pilate wounded by Zealots; his slow recovery fills the summer

**33 AD**—Bar Abbas captured; Jesus crucified, Day of Pentecost

**34 AD**—John heals Pilate's son; Herod begins persecuting the church, Stephen martyred

**35 AD**—Porcia becomes a follower of Jesus

**37 AD**—Pilate orders an attack on the Samaritan followers of Moses ben Judah, then recalled to Rome; Tiberius dies, Caligula becomes Emperor, and Pilate and his family become fugitives

**38 AD**—Lucius Pontius Pilate redeems himself

# GLOSSARY OF LATIN TERMS USED IN THIS BOOK

*Absolvo:* A verdict of "Not Guilty" declared by a Roman judge or jury

*Amuensis:* A scribe or secretary who penned letters dictated by another

*Arctoritas:* the circle of influence and prestige enjoyed by a member of the Roman aristocracy – it was measured by the number of clients one had, the respect one commanded from his peers, and one's public reputation

*Armillae:* A golden armband awarded to legionaries who slew an enemy in hand to hand combat

*Ave:* "Greetings!" – a common Latin salutation, "Hello" in English

*Cacat:* Latin slang for human feces; sometimes also used as an expletive

*Calvarium:* the skull

*Centurion:* A noncommissioned officer in a Roman legion who commanded 100 legionaries and around 20 auxiliaries

*Condemno:* A verdict of "Guilty" from a Roman court or magistrate

*Consul:* The Chief executives of the Roman Republic; two in number, they were elected by the citizens of Rome and served a one year term. Under the Emperors, the office held less power, but still carried great prestige.

*Conterburnalis:* A junior officer in the Roman military, equivalent to an ensign or field cadet.

*Corona Civitas:* the Civic Crown, Rome's second highest military decoration. It was awarded to any soldier who saved the life of a comrade, held his ground throughout the battle, and personally killed at least one of the enemy.

*Corona Granicus:* Rome's highest decoration, a simple crown woven from the grass of the battlefield where it was won. This award was given to any soldier who single-handedly saved an entire legion from destruction.

# THE REDEMPTION OF PONTIUS PILATE

*Culus:* slang term for the anus

*Curia Julia:* the Court of Julia, a public building erected by Gaius Julius Caesar in honor of his daughter Julia, which became the customary meeting place of the Roman Senate in Augustus' time

*Cursus Honorum:* The "ladder of honors" – the succession of offices that a successful Roman was expected to occupy on his way to the highest elected position, that of Consul.

*Denarius:* a common Roman coin, made of silver, which represented one day's wage for an average laborer.

*Divus Julius:* the "Divine Julius" – the title granted to Gaius Julius Caesar after his death and deification

*Ecastor:* "By Castor!" – a mild expletive used by Roman men and women in polite conversation to express dismay or disbelief

*Edepol:* "By Pollux!" a companion expletive used more often by Roman men than women

*Fortuna:* the Roman Goddess of Luck, believed to favor certain individuals

*Gens humana:* the human race; mankind

*Gladius:* A Roman shortsword. The blade was double edged, and typically 16 to 18 inches in length

*Hubris:* (actually Greek rather than Latin) a pride so great that it offends the gods

*Imperator:* lit. "conqueror," this was the designation normally given to any Roman commander who vanquished an enemy army on the field. Later, it became the title of Rome's rulers, and passed into English as the word "Emperor"

*Imperium:* The right to command; conferred by the Senate and People of Rome, or later by the Emperor. There were different levels of *imperium,* according to one's rank.

*Legate (also Legatus):* The commander of a Roman Army, while a Junior Legate commanded individual legions within the Army.

*Lictors:* The honor guards assigned to Roman officials - the greater the number of lictors, the higher the rank. The senior lictor would carry the *fasces* which represented the official's *imperium*

*Ludus Magnus:* Rome's largest gladiator training facility

406

***Mare Nostrum:*** "Our Sea," the Romans' nickname for the Mediterranean

***Mos Maorum:*** The traditions of the Roman Republic, the way things had always been done, similar to the Biblical "traditions of our elders."

***Paterfamilias:*** "Head of the Family;" the formal position of the father in a Roman home. As head, he literally had the power of life and death over family members.

***Pax Romana:*** The "Peace of Rome," begun during the reign of Augustus, which would last for nearly 200 years without large-scale wars

***Phalerae:*** a disc worn on the breastplate; could be gold, silver, or bronze according to the valor of the act it was awarded for

***Pilae (pilus*** singular): the standard spear used by Roman legionaries, about five feet in length, with a forged iron head. They were designed to be thrown, although they could also be useful in short-range combat as a thrusting lance

***Plebeian:*** The historically "common" classes of the Roman Republic, although by Pilate's time plebs were eligible to hold any political office, and comprised more than half the membership of the Senate.

***Podex:*** The part of the anatomy one sits on; the buttocks

***Pomerium:*** The sacred boundary of the city of Rome. By tradition, no military commander could cross it without laying down his *imperium.*

***Praetor:*** A local magistrate, elected by the citizens of Rome. The Urban Praetors were in charge of maintaining the city of Rome's infrastructure, including roads, aqueducts, and sewers, as well as public buildings.

***Praetorian Guard:*** The personal bodyguards of the Emperor of Rome

***Prefect:*** A Roman official who was appointed by the Senate or Emperor rather than elected; there were both military and civilian prefects

***Primus Pilus (*** also ***Primipilus):*** Lit. "First Spear," the highest ranking centurion in a legion of Roman soldiers.

***Princeps:*** One of the Emperor's official titles, loosely translated to "First Citizen"

***Princeps Senatus:*** The senior member and leader of the Roman Senate

***Proconsul:*** A Roman governor who has held the rank of Consul before being sent to his province

***Publicani:*** also called tax farmers, they were usually local residents who contracted to collect taxes from the native population. Called "Publicans" in the New Testament, they were universally despised.

***Quaestor:*** an elected magistrate of the Roman Republic, whose members automatically qualified for a seat in the Senate.

***Retarius:*** A gladiator who fought with a net and a trident as his weapons

***Rudis:*** a wooden sword used for training purposes

***Sagum:*** A leather cloak worn by soldiers on campaign; it was oiled to keep it supple and waterproof

***Secutor:*** A gladiator who fought with the sword and shield

***Spartacanii:*** The army of slaves that followed Spartacus in his rebellion against Rome in 70 BC

***Stadia:*** a unit of measurement, approximately 600 feet

***Stibium:*** Makeup favored by prostitutes and older women in the East; believed to have been invented in Egypt

***Tata:*** childish name for one's father, equivalent to "Daddy"

***Tetrarch:*** One who governs one fifth of a kingdom – a title given to Herod the Great's sons after their father's kingdom was split between them

***Torcs:*** a golden necklet awarded for valor in combat

***Tribune:*** An elected official who represents the interests of the electorate. Military Tribunes acted as liaisons between the soldiers and their commander; Tribune of the Plebs was a very important political office that automatically enrolled its members in the Senate. Historically, Tribunes of the Plebs could introduce legislation and veto any proposal from the Consuls or the Senate. Although their powers were reduced under the Principate, the office still carried great honor and was highly sought after.

***Vestal Virgins:*** these were the ten priestesses of Vesta, the goddess of hearth and home, bound for the duration of their office to remain pure. They were usually pledged to Vesta at age 8 and released from their vows at the age of 35.

Made in the USA
Monee, IL
08 January 2020

20066673R00227